Joseph Wheeler

A biographical dictionary of freethinkers of all ages and nations

Joseph Wheeler

A biographical dictionary of freethinkers of all ages and nations

ISBN/EAN: 9783337283247

Printed in Europe, USA, Canada, Australia, Japan

Cover: Foto ©Raphael Reischuk / pixelio.de

More available books at **www.hansebooks.com**

A
BIOGRAPHICAL DICTIONARY

OF

FREETHINKERS

OF

ALL AGES AND NATIONS.

BY

J. M. WHEELER.

———————

London:

PROGRESSIVE PUBLISHING COMPANY,
28 STONECUTTER STREET, E.C.

1889.

PREFACE.

JOHN STUART MILL in his "Autobiography" declares with truth that "the world would be astonished if it knew how great a proportion of its brightest ornaments, of those most distinguished even in popular estimation for wisdom and virtue are complete sceptics in religion." Many of these, as Mill points out, refrain from various motives from speaking out. The work I have undertaken will, I trust, do something to show how many of the world's worthiest men and women have been Freethinkers.

My Dictionary does not pretend to be a complete list of those who have rendered services to Freethought. To form such a compilation would rather be the task of an international society than of an individual. Moreover details concerning many worthy workers are now inaccessible. Freethought boasts its noble army of martyrs of whom the world was not worthy, and who paid the penalty of their freedom in prison or at the stake. Some of the names of these are only known by the vituperation of their adversaries. I have done my best to preserve some trustworthy record of as many as possible.

The only complete work with a similar design of which I have any knowledge, is the *Dictionnaire des Athées anciens et modernes*, by Sylvain Maréchal with its supplements by Jerome de Lalande the Astronomer, An. VIII. (1800)-1805. That work, which is now extremely rare, gave scarcely any biographical details, and unfortunately followed previous orthodox atheographers, such as Buddeus, Reimmann, Hardouin, Garasse, Mersenne, in classing as Atheists those to whom the title was inapplicable. I have taken no names from these sources without examining the evidence.

A work was issued by Richard Carlile in 1826, entitled *A Dictionary of Modern Anti-Superstionists;* or, "an account, arranged alphabetically, of those who, whether called Atheists, Sceptics, Latitudinarians, Religious Reformers, or etc., have during the last ten centuries contributed towards the diminution of superstition. Compiled by a searcher after Truth." The compiler, as I have reason to know, was Julian Hibbert, who brought to his task adequate scholarship and leisure. It was, however, conceived on too extensive a scale, and in 128 pages, all that was issued, it only reached to the name of Annet. Julian Hibbert also compiled chronological tables of English Freethinkers, which were published in the *Reasoner* for 1855.

Of the *Anti-Trinitarian Biography* of the Rev. Robert Wallace, or of the previous compilations of Saudius and Bock, I have made but little use. To include the names of all who reject some of the Christian dogmas was quite beside my purpose, though I have included those of early Unitarians and Universalists who, I conceive, exhibited the true spirit of free inquiry in the face of persecution. To the *Freydenker Lexikon* of J. A. Trinius (1759) my obligations are slight, but should be acknowledged. To Bayle's *Dictionary*, Hoefer's *Nouvelle Biographie Generale*, Meyer's *Konversations Lexikon*, Franck's *Dictionnaire des Sciences Philosophiques*, and to Larousse's *Grand Dictionnaire Universel* I must also express my indebtedness. In the case of disputed dates I have usually found Haydn's *Dictionary of Biography* (1886) most trustworthy, but I have also consulted Oettinger's valuable *Moniteur des Dates.*

The particulars have in all cases been drawn from the best available sources. I have not attempted to give a full view of any of the lives dealt with, but merely sought to give some idea of their services and relation to Freethought. Nor have I enumerated the whole of the works of authors who have often dealt with a variety of subjects. As full a list as is feasible has, however, been given of their distinctive Freethought works; and the book will, I hope, be useful to anyone wishing information as to the bibliography of Freethought. The only work of a bibliographical kind is the *Guide du Libre Penseur*, by M. Alfred Verlière, but his list is very far from complete even of the French authors, with whom it is almost entirely occupied. I should also mention *La Lorgnette Philosophique*, by M. Paquet, as giving lively sketches, though not biographies, of some modern French Freethinkers.

In the compilation of my list of names I have received assistance from my friends, Mr. G. W. Foote (to whom I am also indebted for the opportunity of publication), Mr. W. J. Birch, Mr. E. Truelove and Mr. F. Malibran. For particulars in regard to some English Freethinkers I am indebted to Mr. Charles Bradlaugh, Mr. George Jacob Holyoake and Mr. E. T. Craig, while Professor Dal Volta, of Florence, has kindly assisted me with some of the Italian names. I must also express my indebtedness to A. de Gubernatis, whose *Dizionario Biografico degli Scrittori Contemporanei.* I have found of considerable service. My thanks are also due to G. K. Fortescue, Esq., for permission to examine the titles of all Freethought works in the British Museum.

Some readers may think my list contains names better omitted, while omitting others well deserving a place. I have, for instance, omitted many foreign Liberal Protestants while including Bishop Colenso, who, ostensibly, did not go so far. But my justification. if any, must be found in my purpose, which is to record the names of those who have contributed in their generation to the *advance* of Freethought. No one can be more conscious of the imperfections of my work than myself, but I console myself with the reflection of Plato, that "though it be the merit of a good huntsman to find game in a wide wood, it is no discredit if he do not find it all"; and the hope that what I have attempted some other will complete.

The most onerous part of my task has been the examination of the claims of some thousand names, mostly foreign, which find no place in this dictionary. But the work throughout has been a labor of love. I designed it as my humble contribution to the cause of Freethought, and leave it with the hope that it will contribute towards the history of "the good old cause"; a history which has yet to be written, and for which, perhaps, the time is not yet ripe.

Should this volume be received with an encouraging share of favor, I hope to follow it with a *History of Freethought in England*, for which I have long been collecting materials.

A BIOGRAPHICAL DICTIONARY
OF FREETHINKERS.

Abælardus (Petrus), b. 1079.   A teacher of philosophy at Paris, renowned for being loved by the celebrated Eloise.   He was accused of teaching erroneous opinions, chiefly about the Creation and the Trinity, and was condemned by a council at Soissons in 1121 and by that of Sens 1140, at the instigation of St. Bernard.   He was hunted about, but spent his last days as a monk at Cluni.   He died 21 April, 1142.   "Abelard," observes Hallam, " was almost the first who awakened mankind, in the age of darkness, to a sympathy with intellectual excellence."

Abano (Petrus de).   See Petrus, *de Abano.*

Abauzit (Firmin), a French writer, descended from an Arabian family which settled in the South of France early in the ninth century, b. Uzes, 11 Nov. 1679.   He travelled in Holland and became acquainted with Bayle, attained a reputation for philosophy, and was consulted by Voltaire and Rousseau.   Among his works are, Reflections on the Gospels, and an essay on the Apocalypse, in which he questions the authority of that work.   Died at Geneva 20 March, 1767. His *Miscellanies* were translated in English by E. Harwood, 1774.

Abbot (Francis Ellingwood).   American Freethinker, b. Boston, 6 Nov. 1836.   He graduated at Harvard University 1859, began life as a Unitarian minister, but becoming too broad for that Church, resigned in 1869.   He started the *Index,* a journal of free religious inquiry and anti-supernaturalism, at Toledo, but since 1874 at Boston.   This he edited 1870-80.   In 1872 appeared his *Impeachment of Christianty.*   In addition to his work on the *Index,* Mr. Abbot has lectured a great deal, and has contributed to the *North American Review* and other periodicals. He was the first president of the American National Liberal League. Mr. Abbot is an evolutionist and Theist, and defends his views in *Scientific Theism*, 1886.

Ablaing van Giessenburg (R. C.) See Giessenburg.

Abu Bakr Ibn Al-Tufail (Abu J'afar) *Al Isbili*. Spanish Arabian philosopher, b. at Guadys, wrote a philosophical romance of pantheistic tendency *Hai Ibn Yakdan*, translated into Latin by Pocock, Oxford 1671, and into English by S. Ockley, 1711, under the title of *The Improvement of Human Reason*. Died at Morocco 1185.

Abu-Fazil (ABU AL FADHL IBN MUBARAK, called *Al Hindi*), vizier to the great Emperor Akbar from 1572. Although by birth a Muhammadan, his investigations into the religions of India made him see equal worth in all, and, like his master, Akbar, he was tolerant of all sects. His chief work is the *Ayin Akbary*, a statistical account of the Indian Empire. It was translated by F. Gladwin, 1777. He was assassinated 1604.

Abul-Abbas-Abdallah III. (Al Mamoun), the seventh Abbasside, caliph, son of Haroun al Rashid, was b. at Bagdad 16 Sept. 786. He was a patron of science and literature, collected Greek and Hebrew manuscripts, and invited the scholars of all nations to his capital. He wrote several treatises and poems. Died in war near Tarsus, 9 Aug. 833.

Abul-Ola (AHMAD IBN ABD ALLAH IBN SULAIMAN), celebrated Arabian poet, b. at Maari, in Syria, Dec., 973. His free opinions gave much scandal to devout Moslems. He was blind through small-pox from the age of four years, but his poems exhibit much knowledge. He called himself " the doubly imprisoned captive," in allusion to his seclusion and loss of sight. He took no pains to conceal that he believed in no revealed religion. Died May, 1057, and ordered the following verse to be written on his tomb :—" I owe this to the fault of my father: none owe the like to mine."

Abu Tahir (al Karmatti), the chief of a freethinking sect at Bahrein, on the Persian Gulf, who with a comparatively small number of followers captured Mecca (930), and took away the black stone. He suddenly attacked, defeated, and took prisoner Abissaj whom, at the head of thirty thousand men, the caliph had sent against him. Died in 943.

Achillini (Alessandro), Italian physician and philosopher b. Bologna 29 Oct. 1463. He expounded the doctrines or Averroes, and wrote largely upon anatomy. Died 2 Aug. 1512. His collected works were published at Venice, 1515.

Ackermann (Louise-Victorine, née CHOQUET), French poetess, b. Paris 30 Nov. 1813. She travelled to Germany and there married (1858) a young theologian, Paul Ackerman, who in preparing for the ministry lost his Christian faith, and who, after becoming teacher to Prince Frederick William (afterwards Frederick III.), died at the age of thirty-four (1846). Both were friends of Proudhon. Madame Ackermann's poems (Paris 1863-74 and 85) exhibit her as a philosophic pessimist and Atheist. "God is dethroned," says M. Caro of her poems (*Revue des Deux Mondes*, 15 May, 1874). She professes hatred of Christianity and its interested professors. She has also published *Thoughts of a Solitary*. Sainte Beuve calls her "the learned solitary of Nice."

Acollas (Pierre Antoine René Paul Emile), French juris-consult and political writer, b. La Châtre 25 June, 1826, studied law at Paris. For participating in the Geneva congress of the International Society in 1867 he was condemned to one year's imprisonment. In 1871 he was appointed head of the law faculty by the Commune. He has published several manuals popular-ising the legal rights of the people, and has written on *Marriage its Past, Present, and Future*, 1880. Mrs. Besant has translated his monograph on *The Idea of God in the Revolution*, published in the Droits de l'Homme.

Acontius (Jacobus—*Italian*, Giacomo Aconzio). Born at Trent early in sixteenth century. After receiving ordination in the Church of Rome he relinquished that faith and fled to Switzerland in 1557. He subsequently came to England and served Queen Elizabeth as a military engineer. To her he dedicated his *Strategems of Satan*, published at Basle 1565. This was one of the earliest latitudinarian works, and was placed upon the *Index*. It was also bitterly assailed by Pro-testant divines, both in England and on the Continent. An English translation appeared in 1648. Some proceedings were taken against Acontius before Bishop Grindall, of the result of which no account is given. Some passages of Milton's *Areo-*

9

pagitica may be traced to Acontius, who, Cheynell informs us, lived till 1623. Stephen's *Dictionary of National Biography* says he is believed to have died shortly after 1566.

Acosta (Uriel). Born at Oporto 1597, the son of a Christianised Jew; he was brought up as a Christian, but on reaching maturity, rejected that faith. He went to Holland, where he published a work equally criticising Moses and Jesus. For this he was excommunicated by the Synagogue, fined and put in prison by the Amsterdam authorities, and his work suppressed. After suffering many indignities from both Jews and Christians, he committed suicide 1647.

Adams (George), of Bristol, sentenced in 1842 to one month's imprisonment for selling the *Oracle of Reason*.

Adams (Robert C.), Canadian Freethought writer and lecturer. Author of *Travels in Faith from Tradition to Reason* (New York, 1881), also *Evolution, a Summary of Evidence*.

Adler (Felix) Ph. D. American Freethinker, the son of a Jewish rabbi, was b. in Alzey, Germany, 13 Aug. 1851. He graduated at Columbia College, 1870, was professor of Hebrew and Oriental literature at Cornell University from '74 to May '76, when he established in New York the Society of Ethical Culture, to which he discourses on Sundays. In 1877 he published a volume entitled *Creed and Deed*, in which he rejects supernatural religion. Dr. Adler has also contributed many papers to the Radical literature of America.

Ænesidemus. A Cretan sceptical philosopher of the first century. He adopted the principle of Heraclitus, that all things were in course of change, and argued against our knowledge of ultimate causes.

Airy (Sir George Biddell). English Astronomer Royal, b. Alnwick 27 July, 1801. Educated at Cambridge, where he became senior wrangler 1823. During a long life Professor Airy did much to advance astronomical science. His *Notes on the Earlier Hebrew Scriptures* 1876, proves him to have been a thorough-going Freethinker.

Aitkenhead (Thomas), an Edinburgh student aged eighteen, who was indicted for blasphemy, by order of the Privy Council, for having called the Old Testament " Ezra's Fables," and having maintained that God and nature were the same. He was found guilty 21 Dec. 1696, and hanged for blasphemy, 8 Jan. 1697.

Aitzema (Lieuwe van), a nobleman of Friesland, b. at Dorckum 19 Nov. 1600, author of a suppressed History of the Netherlands, between 1621-68. Is classed by Reimmann as an Atheist. Died at the Hague 23 Feb. 1669.

Akbar (Jalal-ed-din Muhammad), the greatest of the emperors of Hindostan, b. 15 Oct. 1542, was famous for his wide administration and improvement of the empire. Akbar showed toleration alike to Christians, Muhammadans, and to all forms of the Hindu faith. He had the Christian gospels and several Brahmanical treatises translated into Persian. The result of his many conferences on religion between learned men of all sects, are collected in the *Dabistan*. Akbar was brought up as a Muhammadan, but became a Theist, acknowledging one God, but rejecting all other dogmas. Died Sept. 1605.

Alberger (John). American author of *Monks, Popes, and their Political Intrigues* (Baltimore, 1871) and *Antiquity of Christianity* (New York, 1874).

Albini (Giuseppe). Italian physiologist, b. Milan. In 1845 he studied medicine in Paris. He has written on embryology and many other physiological subjects.

Alchindus. YAKUB IBN IS'HAK IBN SUBBAH (Abú Yúsuf) called *Al Kindi*, Arab physician and philosopher, the great grandson of one of the companions of Muhammad, the prophet, flourished from 814 to about 840. He was a rationalist in religion, and for his scientific studies he was set down as a magician.

Alciati (Giovanni Paolo). A Milanese of noble family. At first a Romanist, he resigned that faith for Calvinism, but gradually advanced to Anti-trinitarianism, which he defends in two letters to Gregorio Pauli, dated Austerlitz 1564 and 1565 Beza says that Alciati deserted the Christian faith and became a Muhammadan, but Bayle takes pains to disprove this. Died at Dantzic about 1570.

Aleardi (Gaetano). Italian poet, known as Aleardo Aleardi,

b. Verona, 4 Nov. 1812. He was engaged in a life-long struggle against the Austrian dominion, and his patriotic poems were much admired. In 1859 he was elected deputy to Parliament for Brescia. Died Verona, 16 July, 1878.

Alembert (Jean le Rond d'), mathematician and philosopher, b. at Paris 16 Nov. 1717. He was an illegitimate son of Canon Destouches and Mme. Tencin, and received his Christian name from a church near which he was exposed as a foundling. He afterwards resided for forty years with his nurse, nor would he leave her for the most tempting offers. In 1741, he was admitted a member of the Academy of Sciences. In 1749, he obtained the prize medal from the Academy of Berlin, for a discourse on the theory of winds. In 1749, he solved the problem of the procession of the equinoxes and explained the mutation of the earth's axis. He next engaged with Diderot, with whose opinions he was in complete accord, in compiling the famous *Encyclopédie*, for which he wrote the preliminary discourse. In addition to this great work he published many historical, philosophical and scientific essays, and largely corresponded with Voltaire. His work on the Destruction of the Jesuits is a caustic and far-reaching production. In a letter to Frederick the Great, he says: " As for the existence of a supreme intelligence, I think that those who deny it advance more than they can prove, and scepticism is the only reasonable course." He goes on to say, however, that experience invincibly proves the materiality of the " soul." Died 29 Oct. 1783. In 1799 two volumes of his posthumous essays were printed in Paris. His works prove d'Alembert to have been of broad spirit and of most extensive knowledge.

Alfieri (Vittorio), Count. Famous Italian poet and dramatist, b. Asti, Piedmont, 17 Jan. 1749, of a noble family. His tragedies are justly celebrated, and in his *Essay on Tyranny* he shows himself as favorable to religious as to political liberty. Written in his youth, this work was revised at a more advanced age, the author remarking that if he had no longer the courage, or rather the fire, necessary to compose it, he nevertheless retained intelligence, independence and judgment enough to approve it, and to let it stand as the last of his literary productions. His attack is chiefly directed against Catholicism, but he does not spare Christianity. " Born among a people," he says, "slavish, ignorant, and already entirely subjugated by priests, the Christian religion knows only how to enjoin the blindest obedience, and is unacquainted even with the name of liberty." Alfieri's tragedy of *Saul* has been prohibited on the English stage. Died Florence, 8 Oct. 1803.

Alfonso X., surnamed the Wise, King of Castille and of Leon; b. in 1223, crowned 1252. A patron of science and lover of astronomy. He compiled a complete digest of Roman, feudal and canon law, and had drawn up the astronomical tables called Alfonsine Tables. By his liberality and example he gave a great impulse to Spanish literature. For his intercourse with Jews and Arabians, his independence towards the Pope and his free disposal of the clerical revenues, he has been stigmatised as an Atheist. To him is attributed the well-known remark that had he been present at the creation of the world he would have proposed some improvents. Father Lenfant adds the pious lie that " The king had scarcely pronounced this blasphemy when a thunderbolt fell and reduced his wife and two children to ashes." Alfonso X. died 4 April, 1284.

Algarotti (Francesco), Count. Italian writer and art critic, b. at Venice, 11 Dec. 1712. A visit to England led him to write *Newtonianism for the Ladies*. He afterwards visited Berlin and became the friend both of Voltaire and of Frederick the Great, who appointed him his Chamberlain. Died with philosophical composure at Pisa, 3 May, 1764.

Alger (William Rounseville), b. at Freetown, Massachusetts, 30 Dec. 1822, educated at Harvard, became a Unitarian preacher of the advanced type. His *Critical History of the Doctrine of a Future Life*, with a complete bibliography of the subject by Ezra Abbot, is a standard work, written from the Universalist point of view.

Allen (Charles Grant Blairfindie), naturalist and author, b. in Kingston, Canada, 24 Feb. 1848. He studied at Merton College, Oxford, and graduated with honors 1871. In 1873 appointed Professor of Logic in Queen's College, Spanish town, Jamaica; from 1874 to '77 he was its principal. Since then he has resided in England, and become known by his popular expositions of Darwinism. His published works include *Physiological Æsthetics* (1877), *The Evolutionist at Large* (1881),

Nature Studies (1883), *Charles Darwin* (1885), and several novels. Grant Allen has also edited the miscellaneous works of Buckle, and has written on *Force and Energy* (1888).

Allen (Ethan) **Col.**, American soldier, b. at Lichfield, Connecticut, 10 Jan. 1737. One of the most active of the revolutionary heroes, he raised a company of volunteers known as the "Green Mountain Boys," and took by surprise the British fortress of Ticonderoga, capturing 100 guns, 10 May, 1775. He was declared an outlaw and £100 offered for his arrest by Gov. Tryon of New York. Afterwards he was taken prisoner and sent to England. At first treated with cruelty, he was eventually exchanged for another officer, 6 May, 1778. He was a member of the state legislature, and succeeded in obtaining the recognition of Vermont as an independent state. He published in 1784 *Reason the only Oracle of Man*, the first publication in the United States openly directed against the Christian religion. It has been frequently reprinted and is still popular in America. Died Burlington, Vermont, 13 Feb. 1789. A statue is erected to him at Montpelier, Vermont.

Allsop (Thomas). "The favorite disciple of Coleridge," b. 10 April, 1794, near Wirksworth, Derbyshire, he lived till 1880. A friend of Robert Owen and the Chartists. He was implicated in the attempt of Orsini against Napoleon III. In his *Letters, Conversations and Recollections of Samuel Taylor Coleridge*, he has imported many of his Freethought views.

Alm (Richard von der). See Ghillany (F. W.)

Alpharabius (Muhammad ibn Muhammad ibn Tarkhan) (Abu Nasr), called *Al Farabi*, Turkish philosopher, termed by Ibn Khallikan the greatest philosopher the Moslems ever had, travelled to Bagdad, mastered the works of Aristotle, and became master of Avicenna. Al Farabi is said to have taught the eternity of the world and to have denied the permanent individuality of the soul. His principal work is a sort of encyclopædia. Rénan says he expressly rejected all supernatural revelation. Died at Damascus Dec. 950, aged upwards of eighty.

Amaury or **Amalric de Chartres**, a heretic of the thirteenth century, was a native of Bene, near Chartres, and lived at Paris, where he gave lessons in logic. In a work bearing the title of *Physion*, condemned by a bull of Pope

Innocent III. (1204), he is said to have taught a kind of Pantheism, and that the reign of the Father and Son must give place to that of the Holy Spirit. Ten of his disciples were burnt at Paris 20 Dec. 1210, and the bones of Amaury were exhumed and placed in the flames.

Amberley (John Russell) Viscount, eldest son of Earl Russell, b. 1843. Educated at Harrow, Edinburgh and Trinity College, Cambridge, where ill-health prevented him reading for honors. He entered Parliament in 1866 as Radical member for Nottingham. Lord Amberley contributed thoughtful articles to the *North British*, the *Fortnightly* and *Theological Reviews*, and will be remembered by his bold *Analysis of Religious Belief* (1876), in which he examines, compares and criticises the various faiths of the world. Lord Amberley left his son to be brought up by Mr. Spalding, a self-taught man of great ability and force of character; but the will was set aside, on appeal to the Court of Chancery, in consideration of Mr. Spalding's heretical views. Died 8 Jan. 1876.

Amman (Hans Jacob), German surgeon and traveller, b Lake Zurich 1586. In 1612 he went to Constantinople, Palestine and Egypt, and afterwards published a curious book called *Voyage in the Promised Land*. Died at Zurich, 1658.

Ammianus (Marcellinus). Roman soldier-historian of the fourth century, b. at Antioch. He wrote the Roman history from the reign of Nerva to the death of Valens in thirty-one books, of which the first thirteen are lost. His history is esteemed impartial and trustworthy. He served under Julian, and compares the rancor of the Christians of the period to that of wild beasts. Gibbon calls him "an accurate and faithful guide." Died about 395 A.D.

Ammonius, surnamed Saccas or the Porter, from his having been obliged in the early part of his life to adopt that calling, was born of Christian parents in Alexandria during the second century. He, however, turned Pagan and opened a school of philosophy. Among his pupils were Origen, Longinus and Plotinus. He undoubtedly originated the Neo-Platonic movement, which formed the most serious opposition to Christianity in its early career. Ammonius died A.D. 243, aged over eighty years.

Anaxagoras, a Greek philosopher of the Ionic school, b. about 499 B.C., lived at Athens and enjoyed the friendship of Pericles. In 450 B.C. he was accused of Atheism for maintaining the eternity of matter and was banished to Lampsacus, where he died in 428 B.C. It is related that, being asked how he desired to be honored after death, he replied, "Only let the day of my death be observed as a holiday by the boys in the schools." He taught that generation and destruction are only the union and separation of elements which can neither be created nor annihilated.

Andre-Nuytz (Louis), author of *Positivism for All*, an elementary exposition of Positive philosophy, to which Littré wrote a preface, 1868.

Andrews (Stephen Pearl). American Sociologist, b. Templeton, Mass., 22 March, 1812. He was an ardent Abolitionist, an eloquent speaker, and the inventor of a universal language called Alwato. His principle work is entitled *The Basic Outline of Universology* (N. Y., 1872). He also wrote *The Church and Religion of the Future* (1886). He was a prominent member and vice-president of the Liberal Club of New York, a contributor to the London *Times*, the New York *Truthseeker*, and many other journals. Died at New York, 21 May, 1886.

Andrieux (Louis). French deputy, b. Trévoux 20 July, 1840. Was called to the bar at Lyons, where he became famous for his political pleading. He took part in the Freethought Congress at Naples in 1869, and in June of the following year he was imprisoned for three months for his attack on the Empire. On the establishment of the Republic he was nominated procureur at Lyons. He was on the municipal council of that city, which he has also represented in the Chamber of Deputies. In 1879 he became Prefect of Police at Paris, but retired in 1881 and was elected deputy by his constituents at Lyons. He has written *Souvenirs of a Prefect of Police* (1885).

Angelucci (Teodoro). Italian poet and philosopher, b. near Tolentino 1549. He advocated Aristotle against F. Patrizi, and was banished from Rome. One of the first emancipators of modern thought in Italy, he also made an excellent translation of the Æneid of Virgil. Died Montagnana, 1600.

Angiulli (Andrea). Italian Positivist, b. Castellana 12 Feb.

16

1837, author of a work on philosophy and Positive research, Naples 1868. He became professor of Anthropology at Naples in 1876, and edits a philosophical review published in that city since 1881.

Annet (Peter). One of the most forcible writers among the English Deists, b. at Liverpool in 1693. He was at one time a schoolmaster and invented a system of shorthand. Priestley learnt it at school and corresponded with Annet. In 1739 he published a pamphlet on *Freethinking the Great Duty of Religion*, by P. A., minister of religion. This was followed by *the Conception of Jesus as the Foundation of the Christian Religion*, in which he boldly attacks the doctrine of the Incarnation as "a legend of the Romanists," and *The Resurrection of Jesus Considered* (1744) in answer to Bishop Sherlock's *Trial of the Witnesses*. This controversy was continued in *The Resurrection Reconsidered* and *The Resurrection Defenders Stript of all Defence*. In *An Examination of the History and Character of St. Paul* he attacks the sincerity of the apostle to the Gentiles and even questions the authenticity of his epistles. In *Supernaturals Examined* (1747) he argues that all miracles are incredible. In 1761 he issued nine numbers of the *Free Inquirer*, in which he attacked the authenticity and credibility of the Pentateuch. For this he was brought before the King's Bench and sentenced to suffer one month's imprisonment in Newgate, to stand twice in the pillory, once at Charing Cross and once at the Exchange. with a label " For Blasphemy," then to have a year's hard labor in Bridewell and to find sureties for good behavior during the rest of his life. It is related that a woman seeing Annet in the pillory said, " Gracious! pilloried for blasphemy. Why, don't we blaspheme every day!" After his release Annet set up a school at Lambeth. Being asked his views on a future life he replied by this apologue: " One of my friends in Italy, seeing the sign of an inn, asked if that was the Angel." " No," was the reply, " do you not see it is the sign of a dragon." " Ah," said my friend, " as I have never seen either angel or dragon, how can I tell whether it is one or the other? " Died 18 Jan. 1769. *The History of the Man after God's Own Heart* (1761) ascribed to Annet, was more probably written by Archibald Campbell. *The View of the Life of King David* (1765) by W. Skilton, Horologist, is also falsely attributed to Annet.

Anthero de Quental, Portuguese writer, b. San Miguel 1843. Educated for the law at the University of Coimbra, he has published both poetry and prose, showing him to be a student of Hartmann, Proudhon and Rénan, and one of the most advanced minds in Portugal.

Anthony (Susan Brownell). American reformer, b. of a Quaker family at South Adams, Massachusetts, 15 Feb. 1820. She became a teacher, a temperance reformer, an opponent of slavery, and an ardent advocate of women's rights. Of the last movement she became secretary. In conjunction with Mrs. E. C. Stanton and Parker Pillsbury she conducted *The Revolutionist* founded in New York in 1868, and with Mrs. Stanton and Matilda Joslyn Gage she has edited the *History of Woman's Suffrage*, 1881. Miss Anthony is a declared Agnostic.

Antoine (Nicolas). Martyr. Denied the Messiahship and divinity of Jesus, and was strangled and burnt at Geneva, 20 April, 1632.

Antonelle (Pierre Antoine) *Marquis d'*, French political economist, b. Arles 1747. He embraced the revolution with ardor, and his article in the *Journal des Hommes Libres* occasioned his arrest with Babœuf. He was, however, acquitted. Died at Arles, 26 Nov. 1817.

Antoninus (Marcus Aurelius). See Aurelius.

Apelt (Ernst Friedrich), German philosopher, b. Reichenau 3 March, 1812. He criticised the philosophy of religion from the standpoint of reason, and wrote many works on metaphysics. Died near Gorlitz, 27 Oct. 1859.

Aquila, a Jew of Pontus, who became a proselyte to Christianity, but afterwards left that religion. He published a Greek version of the Hebrew scriptures to show that the prophecies did not apply to Jesus (A.D. 128). The work is lost. He has been identified by E. Deutsch with the author of the Targum of Onkelos.

Arago (Dominique François Jean), French academician, politician, physicist and astronomer, b. Estagel, 26 Feb. 1786. He was elected to the French Academy of Sciences at the age of twenty-three. He made several optical and electro-magnetic discoveries, and advocated the undulatory theory of light. He was an ardent Republican and Freethinker, and took part in the provisional Government of 1848. He opposed the election of Louis Napoleon, and refused to take the oath of allegiance after the *coup d'état* of December, 1851. Died 2 Oct. 1853. Humboldt calls him a "zealous defender of the interests of Reason."

Ardigo (Roberto), Italian philosopher, b. at Casteldidone (Cremona) 28 Jan. 1828, was intended for the Church, but took to philosophy. In 1869 he published a discourse on Peitro Pomponazzi, followed next year by *Psychology as a Positive Science.* Signor Ardigo has also written on the formation of the solar system and on the historical formation of the ideas of God and the soul. An edition of his philosophical works was commenced at Mantua in 1882. Ardigo is one of the leaders of the Italian Positivists. His *Positivist Morals* appeared in Padua 1885.

Argens (Jean Baptiste de BOYER) *Marquis d'*, French writer, b. at Aix, in Provence, 24 June 1704. He adopted a military life and served with distinction. On the accession of Frederick the Great he invited d'Argens to his court at Berlin, and made him one of his chamberlains. Here he resided twenty-five years and then returned to Aix, where he resided till his death 11 June, 1771. His works were published in 1768 in twenty-four volumes. Among them are *Lettres Juives, Lettres Chinoises* and *Lettres Cabalistiques,* which were joined to *La Philosophie du bon sens.* He also translated Julian's discourse against Christianity and Ocellus Lucanus on the Eternity of the World. Argens took Bayle as his model, but he was inferior to that philosopher.

Argental (Charles Augustin de FERRIOL) *Count d'*, French diplomat, b. Paris 20 Dec. 1700, was a nephew of Mme. de Tencin, the mother of D'Alembert. He is known for his long and enthusiastic friendship for Voltaire. He was said to be the author of *Mémoires du Comte de Comminge* and *Anecdotes de la cour d'Edouard.* Died 5 Jan. 1788.

Aristophanes, great Athenian comic poet, contemporary with Socrates, Plato, and Euripides, b. about 444 B.C. Little is known of his life. He wrote fifty-four plays, of which only eleven remain, and was crowned in a public assembly for his attacks on the oligarchs. With the utmost boldness he satirised

19

not only the the political and social evils of the age, but also the philosophers, the gods, and the theology of the period. Plato is said to have died with Aristophanes' works under his pillow.   Died about 380 B.C.

Aristotle, the most illustrious of ancient philosophers, was born at Stagyra, in Thrace, 384 B.C.   He was employed by Philip of Macedon to instruct his son Alexander.   His inculcation of ethics as apart from all theology, justifies his place in this list.   After the death of Alexander, he was accused of impiety and withdrew to Chalcis, where he died B.C. 322. Grote says: "In the published writings of Aristotle the accusers found various heretical doctrines suitable for sustaining their indictment; as, for example, the declaration that prayer and sacrifices to the gods were of no avail."   His influence was predominant upon philosophy for nearly two thousand years.   Dante speaks of him as "the master of those that know."

Arnold of Brescia, a pupil of Abelard.   He preached against the papal authority and the temporal power, and the vices of the clergy.   He was condemned for heresy by a Lateran Council in 1139, and retired from Italy.   He afterwards returned to Rome and renewed his exertions against sacerdotal oppression, and was eventually seized and burnt at Rome in 1155.   Baronius calls him "the patriarch of political heretics."

Arnold (Matthew), LL.D. poet and critic, son of Dr. Arnold of Rugby, b. at Laleham 24 Dec. 1822.   Educated at Winchester, Rugby, and Oxford, where he won the Newdigate prize.   In 1848 he published the *Strayed Reveller, and other Poems*, signed A. In 1851 he married and became an inspector of schools.   In 1853 appeared *Empedocles on Etna*, a poem in which, under the guise of ancient teaching he gives much secular philosophy. In 1857 he was elected Professor of Poetry at Oxford.   In 1871 he published an essay entitled *St. Paul and Protestantism;* in 1873 *Literature and Dogma*, which, from its rejection of supernaturalism, occasioned much stir and was followed by *God and the Bible*.   In 1877 Mr. Arnold published *Last Essays on Church and State*.   Mr. Arnold has a lucid style and is abreast of the thought of his age, but he curiously unites rejection of supernaturalism, including a personal God, with a fond regard for the Church of England. He may be said in his own words to wander "between two worlds, one dead, the other powerless to be born." Died 15 April, 1888.

Arnould (Arthur), French writer, b. Dieuze 7 April, 1833. As journalist he wrote on *l'Opinion Nationale*, the *Rappel, Reforme* and other papers. In 1864 he published a work on Beranger, and in '69 a *History of the Inquisition*. In Jan. 1870 he founded *La Marseillaise* with H. Rochefort, and afterwards the *Journal du Peuple* with Jules Valles. He was elected to the National Assembly and was member of the Commune, of which he has written a history in three volumes. He has also written many novels and dramas.

Arnould (Victor), Belgian Freethinker, b. Maestricht, 7 Nov. 1838, advocate at the Court of Appeal, Brussels. Author of a *History of the Church* 1874, and a little work on the *Philosophy of Liberalism* 1877.

Arouet (François Marie). See Voltaire.

Arpe (Peter Friedrich). Philosopher, b. Kiel, Holstein, 10 May, 1682. Wrote an apology for Vanini dated Cosmopolis (*i.e.*, Rotterdam, 1712). A reply to La Monnoye's treatise on the book *De Tribus Impostoribus* is attributed to him. Died, Hamburgh, 4 Nov. 1740.

Arthur (John) is inserted in Maréchal's *Dictionnaire des Athées* as a mechanic from near Birmingham, who took a prize at Paris and republished the *Invocation to Nature* in the last pages of the *System of Nature*. Julian Hibbert inserted his name in his *Chronological Tables of Anti-Superstitionists*, with the date of death 1792.

Asseline (Louis). French writer, b. at Versailles in 1829, became an advocate in 1851. In 1866 he established *La Libre Pensée*, a weekly journal of scientific materialism, and when that was suppressed *La Pensée Nouvelle*. He was one of the founders of the *Encyclopédie Générale*. He wrote *Diderot and the Nineteenth Century*, and contributed to many journals. After the revolution of 4 Sept. 1870 he was elected mayor of the fourteenth arrondissement of Paris, and was afterwards one of the Municipal Council of that city. Died 6 April, 1878.

Assezat (Jules). French writer, b. at Paris 21 Jan. 1832 was a son of a compositor on the *Journal des Debats*, on which Jules obtained a position and worked his way to the editorial chair. He was secretary of the Paris Society of Anthropology, contributed to *La Pensée Nouvelle*, edited the *Man Machine* of Lamettrie, and edited the complete works of Diderot in twenty volumes. Died 24 June, 1876.

Assollant (Jean, Baptiste Alfred). French novelist, b. 20 March, 1827. Larousse says he has all the scepticism of Voltaire.

Ast (Georg Anton Friedrich). German Platonist, b. Gotha 29 Dec. 1778. Was professor of classical literature at Landshut and Munich. Wrote *Elements of Philosophy*, 1809, etc. Died Munich 31 Dec. 1841.

Atkinson (Henry George). Philosophic writer, b. in 1818. Was educated at the Charterhouse, gave attention to mesmerism, and wrote in the *Zoist*. In 1851 he issued *Letters on the Laws of Man's Nature and Development*, in conjunction with Harriet Martineau, to whom he served as philosophic guide. This work occasioned a considerable outcry. Mr. Atkinson was a frequent contributor to the *National Reformer* and other Secular journals. He died 28 Dec. 1884, at Boulogne, where he had resided since 1870.

Aubert de Verse (Noel). A French advocate of the seventeenth century, who wrote a history of the Papacy (1685) and was accused of blasphemy.

Audebert (Louise). French authoress of the *Romance of a Freethinker* and of an able *Reply of a Mother to the Bishop of Orleans*, 1868.

Audifferent (Georges). Positivist and executor to Auguste Comte, was born at Saint Pierre (Martinque) in 1823, settled at Marseilles, and is the author of several medical and scientific works.

Aurelius (Marcus Antoninus). Roman Emperor and Stoic philosopher, b. at Rome 26 April, 121. Was carefully educated, and lived a laborious, abstemious life. On the death of his uncle Antoninus Pius, 161, the Senate obliged him to take the government, but he associated with himself L. Verus.

On the death of Verus in 169 Antoninus possessed sole authority, which he exercised with wise discretion and great glory. Much of his time was employed in defending the northern frontiers of the empire against Teutonic barbarians. He had no high opinion of Christians, speaking of their obstinacy, and it is pretended many were put to death in the reign of one of the best emperors that ever ruled. If so we may be assured it was for their crimes. Ecclesiastical historians have invented another pious miracle in a victory gained through the prayers of the Christians. Antoninus held that duty was indispensable even were there no gods. His *Meditations*, written in the midst of a most active life, breathe a lofty morality, and are a standing refutation of the view that pure ethics depend upon Christian belief. Died 17 March, 180.

Austin (Charles), lawyer and disciple of Bentham, b. Suffolk 1799. At Cambridge, where he graduated B.A. in 1824 and M.A. in 1827, he won, much to the amazement of his friends, who knew his heterodox opinions, the Hulsean prize for an essay on Christian evidences. For this he was sorry afterwards, and told Lord Stanley of Alderley "I could have written a much better essay on the other side." He afterwards wrote on the other side in the *Westminster Review*. Successful as a lawyer, he retired in ill-health. J. S. Mill writes highly of his influence. The Hon. L. A. Tollemache gives a full account of his heretical opinions. He says "He inclined to Darwinism, because as he said, it is so antecedently probable; but, long before this theory broke the back of final causes, he himself had given them up." Died 21 Dec. 1874.

Austin (John), jurist, brother of above, was born 3 March, 1790. A friend of James Mill, Grote and Bentham, whose opinions he shared, he is chiefly known by his profound works on jurisprudence. Died 17 Dec. 1859.

Avempace, *i.e.*, Muhammad ibn Yahya ibn Bajjat (Abu Bekr), called *Ibn al-Saigh* (the son of the goldsmith), Arabian philosopher and poet, b. at Saragossa, practised medicine at Seville 1118, which he quitted about 1120, and became vizier at the court of Fez, where he died about 1138. An admirer of Aristotle, he was one of the teachers of Averroes. Al-Fath Ibn Khâkân represents him as an infidel and Atheist, and says:

"Faith disappeared from his heart and left not a trace behind; his tongue forgot the Merciful, neither did [the holy] name cross his lips." He is said to have suffered imprisonment for his heterodoxy.

Avenel (Georges), French writer, b. at Chaumont 31 Dec. 1828. One of the promoters of the *Encyclopédie Générale*. His vindication of Cloots (1865) is a solid work of erudition. He became editor of *la République Française* and edited the edition of Voltaire published by *Le Siècle* (1867-70). Died at Bougival, near Paris, 1 July, 1876, and was, by his express wish, buried without religious ceremony.

Averroes (Muhammad Ibn-Ahmad Ibn Rushd), *Abu al Walid*, Arabian philosopher, b. at Cordova in 1126, and died at Morocco 10 Dec. 1198. He translated and commented upon the works of Aristotle, and resolutely placed the claims of science above those of theology. He was prosecuted for his heretical opinions by the Muhammadan doctors, was spat upon by all who entered the mosque at the hour of prayer, and afterwards banished. His philosophical opinions, which incline towards materialism and pantheism, had the honor of being condemned by the University of Paris in 1240. They were opposed by St. Thomas Aquinas, and when profoundly influencing Europe at the Rennaisance through the Paduan school were again condemned by Pope Leo X. in 1513.

Avicenna (Husain Ibn Abdallah, called *Ibn Sina*), Arabian physician and philosopher, b. Aug. 980 in the district of Bokhara. From his early youth he was a wonderful student, and at his death 15 June, 1037, he left behind him above a hundred treatises. He was the sovereign authority in medical science until the days of Harvey. His philosophy was pantheistic in tone, with an attempt at compromise with theology

Aymon (Jean), French writer, b. Dauphiné 1661. Brought up in the Church, he abjured Catholicism at Geneva, and married at the Hague. He published *Metamorphoses of the Romish Religion*, and is said to have put forward a version of the *Esprit de Spinoza* under the famous title *Treatise of Three Impostors*. Died about 1734.

Bagehot (Walter), economist and journalist, b. of Unitarian parents, Langport, Somersetshire, 3 Feb. 1826; he died at the same place 24 March, 1877.   He was educated at London University, of which he became a fellow.   For the last seventeen years of his life he edited the *Economist* newspaper.   His best-known works are *The English Constitution, Lombard Street* and *Literary Studies.*   In *Physics and Politics* (1872), a series of essays on the Evolution of Society, he applies Darwinism to politics.   Bagehot was a bold, clear, and very original thinker, who rejected historic Christianity.

Baggesen (Jens Immanuel), Danish poet, b. Kösor, Zealand. 15 Feb. 1764.   In 1789 he visited Germany, France, and Switzerland; at Berne he married the grand-daughter of Haller.   He wrote popular poems both in Danish and German, among others *Adam and Eve*, a humorous mock epic (1826). He was an admirer of Voltaire.   Died Hamburg, 3 Oct. 1826.

Bahnsen (Julius Friedrich August), pessimist, b. Tondern, Schleswig-Holstein, 30 Mar. 1830.   Studied philosophy at Keil, 1847.   He fought against the Danes in '49, and afterwards studied at Tübingen.   Bahnsen is an independent follower of Schopenhauer and Hartmann, joining monism to the idealism of Hegel.   He has written several works, among which we mention *The Philosophy of History*, Berlin, 1872, and *The Contradiction between the Knowledge and the Nature of the World* (2 vols),   Berlin 1880-82.

Bahrdt (Karl Friedrich), German deist, b. in Saxony, 25 Aug. 1741.   Educated for the Church, in 1766 he was made professor of biblical philology.   He was condemned for heresy, and wandered from place to place.   He published a kind of expurgated Bible, called *New Revelations of God: A System of Moral Religion for Doubters and Thinkers*, Berlin, 1787, and a *Catechism of Natural Religion*, Halle, 1790.   Died near Halle, 23 April, 1792.

Bailey (James Napier), Socialist, edited the *Model Republic*, 1843, the *Torch*, and the *Monthly Messenger.*   He published *Gehenna: its Monarch and Inhabitants ; Sophistry Unmasked*, and several other tracts in the "Social Reformer's Cabinet Library," and some interesting *Essays on Miscellaneous Subjects.* at Leeds, 1842.

Bailey (Samuel), philosophical writer, of Sheffield, b. in 1791. His essay on the *Formation and Publication of Opinions* ap-

25

peared in 1821. He vigorously contends that man is not responsible for his opinions because they are independent of his will, and that opinions should not be the subject of punishment. Another anonymous Freethought work was *Letters from an Egyptian Kaffir on a Visit to England in Search of Religion*. This was at first issued privately 1839, but afterwards printed as a *Reasoner* tract. He also wrote *The Pursuit of Truth*, 1829, and a *Theory of Reasoning*, 1851. He was acquainted with both James and John Stuart Mill, and shared in most of the views of the philosophical Radicals of the period. Died 18 Jan. 1870, leaving £90,000 to his native town.

Bailey (William S.), editor of the *Liberal*, published in Nashville, Tennessee, was an Atheist up till the day of death, March, 1886. In a slave-holding State, he was the earnest advocate of abolition.

Baillie (George), of Garnet Hill, Glasgow. Had been a sheriff in one of the Scotch counties. He was a liberal subscriber to the Glasgow Eclectic Institute. In 1854 he offered a prize for the best essay on Christianity and Infidelity, which was gained by Miss Sara Hennell. In 1857 another prize was restricted to the question whether Jesus prophesied the coming of the end of the world in the life-time of his followers. It was gained by Mr. E. P. Meredith, and is incorporated in his *Prophet of Nazareth*. In 1863 Mr. Baillie divested himself of his fortune (£18,000) which was to be applied to the erection and endowment of an institution to aid the culture of the operative classes by means of free libraries and unsectarian schools, retaining only the interest for himself as curator. He only survived a few years.

Baillière (Gustave-Germer), French scientific publisher, b. at Paris 26 Dec. 1837. Studied medicine, but devoted himself to bringing out scientific publications such as the *Library of Contemporary Philosophy*, and the *International Scientific Series*. He was elected 29 Nov. 1871 as Republican and anti-clerical member of the Municipal Council of Paris.

Bain (Alexander) LLD. Scotch philosopher, b. at Aberdeen in 1818. He began life as a weaver but studied at Marischal College 1836-40, and graduated M.A. in 1840. He then began to contribute to the *Westminster Review*, and became acquainted with John Stuart Mill, whose *Logic* he discussed in manuscript. In 1855 he published *The Senses and The Intellect*, and in 1859 *The Emotions and the Will*, constituting together a systematic exposition of the human mind. From 1860 to 1880 he occupied the Chair of Logic in the University of Aberdeen, his accession being most obnoxious to the orthodox, and provoking disorder among the students. In 1869 he received the degree of LLD. In additon to numerous educational works Dr. Bain published a *Compendium of Mental and Moral Science* (1868), *Mind and Body* (1875), and *Education as a Science* (1879), for the International Scientific Series. In 1882 he published *James Mill, a Biography*, and *John Stuart Mill: a Criticism, with Personal Recollections*. In 1881 he was elected Lord Rector of the University of Aberdeen, and this honor was renewed in 1884, in which year he published *Practical Essays*.

Bainham (James), martyr. He married the widow of Simon Fish, author of the *Supplycacion of Beggars*, an attack upon the clergy of the period. In 1531 he was accused of heresy, having among other things denied transubstantiation, the confessional, and " the power of the keys." It was asserted that he had said that he would as lief pray to his wife as to " our lady," and that Christ was but a man. This he denied, but admitted holding the salvation of unbelievers. He was burnt 30 April, 1532.

Baissac (Jules), French *littérateur*, b. Vans, 1827, author of several studies in philology and mythology. In 1878 he published *Les Origines de la Religion* in three volumes, which have the honor of being put upon the Roman *Index*. This was followed by *l'Age de Dieu*, a study of cosmical periods and the feast of Easter. In 1882 he began to publish *Histoire de la Diablerie Chrétienne*, the first part of which is devoted to the person and " personnel " of the devil.

Bakunin (Mikhail Aleksandrovich), Russian Nihilist, b. Torshok (Tver) 1814, of an ancient aristocratic family. He was educated at St. Petersburg, and entered as an ensign in the artillery. Here he became imbued with revolutionary ideas. He went to Berlin in 1841, studied the Hegelian philosophy, and published some philosophical writings under the name of Jules Elisard. In '43 he visited Paris and became a disciple of

Proudhon. In '48 he was expelled from France at the demand of Russia, whose government set the price of 10,000 silver roubles on his head, went to Dresden and became a member of the insurrectionary government. He was arrested and condemned to death, May '50, but his sentence was commuted to imprisonment for life. He escaped into Austria, was again captured and sentenced to death, but was handed over to Russia and deported to Siberia. After several years' penal servitude he escaped, travelled over a thousand miles under extreme hardship, reached the sea and sailed to Japan. Thence he sailed to California, thence to New York and London, where with Herzen he published the *Kolokol*. He took part in the establishment of the International Society, but being at issue with Karl Marx abandoned that body in 1873. He died at Berne 1 July 1876, leaving behind a work on *God and the State*, both being vigorously attacked. Laveleye writes of him as "the apostle of universal destruction."

Ball (William Platt), b. at Birmingham 28 Nov. 1844. Educated at Birkbeck School, London. Became schoolmaster but retired rather than teach religious doctrines. Matriculated at London University 1866. Taught pyrotechny in the Sultan's service 1870–71. Received the order of the Medjidieh after narrow escape from death by the bursting of a mortar. Upon his return published *Poems from Turkey* (1872). Mr. Ball has contributed to the *National Reformer* since 1878 and since 1884 has been on the staff of the *Freethinker*. He has published pamphlets on *Religion in Schools*, the *Ten Commandments* and *Mrs Besant's Socialism*, and has compiled with Mr. Foote the *Bible Handbook*. Mr. Ball is a close thinker and a firm supporter of Evolutional Malthusianism, which he has ably defended in the pages of *Progress*. He has of late been engaged upon the question: Are the Effects of Use and Disuse Inherited?

Ballance (John), New Zealand statesman, b. Glenary, Antrim Ireland, March 1839. Going out to New Zealand he became a journalist and started the *Wanganui Herald*. He entered Parliament in 1875 and became Colonial Treasurer in '78. With Sir Robert Stout he has been a great support to the Freethought cause in New Zealand.

Baltzer (Wilhelm Eduard). German rationalist, b. 24 Oct.

1814, at Hohenleine in Saxony. He was educated as a Protestant minister, but resigned and founded at Nordhausen in 1847 a free community. He took part in the Parliament of Frankfort in '48 ; has translated the life of Apollonius of Tyana, and is the author of a history of religion and numerous other works. Died 24 June, 1887.

Bancel (François Désiré). French politician, b. Le Mastre, 2 Feb. 1822. Became an advocate. In 1849, he was elected to the Legislative Assembly. After the *coup d'état* he retired to Brussels, where he became Professor at the University. In 1869 he was elected deputy at Paris in opposition to M. Ollivier. He translated the work on Rationalism by Ausonio Franchi, and wrote on *Mysteries*, 1871, besides many political works. Died 23 June, 1871.

Barbier (Edmond). French translator of the works of Darwin, Lubbock, and Tylor. Died 1883.

Barbier d'Aucour (Jean). French critic and academician, b. Langres, 1642. Most of his writings are directed against the Jesuits. Died Paris, 13 Sept. 1694.

Barlow (George). Poet, b. in London, 19 June, 1847. In his volumes, *Under the Dawn* and *Poems, Real and Ideal*, he gives utterance to many Freethought sentiments.

Barlow (Joel). American statesman, writer and poet, b. Reading, Connecticut, 24 March, 1754. Served as a volunteer in the revolutionary war, became a chaplain, but resigned that profession, taking to literature. In England, in 1791, he published *Advice to the Privileged Orders*. In France he translated Volney's *Ruins of Empires*, and contributed to the political literature of the Revolution. Paine entrusted him with the MS. of the first part of the *Age of Reason*. His chief work is entitled the *Columbiad*, 1808. He was sent as minister to France, 1811, and being involved in the misfortunes following the retreat from Moscow, died near Cracow, Poland, 24 Dec. 1812.

Barni (Jules Romain). French philosophic writer, b. Lille, 1 June, 1818. He became secretary to Victor Cousin, and translated the works of Kant into French. He contributed to *La Liberté de Penser* (1847-51) and to *l'Avenir* (1855). During the Empire he lived in Switzerland and published *Martyrs de* *la Libre Pensée* (1862), *La Morale dans la Démocratie* (1864), and a work on the French Moralists of the Eighteenth Century (1873). He was elected to the National Assembly, 1872, and to the Chamber of Deputies, 1876. Died at Mers, 4 July, 1878. A statue is erected to him at Amiens.

Barnout (Hippolyte). French architect and writer, b. Paris 1816, published a *Rational Calendar* 1859 and 1860. In May 1870 he established a journal entitled *L'Athée*, the Atheist, which the clerical journals declared drew God's vengeance upon France. He is also author of a work on aerial navigation.

Barot (François Odysse). French writer, b. at Mirabeau 1830. He has been a journalist on several Radical papers, was secretary to Gustave Flourens, and has written on the Birth of Jesus (1864) and *Contemporary Literature in England* (1874).

Barrett (Thomas Squire). Born 9 Sept. 1842, of Quaker parents, both grandfathers being ministers of that body; educated at Queenwood College, obtained diploma of Associate in Arts from Oxford with honors in National Science and Mathematics, contributed to the *National Reformer* between 1865 and 1870, published an acute examination of Gillespie's argument, *à priori*, for the existence of God (1869), which in 1871 reached a second edition. He also wrote *A New View of Causation* (1871), and an *Introduction to Logic and Metyphysics* (1877). Mr. Barrett has been hon. sec. of the London Dialectical Society, and edited a short-lived publication, *The Present Day*, 1886.

Barrier (F. M.). French Fourierist, b. Saint Etienne 1815, became professor of medicine at Lyons, wrote *A Sketch of the Analogy of Man and Humanity* (Lyons 1846), and *Principles of Sociology* (Paris 1867), and an abridgment of this entitled *Catechism of Liberal and Rational Socialism*. Died Montfort-L'Amaury 1870.

Barrillot (François). French author, b. of poor parents at Lyons in 1818. An orphan at seven years of age, he learnt to read from shop signs, and became a printer and journalist. Many of his songs and satires acquired popularity. He has also wrote a letter to Pope Pius IX. on the Œcumenical Council (1871), signed Jean Populus, and a philosophical work entitled *Love is God*. Died at Paris, 11 Dec. 1874.

Barthez (Paul Joseph), French physician, b. Montpelier 11 Dec. 1734. A friend of D'Alembert, he became associate editor of the *Journal des Savants* and *Encyclopédie Méthodique*. He was made consulting physician to the king and a councillor of State. Shown by the Archbishop of Sens a number of works relating to the rites of his see he said, " These are the ceremonies of Sens, but can you show me the sense [Sens] of ceremonies." His principal work is *New Elements of the Science of Man*. Died 15 Oct. 1806.

Basedow (Johann Bernhard), German Rationalist and educational reformer, b. at Hamburg 11 Sept. 1723. He studied theology at Leipsic, became professor at the Academy of Sora, in Denmark, 1753-1761, and at Altona, 1761-1768. While here he published *Philalethea*, the *Grounds of Religion*, and other heterodox works, which excited so much prejudice that he was in danger of being stoned. He devoted much attention to improving methods of teaching. Died at Magdeburg 25 July, 1790.

Baskerville (John), famous printer, b. Sion Hill, Wolverley, Worcestershire, 28 Jan. 1706. Lived at Birmingham. He was at first a stone-mason, then made money as an artistic japanner, and devoted it to perfecting the art of type-founding and printing. As a printer-publisher he produced at his own risk beautiful editions of Milton, Addison, Shaftesbury, Congreve, Virgil, Horace, Lucretius, Terence, etc. He was made printer to Cambridge University 1758. Wilkes once visited him and was "shocked at his infidelity" (!) He died 8 Jan. 1775, and was buried in a tomb in his own garden. He had designed a monumental urn with this inscription : " Stranger, beneath this cone in unconsecrated ground a friend to the liberties of mankind directed his body to be inurned. May the example contribute to emancipate thy mind from the idle fears of superstition and the wicked arts of priesthood." His will expresses the utmost contempt for Christianity. His type was appropriately purchased to produce a complete edition of Voltaire.

Bassus (Aufidus). An Epicurean philosopher and friend of Seneca in the time of Nero. Seneca praises his patience and courage in the presence of death.

Bate (Frederick), Socialist, author of *The Student* 1842 a drama in which the author's sceptical views are put forward.

Mr. Bate was one of the founders of the social experiment at New Harmony, now Queenswood College, Hants, and engraved a view representing the Owenite scheme of community.

Baudelaire (Charles Pierre), French poet, b. Paris, 9 April 1821, the son of a distinguished friend of Cabanis and Condorcet. He first became famous by the publication of *Fleurs du Mal*, 1857, in which appeared *Les Litanies de Satan*. The work was prosecuted and suppressed. Baudelaire translated some of the writings of E. A. Poe, a poet whom he resembled much in life and character. The divine beauty of his face has been celebrated by the French poet, Théodore de Banville, and his genius in some magnificent stanzas by the English poet, Algernon Swinburne. Died Paris 31 Aug. 1867.

Baudon (P. L.), French author of a work on the *Christian Superstition*, published at Brussels in 1862 and dedicated to Bishop Dupanloup under the pseudonym of "Aristide."

Bauer (Bruno), one of the boldest biblical critics of Germany, b. Eisenberg, 6 Sept. 1809. Educated at the University of Berlin, in 1834 he received a professorship of theology. He first attained celebrity by a review of the *Life of Jesus* by Strauss (1835). This was followed by his *Journal of Speculative Theology* and *Critical Exposition of the Religion of the Old Testament*. He then proceeded to a *Review of the Gospel History*, upon the publication of which (1840) he was deprived of his professorship at Bonn. To this followed *Christianity Unveiled* (1843), which was destroyed at Zurich before its publication. This work continued his opposition to religion, which was carried still further in ironical style in his *Proclamation of the Day of Judgement concerning Hegel the Atheist*. Bauer's heresy deepened with age, and in his *Review of the Gospels and History of their Origin* (1850), to which *Apostolical History* is a supplement, he attacked the historical truth of the New Testament narratives. In his *Review of the Epistles attributed to St. Paul* (1852) he tries to show that the first four epistles, which had hardly ever before been questioned, were not written by Paul, but are the production of the second century. In his *Christ. and the Cæsars* he shows the influence of Seneca and Greco-Roman thought upon early Christianity. He died near Berlin, 13 April, 1882.

Bauer (Edgar), b. Charlottenburg, 7 Oct. 1820, brother of the preceding, collaborated in some of his works. His brochure entitled *Bruno Bauer and his Opponents* (1842) was seized by the police. For his next publication, *The Strife of Criticism with Church and State* (1843), he was imprisoned for four years. He has also written on English freedom, Capital, etc.

Baume-Desdossat (Jacques François, de la), b. 1705, a Canon of Avignon who wrote *La Christiade* (1753), a satire on the gospels, in which Jesus is tempted by Mary Magdalene. It was suppressed by the French Parliament and the author fined. He died 30 April, 1756.

Baur (Ferdinand Christian von), distinguished theological critic, b. 21 June, 1792, near Stuttgart. His father was a clergyman. He was educated at Tübingen, where in 1826 he became professor of Church history. Baur is the author of numerous works on dogmatic and historic theology, in which he subverts all the fundamental positions of Christianity. He was an Hegelian Pantheist. Among his more important works are *Christianity and the Church in the First Three Centuries* and *Paul: His Life and Works.* These are translated into English. He acknowledges only four of the epistles of Paul and the Revelation as genuine products of the apostolic age, and shows how very far from simplicity were the times and doctrines of primitive Christianity. After a life of great literary activity he died at Tübingen, 2 Dec. 1860.

Bayle (Pierre), learned French writer, b. 18 Nov. 1647, at Carlat, France, where his father was a Protestant minister. He was converted to Romanism while studying at the Jesuit College, Toulouse, 1669. His Romanism only lasted seventeen months. He abjured, and fled to Switzerland, becoming a sceptic, as is evident from *Thoughts on the Comet,* in which he compares the supposed mischiefs of Atheism with those of fanaticism, and from many articles in his famous *Dictionnaire Critique,* a work still of value for its curious learning and shrewd observation. In his journal *Nouvelles de la République des Lettres* he advocates religious toleration on the ground of the difficulty of distinguishing truth from error. His criticism of Maimbourg's *History of Calvinism* was ordered to be burnt by the hangman. Jurieu persecuted him, and he was ordered to be more careful in preparing the second edition of his dictionary. He died at Rotterdam, 28 Dec. 1706. Bayle has been called the father of free discussion in modern times.

Bayrhoffer (Karl Theodor), German philosopher, b. Marburg, 14 Oct., 1812, wrote *The Idea and History of Philosophy* (1838), took part in the revolution of '48, emigrated to America, and wrote many polemical works. Died near Monroe, Wisconsin, 3 Feb. 1888.

Beauchamp (Philip). See Bentham and Grote.

Beausobre (Louis de), b. at Berlin, 22 Aug. 1730, was adopted by Frederick the Great out of esteem for his father, Isaac Beausobre, the author of the History of Manicheanism. He was educated first at Frankfort-on-Oder, then at Paris. He wrote on the scepticism of the wise (*Pyrrhonisme du Sage*, Berlin, 1754), a work condemned to be burnt by the Parliament of Paris. He also wrote anonymously *The Dreams of Epicurus*, and an essay on Happiness (Berlin, 1758), reprinted with the *Social System* of Holbach in 1795. Died at Berlin, 3 Dec. 1783.

Bebel (Ferdinand August). German Socialist, b. Cologne, 22 Feb. 1840. Brought up as a turner in Leipsic. Since '63, he became distinguished as an exponent of social democracy, and was elected to the German Reichstag in '71. In the following year he was condemned (6 March) to two years' imprisonment for high treason. He was re-elected in '74. His principal work is *Woman in the Past, Present and Future* which is translated by H. B. A. Walther, 1885. He has also written on the *Mohammedan Culture Period* (1884) and on *Christianity and Socialism*.

Beccaria (Bonesana Cesare), an Italian marquis and writer, b. at Milan, 15 March, 1738. A friend of Voltaire, who praised his treatise on *Crimes and Punishments* (1769), a work which did much to improve the criminal codes of Europe. Died Milan, 28 Nov. 1794.

Beesly (Edward Spencer), Positivist, b. Feckenham, Worcestershire, 1831. Educated at Wadham College, Oxford, where he took B.A. in 1854, and M.A. in '57. Appointed Professor of History, University College, London, in 1860. He is one of the translators of Comte's *System of Positive Polity,* and has published several pamphlets on political and social questions.

Beethoven (Ludwig van), one of the greatest of musical composers, b. Bonn 16 Dec. 1770. His genius early displayed itself, and at the age of five he was set to study the works of Handel and Bach. His many compositions are the glory of music. They include an opera " Fidelio," two masses, oratorios, symphonies, concertos, overtures and sonatas, and are characterised by penetrating power, rich imagination, intense passion, and tenderness. When about the age of forty he became totally deaf, but continued to compose till his death at Vienna, 26 March, 1827. He regarded Goethe with much the same esteem as Wagner showed for Schopenhauer, but he disliked his courtliness. His Republican sentiments are well known, and Sir George Macfarren, in his life in the *Imperial Dictionary of Universal Biography*, speaks of him as a " Freethinker,' and says the remarkable mass in C. " might scarcely have proceeded from an entirely orthodox thinker." Sir George Grove, in his *Dictionary of Music and Musicians*, says : " Formal religion he apparently had none," and " the Bible does not appear to have been one of his favorite books." At the end of his arrangement of " Fidelio " Moscheles had written, " Fine. With God's help." To this Beethoven added, " O man, help thyself."

Bekker (Balthasar), Dutch Rationalist, b. Metslawier (Friesland) 20 March, 1634. He studied at Gronigen, became a doctor of divinity, and lived at Francker, but was accused of Socinianism, and had to fly to Amsterdam, where he raised another storm by his *World Bewitched* (1691), a work in which witchcraft and the power of demons are denied. His book, which contains much curious information, raised a host of adversaries, and he was deposed from his place in the Church. It appeared in English in 1695. Died, Amsterdam, 11 June, 1698. Bekker was remarkably ugly, and he is said to have " looked like the devil, though he did not believe in him."

Belinsky (Vissarion Grigorevich), Russian critic, b. Pensa 1811, educated at Pensa and Moscow, adopted the Pantheistic philosophy of Hegel and Schelling. Died St. Petersburg, 28 May, 1848. His works were issued in 12 volumes, 1857-61.

Bell (Thomas Evans), Major in Madras Army, which he entered in 1842. He was employed in the suppression of

Thugee. He wrote the *Task of To-Day*, 1852, and assisted the *Reasoner*, both with pen and purse, writing over the signature "Undecimus." He contemplated selling his commission to devote himself to Freethought propaganda, but by the advice of his friends was deterred. He returned to India at the Mutiny. In January, 1861, he became Deputy-Commissioner of Police at Madras. He retired in July, 1865, and has written many works on Indian affairs. Died 12 Sept. 1887.

Bell (William S.), b. in Alleghany city, Pennsylvania, 10 Feb. 1832. Brought up as a Methodist minister, was denounced for mixing politics with religion, and for his anti-slavery views. In 1873 he preached in the Universalist Church of New Bedford, but in Dec. '74, renounced Christianity and has since been a Freethought lecturer. He has published a little book on the French Revolution, and some pamphlets.

Bender (Wilhelm), German Rationalist, professor of theology at Bonn, b. 15 Jan. 1845, who created a sensation at the Luther centenary, 1883, by declaring that the work of the Reformation was incompleted and must be carried on by the Rationalists.

Bennett (De Robigne Mortimer), founder and editor of the New York *Truthseeker*, b. of poor parents, Springfield (N.Y.), 23 Dec. 1818. At the age of fifteen he joined the Shaker Society in New Lebanon. Here he stayed thirteen years and then married. Having lost faith in the Shaker creed, he went to Louisville, Kentucky, where he started a drug store. The perusal of Paine, Volney, and similar works made him a Freethinker. In 1873, his letters to a local journal in answer to some ministers having been refused, he resolved to start a paper of his own. The result was the *Truthseeker*, which in January, 1876 became a weekly, and has since become one of the principal Freethought organs in America. In 1879 he was sentenced to thirteen months' imprisonment for sending through the post a pamphlet by Ezra H. Heywood on the marriage question. A tract, entitled *An Open Letter to Jesus Christ*, was read in court to bias the jury. A petition bearing 200,000 names was presented to President Hayes asking his release, but was not acceeded to. Upon his release his admirers sent him for a voyage round the world. He wrote *A Truthseeker's Voyage Round the World, Letters from Albany Penitentiary, Answers to*

Christian Questions and Arguments, two large volumes on *The Gods*, another on the *World's Sages, Infidels and Thinkers*, and published his discussions with Humphrey, Mair, and Teed, and numerous tracts. He died 6 Dec. 1882.

Bentham (Jeremy), writer on ethics, jurisprudence, and political economy, b. 15 Feb. 1748. A grand uncle named Woodward was the publisher of Tindal's *Christianity as Old as the Creation*. Was educated at Westminster and Oxford, where he graduated M.A. 1767. Bentham is justly regarded as the father of the school of philosophical Radicalism. In philosophy he is the great teacher of Utilitarianism ; as a jurist he did much to disclose the defects of and improve our system of law. Macaulay says he "found jurisprudence a gibberish and left it a science." His most pronounced Freethought work was that written in conjunction with Grote, published as *An Analysis of the Influence of Natural Religion*, by Philip Beauchamp, 1822. Among his numerous other works we can only mention *Deontology, or the Science of Morality*, an exposition of utilitarianism ; *Church of Englandism and its Catechism Examined; Not Paul, but Jesus*, published under the pseudonym of Gamaliel Smith. Died 6 June, 1832, leaving his body for the purposes of science.

Beranger (Jean Pierre de), celebrated French lyrical poet, b. Paris, 19 Aug. 1780. His satire on the Bourbons twice ensured for him imprisonment. He was elected to the Constituant Assembly 1848. Béranger has been compared not inaptly to Burns. All his songs breathe the spirit of liberty, and several have been characterised as impious. He died 16 July, 1857.

Bergel (Joseph), Jewish Rationalist, author of *Heaven and Its Wonders*, Leipsic, 1881, and *Mythology of the Ancient Hebrews*, 1882.

Berger (Moriz), author of a work on *Materialism in Conflict with Spiritualism and Idealism*, Trieste, 1883.

Bergerac de (Savinien Cyrano). See Cyrano.

Bergk (Johann Adam), German philosopher, b. Hainechen, Zeitz, 27 June, 1769 ; became a private teacher at Leipsic and wrote many works, both under his own name and psuedonyms. He published the *Art of Thinking*, Leipsic, 1802, conducted the *Asiatic Magazine*, 1806, and wrote under the name of

Frey the *True Religion*, "recommended to rationalists and destined for the Radical cure of supernaturalists, mystics, etc." Died Leipsic, 27 Oct. 1834.

Bergk (Theodor), German humanist, son of the above, b. Leipsic, 22 May, 1812, author of a good *History of Greek Literature*, 1872.

Berigardus (Claudius), or **Beauregard** (Claude Guillermet), French physician and philosopher, b. at Moulins about 1591. He became a professor at Pisa from 1628 till 1640, and then went to Padua. His *Circulus Pisanus*, published in 1643, was considered an Atheistic work. In the form of a dialogue he exhibits the various hypotheses of the formation of the world The work was forbidden and is very rare. His book entitled *Dubitationes in Dialogum Galilæi*, also brought on him a charge of scepticism. Died in 1664.

Berkenhout (Dr. John), physician and miscellaneous writer, b. 1731, the son of a Dutch merchant who settled at Leeds. In early life he had been a captain both in the Prussian and English service, and in 1765 took his M.D. degree at Leyden. He published many books on medical science, a synopsis of the natural history of Great Britain and Ireland, and several humorous pieces, anonymously. His principal work is entitled *Biographia Literaria*, a biographical history of English literature, 1777. Throughout the work he loses no opportunity of displaying his hostility to the theologians, and is loud in his praises of Voltaire. Died 3 April, 1791.

Berlioz (Louis Hector). The most original of French musical composers, b. Isère, 11 Dec. 1803. He obtained fame by his dramatic symphony of *Romeo and Juliet* (1839), and was made chevalier of the Legion of Honor. Among his works is one on the *Infancy of Christ*. In his *Memoirs* he relates how he scandalised Mendelssohn "by laughing at the Bible." Died Paris, 9 March, 1869.

Bernard (Claude), French physiologist, b. Saint Julien 12 July, 1813. Went to Paris 1832, studied medicine, became member of the Institute and professor at the Museum of Natural History, wrote *La Science Expérimentale*, and other works on physiology. Died 10 Feb. 1878, and was buried at the expense of the Republic. Paul Bert calls him the introducer of determinism in the domain of physiology.

Bernier (Abbé). See Holbach.

Bernier (François), French physician and traveller, b. Angers about 1625. He was a pupil of Gassendi, whose works he abridged, and he defended Descartes against the theologians. He is known as *le joli philosophe*. In 1654 he went to Syria and Egypt, and from thence to India, where he became physician to Aurungzebe. On his return he published an account of his travels and of the Empire of the Great Mogul, and died at Paris 22 Sept. 1688.

Bernstein (Aaron), a rationalist, b. of Jewish parents Dantzic 1812. His first work was a translation of the *Song of Songs*, published under the pseudonym of A. Rebenstein (1834). He devoted himself to natural science and published works on *The Rotation of Planets, Humboldt and the Spirit of the Time*, etc. His essay on *The Origin of the Legends of Abraham, Isaac, and Jacob* was translated by a German lady and published by Thomas Scott of Ramsgate (1872). Died Berlin, 12 Feb. 1884.

Berquin (Louis de), French martyr, b. in Artois, 1489. Erasmus, his friend, says his great crime was openly professing hatred of the monks. In 1523 his works were ordered to be burnt, and he was commanded to abjure his heresies. Sentence of perpetual banishment was pronounced on him on April 16, 1529. He immediately appealed to the Parliament. His appeal was heard and rejected on the morning of the 17th. The Parliament reformed the judgment and condemned him to be burnt alive, and the sentence was carried out on the same afternoon at the Place de la Grève. He died with great constancy and resolution.

Bert (Paul), French scientist and statesman, b. at Auxerre, 17 Oct. 1833. In Paris he studied both law and medicine, and after being Professor in the Faculty of Science at Bordeaux, he in 1869 obtained the chair of physiology in the Faculty of Science at Paris, and distinguished himself by his scientific experiments. In '70 he offered his services to the Government of National Defence, and in '72 was elected to the National Assembly, where he signalised himself by his Radical opinions. Gambetta recognised his worth and made him Minister of Public Instruction, in which capacity he organised French education on a Secular basis. His *First Year of Scientific*

Instruction is almost universally used in the French primary schools. It has been translated into English by Josephine Clayton (Madame Paul Bert). His strong anti-clerical views induced much opposition. He published several scientific and educational works and attacked *The Morality of the Jesuits*, '80. In '86 he was appointed French Resident Minister at Tonquin, where he died 11 Nov. '86. His body was brought over to France and given a State funeral, a pension being also accorded to his widow.

Bertani (Agostino), Italian patriot, b. 19 Oct. 1812, became a physician at Genoa, took part with Garibaldi and Mazzini, organising the ambulance services. A declared Freethinker, he was elected deputy to the Italian Parliament. Died Rome 30 April, '86.

Berti (Antonio), Italian physician, b. Venice 20 June, 1816· Author of many scientific works, member of the Venice Municipal Council and of the Italian Senate. Died Venice 24 March, 1879.

Bertillon (Louis Adolphe), French Anthropologist and physician, b. Paris 1 April, 1821. His principal work is a statistical study of the French population, Paris '71. He edits in conjunction with A. Hovelacque and others, the *Dictionary of the Anthropological Sciences* ('83 etc.) His sons, Jacques (b. '51) and Alphonse (b. '53), prosecute similar studies.

Bertrand de Saint-Germain (Guillaume Scipion), French physician, b. Puy-en Velay 25 Oct. 1810. Became M.D. 1840, wrote on *The Original Diversity of Human Races* (1847), and a materialistic work on *Manifestation of Life and Intelligence through Organisation*, 1848. Has also written on *Descartes as a Physiologist*, 1869.

Berwick (George J.) M.D., appointed surgeon to the East India Company in 1828, retired in '52. Author of *Awas-i-hind*, or a Voice from the Ganges ; being a solution of the true source of Christianity. By an Indian Officer ; London, 1861. Also of a work on *The Forces of the Universe*, '70. Died about 1872.

Besant (Annie) née Wood. B. London, 1 Oct. 1847. Educated in Evangelicalism by Miss Marryat, sister of novelist, but turned to the High Church by reading Pusey and others. In " Holy Week " of 1866 she resolved to write the story of the week from the gospel. Their contradictions startled her but she regarded her doubts as sin. In Dec. '67 she married the Rev. F. Besant, and read and wrote extensively. The torment a child underwent in whooping-cough caused doubts as to the goodness of God. A study of Greg's *Creed of Christendom* and Arnold's *Literature and Dogma* increased her scepticism. She became acquainted with the Rev. C. Voysey and Thomas Scott, for whom she wrote an *Essay on the Deity of Jesus of Nazareth*, " by the wife of a beneficed clergyman." This led to her husband insisting on her taking communion or leaving. She chose the latter course, taking by agreement her daughter with her. Thrown on her own resources, she wrote further tracts for Mr. Scott, reprinted in *My Path to Atheism* ('77). Joined the National Secular Society, and in '74 wrote in the *National Reformer* over the signature of "Ajax." Next year she took to the platform and being naturally eloquent soon won her way to the front rank as a Freethought lecturess, and became joint editor of the *National Reformer*. Some lectures on the French Revolution were republished in book form. In April, '77, she was arrested with Mr. Bradlaugh for publishing the *Fruits of Philosophy*. After a brilliant defence, the jury exonerated the defendants from any corrupt motives, and although they were sentenced the indictment was quashed in Feb. '78, and the case was not renewed. In May, '78, a petition in Chancery was presented to deprive Mrs. Besant of her child on the ground of her Atheistic and Malthusian views. Sir G. Jessell granted the petition. In '80 Mrs. Besant matriculated at the London University and took 1st B.Sc. with honors in '82. She has debated much and issued many pamphlets to be found in *Theological Essays and Debates*. She wrote the second part of the *Freethinkers' Text Book* dealing with Christian evidence ; has written on the *Sins of the Church*, 1886, and the *Evolution of Society*. She has translated Jules Soury's *Religion of Israel*, and *Jesus of the Gospels;* Dr. L. Büchner on the *Influence of Heredity* and *Mind in Animals*, and from the fifteenth edition of *Force and Matter*. From '83 to '88 she edited *Our Corner*, and since '85 has given much time to Socialist propaganda, and has written many Socialist pamphlets. In Dec. '88, Mrs. Besant was elected a member of the London School Board.

Beverland (Hadrianus), Dutch classical scholar and nephew of Isaac Vossius, b. Middleburg 1654. He took the degree of doctor of law and became an advocate, but devoted himself to literature. He was at the university of Oxford in 1672. His treatise on Original Sin, *Peccatum Originale* (Eleutheropoli, 1678), in which he contends that the sin of Adam and Eve was sexual inclination, caused a great outcry. It was burnt, Beverland was imprisoned and his name struck from the rolls of Leyden University. He wrote some other curious works and died about 1712.

Bevington (Louisa S.), afterwards GUGGENBERGER; English poetess and authoress of *Key Notes*, 1879; *Poems, Lyrics and Sonnets*, '82; wrote "Modern Atheism and Mr. Mallock" in the *Nineteenth Century* (Oct. and Dec. '79), and on "The Moral Demerits of Orthodoxy" in *Progress*, Sept. '84.

Beyle (Marie Henri), French man of letters, famous under the name of de Stendhal, b. Grenoble, 23 Jan. 1783. Painter, soldier, merchant and consul, he travelled largely, a wandering life being congenial to his broad and sceptical spirit. His book, *De l'Amour* is his most notable work. He was an original and gifted critic and romancer. Balzac esteemed him highly. He died at Paris, 23 March, 1842. Prosper Merimée has published his correspondence. One of his sayings was "Ce qui excuse Dieu, c'est qu'il n'existe pas"—God's excuse is that he does not exist.

Bianchi (Angelo), known as BIANCHI-GIOVINI (Aurelio) Italian man of letters, b. of poor parents at Como, 25 Nov. 1799 He conducted several papers in various parts of Piedmont and Switzerland. His *Life of Father Paoli Sarpi*, 1836, was put on the Index, and thenceforward he was in constant strife with the Roman Church. For his attacks on the clergy in *Il Republicano*, at Lugano, he was proscribed, and had to seek refuge at Zurich, 1839. He went thence to Milan and there wrote a *History of the Hebrews*, a monograph on *Pope Joan*, and an account of the Revolution. His principal works are the *History of the Popes* until the great schism of the West (Turin, 1850–64) and a *Criticism of the Gospels*, 1853, which has gone through several editions. Died 16 May, 1862.

Biandrata or BLANDRATA (Giorgio), Italian anti-trinitarian reformer, b. Saluzzo about 1515. Graduated in arts and medicine at Montpellier, 1533. He was thrown into the prison of the Inquisition at Pavia, but contrived to escape to Geneva, where he become obnoxious to Calvin. He left Geneva in 1558 and went to Poland where he became a leader of the Socinian party. He was assassinated 1591.

Bichat (Marie François Xavier), a famous French anatomist and physiologist, b Thoirette (Jura), 11 Nov. 1771. His work on the *Physiology of Life and Death* was translated into English. He died a martyr to his zeal for science, 22 July, 1802.

Biddle or BIDLE (John), called the father of English Unitarianism, b. Wotton-under-Edge, Gloucestershire, 14 Jan. 1615. He took his M.A. degree at Oxford, 1641, and became master of the Gloucester Grammar School, but lost the situation for denying the Trinity. He was also imprisoned there for some time, and afterwards cited at Westminster. He appealed to the public in defence, and his pamphlet was ordered to be burnt by the hangman, 6 Sept. 1647. He was detained in prison till 1652, after which he published several pamphlets, and was again imprisoned in 1654. In Oct. 1655, Cromwell banished him to the Scilly Isles, making him an allowance. He returned to London 1658, but after the publication of the Acts of Uniformity was again seized, and died in prison 22 Sept. 1662.

Bierce (M. H.) see GRILE (Dod).

Billaud-Varenne (Jean Nicolas), French conventionalist b. La Rochelle, 23 April, 1756. About 1785 became advocate to Parliament; denounced the government and clergy 1789. Proposed abolition of the monarchy 1 July, 1791, and wrote *Elements of Republicanism*, 1793. Withdrew from Robespierre after the feast of the Supreme Being, saying "Thou beginnest to sicken me with thy Supreme Being." Was exiled 1 April, 1795, and died at St. Domingo, 3 June, 1819.

Bion, of Borysthenes, near the mouth of the Dneiper. A Scythian philosopher who flourished about 250 B.C. He was sold as a slave to a rhetorician, who afterwards gave him freedom and made him his heir. Upon this he went to Athens and applied himself to the study of philosophy. He had several teachers, but attached himself to Theodorus the Atheist. He was famous for his knowledge of music, poetry, and philosophy. Some shrewd sayings of his are preserved, as that "only the votive tablets of the preserved are seen in the temples, not those of the drowned" and "it is useless to tear our hair when in grief since sorrow is not cured by baldness."

Birch (William John), English Freethinker, b. London 4 Jan. 1811. Educated at Baliol College, Oxford, graduated M.A. at New Inn Hall. Author of *An Inquiry into the Philosophy and Religion of Shakespeare*, 1848; *An Inquiry into the Philosophy and Religion of the Bible*, 1856; this work was translated into Dutch by "Rudolf Charles;" *Paul an Idea, not a Fact;* and the *Real and Ideal.* In the stormy time of '42 Mr. Birch did much to support the prosecuted publications. He brought out the *Library of Reason* and supported *The Reasoner* and *Investigator* with both pen and purse. Mr. Birch has resided much in Italy and proved himself a friend to Italian unity and Freedom. He is a member of the Italian Asiatic Society. Mr. Birch has been a contributor to *Notes and Queries* and other journals, and has devoted much attention to the early days of Christianity, having many manuscripts upon the subject.

Bithell (Richard), Agnostic, b. Lewes, Sussex, 22 March 1821, of pious parents. Became teacher of mathematics and chemistry. Is Ph.D. of Gottingen and B.Sc. of London University. In '65 he entered the service of the Rothschilds. Has written *Creed of a Modern Agnostic*, 1883; and *Agnostic Problems*, 1887.

Bjornson (Björnstjerne), Norwegian writer, b. Quickne 8 Dec. 1832. His father was a Lutheran clergyman. Has done much to create a national literature for Norway. For his freethinking opinions he was obliged to leave his country and reside in Paris. Many of his tales have been translated into English. In 1882 Björnson published at Christiania, with a short introduction, a resumé of C. B. Waite's *History of the Christian Religion*, under the title of *Whence come the Miracles of the New Testament?* This was the first attack upon dogmatic Christianity published in Norway, and created much discussion. The following year he published a translation of Colonel Ingersoll's article in the *North American Review* upon the "Christian Religion," with a long preface, in which he attacks the State Church and Monarchy. The translation was entitled *Think for Yourself.* The first edition rapidly sold out and a second one appeared. He has since, both in speech and writing, repeatedly avowed his Freethought, and has had several controversies with the clergy.

Blagosvyetlov (Grigorevich E.), Russian author, b. in the Caucasus, 1826. Has written on Shelley, Buckle, and Mill, whose *Subjection of Women* he translated into Russian. He edited a magazine Djelo (Cause). Died about 1885.

Blanqui (Louis Auguste), French politician, b. near Nice, 7 Feb. 1805, a younger brother of Jerome Adolphe Blanqui, the economist. Becoming a Communist, his life was spent in conspiracy and imprisonment under successive governments. In '39 he was condemned to death, but his sentence commuted to imprisonment for life, and was subject to brutal treatment till the revolution of '48 set him at liberty. He was soon again imprisoned. In '65 he wrote some remarkable articles on Monotheism in *Le Candide*. After the revolution of 4 Sept. '70, Blanqui demanded the suppression of worship. He was again imprisoned, but was liberated and elected member of the Commune, and arrested by Thiers. In his last imprisonment he wrote a curious book, *Eternity and the Stars*, in which he argues from the eternity and infinity of matter. Died Paris, 31 Dec. 1880. Blanqui took as his motto " Ni Dieu ni maître "—Neither God nor master.

Blasche (Bernhard Heinrich), German Pantheist, b. Jena 9 April, 1776. His father was a professor of theology and philosophy. He wrote *Kritik des Modernen Geisterglaubens* (Criticism of Modern Ghost Belief), *Philosophische Unsterblich-keitsl hre* (Teaching of Philosophical Immortality), and other works. Died near Gotha 26 Nov. 1832.

Blignieres (Célestin de), French Positivist, of the Polytechnic school. Has written a popular exposition of Positive philosophy and religion, Paris 1857; The *Positive Doctrine*, 1867 ; *Studies of Positive Morality*, 1868 ; and other works.

Blind (Karl), German Republican, b. Mannheim, 4 Sept. 1826. Studied at Heidelberg and Bonn. In 1848 he became a revolutionary leader among the students and populace, was wounded at Frankfort, and proscribed. In Sept. '48 he led the second republican revolution in the Black Forest. He was made prisoner and sentenced to eight year's imprisonment. In the spring of

'49 he was liberated by the people breaking open his prison. Being sent on a mission to Louis Napoleon, then president of the French Republic at Paris, he was arrested and banished from France. He went to Brussels, but since '52 has lived in in England, where he has written largely on politics, history, and mythology. His daughter Mathilde, b. at Mannheim, opened her literary career by publishing a volume of poems in 1867 under the name of *Claude Lake*. She has since translated Straus's *Old Faith and the New*, and written the volumes on George Eliot and Madame Roland in the *Eminent Women* series.

Blount (Charles), English Deist of noble family, b. at Holloway 27 April, 1654. His father, Sir Henry Blount, probably shared in his opinions, and helped him in his arti-religious work, *Anima Mundi*, 1678. This work Bishop Compton desired to see suppressed. In 1680 he published *Great is Diana of the Ephesians*, or the Origin of Idolatry, and the two first books of *Apollonius Tyanius*, with notes, in which he attacks priestcraft and superstition. This work was condemned and suppressed. Blount also published *The Oracles of Reason*, a number of Freethought Essays. By his *Vindication of Learning and Liberty of the Press*, and still more by his hoax on Bohun entitled *William and Mary Conquerors*, he was largely instrumental in doing away with the censorship of the press. He shot himself, it is said, because he could not marry his deceased wife's sister (August, 1693). His miscellaneous works were printed in one volume, 1695.

Blumenfeld (J. C.), wrote *The New Ecce Homo or the Self Redemption of Man*, 1839. He is also credited with the authorship of *The Existence of Christ Disproved* in a series of Letters by " A German Jew," London, 1841.

Boerne (Ludwig), German man of letters and politician, b. Frankfort 22 May, 1786. In 1818 he gave up the Jewish religion, in which he had been bred, nominally for Protestantism, but really he had, like his friend Heine, become a Freethinker. He wrote many works in favor of political liberty and translated Lammenais' *Paroles d'un Croyant*. Died 12 Feb. 1837.

Bodin (Jean), French political writer, b. Angers 1530. He studied at Toulouse and is said to have been a monk but turned to the law, and became secretary to the Duc d'Alençon. His

46

book *De la Republique* is highly praised by Hallam, and is said to have contained the germ of Montesquieu's "Spirit of the Laws." He wrote a work on demonomaina, in which he seems to have believed, but in his *Colloquium Heptaplomeron* coloquies of seven persons : a Catholic, a Lutheran, a Calvinist, a Pagan, a. Muhammadan, a Jew, and a Deist, which he left in manuscript, he put some severe attacks on Christianity. Died of the plague at Laon in 1596.

Boggis (John) is mentioned by Edwards in his *Gangrena*, 1645, as an Atheist and disbeliever in the Bible.

Boichot (Jean Baptiste), b. Villier sur Suize 20 Aug. 1820, entered the army. In '49 he was chosen representative of the people. After the *coup d'etat* he came to England, returned to France in '54, was arrested and imprisoned at Belle Isle. Since then he has lived at Brussels, where he has written several works and is one of the council of International Freethinkers.

Boindin (Nicolas) French litterateur, wit, playwright and academician, b. Paris 29 May, 1676. He publicly professed Atheism, and resorted with other Freethinkers to the famous café Procope. There, in order to speak freely, they called the soul Margot, religion Javotte, liberty Jeanneton, and God M. de l'Etre. One day a spy asked Boindin, "Who is this M. de l'Etre with whom you seem so displeased?" "Monsieur," replied Boindin, "he is a police spy." Died 30 Nov. 1751. His corpse was refused "Christian burial."

Boissiere (Jean Baptiste Prudence), French writer, b. Valognes Dec. 1806, was for a time teacher in England. He compiled an analogical dictionary of the French language. Under the name of Sièrebois he has published the *Autopsy of the Soul* and a work on the foundations of morality, which he traces to interest. He has also written a book entitled *The Mechanism of Thought*, '84.

Boissonade (J. A.), author of *The Bible Unveiled*, Paris, 1871.

Boito (Arrigo), Italian poet and musician, b. at Padua, whose opera "Mefistofele," has created considerable sensation by its boldness.

Bolingbroke (Henry SAINT JOHN) Lord, English statesman and philosopher, b. at Battersea, 1 Oct. 1672. His political life was a stormy one. He was the friend of Swift and of Pope, who in his *Essay on Man* avowedly puts forward the views of Saint John. He died at Battersea 12 Dec. 1751, leaving by will his MSS. to David Mallet, who in 1754 published his works, which included *Essays Written to A. Pope, Esq*, *on Religion and Philosophy*, in which he attacks Christianity with both wit and eloquence. Bolingbroke was a Deist, believing in God but scornfully rejecting revelation. He much influenced Voltaire, who regarded him with esteem.

Bonavino (Francesco Cristoforo) see FRANCHI (Ausonio).

Boni (Filippo de), Italian man of letters, b. Feltre, 1820. Editor of a standard *Biography of Artists*, published at Venice, 1840. He also wrote on the Roman Church and Italy and on *Reason and Dogma*, Siena, '66, and contributed to Stefanoni's *Libero Pensiero*. De Boni was elected deputy to the Italian Parliament. He has written on " Italian Unbelief in the Middle Ages " in the *Annuario Filosofico del Libero Pensiero,* '68.

Boniface VIII., Pope (Benedetto Gaetano), elected head of Christendom, 24 Dec. 1204. During his quarrel with Philip the Fair of France charges were sworn on oath against Pope Boniface that he neither believed in the Trinity nor in the life to come, that he said the Virgin Mary " was no more a virgin than my mother"; that he did not observe the fasts of the Church, and that he spoke of the cardinals, monks, and friars as hypocrites. It was in evidence that the Pope had said "God may do the worst with me that he pleases in the future life; I believe as every educated man does, the vulgar believe otherwise. We have to speak as they do, but we must believe and think with the few." Died 11 Oct. 1303.

Bonnycastle (John), mathematician, b. Whitchurch, Bucks, about 1750. He wrote several works on elementary mathematics and became Professor of mathematics at the Royal Military Academy, Woolwich, where he died 15 May, 1821. He was a friend of Fuseli, and private information assures me he was a Freethinker.

Booms (Marinus Adriaansz), Dutch Spinozist, a shoemaker by trade, who wrote early in the eigthteenth century, and on 1 Jan. 1714, was banished.

Bonnot de Condillac (Etienne) see CONDILLAC.

Bonstetten (Karl Victor von), Swiss Deist, b. Berne, 3 Sept· 1745. Acquainted with Voltaire and Rousseau he went to Leyden and England to finish his education. Among his works are *Researches on the Nature and Laws of the Imagination*, 1807 ; and *tudies on Man*, 1821. Died Geneva, 3 Feb. 1832.

Borde (Frédéric), editor of *La Philosophie de l'Avenir*, Paris, 1875, etc. Born La Rochelle 1811. Has written on Liberty of Instruction, etc.

Born (Ignaz von) baron, b. Carlsruhe, 26 Dec. 1742. Bred by the Jesuits, he became an ardent scientist and a favorite of the Empress Marie Theresa, under whose patronage he published works on Mineralogy. He was active as a Freemason, and Illuminati, and published with the name Joannes Physiophilus a stinging illustrated satire entitled *Monchalogia*, or the natural history of monks.

Bosc (Louis Augustin Guillaume), French naturalist, b. Paris, 29 Jan. 1759; was tutor and friend to Madame Roland whose *Memoirs* he published. He wrote many works on natural history. Died 10 July, 1828.

Boucher (E. Martin), French writer, b. Beaulieu, 1809 ; contributed to the *Rationalist* of Geneva, where he died 1882. Author of a work on Revelation and Rationalism, entitled *Search for the Truth*, Avignon, 1884.

Bougainville (Louis Antoine de) Count, the first French voyager who made the tour around the world ; b. Paris, 11 Nov. 1729. Died 31 Aug. 1811. He wrote an interesting account of his travels.

Bouillier (Francisque), French philosopher, b. Lyons 12 July 1813, has written several works on psychology, and contributed to *la Liberté de Penser*. His principal work is a History of the Cartesian Philosophy." He is a member of the Institute and writes in the leading reviews.

Bouis (Casimir), French journalist, b. Toulon 1848, edited *La Libre Pensée* and wrote a satire on the Jesuits entitled *Calottes et Soutanes*, 1870. Sent to New Caledonia for his participation in the Commune, he has since his return published a volume of political verses entitled *Après le Naufrage*, After the Shipwreck, 1880.

Boulainvilliers (Henri de), Comte de St. Saire, French historian and philosopher, b. 11 Oct. 1658. His principal historical work is an account of the ancient French Parliaments. He also wrote a defence of Spinozism under pretence of a refutation of Spinoza, an analysis of Spinoza's Tractus Theologico-Politicus, printed at the end of *Doubts upon Religion*, Londres, 1767. A *Life of Muhammad*, the first European work doing justice to Islam, and a *History of the Arabs* also proceeded from his pen, and he is one of those to whom is attributed the treatise with the title of the *Three Impostors*, 1755. Died 23 Jan. 1722.

Boulanger (Nicolas-Antoine), French Deist, b. 11 Nov. 1722. Died 16 Sept. 1759. He was for some time in the army as engineer, and afterwards became surveyor of public works. After his death his works were published by D'Holbach who rewrote them. His principal works are *Antiquity Unveiled* and *Researches on the Origin of Oriental Despotism*. *Christianity Unveiled*, attributed to him and said by Voltaire to have been by Damilavile, was probably written by D'Holbach, perhaps with some assistance from Naigeon. It was burnt by order of the French Parliament 18 Aug. 1770. *A Critical Examination of the Life and Works of St. Paul*, attributed to Boulanger, was really made up by d'Holbach from the work of Anuet. Boulanger wrote dissertations on Elisha, Enoch and St. Peter, and some articles for the *Encyclopédie*.

Bourdet (Dr.) Eugene, French Positivist, b. Paris, 1818. Author of several works on medicine and Positivist philosophy and education.

Boureau-Deslands (A. F.) See Deslandes.

Bourget (Paul), French littérateur, b. at Amiens in 1852. Has made himself famous by his novels, essays on contemporary psychology, studies of M. Rénan, etc. He belongs to the Naturalist School, but his methods are less crude than those of some of his colleagues. His insight is most subtle, and his style is exquisite.

Boutteville (Marc Lucien), French writer, professor at the Lycée Bonaparte; has made translations from Lessing and published an able work on the Morality of the Church and Natural Morality, 1866, for which the clergy turned him out of a professorship he held at Sainte-Barbe.

Bovio (Giovanni), Professor of Political Economy in the University of Naples and deputy to the Italian parliament; is an ardent Freethinker. Both in his writings and in parliament Prof. Bovio opposes the power of the Vatican and the reconciliation between Church and State. He has constantly advocated liberty of conscience and has promoted the institution of a Dante chair in the University of Rome. He has written a work on *The History of Law*, a copy of which he presented to the International Congress of Freethinkers, 1887.

Bowring (Sir John, K.B., LL D.), politician, linguist and writer, b. Exeter, 17 Oct., 1792. In early life a pupil of Dr. Lant Carpenter and later a disciple of Jeremy Bentham, whose principles he maintained in the *Westminster Review*, of which he was editor, 1825. Arrested in France in 1822, after a fortnight's imprisonment he was released without trial. He published Bentham's *Deontology* (1834), and nine years after edited a complete collection of the works of Bentham. Returned to Parliament in '35, and afterwards was employed in important government missions. In '55 he visited Siam, and two years later published an account of *The Kingdom and People of Siam*. He translated Goethe, Schiller, Heine, and the poems of many countries; was an active member of the British Association and of the Social Science Association, and did much to promote rational views on the Sunday question. Died 23 Nov. 1872.

Boyle (Humphrey), one of the men who left Leeds for the purpose of serving in R. Carlile's shop when the right of free publication was attacked in 1821. Boyle gave no name, and was indicted and tried as "a man with name unknown" for publishing a blasphemous and seditious libel. In his defence he ably asserted his right to hold and publish his opinions. He read portions of the Bible in court to prove he was justified in calling it obscene. Upon being sentenced, 27 May, 1822, to eighteen months' imprisonment and to find sureties for five years, he remarked "I have a mind, my lord, that can bear such a sentence with fortitude."

Bradlaugh (Charles). Born East London, 26 Sept. 1833. Educated in Bethnal Green and Hackney. He was turned from his Sunday-school teachership and from his first situation through the influence of the Rev. J. G. Packer, and found refuge with the widow of R. Carlile. In Dec. 1850 he entered the Dragoon Guards and proceeded to Dublin. Here he met James Thomson, the poet, and contracted a friendship which lasted for many years. He got his discharge, and in '53 returned to London and became a solicitor's clerk. He began to write and lecture under the *nom de guerre* of " Iconoclast," edited the *Investigator*, '59 ; and had numerous debates with ministers and others. In 1860 he began editing the *National Reformer*, which in '68–9 he successfully defended against a prosecution of the Attorney General, who wished securities against blasphemy. In '68 he began his efforts to enter Parliament, and in 1880 was returned for Northampton. After a long struggle with the House, which would not admit the Atheist, he at length took his seat in 1885. He was four times re-elected, and the litigation into which he was plunged will become as historic as that of John Wilkes. Prosecuted in '76 for publishing *The Fruits of Philosophy*, he succeeded in quashing the indictment. Mr. Bradlaugh has had numerous debates, several of which are published. He has also written many pamphlets, of which we mention New Lives of Abraham, David, and other saints, *Who was Jesus Christ? What did Jesus Teach? Has Man a Soul, Is there a God?* etc. His *Plea for Atheism* reached its 20th thousand in 1880. Mr. Bradlaugh has also published *When were our Gospels Written*, 1867 ? *Heresy, its Utility and Morality*, 1870 ; *The Inspiration of the Bible*, 1873 ; *The Freethinker's Text Book*, part i., dealing with natural religion, 1876 ; *The Laws Relating to Blasphemy and Heresy*, 1878 ; *Supernatural and Rational Morality*, 1886. In 1857 Mr. Bradlaugh commenced a commentary on the Bible, entitled *The Bible, What is it?* In 1865 this appeared in enlarged form, dealing only with the Pentateuch. In 1882 he published *Genesis, Its Authorship and Authenticity*. In Parliament Mr. Bradlaugh has become a conspicuous figure, and has introduced many important measures. In 1888 he succeeded in passing an Oaths Bill, making affirmations permissible instead of oaths. His elder daughter, Alice, b. 30 April, 1856, has written on *Mind Considered as a Bodily Function*, 1884. Died 2 Dec. 1888. His second daughter, Hypatia Bradlaugh Bonner, b. 31 March, 1858, has written " Princess Vera " and other stories, " Chemistry of Home," etc.

Brækstad (Hans Lien), b. Throndhjem, Norway, 7 Sept. 1845. Has made English translations from Björnson, Asbjörnsen. Andersen, etc., and has contributed to *Harper's Magazine* and other periodical literature.

Brandes (Georg Morris Cohen), Danish writer, by birth a Jew, b. Copenhagen, 4 Feb. 1842. In 1869 he translated J. S. Mills' *Subjection of Women*, and in the following year took a doctor's degree for a philosophical treatise. His chief work is entitled the *Main Current of Literature in the Nineteenth Century*. His brother, Dr. Edvard Brandes, was elected to the Danish Parliament in 1881, despite his declaration that he did not believe either in the God of the Christians or of the Jews.

Bray (Charles), philosophic writer, b. Coventry, 31 Jan. 1811, He was brought up as an Evangelical, but found his way to Freethought. Early in life he took an active part in promoting unsectarian education. His first work (1835) was on *The Education of the Body*. This was followed by *The Education of the Feelings*, of which there were several editions. In 1836 he married Miss Hennell, sister of C. C. Hennell, and took the *System of Nature* and Volney's *Ruins of Empires* " to enliven the honeymoon." Among his friends was Mary Ann Evans (" George Eliot "), who accompanied Mr. and Mrs. Bray to Italy. His works on *The Philosophy of Necessity* (1841) and *Cerebral Psychology* (1875) give the key to all his thought. He wrote a number of Thomas Scott's series of tracts : *Illusion and Delusion, The Reign of Law in Mind as in Matter, Toleration* with remarks on Professor Tyndall's " Address," and a little book, *Christianity in the Light of our Present Knowledge and Moral Sense* (1876). He also wrote *A Manual of Anthropology* and similar works. In a postscript to his last volume, *Phases of Opinion and Experience During a Long Life*, dated 18 Sept. 1884, he stated that he has no hope or expectation or belief even in the possibility of continued individuality after death, and that as his opinions have done to live by " they will do to die by." He died 5 Oct. 1884.

Bresson (Léopold), French Positivist, b. Lamarche, 1817. Educated at the Polytechnic School, which he left in 1840 and served on public works. For seventeen years was director of an Austrian Railway Company. Wrote *Idées Modernes*, 1880.

Bridges (John Henry), M.D. English Positivist, b. 1833, graduated B.A. at Oxford 1855, and B.M. 1859; has written on *Religion and Progress*, contributed to the *Fortnightly Review*, and translated Comte's *General View of Positivism* (1865) and *System of Positive Polity* (1873).

Bril (Jakob), Dutch mystical Pantheist, b. Leyden, 21 Jan. 1639. died 1700. His works were published at Amsterdam, 4705.

Brissot (Jean Pierre) DE WARVILLE, active French revolutionist, b. Chartres, 14 Jan. 1754. He was bred to the law, but took to literature. He wrote for the *Courier de l'Europe*, a revolutionary paper suppressed for its boldness, published a treatise on Truth, and edited a Philosophical Law Library, 1782—85. He wrote against the legal authority of Rome, and is credited with *Philosophical Letters upon St. Paul and the Christian Religion*, Neufchatel, 1783. In 1784 he was imprisoned in the Bastille for his writings. To avoid a second imprisonment he went to England and America, returning to France at the outbreak of the Revolution. He wrote many political works, became member of the Legislative Assembly, formed the Girondist party, protested against the execution of Louis XVI., and upon the triumph of the Mountain was executed with twenty-one of his colleagues, 31 Oct., 1793. Brissot was a voluminous writer, honest, unselfish, and an earnest lover of freedom in every form.

Bristol (Augusta), née COOPER, American educator, b. Croydon, New Haven, 17 April, 1835. In 1850 became teacher and gained repute by her *Poems*. In Sept. 1880, she represented American Freethinkers at the International Conference at Brussels. She has written on *Science and its Relations to Human Character* and other works.

Broca (Pierre Paul), French anthropologist, b. 28 June, 1821. A hard-working scientist, he paid special attention to craniology. In 1875 he founded the School of Anthropology and had among his pupils Gratiolet, Topinard, Hovelacque and Dr. Carter Blake, who translated his treatise on *Hybridity*. He established *The Review of Anthropology*, published numerous scientific works and was made a member of the Legion of onor. In philosophy he inclined to Positivism. Died Paris, 9 July, 1880.

Brooksbank (William), b. Nottingham 6 Dec. 1801. In 1824 he wrote in Carlile's *Lion*, and has since contributed to the *Reasoner*, the *Pathfinder*, and the *National Reformer*. He was an intimate friend of James Watson. He wrote *A Sketch of the Religions of the Earth, Revelation Tested by Astronomy, Geography, Geology*, etc., 1856, and some other pamphlets. Mr. Brooksbank is still living in honored age at Nottingham.

Brothier (Léon), author of a *Popular History of Philosophy*, 1861, and other works in the *Bibliothèque Utile*. He contributed to the *Rationalist* of Geneva.

Broussais (François Joseph Victor), French physician and philosopher, b. Saint Malo, 17 Dec. 1772. Educated at Dinan, in 1792 he served as volunteer in the army of the Republic. He studied medicine at St. Malo and Brest, and became a naval surgeon. A disciple of Bichat, he did much to reform medical science by his *Examination of Received Medical Doctrines* and to find a basis for mental and moral science in physiology by his many scientific works. Despite his bold opinions, he was made Commander of the Legion of Honor. He died poor at St. Malo 17 Nov. 1838, leaving behind a profession of faith, in which he declares his disbelief in a creator and his being " without hope or fear of another life."

Brown (George William), Dr., of Rockford, Illinois, b. in Essex Co., N.Y., Oct. 1820, of Baptist parents. At 17 years of age he was expelled the church for repudiating the dogma of an endless hell. Dr. Brown edited the *Herald of Freedom*, Kansas. In 1856 his office was destroyed by a pro-slavery mob, his type thrown into the river, and himself and others arrested but was released without trial. Dr. Brown has contributed largely to the *Ironclad Age* and other American Freethought papers, and is bringing out a work on the Origin of Christianity.

Brown (Titus L.), Dr., b. 16 Oct. 1823, at Hillside (N.Y.). Studied at the Medical College of New York and graduated at the Homœopathic College, Philadelphia. He settled at Binghamton where he had a large practice. He contributed to the

Boston Investigator and in 1877 was elected President of the Freethinkers Association. Died 17 Aug. 1887.

Browne (Sir Thomas), physician and writer, b. London, 19 Oct. 1605. He studied medicine and travelled on the Continent, taking his doctor's degree at Leyden (1633). He finally settled at Norwich, where he had a good practice. His treatise *Religio Medici*, famous for its fine style and curious mixture of faith and scepticism, was surreptitiously published in 1612. It ran through several editions and was placed on the Roman *Index*. His *Pseudodoxia Epidemica; Enquiries into Vulgar and Common Errors*, appeared in 1646. While disputing many popular superstitions he showed he partook of others This curious work was followed by *Hydriotaphia, or Urn-Burial*, in which he treats of cremation among the ancients. To this was added *The Garden of Cyrus.* He died 19 Oct. 1682.

Bruno (Giordano), Freethought martyr, b. at Nola, near Naples, about 1548. He was christened Filippo which he changed to Filoteo, taking the name of Giordano when he entered the Dominican order. Religious doubts and bold strictures on the monks obliged him to quit Italy, probably in 1580. He went to Geneva but soon found it no safe abiding place, and quitted it for Paris, where he taught, but refused to attend mass. In 1583 he visited England, living with the French ambassador Castelnau. Having formed a friendship with Sir Philip Sidney, he dedicated to him his *Spaccio della Bestia Triomfante*, a satire on all mythologies. In 1585 he took part in a logical tournament, sustaining the Copernican theory against the doctors of Oxford. The following year he returned to Paris, where he again attacked the Aristotelians. He then travelled to various cities in Germany, everywhere preaching the broadest heresy. He published several Pantheistic, scientific and philosophical works. He was however induced to return to Italy, and arrested as an heresiarch and apostate at Venice, Sept. 1592. After being confined for seven years by the Inquisitors, he was tried, and burnt at Rome 17 Feb. 1600. At his last moments a crucifix was offered him, which he nobly rejected. Bruno was vastly before his age in his conception of the universe and his rejection of theological dogmas. A statue of this heroic apostle of liberty and light, executed by one of the first sculptors of Italy, is to be erected on the spot where he perished, the Municipal Council of Rome having granted the site in face of the bitterest opposition of the Catholic party. The list of subscribers to this memorial comprises the principal advanced thinkers in Europe and America.

Brzesky (Casimir Liszynsky Podsedek). See Liszinski.

Bucali or BUSALI (Leonardo), a Calabrian abbot of Spanish descent, who became a follower of Servetus in the sixteenth century, and had to seek among the Turks the safety denied him in Christendom. He died at Damascus.

Buchanan (George), Scotch historian and scholar, b. Killearn, Feb. 1506. Evincing an early love of study, he was sent to Paris at the age of fourteen. He returned to Scotland and became distinguished for his learning. James V. appointed him tutor to his natural son. He composed his *Franciscanus et Fratres*, a satire on the monks, which hastened the Scottish reformation. This exposed him to the vengeance of the clergy. Not content with calling him Atheist, Archbishop Beaton had him arrested and confined in St. Andrew's Castle, from whence he escaped and fled to England. Here he found, as he said, Henry VIII. burning men of opposite opinions at the same stake for religion. He returned to Paris, but was again subjected to the persecution of Beaton, the Scottish Ambassador. On the death of a patron at Bordeaux, in 1548, he was seized by the Inquisition and immured for a year and a half in a monastery, where he translated the Psalms into Latin. He eventually returned to Scotland, where he espoused the party of Moray. After a most active life, he died 28 Sept. 1582, leaving a History of Scotland, besides numerous poems, satires, and political writings, the most important of which is a work of republican tendency, *De Jure Regni*, the *Rights of Kings*.

Buchanan (Robert), Socialist, b. Ayr, 1813. He was successively a schoolmaster, a Socialist missionary and a journalist. He settled in Manchester, where he published works on the *Religion of the Past and Present*, 1839; the *Origin and Nature of Ghosts*, 1840. An Exposure of Joseph Barker, and a *Concise History of Modern Priestcraft* also bear the latter date. At this time the Socialists were prosecuted for lecturing on Sunday, and Buchanan was fined for refusing to take the oath of supremacy, etc. After the decline of Owenism, he wrote for the

Northern Star, and edited the Glasgow *Sentinel*. He died at the home of his son, the poet, at Bexhill, Sussex, 4 March, 1866.

Buchanan (Joseph Rhodes), American physician, b. Frankfort, Kentucky, 11 Dec. 1814. He graduated M.D. at Louisville University, 1842, and has been the teacher of physiology at several colleges. From 1849–56 he published *Buchanan's Journal of Man*, and has written several works on Anthropology.

Buchner (Ludwig). See Buechner.

Buckle (Henry Thomas), philosophical historian, b. Lee, Kent, 24 Nov. 1821. In consequence of his delicate health he was educated at home. His mother was a strict Calvinist, his father a strong Tory, but a visit to the Continent made him a Freethinker and Radical. He ever afterwards held travelling to be the best education. It was his ambition to write a *History of Civilisation in England*, but so vast was his design that his three notable volumes with that title form only part of the ntroduction. The first appeared in 1858, and created a great sensation by its boldness. In the following year he championed the cause of Pooley, who was condemned for blasphemy, and dared the prosecution of infidels of standing. In 1861 he visited the East, in the hope of improving his health, but died at Damascus, 29 May, 1862. Much of the material collected for his History has been published in his *Miscellaneous and Posthumous Works*, edited by Helen Taylor, 1872. An abridged edition, edited by Grant Allen, appeared in 1886.

Buechner (Friedrich Karl Christian Ludwig), German materialist, b. Darmstadt, 29 March, 1824. Studied medicine in Geissen. Strassburg and Vienna. In '55 he startled the world with his bold work on *Force and Matter*, which has gone through numerous editions and been translated into nearly all the European languages. This work lost him the place of professor which he held at Tübingen, and he has since practised in his native town. Büchner has developed his ideas in many other works such as *Nature and Spirit* (1857). *Physiological Sketches*, '61 ; *Nature and Science*, '62 ; *Conferences on Darwinism*, '69 ; *Man in the Past, Present and Future*, '69 ; *Materialism its History and Influence on Society*, '73 ; *The Idea of God*, '74 ; *Mind in Animals*, '80 ; and *Light and Life*, '82. He also contributes to the *Freidenker*, the *Dageraad*, and other journals.

Buffon (Georges Louis LECLERC), *Count de*, French naturalist, b. Montford, Burgundy, 7 Sept. 1707. An incessant worker. His *Natural History* in 36 volumes bears witness to the fertility of his mind and his capacity for making science attractive. Buffon lived much in seclusion, and attached himself to no sect or religion. Some of his sentences were attacked by the Sorbonne. Hérault de Séchelles says that Buffon said : " I have named the Creator, but it is only necessary to take out the word and substitute the power of nature." Died at Paris 16 April, 1788.

Buitendijk or **Buytendyck** (Gosuinus van), Dutch Spinozist, who wrote an Apology at the beginning of the eighteenth century and was banished 1716.

Bufalini (Maurizio), Italian doctor, b. Cesena 2 June, 1787. In 1813 he published an essay on the *Doctrine of Life* in opposition to vitalism, and henceforward his life was a conflict with the upholders of that doctrine. He was accused of materialism, but became a professor at Florence and a member of the Italian Senate in 1860. Died at Florence 31 March, 1875.

Burdach (Karl Friedrich), German physiologist, b. Leipsic 12 June, 1776. He occupied a chair at the University of Breslau. His works on physiology and anthropology did much to popularise those sciences, and the former is placed on the *Index Librorum Prohibitorum* for its materialistic tendency. He died at Konigsberg, 16 July, 1847.

Burdon (William), M.A., writer, b. Newcastle, 11 Sept. 1764. Graduated at Emmanuel College, Cambridge, 1788. He was intended for a clergyman, but want of faith made him decline that profession. His principal work is entitled *Materials for Thinking*. Colton largely availed himself of this work in his *Lacon*. It went through five editions in his lifetime, and portions were reprinted in the *Library of Reason*. He also addressed *Three Letters to the Bishop of Llandaff*, wrote a *Life and Character of Bonaparte*, translated an account of the Revolution in Spain, edited the Memoirs of Count Boruwlaski, and wrote some objections to the annual subscription to the Sons of the Clergy. Died in London, 30 May, 1818.

Burigny (Jean LEVESQUE DE), French writer, b. Rheims, 1692. He became a member of the French Academy, wrote a treatise on the Authority of the Pope, a History of Pagan Philosophy and other works, and is credited with the *Critical Examination of the Apologists of the Christian Religion*, published under the name of Freret by Naigeon, 1766. Levesque de Burigny wrote a letter in answer to Bergier's *Proofs of Christianity*, which is published in Naigeon's *Recueil Philosophique*. Died at Paris, 8 Oct. 1785.

Burmeister (Hermann), German naturalist, b. Stralsund, 15 Jan. 1807. In 1827 he became a doctor at Halle. In '48 he was elected to the National Assembly. In 1850 he went to Brazil. His principal work is *The History of Creation*, 1843.

Burmeister or BAURMEISTER (Johann Peter Theodor) a German Rationalist and colleague of Ronge. Born at Flensburg, 1805. He resided in Hamburg, and wrote in the middle of the present century under the name of J. P. Lyser.

Burnet (Thomas), b. about 1635 at Croft, Yorkshire, Through the interest of a pupil, the Duke of Ormonde, he obtained the mastership of the Charterhouse, 1685. In 1681 the first part of his *Telluris Theoria Sacra*, or Sacred Theory of the Earth, appeared in Latin, and was translated and modified in 1684. In 1692 Burnet published, both in English and in Latin, his *Archæologiæ Philosophicæ*, or the Ancient Doctrine of the Origin of Things. He professes in this to reconcile his theory with Genesis, which receives a figurative interpretation; and a ludicrous dialogue between Eve and the serpent gave great offence. In a popular ballad Burnet is represented as saying—

> That all the books of Moses
> Were nothing but supposes.

He had to resign a position at court. In later life he wrote *De Fide et Officiis Christianorum* (on Christian Faith and Duties), in which he regards historical religions as based on the religion of nature, and rejects original sin and the "magical" theory of sacraments; and *De Statu Mortuorum et Resurgentium*, on the State of the Dead and Resurrected, in which he opposed the doctrine of eternal punishment and shadowed forth a scheme of Deism. These books he kept to himself to avoid a prosecution for heresy, but had a few copies printed for private friends. He died in the Charterhouse 27 Sept. 1715. A tract entitled *Hell Torments not Eternal* was published in 1739.

Burnett (James), Lord Monboddo, a learned Scotch writer and judge, was b. Monboddo, Oct. 1714. He adopted the law as his profession, became a celebrated advocate, and was made a judge in 1767. His work on the *Origin and Progress of Language* (published anonymously 1773-92), excited much derision by his studying man as one of the animals and collecting facts about savage tribes to throw light on civilisation. He first maintained that the orang-outang was allied to the human species. He also wrote on *Ancient Metaphysics*. He was a keen debater and discussed with Hume, Adam Smith, Robertson, and Lord Kames. Died in Edinburgh, 26 May, 1799.

Burnouf (Emile Louis), French writer, b. Valonges, 25 Aug. 1821. He became professor of ancient literature to the faculty of Nancy. Author of many works, including a translation of selections from the *Novum Organum* of Bacon, the Bhagvat-Gita, an Introduction to the Vedas, a history of Greek Literature, Studies in Japanese, and articles in the *Revue des deux Mondes*. His heresy is pronounced in his work on the *Science of Religions*, 1878, in his *Contemporary Catholicism*, and *Life and Thought*, 1886.

Burnouf (Eugène), French Orientalist, cousin of the preceding; b. Paris, 12 Aug. 1801. He opened up to the Western world the Pali language, and with it the treasures of Buddhism, whose essentially Atheistic character he maintained. To him also we are largely indebted for a knowledge of Zend and of the Avesta of the Zoroastrians. He translated numerous Oriental works and wrote a valuable *Introduction to the History of Indian Buddhism*. Died at Paris, 28 May, 1852.

Burns (Robert), Scotland's greatest poet, b. near Ayr, 25 Jan. 1759. His father was a small farmer, of enlightened views. The life and works of Burns are known throughout the world. His Freethought is evident from such productions as the " Holy Fair," " The Kirk's Alarm," and " Holy Willie's Prayer," and many passages in private letters to his most familiar *male* friends. Died at Dumfries, 21 July, 1796.

Burr (William Henry), American author, b. 1819, Gloversville, N.Y., graduated at Union College, Schenectady, became a shorthand reporter to the Senate. In 1869 he retired and devoted himself to literary research. He is the anonymous author of *Revelations of Antichrist*, a learned book which exposes the obscurity of the origin of Christianity, and seeks to show that the historical Jesus lived almost a century before the Christian era. He has also written several pamphlets: *Thomas Paine was Junius*, 1880: *Self Contradictions of the Bible; Is the Bible a Lying Humbug? A Roman Catholic Canard*, etc. He has also frequently contributed to the *Boston Investigator*, the New York *Truthseeker*, and the *Ironclad Age* of Indianopolis.

Burton (Sir Richard Francis), traveller, linguist, and author, b. Barham House, Herts, 19 March, 1821. Intended for the Church, he matriculated at Oxford, but in 1842 entered the East India Company's service, served on the staff of Sir C. Napier, and soon acquired reputation as an intrepid explorer. In '51 he returned to England and started for Mecca and Medina, visiting those shrines unsuspected, as a Moslem pilgrim. He was chief of the staff of the Osmanli cavalry in the Crimean war, and has made many remarkable and dangerous expeditions in unknown lands; he discovered and opened the lake regions in Central Africa and explored the highlands of Brazil. He has been consul at Fernando Po, Santos, Damascus, and since 1872 at Trieste, and speaks over thirty languages. His latest work is a new translation of *The Thousand Nights and a Night* in 10 vols. Being threatened with a prosecution, he intended justifying "literal naturalism" from the Bible. Burton's knowledge of Arabic is so perfect that when he used to read the tales to Arabs, they would roll on the ground in fits of laughter.

Butler (Samuel), poet, b. in Strensham, Worcestershire, Feb. 1612. In early life he came under the influence of Selden. He studied painting, and is said to have painted a head of Cromwell from life. He became clerk to Sir Samuel Luke, one of Cromwell's Generals, whom he has satirised as Hudibras. This celebrated burlesque poem appeared in 1663 and became famous, but, although the king and court were charmed with its wit, the author was allowed to remain in poverty and obscurity till he died at Covent Garden, London, 25 Sept. 1680. Butler expressed the opinion that

> "Religion is the interest of churches
> That sell in other worlds in this to purchase."

Buttmann (Philipp Karl), German philologist, b. Frankfort, 5 Dec. 1764. Became librarian of the Royal Library at Berlin. He edited many of the Greek Classics, wrote on the *Myth of the Deluge*, 1819, and a learned work on Mythology, 1828. Died Berlin, 21 June, 1829.

Buzot (François Léonard Nicolas), French Girondin, distinguished as an ardent Republican and a friend and lover of Madame Roland. Born at Evreux, 1 March, 1760 ; he died from starvation when hiding after the suppression of his party June, 1793.

Byelinsky (Vissarion G.) See Belinsky.

Byron (George Gordon Noel) Lord, b. London, 22 Jan. 1788, He succeeded his grand-uncle William in 1798 ; was sent to. Harrow and Cambridge. In 1807 he published his *Hours of Idleness*, and awoke one morning to find himself famous. His power was, however, first shown in his *English Bards and Scotch Reviewers*, in which he satirised his critics, 1809. He then travelled on the Continent, the result of which was seen in his *Childe Harold's Pilgrimage* and other works. He married 2 Jan. 1815, but a separation took place in the following year. Lord Byron then resided in Italy, where he made the acquaintance of Shelley. In 1823 he devoted his name and fortune to the cause of the Greek revolution, but was seized with fever and died at Missolonghi, 19 April, 1824. His drama of *Cain: a Mystery*, 1822, is his most serious utterance, and it shows a profound contempt for religious dogma. This feeling is also exhibited in his magnificent burlesque poem, *The Vision of Judgment*, which places him at the head of English satirists. In his letters to the Rev. Francis Hodgson, 1811, he distinctly says : " I do not believe in any revealed religion. . . . I will have nothing to do with your immortality ; we are miserable enough in this life, without the absurdity of speculating upon another. . . . The basis of your religion is injustice ; the Son of God, the pure, the immaculate, the innocent, is sacrificed for the guilty," etc.

Cabanis (Pierre Jean George), called by Lange " the father of the materialistic physiology," b. Conac, 5 June, 1757. Became pupil of Condillac and friend of Mirabeau, whom he attended in his last illness, of which he published an account

1791. He was also intimate with Turgot, Condorcet, Holbach, Diderot, and other distinguished Freethinkers, and was elected member of the Institute and of the Council of Five Hundred in the Revolution. His works are m ostly medical, the chief being *Des Rapports du Physique et du Morale de l'Homme*, in which he contends that thoughts are a secretion of the brain. Died Rueil, near Paris, 5 May, 1808.

Cæsalpinus (Andreas), Italian philosopher of the Renaissance, b. Arezzo, Tuscany, 1519. He became Professor of Botany at Pisa, and Linnæus admits his obligations to his work, *De Plantis*, 1583. He also wrote works on metals and medicine, and showed acquaintance with the circulation of the blood. In a work entitled *Demonum Investigatio*, he contends that "possession" by devils is amenable to medical treatment. His *Quæstionum Peripateticarum*, in five books, Geneva, 1588, was condemned as teaching a Pantheistic doctrine similar to that of Spinoza. Bishop Parker denounced him. Died 23 Feb. 1603.

Cæsar (Caius Julius). the "foremost man of all this world,'' equally renowned as soldier, statesman, orator, and writer, b. 12 July, 100 B.C., of noble family. His life, the particulars of which are well known, was an extraordinary display of versatility, energy, courage, and magnanimity. He justified the well-known line of Pope, "Cæsar the world's great master and his own." His military talents elevated him to the post of dictator, but this served to raise against him a band of aristocratic conspirators, by whom he was assassinated, 15 March, 44 B.C. His *Commentaries* are a model of insight and clear expression. Sallust relates that he questioned the existence of a future state in the presence of the Roman senate. Froude says : "His own writings contain n othing to indicate that he himself had any religious belief at all. He saw no evidence that the gods practically interfered in human affairs. . . . He held to the facts of this life and to his own convictions; and as he found no reason for supposing that there was a life beyond the grave he did not pretend to expect it."

Cahuac (John), bookseller, revised an edition of Palmer's *Principles of Nature*, 1819. For this he was prosecuted at the instance of the "Vice Society," but the matter was compromised. He was also prosecuted for selling the *Republican*, 1820.

Calderino (Domizio), a learned writer of the Renaissance, b. in 1445, in the territory of Verona, and lived at Rome, where he was professor of literature, in 1477. He edited and commented upon many of the Latin poets. Bayle says he was without religion. Died in 1478.

Calenzio (Eliseo), an Italian writer, b. in the kingdom of Naples about 1440. He was preceptor to Prince Frederic, the son of Ferdinand, the King of Naples. He died in 1503, leaving behind a number of satires, fables and epigrams, some of which are directed against the Church.

Call (Wathen Mark Wilks), English author, b. 7 June, 1817. Educated at Cambridge, entered the ministry in 1843, but resigned his curacy about 1856 on account of his change of opinions, which he recounts in his preface to *Reverberations*, 1876. Mr. Call is of the Positivist school, and has contributed largely to the *Fortnightly* and *Westminster Reviews*.

Callet (Pierre Auguste), French politician, b. St. Etienne, 27 Oct. 1812; became editor of the *Gazette* of France till 1840. In 1848 he was nominated Republican representative. At the *coup d'état* of 2 Dec. 1851, he took refuge in Belgium. He returned to France, but was imprisoned for writing against the Empire. In 1871, Callet was again elected representative for the department of the Loire. His chief Freethought work is *L'Enfer*, an attack upon the Christian doctrine of hell, 1861.

Camisani (Gregorio), Italian writer, b. at Venice, 1840. A Professor of Languages in Milan. He has translated the *Upas* of Captain R. H. Dyas and other works.

Campanella (Tommaso), Italian philosopher, b. Stilo, Calabria, 5 Sept. 1568. He entered the Dominican order, but was too much attracted by the works of Telesio to please his superiors. In 1590 his *Philosophia Sensibus Demonstratio* was printed at Naples. Being prosecuted, he fled to Rome, and thence to Florence, Venice, and Padua. At Bologna some of his MS. fell into the hands of the Inquisition, and he was arrested. He ably defended himself and was acquitted. Returning to Calabria in 1599, he was arrested on charges of heresy and conspiracy against the Spanish Government of Naples, and having appealed to Rome, was sentenced to perpetual imprisonment in the prison of the Holy Office. He

65

was put to the torture seven times, his torments on one occasion extending over forty hours, but he refused to confess. He was dragged from one prison to another for twenty-seven year, during which he wrote some sonnets, a history of the Spanish monarchy, and several philosophical works. On 15 May, 1626, he was released by the intervention of Pope Urban VIII. He was obliged to fly from Rome to France, where he met Gassendi. He also visited Descartes in Holland. Julian Hibbert remarked that his *Atheismus Triumphatus*—Atheism Subdued, 1631, would be better entitled *Atheismus Triumphans*—Atheism Triumphant—as the author puts his strongest arguments on the heterodox side. In his *City of the Sun*, Campanella follows Plato and More in depicting an ideal republic and a time when a new era of earthly felicity should begin. Hallam says "The strength of Campanella's genius lay in his imagination." His "Sonnets" have been translated by J. A. Symonds. Died Paris, 21 May, 1639.

Campbell (Alexander), Socialist of Glasgow, b. about the beginning of the century. He early became a Socialist, and was manager at the experiment at Orbiston under Abram Combe, of whom he wrote a memoir. Upon the death of Combe, 1827, he became a Socialist missionary in England. He took an active part in the co-operative movement, and in the agitation for an unstamped press, for which he was tried and imprisoned at Edinburgh, 1833-4. About 1849 he returned to Glasgow and wrote on the *Sentinel*. In 1867 he was presented with a testimonial and purse of 90 sovereigns by admirers of his exertions in the cause of progress. Died about 1873.

Campion (William), a shoemaker, who became one of R. Carlile's shopmen; tried 8 June, 1824, for selling Paine's *Age of Reason*. After a spirited defence he was found guilty and sentenced to three years' imprisonment. In prison he edited, in conjunction with J. Clarke, R. Hassell, and T. R. Perry, the *Newgate Monthly Magazine*, to which he contributed some thoughtful papers, from Sept. 1824, to Aug. 1826, when he was removed to the Compter.

Canestrini (Giovanni), Italian naturalist, b. Rerò, 1835. He studied at Vienna, and in '60 was nominated Professor of Natural History at Geneva. Signor Canestrini contributed to the *Annuario Filosofico del Libero Pensiero*, and is known for his popularisation of the works of Darwin, which he has translated into Italian. He has written upon the *Origin of Man*, which has gone through two editions, Milan, '66–'70, and on the *Theory of Evolution*, Turin, '77. He was appointed Professor of Zoology, Anatomy and Comparative Physiology at Padua, where he has published a Memoir of Charles Darwin, '82.

Cardano (Girolamo), better known as JEROME CARDAN, Italian mathematician, and physician, b. Pavia, 24 Sept. 1501. He studied medicine, but was excluded from the Milan College of Physicians on account of illegitimate birth. He and his young wife were at one time compelled to take refuge in the workhouse. It is not strange that his first work was an exposure of the fallacies of the faculty. A fortunate cure brought him into notice and he journeyed to Scotland as the medical adviser of the Archbishop of St. Andrews, 1551. In 1563 he was arrested at Bologna for heresy, but was released, although deprived of his professorship. He died at Rome, 20 Sept. 1576, having, it is said, starved himself to verify his own prediction of his death. Despite some superstition, Cardano did much to forward science, especially by his work on Algebra, and in his works *De Subtilitate Rerum* and *De Varietate Rerum*, amid much that is fanciful, perceived the universality of natural law and the progressive evolution of life. Scaliger accused him of Atheism. Pünjer says " Cardanus deserves to be named along with Telesius as one of the principal founders of Natural Philosophy."

Carducci (Giosuè), Italian poet and Professor of Italian Literature at the University of Bologna, b. Pietrasantra, in the province of Lucca, 27 July, 1836. As early as '49 he cried, *Abasso tutti i re: viva la republica*—Down with all kings ! Long live the republic ! Sprung into fame by his *Hymn to Satan*, '69, by which he intended the spirit of resistance. He has written many poems and satires in which he exhibits himself an ardent Freethinker and Republican. At the end of '57 he wrote his famous verse " Il secoletto vil che cristianeggia "—" This vile christianising century." In '60 he became professor of Greek in Bologna University, being suspended for a short while in '67 for an address to Mazzini. In '76 he was elected as republican deputy to the Italian Parliament for Lugo di Romagna.

Carlile (Eliza Sharples), second wife of Richard Carlile, came from Lancashire during the imprisonment of Carlile and Taylor, 1831, delivered discourses at the Rotunda, and started a journal, the *Isis*, which lasted from 11 Feb. to 15 Dec. 1832. The *Isis* was dedicated to the young women of England "until super-stition is extinct," and contained Frances Wright's discourses, in addition to those by Mrs. Carlile, who survived till '61. Mr. Bradlaugh lodged with Mrs. Carlile at the Warner Place Insti-tute, in 1849. She had three children, Hypatia, Theophila and Julian, of whom the second is still living.

Carlile (Jane), first wife of R. Carlile, who carried on his business during his imprisonment, was proceeded against, and sentenced to two years' imprisonment, 1821. She had three children, Richard, Alfred, and Thomas Paine Carlile, the last of whom edited the *Regenerator*, a Chartist paper published at Manchester, 1839.

Carlile (Richard), foremost among the brave upholders of an English free press, b. Ashburton, Devon, 8 Dec. 1790. He was apprenticed to a tin-plate worker, and followed that business till he was twenty-six, when, having read the works of Paine, he began selling works like Wooler's *Black Dwarf*, which Government endeavored to suppress. Sherwin offered him the dangerous post of publisher of the *Republican*, which he accepted. He then published Southey's *Wat Tyler*, reprinted the political works of Paine and the parodies for which Hone was tried, but which cost Carlile eighteen weeks' imprisonmen t. In 1818 he published Paine's Theological Works. The prosecution insti-tuted induced him to go on printing similar works, such as Palmer's *Principles of Nature, Watson Refuted, Jehovah Unveiled*, etc. By Oct. 1819, he had six indictments to answer, on two of which he was tried from 12 to 16 October. He read the whole of the *Age of Reason* in his defence, in order to have it in the report of the trial. He was found guilty and sentenced (16 Nov.) to fifteen hundred pounds fine and three years' imprisonment in Dorchester Gaol. During his imprisonment his business was kept on by a succession of shopmen. Refusing to find securities not to publish, he was kept in prison till 18

Nov. 1835, when he was liberated unconditionally. During his imprisonment he edited the *Republican*, which extended to fourteen volumes. He also edited the *Deist*, the *Moralist*, the *Lion* (four volumes), the *Prompter* (for No. 3 of which he again suffered thirty-two months' imprisonment), and the *Gauntlet*. Amongst his writings are *An Address to Men of Science*, *The Gospel according to R. Carlile*, *What is God? Every Woman's Book*, etc. He published *Doubts of Infidels*, *Janus on Sion*, *Sepher Toldoth Jeshu*, D'Holbach's *Good Sense*, Volney's *Ruins*, and many other Freethought works. He died 10 Feb. 1843, bequeathing his body to Dr. Lawrence for scientific purposes.

Carlyle (Thomas), one of the most gifted and original writers of the century, b. 4 Dec. 1795, at Ecclefechan, Dumfriesshire, where his father, a man of intellect and piety, held a small farm. Showing early ability he was intended for the Kirk, and educated at the University of Edinburgh. He, however, became a tutor, and occupied his leisure in translating from the German. He married Jane Welsh 17 Oct. 1826, and wrote in the *London Magazine* and *Edinburgh Review* many masterly critical articles, notably on Voltaire, Diderot, Burns, and German literature. In 1833-4 his *Sartor Resartus* appeared in *Fraser's Magazine*. In '34 he removed to London and began writing the *French Revolution*, the MS. of the first vol. of which he confided to Mill, with whom it was accidentally burnt. He re-wrote the work without complaint, and it was published in '37. He then delivered a course of lectures on " German Literature " and on " Heroes, Hero-Worship, and the Heroic in History," in which he treats Mahomet as the prophet " we are freest to speak of." His *Past and Present* was published in '43. In '45 appeared *Oliver Cromwell's Letters and Speeches*. In '50 he published *Latter-Day Pamphlets*, which contains his most distinctive political and social doctrines, and in the following year his *Life of John Sterling*, in which his heresy clearly appears. His largest work is his *History of the Life and Times of Frederick the Great*, in 10 vols. He was elected rector of Edinburgh University in '65. Died 5 Feb. 1881. Mr. Froude, in his *Biography of Carlyle*, says, " We have seen him confessing to Irving that he did not believe as his friend did in the Christian religion.". . . . " the special miraculous occurrences of sacred history were not credible to him."

69

Carneades, sceptical philosopher, b. Cyrene about B.C. 213. He went early to Athens, and attended the lectures of the Stoics, learning logic from Diogenes. In the year 155, he was chosen with other deputies to go to Rome to deprecate a fine which had been placed on the Athenians. During his stay at Rome he attracted great attention by his philosophical orations. Carneades attacked the very idea of a God at once infinite and an individual. He denied providence and design. Many of his arguments are preserved in Cicero's *Academics* and *De Natura Deorum.* Carneades left no written works; his views seem to have been systematised by his follower Clitomachus. He died B.C. 129. Carneades is described as a man of unwearied industry. His ethics were of elevated character.

Carneri (Bartholomäus von), German writer, b. Trieste, 3 Nov. 1821. Educated at Vienna. In 1870 he sat in the Austrian Parliament with the Liberals. Author of an able work on *Morality and Darwinism,* Vienna, 1871. Has also written *Der Mensch als Selbstweck,* " Humanity as its own proper object," 1877 ; *Grundlegung der Ethik,* Foundation of Morals, 1881 ; and Ethical Essays on Evolution and Happiness, Stuttgart, 1886.

Carra (Jean Louis), French man of letters and Republican, b. 1743 at Pont de Veyle. He travelled in Germany, Italy, Turkey, Russia, and Moldavia, where he became secretary to the hospodar. On returning to France he became employed in the King's library and wrote a *History of Moldavia* and an *Essay on Aerial Navigation.* He warmly espoused the revolution and was one of the most ardent orators of the Jacobin club. In the National Assembly he voted for the death of Louis XVI., but was executed with the Girondins, 31 Oct. 1793. His Freethought sentiments are evident from his *System of Reason,* 1773 ; his *Spirit of Morality and Philosophy,* 1777 ; *New Principles of Physic,* 1782–3, and other works.

Carrel (Jean Baptiste Nicolas Armand), called by Saint Beuve " the Junius of the French press," b. Rouen, 8 May, 1800. He became a soldier, but, being a Republican, fought on behalf of the Spanish revolution. Being taken prisoner, he was condemned to death, but escaped through some informality. He became secretary to Thierry, edited the works of P. L. Courier, and established the *Nation* in conjunction with Thiers and Mignet.   J. S. Mill writes of him in terms of high praise.   The leading journalist of his time, his slashing articles led to several duels, and in an encounter with Emile de Girardin (22 July, 1836) he was fatally wounded.   On his death-bed, says M. Littré, he said "*Point de prêtres, point d'église*" —no priests nor church.   Died 21 July, 1836.   He wrote a *History of the Counter-Revolution in England,* with an eye to events in his own country.

Carus (Julius Viktor), German zoologist, b. Leipsic, 25 Aug. 1825.   Has been keeper of anatomical museum at Oxford, and has translated Darwin's works and the philosophy of G. H. Lewes.

Carus (Karl Gustav), German physiologist and Pantheist, b. Leipsic, 3 Jan. 1789.   He taught compatative anatomy at the university of that town, and published a standard introduction to that subject.   He also wrote *Psyche,* a history of the development of the human soul, 1846, and *Nature and Idea,* 1861.   Died at Dresden, 28 July, 1869.

Castelar y Ripoll (Emilio), Spanish statesman, b. Cadiz, 8 Sept. 1832.   He began as a journalist, and became known by his novel *Ernesto,* 1855.   As professor of history and philosophy, he delivered lectures on "Civilisation during the first three centuries of Christendom."   *La Formula del Progresso* contains a sketch of democratic principles.   On the outbreak of the revolution of '68 he advocated a Federal Republic in a magnificent oration.   The Crown was however offered to Amadeus of Savoy.   "Glass, with care," was Castelar's verdict on the new dynesty, and in Feb. '73 Castelar drew up a Republican Constitution ; and for a year was Dictator of Spain. Upon his retirement to France he wrote a sketchy *History of the Republican Movement in Europe.*   In '76 he returned to Spain and took part in the Cortes, where he has continued to advocate Republican views.   His *Old Rome and New Italy,* and *Life of Lord Byron* have been translated into English.

Castelli (David), Italian writer, b. Livorno, 30 Dec. 1836. Since 1873 he has held the chair of Hebrew in the Institute of Superior Studies at Florence.   He has translated the book of Ecclesiastes with notes, and written rationalistic works on *Talmudic Legends,* 1869 ; *The Messiah According to the Hebrews,*

'74; the *Bible Prophets*, '82; and *The History of the Israelites*, 1887.

Castilhon (Jean Louis), French man of letters, b. at Toulouse in 1720. He wrote in numerous publications, and edited the *Journal of Jurisprudence*. His history of dogmas and philosophical opinions had some celebrity, and he shows himself a Freethinker in his *Essay on Ancient and Modern Errors and Superstitions*, Amsterdam, 1765; his *Philosophical Almanack*, 1767; and his *History of Philosophical Opinions*, 1769. Died 1793.

Cattell (Christopher Charles), writer in English Secular journals, author of *Search for the First Man; Against Christianity; The Religion of this Life*, etc.

Caumont (Georges), French writer of genius, b. about 1845. Suffering from consumption, he wrote *Judgment of a Dying Man upon Life*, and humorous and familiar *Conversations of a Sick Person with the Divinity*. Died at Madeira, 1875.

Cavalcante (Guido), noble Italian poet and philosopher, b. Florence, 1230. A friend of Dante, and a leader of the Ghibbelin party. He married a daughter of Farinata delgi Uberti. Bayle says, "it is said his speculation has as their aim to prove their is no God. Dante places his father in the hell of Epicureans, who denied the immortality of the soul." Guido died in 1300. An edition of his poems was published in 1813.

Cavallotti (Felice Carlo Emanuel), Italian poet and journalist, b. Milan, 6 Nov. 1842, celebrated for his patriotic poems; is a pronounced Atheist. He was elected member of the Italian parliament in 1873.

Cayla (Jean Mamert), French man of letters and politician, b. Vigan (Lot) 1812. Became in '37 editor of the *Emancipator* of Toulouse, a city of which he wrote the history. At Paris he wrote to the *Siècle*, the *République Française* and other journals, and published *European Celebrities* and numerous anti-clerical brochures, such as *The Clerical Conspiracy*, '61; *The Devil, his Grandeur and Decay*, '64; *Hell Demolished*, '65; *Suppression of Religious Orders*, '70; and *The History of the Mass*, '74. He died 2 May, 1877.

Cazelles (Emile), French translator of Bentham's *Influence of*

Natural Religion, Paris, 1875. Has also translated Mill's *Subjection of Women* and his *Autobiography* and *Essays on Religion.*

Cecco d'Ascoli, *i.e.*, STABILI (Francesco degli), Italian poet, b. Ascoli, 1257. He taught astrology and philosophy at Bologna. In 1324 he was arrested by the Inquisition for having spoken against the faith, and was condemned to fine and penitence. He was again accused at Florence, and was publicly burnt as an heretic 16 Sept. 1327. His best known work is entitled *Acerba*, a sort of encyclopædia in rhyme.

Cellarius (Martin), Anabaptist, who deserves mention as the first avowed Protestant Anti-trinitarian. He studied Oriental languages with Reuchlin and Melancthon, but having discussed with Anabaptists acknowledged himself converted, 1522, and afterwards gave up the deity of Christ. He was imprisoned, and on his release went to Switzerland, where he died 11 Oct. 1564.

Celsus, a Pagan philosopher, who lived in the second century. He was a friend of Lucian, who dedicated to him his treatise on the False Prophet. He wrote an attack on Christianity, called *The True Word*. The work was destroyed by the early Christians. The passages given by his opponent, Origen, suffice to show that he was a man of high attainments, well acquainted with the religion he attacked, and that his power of logic and irony was most damaging to the Christian faith.

Cerutti (Guiseppe Antonio Gioachino), poet, converted Jesuit, b. Turin, 13 June, 1738. He became a Jesuit, and wrote a defence of the Society. He afterwards became a friend of Mirabeau adopted the principles of 1789, wrote in defence of the Revolution, and wrote and published a *Philosophical Breviary*, or history of Judaism, Christianity, and Deism, which he attributed to Frederick of Prussia. His opinions may also be gathered from his poem, *Les Jardins de Betz*, 1792. Died Paris, 3 Feb. 1792.

Chaho (J. Augustin), Basque man of letters, b. Tardets, Basses-Pyrénées) 10 Oct. 1811. His principal works are a *Philosophy of Comparative Religion*, and a Basque dictionary. At Bayonne he edited the *Ariel*. In 1852 this was suppressed and he was exiled. Died 23 Oct. 1858.

Chaloner (Thomas), M.P., Regicide, b. Steeple Claydon, Bucks, 1595. Educated at Oxford, he became member for Richmond

(Yorks),1645. Was a witness against Archbishop Laud, and one of King Charles's Judges. In 1651 he was made Councillor of State. Wood says he " was as far from being a Puritan as the east is from the west," and that he " was of the natural religion."   He wrote a pretended *True and Exact Relation of the Finding of Moses His Tomb*, 1657, being a satire directed against the Presbyterians. Upon the Restoration he fled to the Low Countries, and died at Middelburg, Zeeland, in 1661.

Chambers (Ephraim), originator of the Cyclopædia of Arts and Sciences, b. Kendal about 1680.   The first edition of his work appeared in 1728, and procured him admission to the Royal Society.   A French translation gave rise to Diderot and D'Alembert's *Encyclopédie*.   Chambers also edited the *Literary Magazine*, 1836, etc.   His infidel opinions were well known, and the Cyclopædia was placed upon the *Index*, but he was buried in the cloisters of Westminster Abbey.   Died 15 May, 1740.

Chamfort (Sébastien Roch Nicolas), French man of letters, b. in Auvergne, near Clermont, 1741.   He knew no parent but his mother, a peasant girl, to supply whose wants he often denied himself necessaries.   At Paris he gained a prize from the Academy for his eulogy on Molière.   About 1776 he published a Dramatic Dictionary and wrote several plays.   In 1781 he obtained a seat in the Academy, being patronised by Mme. Helvetius.   He became a friend of Mirabeau, who called him *une tête électrique*.   In 1790 he commenced a work called *Pictures of the Revolution*.   In the following year he became secretary of the Jacobin Club and National Librarian.   Arrested by Robespierre, he desperately, but vainly, endeavored to commit suicide.   He died 13 April, 1794, leaving behind numerous works and a collection of *Maxims, Thoughts, Characters, and Anecdotes*, which show profound genius and knowledge of human nature.

Chapman (John), M.R.C.S., b. 1839.   Has written largely in the *Westminster Review*, of which he is proprietor.

Chappellsmith (Margaret), née REYNOLDS, b. Aldgate, 22 Feb. 1806.   Early in life she read the writings of Cobbett. In '36 she began writing political articles in the *Dispatch*, and afterwards became a Socialist and Freethought lecturess.   She married John Chappellsmith in '39, and in '42 she began

buisness as a bookseller. In '37 she expressed a preference for the development theory before that of creation.
In '50 they emigrated to the United States, where Mrs. Chappellsmith contributed many articles to the *Boston Investigator.*

Charles (Rudolf). See Giessenburg.

Charma (Antoine), French philosopher, b. 15 Jan. 1801. In
'30 he was nominated to the Chair of Philosophy at Caen. He
was denounced for his impiety by the Count de Montalembert
in the Chamber of peers, and an endeavor was made to unseat
him. He wrote many philosophical works, and an account of
Didron's *Histoire de Dieu.* Died 5 Aug. 1869.

Charron (Pierre), French priest and sceptic, b. Paris, 1513.
He was an intimate friend of Montaigne. His principal work
is a *Treatise on Wisdom,* 1601, which was censured as irreligious
by the Jesuits. Franck says "the scepticism of Charron in-
clines visibly to 'sensualisme' and even to materialism." Died
Paris, 16 Nov. 1603.

Chassebœuf de Volney (Constantin François). See Volney.

Chastelet du or **Chatelet Lomont** (Gabrielle Emilie LE
TONNELIER DE BRETEUIL), Marquise, French *savante*, b. Paris,
17 Dec. 1706. She was learned in mathematics and other sciences,
and in Latin, English and Italian. In 1740 she published a work on
physical philosophy entitled *Institutions de Physique.* She afterwards made a good French translation of Newton's *Principia.*
She lived some years with Voltaire at Cirey between 1735 and
1747, and addressed to him *Doubts on Revealed Religions,* published in 1792. She also wrote a *Treatise on Happiness,* which
was praised by Condorcet.

Chastellux (François Jean de), Marquis. A soldier, traveller
and writer, b. Paris 1734. Wrote *On Public Happiness* (2 vols.,
Amst. 1776), a work Voltaire esteemed highly. He contributed
to the *Encyclopédie;* one article on "Happiness," being suppressed by the censor because it did not mention God. Died
Paris, 28 Oct. 1788.

Chatterton (Thomas), the marvellous boy poet, b. Bristol,
20 Nov, 1752. His poems, which he pretended were written
by one Thomas Rowley in the fourteenth century and dis-

covered by him in an old chest in Redcliffe Church, attracted much attention. In 1769 he visited London in hopes of rising by his talents, but after a bitter experience of writing for the magazines, destroyed himself in a fit of despair 25 Aug. 1770. Several of his poems betray deistic opinions.

Chaucer (Geoffrey), the morning star of English poetry and first English Humanist, b. London about 1340. In 1357 he was attached to the household of Lionel, third son of Edward III. He accompanied the expedition to France 1359—60, was captured by the French, and ransomed by the king. He was patronised by John of Gaunt, and some foreign missions were entrusted to him, one of them being to Italy, where he met Petrarch. All his writings show the influence of the Renaissance, and in his *Canterbury Pilgrims* he boldly attacks the vices of the ecclesiastics. Died 25 Oct. 1400, and was buried in Westminster Abbey.

Chaumette (Pierre Gaspard), afterwards Anaxagoras, French revolutionary, b. Nevers, 24 May, 1763. The son of a shoemaker, he was in turn cabin boy, steersman, and attorney's clerk. In early youth he received lessons in botany from Rousseau. He embraced the revolution with ardor, was the first to assume the tri-color cockade, became popular orator at the club of the Cordeliers, and was associated with Proudhomme in the journal *Les Revolutions de Paris.* Nominated member of the Commune 10 Aug. 1792, he took the name of Anaxagoras to show his little regard for his baptismal saints. He was elected Procureur Syndic, in which capacity he displayed great activity. He abolished the rod in schools, suppressed lotteries, instituted workshops for fallen women, established the first lying-in-hospital, had books sent to the hospitals, separated the insane from the sick, founded the Conservatory of Music, opened the public libraries every day (under the *ancien régime* they were only open two hours per week), replaced books of superstition by works of morality and reason, put a graduated tax on the rich to provide for the burial of the poor, and was the principal mover in the feasts of Reason and closing of the churches. He was accused by Robespierre of conspiring with Cloots " to efface all idea of the Deity," and was guillotined 13 April, 1794.

Chaussard (Pierre Jean Baptiste), French man of letters, b. Paris, 8 Oct. 1766. At the Revolution he took the name of Publicola, and published patriotic odes, *Esprit de Mirabeau*, and other works. He was preacher to the Theophilanthropists, and became professor of *belles lettres* at Orleans. Died 9 Jan. 1823.

Chemin-Dupontes (Jean Baptiste), b. 1761. One of the founders of French Theophilanthropy; published many writings, the best known of which is entitled *What is Theophilanthropy ?*

Chenier (Marie André de), French poet, b. Constantinople, 29 Oct. 1762. His mother, a Greek, inspired him with a love for ancient Greek literature. Sent to college at Paris, he soon manifested his genius by writing eclogues and elegies of antique simplicity and sensibility. In 1787 he came to England as Secretary of Legation. He took part in the legal defence of Louis XVI., eulogised Charlotte Corday, and gave further offence by some letters in the *Journal de Paris*. He was committed to prison, and here met his ideal in the Comtesse de Coigny. Confined in the same prison, to her he addressed the touching verses, The Young Captive (La jeune Captive). He was executed 25 July, 1794, leaving behind, among other poems, an imitation of Lucretius, entitled *Hermes*, which warrants the affirmation of de Chênedolle, that "Andre Chénier etait athée avec délices."

Chenier (Marie Joseph de), French poet and miscellaneous writer, brother of the preceding, b. Constantinople, 28 Aug· 1764. He served two years in the army, and then applied himself to literature. His first successful drama, "Charles IX.," was produced in 1789, and was followed by others. He wrote many patriotic songs, and was made member of the Convention. He was a Voltairean, and in his *Nouveaux Saints* (1801) satirised those who returned to the old faith. He wrote many poems and an account of French literature. Died Paris, 10 Jan. 1811.

Chernuishevsky or **Tchernycheiosky** (Nikolai Gerasimovich), Russian Nihilist, b. Saratof, 1829. Educated at the University of St. Petersburg, translated Mill's *Political Economy*, and wrote on *Superstition and the Principles of Logic*, '59. His bold romance, *What is to be Done?* was published '63.   In the following year he was sentenced to the Siberian mines, where, after heartrending cruelties, he has become insane.

Chesneau Du Marsais (César).   See Dumarsais.

Chevalier (Joseph Philippe), French chemist, b. Saint Pol 21 March, 1806, is the author of an able book on " The Soul from the standpoint of Reason and Science," Paris, '61.   He died at Amiens in 1865.

Chies y Gomez (Ramon), Spanish Free thinker, b. Medina de Pomar, Burgos, 13 Oct. 1845.   His father, a distinguished Republican, educated him without religion.   In '65 Chies went to Madrid, and followed a course of law and philosophy at the University, and soon after wrote for a Madrid paper *La Discusion*.   He took an active part in the Revolution of '65, and at the proclamation of the Republic, '73, became civil governor of Valencia.   In '81 he founded a newspaper *El Voto Nacional*, and since '83 has edited *Las Dominicales del Libre Pensamiento*, which he also founded.   Ramon Chies is one of the foremost Freethought champions in Spain and lectures as well as writes.

Child (Lydia Maria) née FRANCIS, American authoress, b. Medford, Mass., 11 Feb. 1802.   She early commenced writing, publishing *Hobomok, a Tale of Early Times*, in '21.   From '25 she kept a private school in Watertown until '28, when she married David Lee Child, a Boston lawyer.   She, with him, edited the *Anti-Slavery Standard*, '41, etc., and by her numerous writings did much to form the opinion which ultimately prevailed.   She was, however, long subjected to public odium, her heterodoxy being well known.   Her principal work is *The Progress of Religious Ideas*, 3 vols. ; '55.   Died Wayland, Mass., 20 Oct. 1880.   She was highly eulogised by Wendell Phillips.

Chilton (William), of Bristol, was born in 1815.   In early life he was a bricklayer, but in '41 he was concerned with Charles Southwell in starting the *Oracle of Reason*, which he set up in type, and of which he became one of the editors.   He contributed some thoughtful articles on the Theory of Development to the *Library of Reason*, and wrote in the *Movement* and the *Reasoner*.   Died at Bristol, 28 May, 1855.

Chubb (Thomas), English Deist, b. East Harnham, near

Salisbury, 29 Sept. 1679, was one of the first to show Rationalism among the common people. Beginning by contending for the *Supremacy of the Father*, he gradually relinquished supernatural religion, and considered that Jesus Christ was of the religion of Thomas Chubb. Died 8 Feb. 1747, leaving behind two vols. which he calls *A Farewell to his Readers*, from which it appears that he rejected both revelation and special providence.

Church (Henry Tyrell), lecturer and writer, edited Tallis's *Shakespeare*, wrote *Woman and her Failings*, 1858, and contributed to the *Investigator* when edited by Mr. Bradlaugh. Died 19 July, 1859.

Clapiers (Luc de). See Vauvenargues.

Claretie (Jules Armand Arsène), French writer, b. Limoges, 3 Dec. 1840. A prolific writer, of whose works we only cite *Free Speech*, '68; his biographies of contemporary celebrities; and his work *Camille Desmoulins*, '75.

Clarke (John), brought up in the Methodist connection, changed his opinion by studying the Bible, and became one of Carlile's shopmen. He was tried 10 June, 1824, for selling a blasphemous libel in number 17, vol. ix., of *The Republican*, and after a spirited defence, in which he read many of the worst passages in the Bible, was sentenced to three years' imprisonment, and to find securities for good behavior during life. He wrote while in prison, *A Critical Review of the Life, Character, and Miracles of Jesus*, a work showing with some bitterness much bold criticism and Biblical knowledge. It first appeared in the *Newgate Magazine* and was afterwards published in book form, 1825 and '39.

Clarke (Marcus), Australian writer, b. Kensington, 1847. Went to Victoria, '63; joined the staff of *Melbourne Argus*. In '76 was made assistant librarian of the Public Library. He has compiled a history of Australia, and written *The Peripatetic Philosopher* (a series of clever sketches), *His Natural Life* (a powerful novel), and some poems. An able Freethought paper, "Civilisation without Delusion," in the *Victoria Review*, Nov. '79, was replied to by Bishop Moorhouse. The reply, with Clarke's answer, which was suppressed, was published in '80. Died 1884.

Claude-Constant, author of a Freethinkers' Catechism published at Paris in 1875.

Clavel (Adolphe), French Positivist and physician, b Grenoble, 1815. He has written on the Principles of 1789, on those of the nineteenth century, on Positive Morality, and some educational works.

Clavel (F. T. B.), French author of a *Picturesque History of Freemasonry*, and also a *Picturesque History of Religions*, 1844, in which Christianity takes a subordinate place.

Clayton (Robert), successively Bishop of Killala, Cork, and Clogher, b. Dublin, 1695. By his benevolence attracted the friendship of Samuel Clarke, and adopted Arianism, which he maintained in several publications. In 1756 he proposed, in the Irish House of Lords, the omission of the Nicene and Athanasian Creeds from the Liturgy, and stated that he then felt more relieved in his mind than for twenty years before. A legal prosecution was instituted, but he died, it is said, from nervous agitation (26 Feb. 1758) before the matter was decided.

Cleave (John), bookseller, and one of the pioneers of a cheap political press. Started the *London Satirist*, and *Cleave's Penny Gazette of Variety*, Oct. 14, 1837, to Jan. 20, '44. He published many Chartist and Socialistic works, and an abridgment of Howitt's *History of Priestcraft*. In May, '40, he was sentenced to four months' imprisonment for selling Haslam's *Letters to the Clergy*.

Clemenceau (Georges Benjamin Eugene), French politician, b. Moulleron-en-Pareds, 28 Sept. 1841. Educated at Nantes and Paris, he took his doctor's degree in '65. His activity as Republican ensured him a taste of gaol. He visited the United States and acted as correspondent on the *Temps*. He returned at the time of the war and was elected deputy to the Assembly. In Jan. 1880 he founded *La Justice*, having as collaborateurs M. C. Pelletan, Prof. Acollas and Dr. C. Letourneau. As one of the chiefs of the Radical party he was largely instrumental in getting M. Carnot elected President.

Clemetshaw (C.), French writer, using the name CILWA. B. 14 Sept. 1864 of English parents; has contributed to many journals, was delegate to the International Congress, London, of '87, and is editor of *Le Danton*.

Clemens (Samuel Langhorne), American humorist, better
known as " Mark Twain," b. Florida, Missouri, 30 Nov. 1835.
In '55 he served as Mississippi pilot, and takes his pen name
from the phrase used in sounding. In *Innocents Abroad, or the
New Pilgrim's Progress*, '69, by which he made his name, there
is much jesting with "sacred" subjects. Mr. Clemens is an
Agnostic.

Clifford (Martin), English Rationalist. Was Master of the
Charterhouse, 1671, and published anonymously a treatise of
Human Reason, London, '74, which was reprinted in the
following year with the author's name. A short while after its
publication Laney, Bishop of Ely, was dining in Charterhouse
and remarked, not knowing the author, " 'twas no matter if all
the copies were burnt and the author with them, because it
made every man's private fancy judge of religion." Clifford
died 10 Dec. 1677. In the *Nouvelle Biographie Générale* Clifford
is amusingly described as an " English theologian of the order
des Chartreux," who, it is added, was " prior of his order."

Clifford (William Kingdon), mathematician, philosopher,
and moralist, of rare originality and boldness, b. Exeter 4 May,
1845. At the age of fifteen he was sent to King's College,
London, where he showed an early genius for mathematics,
publishing the *Analogues of Pascal's Theorem* at the age of
eighteen. Entered Trinity College, Cambridge, in '63. In '67
he was second wrangler. Elected fellow of his college, he
remained at Cambridge till 1870, when he accompanied the
eclipse expedition to the Medeterranean. The next year he
was appointed Professor of mathematics at London University,
a post he held till his death. He was chosen F.R.S. '74.
Married Miss Lucy Lane in April, '75. In the following year
symptoms of consumption appeared, and he visited Algeria
and Spain. He resumed work, but in '79 took a voyage to
Madeira, where he died 3 March. Not long before his death
appeared the first volume of his great mathematical work.
Elements of Dynamic. Since his death have been published
The Common Sense of the Exact Sciences, and *Lectures and Essays*, in
two volumes, edited by Leslie Stephen and Mr. F. Pollock.
These volumes include his most striking Freethought lectures
and contributions to the *Fortnightly* and other reviews. He

intended to form them into a volume on *The Creed of Science.*
Clifford was an outspoken Atheist, and he wrote of Christianity
as a religion which wrecked one civilisation and very nearly
wrecked another.

Cloots or **Clootz** (Johann Baptist, afterwards Anacharsis)
Baron du Val de Grâce, Prussian enthusiast, b. near Cleves,
24 June, 1755, was a nephew of Cornelius de Pauw. In 1780
he published the The *Certainty of the Proofs of Mohammedanism,*
under the pseudonym of Ali-gier-ber, an anagram of Bergier,
whose *Certainty of the Proofs of Christianity* he parodies. He
travelled widely, but became a resident of Paris and a warm
partisan of the Revolution, to which he devoted his large
fortune. He wrote a reply to Burke, and continually wrote
and spoke in favor of a Universal Republic. On 19 June,
1790, he, at the head of men of all countries, asked a place
at the feast of Federation, and henceforward was styled
" orator of the human race." He was, with Paine, Priestley,
Washington and Klopstock, made a French citizen, and in 1792
was elected to the Convention by two departments. He debap-
tised himself, taking the name Anacharsis, was a prime mover
in the Anti-Catholic party, and induced Bishop Gobel to resign.
He declared there was no other God but Nature. Incurring
the enmity of Robespierre, he and Paine were arrested as
foreigners. After two and a half months' imprisonment at
St. Lazare, he was brought to the scaffold with the Hébertistes,
24 March, 1794. He died calmly, uttering materialist sentiments to the last.

Clough (Arthur Hugh), poet, b. Liverpool, 1 Jan. 1819. He
was educated at Rugby, under Dr. Arnold, and at Oxford,
where he showed himself of the Broad School. Leslie Stephen
says, " He never became bitter against the Church of his childhood, but he came to regard its dogmas as imperfect and
untenable." In '48 he visited Paris, and the same year
produced his *Bothie of Toper-na-Fuosich :* a Long-Vacation
Pastoral. Between '49 and '52 he was professor of English
literature in London University. In '52 he visited the United
States, where he gained the friendship of Emerson and
Longfellow, and revised the Dryden translation of *Plutarch's
Lives.* Died at Florence, 13 Nov. 1861. His *Remains* are published
in two volumes, and include an essay on Religious Tradition and

some notable poems. He is the Thyrsis of Matthew Arnold's exquisite Monody.

Cnuzius (Matthias). See Knutzen.

Coke (Henry), author of *Creeds of the Day*, or collated opinions of reputable thinkers, in 2 vols, London, 1883.

Cole (Peter), a tanner of Ipswich, was burnt for blasphemy in the castle ditch, Norwich, 1587. A Dr. Beamond preached to him before the mayor, sheriffs, and aldermen, " but he would not recant." See Hamont.

Colenso (John William), b. 24 Jan. 1814. Was educated at t. John's, Cambridge, and became a master at Harrow. After acquiring fame by his valuable *Treatise on Algebra*, '49, he became first Bishop of Natal, '54. Besides other works, he published *The Pentateuch and Book of Joshua Critically Examined*, 1862–79, which made a great stir, and was condemned by both Houses of Convocation and its author declared deposed. The Privy Council, March '65, declared this deposition " null and void in law." Colenso pleaded the cause of the natives at the time of the Zulu War. He died 20 June, 1883.

Colins (Jean Guillaume César Alexandre Hippolyte) Baron de, Belgian Socialist and founder of " Collectivism," b. Brussels, 24 Dec. 1783. Author of nineteen volumes on Social Science. He denied alike Monotheism and Pantheism, but taught the natural immortality of the soul. Died at Paris, 12 Nov. 1859. A number of disciples propagate his opinions in the *Philosophie de l'Avenir*.

Collins (Anthony), English Deist, b. Heston, Middlesex, 21 June, 1676. He studied at Cambridge and afterwards at the Temple, and became Justice of the Peace and Treasurer of the County of Essex. He was an intimate friend of Locke, who highly esteemed him and made him his executor. He wrote an *Essay on Reason*, 1707 ; *Priestcraft in Perfection*, 1710 ; a *Vindication of the Divine Attributes*, and a *Discourse on Freethinking*, 1713. This last occasioned a great outcry, as it argued that all belief must be based on free inquiry, and that the use of reason would involve the abandonment of supernatural revelation. In 1719 he published *An Inquiry Concerning Human Liberty*, a brief, pithy defence of necessitarianism, and in 1729 *A Discourse on Liberty* *and Necessity.* In 1724 appeared his *Discourse on the Grounds and Reasons of the Christian Religion,* and this was followed by *The Scheme of Literal Prophecy Considered,* 1726. He was a skilful disputant, and wrote with great ability. He is also credited with *A Discourse Concerning Ridicule and Irony in Writing.* Died at London, 13 Dec. 1729. Collins, says Mr. Leslie Stephen, "appears to have been an amiable and upright man, and to have made all readers welcome to the use of a free library." Professor Fraser calls him "a remarkable man," praises his "love of truth and moral courage," and allows that in answering Dr. Samuel Clarke on the question of liberty and necessity he "states the arguments against human freedom with a logical force unsurpassed by any necessitarian." A similar testimony to Collins as a thinker and dialectician is borne by Professor Huxley.

Colman (Lucy N.), American reformer, b. 26 July, 1817, has spent most of her life advocating the abolition of slavery, women's rights, and Freethought. She has lectured widely, written Reminisences in the *Life of a Reformer of Fifty Years,* and contributed to the *Truthseeker* and *Boston Investigator.*

Colotes, of Lampsacus, a hearer and disciple of Epicurus, with whom he was a favorite. He wrote a work in favor of his master's teachings. He held it was unworthy of a philosopher to use fables.

Combe (Abram), one of a noted Scotch family of seventeen, b. Edinburgh, 15 Jan. 1785. He traded as a tanner, but, becoming acquainted with Robert Owen, founded a community at Orbiston upon the principle of Owen's New Lanark, devoting nearly the whole of his large fortune to the scheme. But his health gave way and he died 11 Aug. 1827. He wrote *Metaphysical Sketches of the Old and New Systems* and other works advocating Owenism.

Combe (Andrew), physician, brother of the above, b. Edinburgh, 27 Oct. 1797; studied there and in Paris; aided his brother George in founding the Phrenological Society; wrote popular works on the *Principles of Physiology* and the *Management of Infancy.* Died near Edinburgh, 9 Aug. 1847.

Combe (George), phrenologist and educationalist, b. Edinburgh, 21 Oct. 1788. He was educated for the law. Became acquainted with Spurzheim, and published *Essays on Phrenology,*

1819, and founded the *Phrenological Journal*. In '28 he published the *Constitution of Man*, which excited great controversy especially for removing the chimeras of special providence and efficacy of prayer. In '33 he married a daughter of Mrs. Siddons. He visited the United States and lectured on Moral Philosophy and Secular Education. His last work was *The Relations between Science and Religion*, '57, in which he continued to uphold Secular Theism. He also published many lectures and essays. Among his friends were Miss Evans (George Eliot), who spent a fortnight with him in '52. He did more than any man of his time, save Robert Owen, for the cause of Secular education. Died at Moor Park, Surrey, 14 Aug. 1858.

Combes (Paul), French writer, b. Paris, 13 June, 1856. Has written on *Darwinism*, '83, and other works popularising science.

Commazzi (Gian-Battista), Count author of *Politica e religione trovate insieme nella persona di Giesù Cristo*, Nicopoli [Vienna] 4 vols., 1706–7, in which he makes Jesus to be a political impostor. It was rigorously confiscated at Rome and Vienna.

Comparetti (Domenico), Italian philologist, b. Rome in 1835. Signor Comparetti is Professor at the Institute of Superior Studies, Rome, and has written many works on the classic writers, in which he evinces his Pagan partialities.

Comte (Isidore Auguste Marie François Xavier), French philosopher, mathematician and reformer, b. at Montpelier, 12 Jan. 1798. Educated at Paris in the Polytechnic School, where he distinguished himself by his mathematical talent. In 1817 he made the acquaintance of St. Simon, agreeing with him as to the necessity of a Social renovation based upon a mental revolution. On the death of St. Simon ('25) Comte devoted himself to the elaboration of an original system of scientific thought, which, in the opinion of some able judges, entitles him to be called the Bacon of the nineteenth century. Mill speaks of him as the superior of Descartes and Leibniz. In '25 he married, but the union proved unhappy. In the following year he lectured, but broke down under an attack of brain fever, which occasioned his detention in an asylum. He speedily recovered, and in '28 resumed his lectures, which were attended by men like Humboldt, Ducrotay, Broussais, Carnot, etc. In '30 he put forward the first volumes of his

Course of Positive Philosophy, which in '42 was completed by the publication of the sixth volume. A condensed English version of this work was made by Harriet Martineau, '53. In '45 Comte formed a passionate Platonic attachement to Mme. Clotilde de Vaux, who died in the following year, having profoundely influenced Comte's life. In consequence of his opinions, he lost his professorship, and was supported by his disciples—Mill, Molesworth and Grote, in England, assisting. Among other works, Comte published *A General View of Positivism,* '48, translated by Dr. Bridges, '65; *A System of Positive Polity,* '51, translated by Drs. Bridges, Beesley, F. Harrison, etc., '75–79; and *A Positive Catechism,* '54, translated by Dr. Congreve, '58. He also wrote on Positive Logic, which he intended to follow with Positive Morality and Positive Industrialism. Comte was a profound and suggestive thinker. He resolutely sets aside all theology and metaphysics, co-ordinates the sciences and substitutes the service of man for the worship of God. Mr. J. Cotter Morison says " He belonged to that small class of rare minds, whose errors are often more valuable and stimulating than other men's truths." He died of cancer in the stomach at Paris, 5 Sept. 1857.

Condillac (Etienne BONNOT DE), French philosopher, b. Grenoble, about 1715. His life was very retired, but his works show much acuteness. They are in 23 vols., the principal being *A Treatise on the Sensations,* 1764; *A Treatise on Animals,* and *An Essay on the Origin of Human Knowledge.* In the first-named he shows that all mental life is gradually built up out of simple sensations. Died 3 Aug. 1780.

Condorcet (Marie Jean Antoine Nicolas CARITAT, Marquis de), French philosopher and politician, b. Ribemont, Picardy, 17 Sept. 1743. Dedicated to the Virgin by a pious mother, he was kept in girl's clothes until the age of 11. Sent to a Jesuit's school, he soon gave up religion. At sixteen he maintained a mathematical thesis in the presence of Alembert. In the next year he dedicated to Turgot a *Profession of Faith.* After some mathematical works, he was made member of the Academy, of which he was appointed perpetual secretary, 1773. In 1776 he published his atheistic *Letters of a Theologian.* He also wrote biographies of Turgot and Voltaire, and in favor of

American independence and against negro slavery. In 1791 he represented Paris in the National Assembly, of which he became Secretary. It was on his motion that, in the following year, all orders of nobility were abolished. Voting against the death of the king and siding with the Gironde drew on him the vengeance of the extreme party. He took shelter with Madame Vernet, but fearing to bring into trouble her and his wife, at whose instigation he wrote his fine *Sketch of the Progress of the Human Mind* while in hiding, he left, but, being arrested, died of exhaustion or by poison self-administered, at Bourg la Reine, 27 March, 1794.

Condorcet (Sophie de Grouchy CARITAT, Marquise de), wife of above, and sister of General Grouchy and of Mme. Cabanis, b. 1765. She married Condorcet 1786, and was considered one of the most beautiful women of her time. She shared her husband's sentiments and opinions and, while he was proscribed, supported herself by portrait painting. She was arrested, and only came out of prison after the fall of Robespierre. She translated Adam Smith's *Theory of the Moral Sentiments*, which she accompanied with eight letters on Sympathy, addressed to Cabanis. She died 8 Sept. 1822. Her only daughter married Gen. Arthur O'Connor.

Confucius (Kung Kew) or Kung-foo-tsze, the philosopher Kung, a Chinese sage, b. in the State of Loo, now part of Shantung, about B.C. 551. He was distinguished by filial piety and learning. In his nineteenth year he married, and three years after began as a teacher, rejecting none who came to him. He travelled through many states. When past middle age he was appointed chief minister of Loo, but finding the Duke desired the renown of his name without adopting his counsel, he retired, and devoted his old age to editing the sacred classics of China. He died about B.C. 478. His teaching, chiefly found in the *Lun-Yu*, or Confucian Analects, was of a practical moral character, and did not include any religious dogmas.

Congreve (Richard), English Positivist, born in 1819. Educated at Rugby under T. Arnold, and Oxford 1840, M.A. 1843; was fellow of Wadham College 1844-51. In '55 he published his edition of *Aristotle Politics*. He became a follower of Comte and influenced many to embrace Positivism. Translated Comte's *Catechism of Positive Philosophy*, 1858, and has written many brochures. Dr. Congreve is considered the head of the strict or English Comtists, and has long conducted a small "Church of Humanity."

Connor (Bernard), a physician, b. Co. Kerry, of Catholic family, 1666. He travelled widely, and was made court physician to John Sobieski, King of Poland. He wrote a work entitled *Evangelium Medici* (1697), in which he attempts to account for the Christian miracles on natural principles. For this he was accused of Atheism. He died in London 27 Oct. 1698.

Constant de Rebecque (Henri Benjamin), Swiss writer, b. Lausanne, 25 Oct. 1767, and educated at Oxford, Erlangen and Edinburgh. In 1795 he entered Paris as a *protégé* of Mme. de Stael, and in 1799 became a member of the Tribunal. He opposed Buonaparte and wrote on *Roman Polytheism* and an important work on *Religion Considered in its Source, its Forms and its Developments* (6 vols.; 1824-32). Died 8 Dec. 1830. Constant professed Protestantism, but was at heart a sceptic, and has been called a second Voltaire. A son was executor to Auguste Comte.

Conta (Basil), Roumanian philosopher, b. Neamtza 27 Nov. 1845. Studied in Italy and Belgium, and became professor in the University of Jassy, Moldavia. In '77 he published a Brussels, in French, a theory of fatalism, which created some stir by its boldness of thought.

Conway (Moncure Daniel), author, b. in Fredericksburg, Stafford co. Virginia, 17 March, 1832. He entered the Methodist ministry '50, but changing his convictions through the influence of Emerson and Hicksite Quakers, entered the divinity school at Cambridge, where he graduated in '54 and became pastor of a Unitarian church until dismissed for his anti-slavery discourses. In '57 he preached in Cincinatti and there published *The Natural History of the Devil*, and other pamphlets. In '63 Mr. Conway came to England and was minister of South Place from the close of '63 until his return to the States in '84. Mr. Conway is a frequent contributor to the press. He has also published *The Earthward Pilgrimage*, 1870, a theory reversing Bunyan's *Pilgrim's Progress*; collected a *Sacred Anthology* from the various sacred books of the world 1873. which he used in his pulpit; has written on *Human Sacrifices*, 1876, and *Idols and Ideals*, 1877. His principal work is *Demonology and Devil Lore*, 1878, containing much information on mythology. He also issued his sermons under the title of *Lessons for the Day*, two vols., 1883, and has published a monograph on the *Wandering Jew*, a biography of Emerson, and is at present engaged on a life of Thomas Paine.

Cook (Kenningale Robert), LL.D., b. in Lancashire 26 Sept. 1845, son of the vicar of Stallbridge. When a boy he used to puzzle his mother by such questions as, "If God was omnipotent could he make what had happened not have happened." He was intended for the Church, but declined to subscribe the articles. Graduated at Dublin in '66, and took LL.D. in '75. In '77 he became editor of the Dublin *University Magazine*, in which appeared some studies of the lineage of Christian doctrine and traditions afterwards published under the title of *The Fathers of Jesus*. Dr. Cook wrote several volumes of choice poems. Died July, 1886.

Cooper (Anthony Ashley), see Shaftesbury.

Cooper (Henry), barrister, b. Norwich about 1784. He was a schoolfellow of Wm. Taylor of Norwich. He served as midshipman at the battle of the Nile, but disliking the service became a barrister, and acquired some fame by his spirited defence of Mary Ann Carlile, 21 July, 1821, for which the report of the trial was dedicated to him by R. Carlile. He was a friend of Lord Erskine, whose biography he commenced. Died 19 Sept. 1824.

Cooper (John Gilbert), poet, b. Thurgaton Priory, Notts, 1723. Educated at Westminster School and Trinity College, Cambridge. An enthusiastic disciple of Lord Shaftesbury. Under the name of "Philaretes" he contributed to Dodsley's Museum. In 1749 he published a *Life of Socrates*, for which he was coarsely attacked by Warburton. He wrote some poems under the signature of Aristippus. Died Mayfair, London, 14 April, 1769.

Cooper (Peter), a benevolent manufacturer, b. N. York, 12 Feb. 1791. He devoted over half a million dollars to the

Cooper Institute, for the secular instruction and elevation of the working classes. Died 4 April, 1883.

Cooper (Robert), Secularist writer and lecturer, b. 29 Dec. 1819, at Barton-on-Irwell, near Manchester. He had the advantage of being brought up in a Freethought family. At fourteen he became teacher in the Co-operative Schools, Salford, lectured at fifteen, and by seventeen became an acknowledged advocate of Owenism, holding a public discussion with the Rev. J. Bromley. Some of his lectures were published—one on *Original Sin* sold twelve thousand copies—when he was scarcely eighteen. The *Holy Scriptures Analysed* (1832) was denounced by the Bishop of Exeter in the House of Lords. Cooper was dismissed from a situation he had held ten years, and in 1841 became a Socialist missionary in the North of England and Scotland. At Edinburgh (1845) he wrote *Free Agency* and *Orthodoxy*, and compiled the *Infidel's Text Book*. About '50 he came to London, lecturing with success at John Street Institution. In '54 he started the *London Investigator*, which he edited for three years. In it appears his lectures on "Science v. Theology," "Admissions of Distinguished Men," etc. Failing health obliged him to retire leaving the *Investigator* to "Anthony Collins" (W. H. Johnson), and afterwards to "Iconoclast" (C. Bradlaugh). At his last lecture he fainted on the platform. In 1858 he remodelled his *Infidel Text-Book* into a work on *The Bible and Its Evidences*. He devoted himself to political reform until his death, 3 May, 1868.

Cooper (Thomas), M.D., LL.D., natural philosopher, politician, jurist and author, b. London, 22 Oct. 1759. Educated at Oxford, he afterwards studied law and medicine; was admitted to the bar and lived at Manchester, where he wrote a number of tracts on "Materialism," "Whether Deity be a Free Agent," etc., 1789. Deputed with James Watt, the inventor, by the Constitutional clubs to congratulate the Democrats of France (April, 1792), he was attacked by Burke and replied in a vigorous pamphlet. In '94 he published *Information Concerning America*, and in the next year followed his friend Priestly to Philadelphia, established himself as a lawyer and was made judge. He also conducted the *Emporium of Arts and Sciences* in that city. He was Professor of Medicine at Carlisle College

'12, and afterwards held the chairs both of Chemistry and Political Economy in South Carolina College, of which he became President, 1820-34. This position he was forced to resign on account of his religious views. He translated from Justinian and Broussais, and digested the Statutes of South Carolina. In philosophy a Materialist, in religion a Freethinker, in politics a Democrat, he urged his views in many pamphlets One on *The Right of Free Discussion*, and a little book on *Geology and the Pentateuch*, in reply to Prof. Silliman, were republished in London by James Watson. Died at Columbia, 11 May, 1810.*

Coornhert (Dirk Volkertszoon), Dutch humanist, poet and writer, b. Amsterdam, 1522. He travelled in his youth through Spain and Portugal. He set up as an engraver at Haarlem, and became thereafter notary and secretary of the city of Haarlem. He had a profound horror of intolerance, and defended liberty against Beza and Calvin. The clergy vituperated him as a Judas and as instigated by Satan, etc. Bayle, who writes of him as Theodore Koornhert, says he communed neither with Protestants nor Catholics. The magistrates of Delft drove him out of their city. He translated Cicero's *De Officiis*, and other works. Died at Gouda, 20 Oct. 1590.

Cordonnier de Saint Hyacinthe. See Saint-Hyacinthe (Themiseuil de).

Corvin-Wiersbitski (Otto Julius Bernhard von), Prussian Pole of noble family, who traced their descent from the Roman Corvinii, b. Gumbinnen, 12 Oct. 1812. He served in the Prussian army, where he met his friend Friedrich von Sallet; retired into the Landwehr 1835, went to Leipsic and entered upon a literary career, wrote the History of the Dutch Revolution, 1811; the *History of Christian Fanaticism*, 1845, which was suppressed in Austria. He took part with the democrats in '48; was condemned to be shot 15 Sept. '49, but the sentence was commuted; spent six years' solitary confinement in prison; came to London, became correspondent to the *Times*; went through American Civil War, and afterwards Franco-Prussian

---

* So varied was the activity of T. Cooper during his long life that his works in the British Museum were catalogued as by six different persons of the same name. I pointed this out, and the six single gentlemen will be rolled into one.

91

War, as a special correspondent. He has written a History of the New Time, 1848–71. Died since 1886.

Cotta (Bernhard), German geologist, b. Little Zillbach, Thuringia, 24 Oct. 1808. He studied at the Academy of Mining, in Freiberg, where he was appointed professor in '42. His first production, *The Dendroliths*, '32, proved him a diligent investigator. It was followed by many geological treatises. Cotta did much to support the nebular hypothesis and the law of natural development without miraculous agency. He also wrote on phrenology. Died at Feirburg., 13 Sept 1879.

Cotta (C. Aurelius), Roman philosopher, orator and states-man, b. B.C. 124. In '75 he became Consul. On the expiration of his office he obtained Gaul as a province. Cicero had a high opinion of him and gives his sceptical arguments in the third book of his *De Natura Deorum*.

Courier (Paul Louis), French writer, b. Paris, 4 Jan. 1772. He entered the army and became an officer of artillery, serving with distinction in the Army of the Republic. He wrote many pamphlets, directed against the clerical restoration, which place him foremost among the literary men of the generation. His writings are now classics, but they brought him nothing but imprisonment, and he was apparently assassinated, 10 April, 1825. He had a presentiment that the bigots would kill him.

Coventry (Henry), a native of Cambridgeshire, b. about 1710, Fellow of Magdalene College, author of *Letters of Philemon to Hydaspus on False Religion* (1736). Died 29 Dec. 1752.

Coward (William), M.D., b. Winchester, 1656. Graduated at Wadham College, Oxford, 1677. Settled first at Northampton, afterwards at London. Published, besides some medical works, *Second Thoughts Concerning Human Soul*, which excited much indignation by denying natural immortality. The House of Commons (17 March, 1704) ordered his work to be burnt. He died in 1725.

Cox (the Right Rev. Sir George William), b. 1827, was educated at Rugby and Oxford, where he took B.C.L. in 1849. Entered the Church, but has devoted himself to history and mythology. His most pretentious work is *Mythology of the Aryan Nations*

(1870). He has also written an *Introduction to Comparative Mytho-logy* and several historical works. In 1886 he became Bishop of Bloemfontein. He is credited with the authorship of the *English Life of Jesus,* published under the name of Thomas Scott. At the Church Congress of 1888 he read an heretical paper on Biblical Eschatology. His last production is a *Life of Bishop Colenso,* 2 vols, 1888.

Coyteux (Fernand), French writer, b. Ruffec, 1800. Author of a materialistic system of philosophy, Brussels, 1853 Studies on physiology, Paris, 1875, etc.

Craig (Edward Thomas), social reformer, b. at Manchester 4 Aug. 1804. He was present at the Peterloo massacre '19; helped to form the Salford Social Institute and became a pioneer of co-operation. In '31 he became editor of the *Lancashire Co-operator.* In Nov. of the same year he undertook the management of a co-operative farm at Rahaline, co. Clare. Of this experiment he has written an history, '72. Mr. Craig has edited several journals and contributed largely to Radical and co-operative literature. He has published a memoir of Dr. Travis and at the age of 84 he wrote on *The Science of Prolonging Life.*

Cramer (Johan Nicolai), Swedish writer, b. Wisby, Gottland, 18 Feb. 1812. He studied at Upsala and became Doctor of Philosophy '36; ordained priest in '42; he resigned in '58. In religion he denies revelation and insists on the separation of Church and State. Among his works we mention *Separation from the Church,* a Freethinker's annotations on the reading of the Bible, Stockholm, 1859. *A Confession of Faith; Forward or Back?* (1862). He has also written on the Punishment of Death (1868), and other topics.

Cranbrook (Rev. James.) Born of strict Calvinistic parents about 1817. Mr. Cranbrook gradually emancipated himself from dogmas, became a teacher, and for sixteen years was minister of an Independent Church at Liscard, Cheshire. He also was professor at the Ladies' College, Liverpool, some of his lectures there being published '57. In Jan. '65, he went to Albany Church, Edinburgh, but his views being too broad for that congregation, he left in Feb. '67 but continued to give Sunday lectures until his death, 6 June, 1869. In '66 he published *Credibilia: an Inquiry into the grounds of Christian faith* and two years later *The Founders of Christianity,* discourses on the origin of Christianity. Other lectures on *Human Depravity, Positive Religion,* etc., were published by Thomas Scott.

Cranch (Christopher Pearse), American painter and poet, b. Alexandria, Virginia, 8 March, 1813, graduated at divinity school, Cambridge, Mass. '35, but left the ministry in '42. He shows his Freethought sentiments in *Satan,* a Libretto, Boston, '74, and other works.

Craven (M. B.), American, author of a critical work on the Bible entitled *Triumph of Criticism,* published at Philadelphia, 1869.

Cremonini (Cesare), Italian philosopher, b. Cento, Ferrara, 1550, was professor of philosophy at Padua from 1591 to 1631, when he died. A follower of Aristotle, he excited suspicion by his want of religion and his tea ching the mortality of the soul. He was frequently ordered by the Jesuits and the Inquisition to refute the errors he gave currency to, but he was protected by the Venetian State, and refused. Like most of the philosophers of his time, he distinguished between religious and philosophic truth. Bayle says. "Il a passé pour un esprit fort, qui ne croyait point l'immortalité de l'âme." Larousse says, "On peut dire qu'il n'etait pas chrétien." Ladvocat says his works "contain many things contrary to religion."

Cross (Mary Ann). See Eliot (George).

Crousse (Louis D.), French Pantheistic philosopher, author of *Principles, or First Philosophy,* 1839, and *Thoughts,* 1845.

Curtis (S. E.), English Free thinker, author of *Theology Displayed,* 1812. He has been credited with *The Protestant's Progress to Infidelity.* See Griffith (Rees). Died 1847.

Croly (David Goodman), American Positivist, b. New York 3 Nov. 1829. He graduated at New York University in '54, and was subsequently a reporter on the *New York Herald.* He became editor of the *New York World* until '72. From '71 to '73 he edited *The Modern Thinker,* an organ of the most advanced thought, and afterwards the *New York Graphic.* Mr. Croly has written a *Primer of Positivism,* '76, and has contributed many articles to periodicals. His wife, Jane Cunningham, who calls herself "Jennie June," b. 1831, also wrote in *The Modern Thinker.*

Cross (Many Ann), see Eliot (George).

Crozier (John Beattie), English writer of Scottish border parentage, b. Galt, Ontario, Canada, 23 April, 1849. In youth he won a scholarship to the grammar school of the town, and thence won another scholarship to the Toronto University, where he graduated '72, taking the University and Starr medals. He then came to London determined to study the great problems of religion and civilisation. He took his diploma from the London College of Physicians in '73. In '77 he wrote his first essay, "God or Force," which, being rejected by all the magazines, he published as a pamphlet. Other essays on the Constitution of the World, Carlyle, Emerson, and Spencer being also rejected, he published them in a book entitled *The Religion of the Future*, '80, which fell flat. He then started his work *Civilisation and Progress*, which appeared in '85, and was also unsuccessful until republished with a few notices in '87, when it received a chorus of applause for its clear and original thoughts. Mr. Crozier is now engaged on his Autobiography, fter which he proposes to deal with the Social question.

Cuffeler (Abraham Johann), a Dutch philosopher and doctor of law, who was one of the first partizans of Spinoza. He lived at Utrecht towards the end of the seventeenth century, and wrote a work on logic in three parts entitled *Specimen Artis Ratiocinandi*, etc., published ostensibly at Hamburg, but really at Amsterdam or Utrecht, 1684. It was without name but with the author's portrait.

Cuper (Frans), Dutch writer, b. Rotterdam. Cuper is suspected to have been one of those followers of Spinoza, who under pretence of refuting him, set forth and sustained his arguments by feeble opposition. His work entitled *Arcana Atheismi Revelato*, Rotterdam 1676, was denounced as written in bad faith. Cuper maintained that the existence of God could not be proved by the light of reason.

Cyrano de Bergerac (Savinien), French comic writer, b. Paris 6 March, 1619. After finishing his studies and serving in the army in his youth he devoted himself to literature. His tragedy "Agrippine" is full of what a bookseller called "belles

95

impiétés," and La Monnoye relates that at its performance the pit shouted "Oh, the wretch ! The Atheist! How he mocks at holy things !" Cyrano knew personally Campanella, Gassendi, Lamothe Le Vayer, Linière, Rohault, etc. His other works consist of a short fragment on *Physic*, a collection of *Letters*, and a *Comic History of the States and Empires of the Moon and the Sun*. Cyrano took the idea of this book from F. Godwin's *Man in the Moon*, 1583, and it in turn gave rise to Swift's *Gulliver's Travels* and Voltaire's *Micromegas*. Died Paris, 1655.

Czolbe (Heinrich), German Materialist, b. near Dantzic, 30 Dec. 1819, studied medicine at Berlin, writing an inaugural dissertation on the *Principles of Physiology*, '44. In '55 he published his *New Exposition of Sensationalism*, in which everything is resolved into matter and motion, and in '65 a work on *The Limits and Origin of Human Knowledge*. He was an intimate friend of Ueberweg. Died at Königsberg, 19 Feb. 1873. Lange says "his life was marked by a deep and genuine morality."

D'Ablaing. See Giessenburg.

Dale (Antonius van), Dutch writer, b. Haarlem, 8 Nov. 1638. His work on oracles was erudite but lumbersome, and to it Fontenelle gave the charm of style. It was translated into English by Mrs. Aphra Behn, under the title of *The History of Oracles and the Cheats of Pagan Priests*, 1699. Van Dale, in another work on *The Origin and Progress of Idolatry and Superstition*, applied the historical method to his subject, and showed that the belief in demons was as old and as extensive as the human race. He died at Haarlem, 28 Nov. 1708.

Damilaville (Etienne Noël), French writer, b. at Bordeaux, 1721. At first a soldier, then a clerk, he did some service for Voltaire, who became his friend. He also made the friendship Diderot, d'Alembert, Grimm, and d'Holbach. He contributed to the *Encyclopédie*, and in 1767 published an attack on the theologians, entitled *Theological Honesty*. The book entitled *Christianity Unveiled* [see Boulanger and Holbach] was attributed by Voltaire, who called it *Impiety Unveiled*, and by La Harpe and Lalande to Damilaville. Voltaire called him "one of our most learned writers." Larousse says "he was an ardent enemy of Christianity." He has also been credited with a share in the *System of Nature*. Died 15 Dec. 1768.

Dandolo (Vincenzo) *Count*, Italian chemist, b. Venice, 26 Oct. 1758, wrote *Principles of Physical Chemistry*, a work in French on *The New Men*, in which he shows his antagonism to religion, and many useful works on vine, timber, and silk culture. Died Varessa, 13 Dec. 1819.

Danton (Georges Jacques), French revolutionist, b. Arcis sur Aube, 28 Oct. 1759. An uncle wished him to enter into orders, but he preferred to study law. During the Revolution his eloquence made him conspicuous at the Club of Cordeliers, and in Feb. 1791, he became one of the administrators of Paris. One of the first to see that after the flight of Louis XVI. he could no longer be king, he demanded his suspension, and became one of the chief organisers of the Republic. In the alarm caused by the invasion he urged a bold and resolute policy. He was a member of the Convention and of the Committee of Public Safety. At the crisis of the struggle with Robespierre Danton declined to strike the first blow and disdained to fly. Arrested March, 1794, he said when interrogated by the judge, " My name is Danton, my dwelling will soon be in annihilation; but my name will live in the Pantheon of history." He maintained his lofty bearing on the scaffold, where he perished 5 April, 1794. For his known scepticism Danton was called *fils de Diderot*. Carlyle calls him "a very Man "

Dapper (Olfert), Dutch physician, who occupied himself with history and geography, on which he produced important works. He had no religion and was suspected of Atheism. He travelled through Syria, Babylonia, etc., in 1650. He translated Herodotus (1664) and the orations of the late Prof. Caspar v. Baerli (1663), and wrote a *History of the City of Amsterdam*, 1663. Died at Amsterdam 1690.

Darget (Etienne), b. Paris, 1712; went to Berlin in 1744 and became reader and private secretary to Frederick the Great (1745–52), who corresponded with him afterwards. Died 1778.

Darwin (Charles Robert), English naturalist, b. Shrewsbury, 12 Feb. 1809. Educated at Shrewsbury, Edinburgh University, and Cambridge. He early evinced a taste for collecting and observing natural objects. He was intended for a clergyman, but, incited by Humboldt's *Personal Narrative*, resolved to travel. He accompanied Captain Fitzroy in the "Beagle" on a voyage of exploration, '31–36, which he narrated in his *Voyage of a Naturalist Round the World,* which obtained great popularity. In '39 he married, and in '42 left London and settled at Down, Kent. His studies, combined with the reading of Lamarck and Malthus, led to his great work on *The Origin of Species by means of Natural Selection,* '59, which made a great outcry and marked an epoch. Darwin took no part in the controversy raised by the theologians, but followed his work with *The Fertilisation of Orchids,* '62 ; *Cross and Self Fertilisation of Plants,* '67 ; *Variations of Plants and Animals under Domestication,* '65 ; and in '71 *The Descent of Man and Selection in relation to Sex,* which caused yet greater consternation in orthodox circles. The following year he issued *The Expression of the Emotions of Men and Animals.* He also published works on the *Movements of Plants, Insectivorous Plants,* the *Forms of Flowers,* and *Earthworms.* He died 19 April, 1882, and was buried in Westminster Abbey, despite his expressed unbelief in revelation. To a German student he wrote, in '79, " Science has nothing to do with Christ, except in so far as the habit of scientific research makes a man cautious in admitting evidence. For myself I do not believe that there ever has been any revelation." In his *Life and Letters* he relates that between 1836 and 1842 he had come to see " that the Old Testament was no more to be trusted than the sacred books of the Hindoos." He rejected design and said " I for one must be content to remain an Agnostic."

Darwin (Erasmus), Dr., poet, physiologist and philosopher, grandfather of the above, was born at Elston, near Newark, 12 Dec. 1731. Educated at Chesterfield and Cambridge he became a physician, first at Lichfield and afterwards at Derby. He was acquainted with Rousseau, Watt and Wedgwood. His principal poem, *The Botanic Garden* was published in 1791, and *The Temple of Nature* in 1803. His principal work is *Zoomania,* or the laws of organic life (1794), for which he was accused of Atheism. He was actually a Deist. He also wrote on female education and some papers in the *Philosophical Transactions.* Died at Derby, 18 April, 1802.

Daubermesnil (François Antoine), French conventionalist. Elected deputy of Tarn in 1792. Afterwards became a member of the Council of Five Hundred. He was one of the founders of Theophilanthropy. Died at Perpignan 1802.

Daudet (Alphonse), French novelist, b. at Nìmes, 13 May 1840, author of many popular romances, of which we mention *L'Evangeliste*, '82, which has been translated into English under the title *Port Salvation*.

Daunou (Pierre Claude François), French politician and historian, b. Boulogne, 18 Aug. 1761. His father entered him in the congregation of the Fathers of the Oratory, which he left at the Revolution. The department of Calais elected him with Carnot and Thomas Paine to the Convention. After the Revolution he became librarian at the Pantheon. He was a friend of Garat, Cabanis, Chenier, Destutt Tracy, Ginguené and Benj. Constant. Wrote *Historical Essay on the Temporal Power of the Popes*, 1810. Died at Paris, 20 June, 1840, noted for his benevolence.

Davenport (Allen), social reformer, b. 1773. He contributed to Carlile's *Republican*; wrote an account of the Life, Writings and Principles of Thomas Spence, the reformer (1826); and published a volume of verse, entitled *The Muses' Wreath* (1827). Died at Highbury, London, 1846.

Davenport (John), Deist, b. London, 8 June, 1789, became a teacher. He wrote *An Apology for Mohammed and the Koran*, 1869; *Curiositates Eroticæ Physiologæ*, or Tabooed Subjects Freely Treated, and several educational works. Died in poverty 11 May, 1877.

David of Dinant, in Belgium, Pantheistic philosopher of the twelfth century. He is said to have visited the Papal Court of Innocent III. He shared in the heresies of Amalric of Châtres, and his work *Quaterini* was condemned and burnt (1209). He only escaped the stake by rapid flight. According to Albert the Great he was the author of a philosophical work *De Tomis*, "Of Subdivisions," in which he taught that all things were one. His system was similar to that of Spinoza.

David (Jacques Louis), French painter, born at Paris, 31 Aug. 1748, was made painter to the king, but joined the Jacobin Club, became a member of the Convention, voted for the king's death and for the civic festivals, for which he made designs.

On the restoration he was banished. Died at Brussels, 29 Dec. 1825. David was an honest enthusiast and a thorough Freethinker.

Davidis or **David** (Ferencz), a Transylvanian divine, b. about 1510. He was successively a Roman Catholic, a Lutheran and an Antitrinitarian. He went further than F. Socinus and declared there was " as much foundation for praying to the Virgin Mary and other dead saints as to Jesus Christ." He was in consequence accused of Judaising and thrown into prison at Deva, where he died 6 June, 1579.

Davies (John C.), of Stockport, an English Jacobin, who in 1797 published a list of contradictions of the Bible under the title of *The Scripturian's Creed,* for which he was prosecuted and imprisoned. The work was republished by Carlile, 1822, and also at Manchester, 1839.

Davidson (Thomas), bookseller and publisher, was prosecuted by the Vice Society in Oct. 1820, for selling the *Republican* and a publication of his own, called the *Deist's Magazine.* For observations made in his defence he was summoned and fined £100, and he was sentenced to two years' imprisonment in Oakham Gaol. He died 16 Dec. 1826.

Debierre (Charles), French writer, author of *Man Before History*, 1888.

De Dominicis. See Dominicis.

De Felice (Francesco), Italian writer, b. Catania, Sicily, 1821, took part in the revolution of '48, and when Garibaldi landed in Sicily was appointed president of the provisional council of war. Has written on the reformation of elementary schools.

De Greef (Guillaume Joseph), advocate at Brussels Court of Appeal, b. at Brussels, 9 Oct. 1842. Author of an important *Introduction to Sociology*, 1886. Wrote in *La Liberté*, 1867–73, and now writes in *La Société Nouvelle.*

De Gubernatis (Angelo), Italian Orientalist and writer, b. Turin, 7 April, 1840; studied at Turin University and became doctor of philosophy. He studied Sanskrit under Bopp and Weber at Berlin. Sig. de Gubernatis has adorned Italian literature with many important works, of which we mention his volumes on *Zoological Mythology*, which has been translated into English, '72 : and on the *Mythology of Plants*. He has compiled and in large part written a *Universal History of Literature*, 18 vols. '82–85 ; edited *La Revista Europea* and the *Revue Internationale*, and contributed to many publications. He is a brilliant writer and a versatile scholar.

De Harven (Emile Jean Alexandre), b. Antwerp, 23 Sept. 1837, the anonymous author of a work on *The Soul: its Origin and Destiny* (Antwerp, 1879).

Dekker (Eduard Douwes), the greatest Dutch writer and Freethinker of this century, b. Amsterdam, 2 March, 1820. In '39 he accompanied his father, a ship's captain, to the Malayan Archipelago. He became officer under the Dutch government in Sumatra, Amboina, and Assistant-Resident at Lebac, Java. He desired to free the Javanese from the oppression of their princes, but the government would not help him and he resigned and returned to Holland, '56. The next four years he spent, in poverty, vainly seeking justice for the Javanese. In '60 he published under the pen name of " Multatuli " *Max Havelaar*, a masterly indictment of the Dutch rule in India, which has been translated into German, French and English. Then follow his choice *Minnebrieven* (Love Letters), '61 ; *Vorsten-school* (A School for Princes), and *Millivenen Studiën* (Studies on Millions). His *Ideën*, 7 vols. '62–79, are full of the boldest heresy. In most of his works religion is attacked, but in the *Ideas* faith is criticised with much more pungency and satire. He wrote " Faith is the voluntary prison-cell of reason." He was an honorary member of the Freethought Society, *De Dageraad*, and contributed to its organ. During the latter years of his life he lived at Wiesbaden, where he died 19 Feb. 1887. His corpse was burned in the crematory at Gotha.

De Lalande (see Lalande).

Delambre (Jean Baptiste Joseph), French astronomer, b. Amiens, 19 Sept. 1749, studied under Lalande and became, like his master, an Atheist. His Tables of the Orbit of Uranus were crowned by the Academy, 1790. In 1807 he succeeded Lalande as Professor of Astronomy at the Collége de France. He is the author of a *History of Astronomy* in five volumes, and of a number of astronomical tables and other scientific works He was appointed perpetual secretary of the Academy of

Sciences. Died 19 Aug. 1822, and was buried at Père la Chaise, Cuvier pronouncing a discourse over his grave.

De la Ramee. See Ouida.

Delbœuf (Joseph Remi Léopold), Belgian writer, b. Liège, 30 Sept. 1831 ; is Professor at the University of Liège, and has written *Psychology as a Natural Science, its Present and its Future; Application of the Experimental Method to the Phenomena of the Soul,* '73, and other works. In his *Philosophical Prolegomena to Geometry* he suggests that even mathematical axioms may have an empirical origin.

Delbos (Léon), linguist, b. 20 Sept. 1849 of Spanish father and Scotch mother. Educated in Paris, Lycée Charlemagne. Is an M.A. of Paris and *officier d'Académie.* Speaks many languages, and is a good Arabic and Sanskrit scholar. Has travelled widely and served in the Franco-German War. Besides many educational works, M. Delbos has written *L'Athée,* the Atheist, a Freethought romance '79, and in English *The Faith in Jesus not a New Faith,* '85. He has contributed to the *Agnostic Annual,* and is a decided Agnostic.

Delepierre (Joseph Octave), Belgian bibliophile, b. Bruges, 12 March, 1802. Was for thirty-five years secretary of Legation to England. His daughter married N. Truebner, who published his work *L'Enfer,* 1876, and many other bibliographical studies. Died London, 18 Aug. 1879.

Delescluze (Louis Charles), French journalist and revolutionary, b. Dreux, 2 Oct. 1809, was arrested in '34 for sedition. Implicated in a plot in '35, he took refuge in Belgium. In '48 he issued at Paris *La Revolution Démocratique et Sociale,* but was soon again in prison. He was banished, came to England with Ledru Rollin, but returning to France in '53 was arrested In '68 he published the *Réveil,* for which he was again fined and sentenced to prison for ten years. In '59 he was amnestied. and imprisoned. He became head of the Commune Committee of Public Safety, and died at the barricade, 25 May, 1871.

Deleyre (Alexandre), French writer, b. Porbats, near Bordeaux, 6 Jan. 1726. Early in life he entered the order of Jesuits, but changed his faith and became the friend of Rousseau and Diderot. He contributed to the *Encyclopédie,* notably the article

102

"Fanatisme," and published an analysis of Bacon and works on the genius of Montesquieu and Saint Evremond, and a History of Voyages. He embraced the Revolution with ardor, was made deputy to the Convention, and in 1795 was made member of the Institute. Died at Paris, 27 March, 1797.

Delisle de Sales. See Isoard Delisle (J. B. C.)

Dell (John Henry), artist and poet, b. 11 Aug. 1832. Contributed to *Progress*, wrote *Nature Pictures*, '71, and *The Dawning Grey*, '85, a volume of vigorous verse, imbued with the spirit of democracy and freethought. Died 31 Jan. 1888.

Deluc (Adolphe), Professor of Chemistry at Brussels, b. Paris, 1 Sept. 1811. Collaborated on *La Libre Recherche*.

De Maillet. See Maillet (Benoît de).

Democritus, a wealthy Atheistic philosopher, b. Abdera, Thrace, B.C. 460. He travelled to Egypt and over a great part of Asia, and is also said to have visited India. He is supposed to have been acquainted with Leucippus, and sixty works were ascribed to him. Died B.C. 357. He taught that all existence consisted of atoms, and made the discovery of causes the object of scientific inquiry. He is said to have laughed at life in general, which Montaigne says is better than to imitate Heraclitus and weep, since mankind are not so unhappy as vain. Democritus was the forerunner of Epicurus, who improved his system.

Demonax, a cynical philosopher who lived in the second century of the Christian era and rejected all religion. An account of him was written by Lucian.

Demora (Gianbattista), director of the *Libero Pensatore* of Milan, and author of some dramatic works.

Denis (Hector), Belgian advocate and professor of political economy and philosophy at Brussels University, b. Braine-le-Comte, 29 April, 1842. Has written largely on social questions and contributed to *La Liberté, la Philosophie Positive*, etc. Is one of the Council of the International Federation of Freethinkers.

Denslow (Van Buren), American writer, author of essays on *Modern Thinkers*, 1880, to which Colonel Ingersoll wrote an introduction. He contributed a paper on the value of irreli-

gion to the *Religio Philosophic* journal of America, Jan. '78, and
has written in the *Truthseeker* and other journals.

Denton (William, F.), poet, geologist, and lecturer, b. Darlington, Durham, 8 Jan. 1823.   After attaining manhood he
emigrated to the United States, '48, and in '56 published *Poems
for Reformers.*   He was a prolific writer, and constant lecturer
on temperance, psychology, geology, and Freethought.   In '72
he published *Radical Discourses on Religious Subjects* (Boston, '72),
and *Radical Rhymes*, '79.   He travelled to Australasia, and died
of a fever while conducting scientific explorations in New
Guinea 26 Aug. 1883.

De Paepe (César) Dr., Belgian Socialist, b. Ostend, 12 July,
1842.   He was sent to the college of St. Michel, Brussels.   He
obtained the Diploma of Candidate of Philosophy, but on the
death of his father became a printer with Désiré Brismée
(founder of Les Solidaires, a Rationalist society).   Proudhon
confided to him the correction of his works.   He became a
physician and is popular with the workmen's societies.   He
was one of the foremost members of the International and
attended all its congresses, as well as those of the International
Federation of Freethinkers.   He has written much on public
hygiene, political economy, and psychology, collaborating in a
great number of the most advanced journals.   Dr. De Paepe is a
short, fair, energetic man, capable both as a speaker and writer

Depasse (Hector), French writer, b. at Armentières in 1843,
is editor of *La République Francaise*, and member of the Paris
Municipal Council.   He has written a striking work on *Clericalism*, in which he urges the separation of Church and State,
1877 ; and is author of many little books on *Contemporary
Celebrities*, among them are Gambetta, Bert, Ranc, etc.

De Ponnat.   See Ponnat (— de), *Baron*.

De Pontan.   See Ponnat.

De Potter (Agathon Louis), Belgian economist, b. Brussels,
11 Nov. 1827.   Has written many works on Social Science, and
has collaborated to *La Ragione* (*Reason*), '56, and *La Philosophie
de l'Avenir.*

De Potter (Louis Antoine Joseph), Belgian politician and
writer, father of the above, b. of noble family, Bruges, 26 April,
1786.   In 1811 he went to Italy and lived ten years at Rome.

In '21 he wrote the *Spirit of the Church*, in 6 vols, which are put on the *Roman Index*. A strong upholder of secular education in Belgium, he was arrested more than once for his radicalism, being imprisoned for eighteen months in '28. In Sept. '30 he became a member of the provisional government. He was afterwards exiled and lived in Paris, where he wrote a philosophical and anti-clerical *History of Christianity*, in 8 vols., 1830-37. He also wrote a *Rational Catechism*, 1854, and a *Rational Dictionary*, 1859, and numerous brochures. Died Bruges, 22 July, 1859.

Deraismes (Maria), French writer and lecturer, b. Paris, 1836. She first made her name as a writer of comedies. She wrote an appeal on behalf of her sex, *Aux Femmes Riches*, 65. The Masonic Lodge of Le Pecq, near Paris, invited her to become a member, and she was duly installed under the Grand Orient of France. The first female Freemason, was president of the Paris Anti-clerical Congress of 1881, and has written much in her journal, *Le Républicain de Seine et Oise*.

De Roberty (Eugene). See Roberty.

Desbarreaux (Jacques Vallée), *Seigneur*, French poet and sceptic, b. Paris, 1602, great-nephew of Geoffrey Vallée, who was burnt in 1574. Many stories are related of his impiety, *e.g.* the well-known one of his having a feasts of eggs and bacon. It thundered, and Des Barreaux, throwing the plate out of window, exclaimed, "What an amount of noise over an omelette." It was said he recanted and wrote a poem beginning, "Great God, how just are thy chastisements." Voltaire, however, assigns this poem to the Abbé Levau. Died at Chalons, 9 May, 1673.

Descartes (René), French philosopher, b. at La Haye, 31 March, 1596. After leaving college he entered the army in '16, and fought in the battle of Prague. He travelled in France and Italy, and in '29 settled in Holland. In '37 he produced his famous *Discourses upon the Method of Reasoning Well*, etc., and in '41 his *Meditations upon First Philosophy*. This work gave such offence to the clergy that he was forced to fly his country "parce qu'il y fait trop chaud pour lui." He burnt his *Traite du Monde* (Treatise on the World) lest he should incur the fate of Gallilei. Though a Theist, like Bacon, he puts aside final causes.   He was offered an asylum by Christina, Queen of Sweden, and died at Stockholm 11 Feb. 1650.

Deschamps (Léger-Marie), known also as Dom Deschamps, a French philosopher, b. Rennes, Poitiers, 10 Jan. 1716.   He entered the Order of Benedictines, but lost his faith by reading an abridgment of the Old Testament.   He became correspondent of Voltaire, Rousseau, d'Alembert, Helvetius, and other philosophers.   "Ce prêtre athée," as Ad. Franck calls him, was the author of a treatise entitled *La Vérité, ou le Vrai Système*, in which he appears to have anticipated all the leading ideas of Hegel.   God, he says, as separated from existing things, is pure nothingness.   An analysis of his remarkable work, which remained in manuscript for three-quarters of a century, has been published by Professor Beaussire (Paris, 1855).   Died at Montreuil-Bellay, 19 April 1774.

Deslandes (André François BOUREAU), b. Pondichery, 1690. Became member of the Berlin Academy and wrote numerous works, mostly under the veil of anonymity, the principal being *A Critical History of Philosophy*, 3 vols (1737).   His *Pygmalion*, a philosophical romance, was condemned by the parliament of Dijon, 1742.   His *Reflexions sur les grands hommes qui sont mort en Plaisantant* (Amsterdam, 1732) was translated into English and published in 1745 under the title, *Dying Merrily*.   Another work directed against religion was *On the certainty of Human Knowledge*, a philosophical examination of the different prerogatives of reason and faith (London, 1741).   Died Paris, 11 April, 1757.

Des Maizeaux (Pierre), miscellaneous writer, b. Auvergne, 1673.   He studied at Berne and Geneva, and became known to Bayle who introduced him to Lord Shaftesbury, with whom he came to London, 1699.   He edited the works of Bayle, Saint Evremond and Toland, whose lives he wrote, as well as those of Hales and Chillingworth.   Anthony Collins was his friend, and at his death left him his manuscripts.   These he transferred to Collins's widow and they were burnt.   He repented and returned the money, 6 Jan. 1730, as the wages of iniquity.   He became Secretary of the Royal Society of London, where he died, 11 July, 1745.

Desmoulins (Lucie Simplice Camille Benôit), French revolutionary writer, b. Guise, 2 March, 1760.   He was a fellow-student of Robespierre at Paris, and became an advocate and an enthusiastic reformer. In July '89 he incited the people to the siege of the Bastille, and thus began the Revolution. On 29 Dec. 1790 he married Lucile Laridon-Duplessis. He edited *Le Vieux Cordelier* and the *Révolutions de France et de Brabant*, in which he stated that Mohammedanism was as credible as Christianity. He was a Deist, preferring Paganism to Christianity. Both creeds were more or less unreasonable; but, folly for folly, he said, I prefer Hercules slaying the Erymanthean boar to Jesus of Nazareth drowning two thousand pigs. He was executed with Danton, 5 April 1794. His amiable wife, Lucile, who was an Atheist (b. 1770), in a few days shared his fate (April 13). Carlyle calls Desmoulins a man of genius, "a fellow of infinite shrewdness, wit—nay, humor."

Des Periers (Jean Bonaventure), French poet and sceptic, b. Arnay le Duc, about 1510. He was brought up in a convent, only to detest the vices of the monks. In 1535 he lived in Dyons and assisted Dolet. He probably knew Rabelais, whom he mentions as "Francoys Insigne." Attached to the court of Marguerite of Valois, he defended Clement Marot when persecuted for making a French version of the Psalms. He wrote the *Cymbalum Mundi*, a satire upon religion, published under the name of Thomas de Clenier à Pierre Tryocan, *i.e.*, Thomas Incrédule à Pierre Croyant, 1537. It was suppressed and the printer, Jehan Morin, imprisoned. Des Periers fled and died (probably by suicide, to escape persecution) before 1544. An English version of *Cymbalum Mundi* was published in 1712. P. G. Brunet, the bibliographer, conjectures that Des Periers was the author of the famous Atheistic treatise, *The Three Impostors*.

Destriveaux (Pierre Joseph), Belgian lawyer and politician, b. Liége, 13 March, 1780. Author of several works on public right. Died Schaerbeck (Brussels), 3 Feb. 1853.

Destutt de Tracy (Antoine Louis de Claude) *Count*, French materialist philosopher, b. 20 July, 1754. His family was of Scotch origin. At first a soldier, he was one of the first noblemen at the Revolution to despoil himself of his title. A friend of Lafayette, Condorcet, and Cabanis, he was a complete sceptic in religion; made an analysis of Dupuis' *Origine de tous les Cultes* (1804), edited Montesquieu and Cabanis, was made a member of the French Academy (1808), and wrote several philosophical works, of which the principal is *Elements of Ideology*. He was a great admirer of Hobbes. Died Paris, 9 March, 1836.

Des Vignes (Pietro), secretary to Frederick II. (1245-49). Mazzuchelli attributes to him the treatise *De Tribus Impostoribus*.

Detrosier (Rowland), social reformer and lecturer, b. 1796, the illegitimate son of a Manchester man named Morris and a Frenchwoman. In his early years he was "for whole days without food." Self-educated, he established the first Mechanics' Institute in England at Hulme, gave Sunday scientific lectures, and published several discourses in favor of secular education. He became secretary of the National Political Union. He was a Deist. Like Bentham, who became his friend, he bequeathed his body for scientific purposes. Died in London, 23 Nov. 1834.

Deubler (Konrad). The son of poor parents, b. Goisern, near Ischl, Upper Austria, 26 Nov. 1814. Self-taught amid difficulties, he became the friend of Feuerbach and Strauss, and was known as "the Peasant Philosopher." In 1854 he was indicted for blasphemy, and was sentenced to two years' hard labor and imprisonment during pleasure. He was incarcerated from 7 Dec. '34, till Nov. '56 at Brünn, and afterwards at Olmutz, where he was released 24 March, 1857. He returned to his native place, and was visited by Feuerbach. In '70 he was made Burgomaster by his fellow-townsmen. Died 30 March, 1884.

Deurhoff (Willem), Dutch writer, b. Amsterdam, March 1650. Educated for the Church, he gave himself to philosophy, translated the works of Descartes, and was accused of being a follower of Spinoza. Forced to leave his country, he took refuge in Brabant, but returned to Holland, where he died 10 Oct. 1717. He left some followers.

De Wette. (See Wette M. L. de).

D'Holbach. See Holbach (P. H. D. von), *Baron*.

Diagoras, Greek poet, philosopher, and orator, known as "the Atheist," b. Melos. A pupil of Democritus, who is said to have freed him from slavery A doubtful tradition reports that he became an Atheist after being the victim of an unpunished perjury. He was accused (B.C. 411) of impiety, and had to fly from Athens to Corinth, where he died. A price was put upon the Atheist's head. His works are not extant, but several anecdotes are related of him, as that he threw a wooden statue of Hercules into the fire to cook a dish of lentils, saying the god had a thirteenth task to perform; and that, being on his flight by sea overtaken by a storm, hearing his fellow-passengers say it was because an Atheist was on board, he pointed to other vessels struggling in the same storm without being laden with a Diagoras.

Di Cagno Politi (Niccola Annibale), Italian Positivist, b. Bari, 1857. Studied at Naples under Angiulli, has written on modern culture and on experimental philosophy in Italy, and contributed articles on Positivism to the *Rivista Europea.*

Diderot (Denis), French philosopher, b. Langres, 6 Oct. 1713. His father, a cutler, intended him for the Church. Educated by Jesuits, at the age of twelve he received the tonsure. He had a passion for books, but, instead of becoming a Jesuit, went to Paris, where he supported himself by teaching and translating. In 1746 he published *Philosophic Thoughts,* which was condemned to be burnt. It did much to advance freedom of opinion. Three years later his *Letters on the Blind* occasioned his imprisonment at Vincennes for its materialistic Atheism. Rousseau, who called him " a transcendent genius," visited Diderot in prison, where he remained three years. Diderot projected the famous *Encyclopédie,* which he edited with Alembert, and he contributed some of the most important articles. With very inadequate recompense, and amidst difficulties that would have appalled an ordinary editor, Diderot superintended the undertaking for many years (1751-65). He also contributed to other important works, such as Raynal's *Philosophic History, L'Esprit,* by Helvetius, and *The System of Nature* and other works of his friend D'Holbach. Diderot's fertile mind also produced dramas, essays, sketches, and novels. Died 30 July, 1784. Comte calls Diderot " the greatest thinker of the eighteenth century."

Diercks (Gustav), German author of able works on the History of the Development of Human Spirit (Berlin, 1881-2) and on Arabian Culture in Spain, 1887. Is a member of the German Freethinkers' Union.

Dilke (Ashton Wentworth), b. 1850. Educated at Cambridge, travelled in Russia and Central Asia, and published a translation of Turgenev's *Virgin Soil*. He purchased and edited the *Weekly Dispatch*; was returned as M.P. for Newcastle in 1880, but, owing to ill health, resigned in favor of John Morley, and died at Algiers 12 March, 1883.

Dinter (Gustav Friedrich), German educationalist, b. Borna, near Leipsic, 29 Feb. 1760. His *Bible for Schoolmsters* is his best-known work. It sought to give rational notes and explanations of the Jew books, and excited much controversy. Died at Konigsberg, 29 May, 1831.

Dippel (Johann Konrad), German alchemist and physician, b. 10 Aug. 1672, at Frankenstein, near Darmstadt. His *Papismus vapulans Protestantium* (1698) drew on him the wrath of the theologians of Geissen, and he had to fly for his life. Attempting to find out the philosopher's stone, he discovered Prussian blue. In 1705 he published his satires against the Protestant Church, *Hirt und eine Heerde*, under the name of Christianus Democritos. He denied the inspiration of the Bible, and after an adventurous life in many countries died 25 April, 1734.

Dobrolyubov (Nikolai Aleksandrovich), Russian author, b. 1836, at Nijni Novgorod, the son of a priest. Educated at St. Petersburg, he became a radical journalist. His works were edited in four vols by Chernuishevsky. Died 17 Nov. 1861.

Dodel-Port (Prof. Arnold), Swiss scientist, b. Affeltrangen, Thurgau, 16 Oct. 1843. Educated at Kreuzlingen, he became in '63 teacher in the Oberschule in Hauptweil; then studied from '64-'69 at Geneva, Zürich, and Munich, becoming *privat docent* in the University of Zürich, '70. In '75 he published *The New History of Creation*. In '78 he issued his world-famous *Botanical Atlas*, and was in '80 made Professor of Botany in the Zürich University and Director of the Botanical Laboratory. He has also written *Biological Fragments* (1885), the *Life and Letters of Konrad Deubler*, "the peasant philosopher" (1886), and has just published *Moses or Darwin? a School*

Question, 1889. Dr. Dodel-Port is an hon. member of the London Royal Society and Vice-President of the German Freethinkers' Union.

Dodwell (Henry), eldest son of the theologian of that name, was b. Shottesbrooke, Berkshire, about the beginning of the eighteenth century. He was educated at Magdalen Hall, when he proceeded B.A., 9 Feb. 1726. In '42 he published a pamphlet entitled *Christianity not Founded on Argument*, which in a tone of grave irony contends that Christianity can only be accepted by faith. He was brought up to the law and was a zealous friend of the Society for the Promotion of Arts, Manufactures, and Commerce. Died 1784.

Doebereiner (Johann Wolfgang), German chemist, b. Bavaria, 15 Dec. 1780. In 1810 he became Professor of Chemistry at Jena, where he added much to science. Died 24 March, 1849. He was friend and instructor to Goethe.

Dolet (Etienne), a learned French humanist, b. Orleans 3 Aug. 1509. He studied in Paris, Padua and Venice. For his heresy he had to fly from Toulouse and lived for some time at Lyons, where he established a printing-press and published some of his works, for which he was imprisoned. He was acquainted with Rabelais, Des Periers, and other advanced men of the time. In 1543 the Parliament condemned his books to be burnt, and in the next year he was arrested on a charge of Atheism. After being kept two years in prison he was strangled and burnt, 3 Aug. 1546. It is related that seeing the sorrow of the crowd, he said : "Non dolet ipe Dolet, sed pia turba dolet."—Dolet grieves not, but the generous crowd grieves. His goods being confiscated, his widow and children were left to beggary. "The French language," says A. F. Didot, "owes him much for his treatises, translations, and poesies." Dolet's biographer, M. Joseph Boulmier, calls him "le Christ de la pensée libre." Philosophy has alone the right, says Henri Martin, to claim Dolet on its side. His English biographer, R. C. Christie, says he was "neither a Catholic nor a Protestant."

Dominicis (Saverio Fausto de), Italian Positivist philosopher, b. Buonalbergo, 1846. Is Professor of Philosophy at Bari, and has written on *Education and Darwinism*.

Dondorf (Dr. A.), See ANDERSON (Marie) in Supplement.

Doray de Longrais (Jean Paul), French man of letters. b. Mauvieux, 1736. Author of a Freethought romance, *Faustin, or the Philosophical Age.* Died at Paris, 1800.

Dorsch (Eduard), German American Freethinker, b. Warzburg 10 Jan. 1822. He studied at Munich and Vienna. In '49 he went to America and settled in Monroe, Michigan, where he published a volume of poems, some being translations from Swinburne. Died 10 Jan. 1887.

Dorsey (J. M.), author of the *The True History of Moses,* and others, an attack on the Bible, published at Boston in 1855.

Draparnaud (Jacques Philippe Raymond), French doctor, b. 3 June, 1772, at Montpelier, where he became Professor of Natural History. His discourses on Life and Vital Functions, and on the Philosophy of the Sciences and Christianity (1801), show his scepticism. Died 1 Feb. 1805.

Draper (John Williams), scientist and historian, b. St. Helens, near Liverpool, 5 May 1811. The son of a Wesleyan minister, he was educated at London University. In '32 he emigrated to America, where he was Professor of Chemistry and Natural History in New York University. He was one of the inventors of photography and the first who applied it to astronomy. He wrote many scientific works, notably on *Human Physiology.* His history of the American Civil War is an important work, but he is chiefly known by his *History of the Intellectual Development of Europe* and *History of the Conflict of Religion and Science,* which last has gone through many editions and been translated into all the principal languages. Died 4 Jan. 1882.

Dreyfus (Ferdinand Camille), author of an able work on the Evolution of Worlds and Societies, 1888.

Droysen (Johann Gustav), German historian, b. Treptoir, 6 July, 1808. Studied at Berlin; wrote in the *Hallische Jahrbücher;* was Professor of History at Keil, 1840; Jena '51 and Berlin '59. Has edited Frederick the Great's Correspondence, and written other important works, some in conjunction with his friend Max Duncker. Died 15 June, 1882.

Drummond (Sir William), of Logie Almond, antiquary and author, b. about 1770; entered Parliament as member for St.

Mawes, Cornwall, 1795. In the following year he became envoy to the court of Naples, and in 1801 ambassader to Constantinople. His principal work is *Origines*, or Remarks on the Origin of several Empires, States, and Cities (4 vols. 1821–29). He also printed privately *The Œdipus Judaicus*, 1811. It calls in question, with much boldness and learning, many legends of the Old Testament, to which it gave an astronomical signification. It was reprinted in '66. Sir William Drummond also wrote anonymously *Philosophical Sketches of the Principles of Society*, 1795. Died at Rome, 29 March, 1828.

Duboc (Julius) German writer and doctor of philosophy b. Hamburgh, 10 Oct. 1829. Educated at Frankfurt and Giessen, is a clever journalist, and has translated the *History of the English Press*. Has written an Atheistic work, *Das Lieben Ohne Gott* (Life without God), with the motto from Feuerbach " No religion is my religion, no philosophy my philosophy," 1875. He has also written on the *Physchology of Love*, and other important works.

Dubois (Pierre), a French sceptic, who in 1835 published *The True Catechism of Believers*—a work ordered by the Court of Assizes to be suppressed, and for which the author (Sept. '35) was condemned to six months' imprisonment and a fine of one thousand francs. He also wrote *The Believer Undeceived*, or Evident Proofs of the Falsity and Absurdity of Christianity ; a work put on the *Index* in '36.

Du Bois-Reymond (Emil), biologist, of Swiss father and French mother, b. Berlin, 7 Nov. 1818. He studied at Berlin and Bonn for the Church, but left it to follow science, '37. Has become famous as a physiologist, especially by his *Researches in Animal Electricity*, '48–60. With Helmholtz he has done much to establish the new era of positive science, wrongly called by opponents Materialism. Du Bois-Reymond holds that thought is a function of the brain and nervous system, and that " soul " has arisen as the gradual results of natural combinations, but in his *Limits of the Knowledge of Nature*, '72, he contends that we must always come to an ultimate incomprehensible. Du Bois-Reymond has written on *Voltaire and Natural Science*, '68 ; *La Mettrie*, '75 ; *Darwin versus Galiani*, '78 ; and *Frederick II.*

and Rousseau, '79. Since '67 he has been perpetual secretary of the Academy of Sciences, Berlin.

Dubuisson (Paul Ulrich), French dramatist and revolutionary, b. Lanat, 1746. A friend of Cloots he suffered with him on the scaffold, 24 March, 1794.

Dubuisson (Paul), living French Positivist, author of *Grand Types of Humanity.*

Du Chatelet Lomont. See Chastelet.

Duclos (Charles Pinot), witty French writer, b. Dinan, 12 Feb. 1704. He was admitted into the French Academy, 1747 and became its secretary, 1755. A friend of Diderot and d'Alembert. His *Considerations sur les Mœurs* is still a readable work. Died 27 March, 1772.

Ducos (Jean François), French Girondist, b. Bordeaux in 1765. Elected to the Legislative Assembly, he, on the 26th Oct. 1791, demanded the complete separation of the State from religion. He shared the fate of the Girondins, 31 Oct. 1793, crying with his last breath, " *Vive la Republique!* "

Du Deffand (Marie), *Marchioness,* witty literary French-woman, b. 1697. Chamfort relates that when young and in a convent she preached irreligion to her young comrades. The abbess called in Massillon, to whom the little sceptic gave her reasons. He went away saying " She is charming." Her house in Paris was for fifty years the resort of eminent authors and statesmen. She corresponded for many years with Horace Walpole, D'Alembert and Voltaire. Many anecdotes are told of her; thus, to the Cardinal de Polignac, who spoke of the miracle of St. Denis walking when beheaded, she said " Il n'y a que le premier pas qui coûte." Died 24 Sept. 1780. To the curé of Saint Sulpice, who came to her death-bed, she said " Ni questions, ni raisons, ni sermons." Larousse calls her "Belle, instruite, spirituelle mais sceptique et materialiste."

Dudgeon (William), a Berwickshire Deist, whose works were published (privately printed at Edinburgh) in 1765.

Dudnevant (A. L. A. Dupin), *Baroness.* See Sand (Georges).

Duehring (Eugen Karl), German writer, b. Berlin, 12 Jan. 1833; studied law. He has, though blind, written many works on science and political economy, also a *Critical History of*

114

Philosophy, '69–78, and *Science Revolutionized*, '78. In Oct. 1879, his death was maliciously reported.

Dulaure (Jacques Antoine), French archeologist and historian, b. Clermont-Ferrand, 3 Dec. 1755. In 1788–90 he published six volumes of a description of France. He wrote many pamphlets, including one on the private lives of ecclesiastics. Elected to the Convention in 1792, he voted for the death of the King. Proscribed as a Girondist, Sept. 1793, he fled to Switzerland. He was one of the Council of Five Hundred, 1796–98. Dulaure wrote a learned *Treatise on Superstitions*, but he is best known by his *History of Paris*, and his *Short History of Different Worships*, 1825, in which he deals with ancient fetishism and phallic worship. Died Paris, 9 Aug. 1835.

Dulaurens (Henri Joseph). French satirist, b. Douay, 27 March, 1719. He was brought up in a convent, and made a priest 12 Nov. 1727. Published a satire against the Jesuits, 1761, he was compelled to fly to Holland, where he lived in poverty. He edited *L'Evangile de la Raison*, a collection of anti-Christian tracts by Voltaire and others, and wrote *L'Anti-papisme révelé* in 1767. He was in that year condemned to perpetual imprisonment for heresy, and shut in the convent of Mariabaum, where he died 1797. Dulaurens was caustic, cynical and vivacious. He is also credited with the *Portfolios of a Philosopher*, mostly taken from the Analysis of. Bayle, Cologne, 1770.

Dulk (Albert Friedrich Benno), German poet and writer, b. Konigsberg, 17 June, 1819; he became a physician, but was expelled for aiding in the Revolution of '48. He travelled in Italy and Egypt. In '65 he published *Jesus der Christ*, embodying rationalism in prose and verse. He has also written *Stimme der Menscheit*, 2 vols., '76, '80, and *Der Irrgang des Lebens Jesu*, '84, besides numerous plays and pamphlets. Died 29 Oct. 1884.

Dumont (Léon), French writer, b. Valenciennes, 1837. Studied for the bar, but took to philosophy and literature. He early embraced Darwinism, and wrote on *Hæckel and the Theory of Evolution*, '73. He wrote in *La Revue Philosophique*, and other journals. Died Valenciennes, 17 Jan. 1877.

115

Dumarsais (César CHESNEAU), French grammarian and philosopher, b. Marseilles, 17 July, 1676. When young he entered the congregation of the oratory. This society he soon quitted, and went to Paris, where he married. A friend of Boindin and Alembert, he wrote against the pretensions of Rome and contributed to the *Encyclopédie*. He is credited with *An Analysis of the Christian Religion* and with the celebrated *Essai sur les Préjugés*, par Mr. D. M., but the latter was probably written by Holbach, with notes by Naigeon. *Le Philosophe*, published in *L'Evangile de la Raison* by Dulaurens, was written by Voltaire. Died 11 June, 1756. Dumarsais was very simple in character, and was styled by D'Alembert the La Fontaine of philosophers.

Dumont (Pierre Etienne Louis), Swiss writer, b. Geneva, 18 July, 1759. Was brought up as a minister, but went to France and became secretary to Mirabeau. After the Revolution he came to England, where he became acquainted with Bentham, whose works he translated. Died Milan, 29 Sept. 1829.

Duncker (Maximilian Wolfgang), German historian, b. Berlin, 15 Oct. 1811. His chief work, the *History of Antiquity*, 1852–57, thoroughly abolishes the old distinction of sacred and profane history, and freely criticises the Jewish records. A translation in six volumes has been made by E. Abbot. Duncker took an active part in the events of '48 and '50, and was appointed Director-General of the State Archives. Died 24 July, 1886.

Dupont (Jacob Louis), a French mathematician and member of the National Convention, known as the Abbé Dupont, who, 14 Dec. 1792, declared himself an Atheist from the tribune of the Convention. Died at Paris in 1813.

Dupont de Nemours (Pierre Samuel), French economist, b. Paris, 14 Dec. 1739. He became President of the Constituent Assembly, and was a Theophilantrophist. Died Delaware, U.S.A., 6 Aug. 1817.

Dupuis (Charles François), French astronomer and philosopher, b. Trie-le-Chateau, 16 Oct. 1742. He was educated for the Church, which he left, and married in 1775. He studied under Lalande, and wrote on the origin of the constellations, 1781. In 1788 he became a member of the Academy of Inscriptions. At the Revolution he was chosen a member of the Convention.

During the Reign of Terror he saved many lives at his own risk. He was afterwards one of the Council of Five Hundred, and president of the legislative body. His chief work is on the *Origin of Religions*, 7 vols., 1795, in which he traces solar worship in various faiths, including Christianity. This has been described as "a monument of the erudition of unbelief." Dupuis died near Dijon, 29 Sept. 1809,

Dutrieux (Pierre Joseph), Belgian physician, b. Tournai, 19 July, 1848. Went to Cairo and became a Bey. Died 1 Jan. 1889.

Dutton (Thomas), M.A., theatrical critic, b. London, 1767. Educated by the Moravians. In 1795 he published a *Vindication of the Age of Reason by Thomas Paine*. He translated Kotzebue's *Pizzaro in Peru*, 1799, and edited the *Dramatic Censor*, 1800, and the *Monthly Theatrical Reporter*, 1815.

Duvernet (Théophile Imarigeon), French writer, b. at Ambert 1730. He was brought up a Jesuit, became an Abbé, but mocked at religion. Duvernet became tutor to Saint Simon. For a political pamphlet he was imprisoned in the Bastille While here he wrote a curious and rare romance, *Les Devotions de Mme. de Bethzamooth*. He wrote on *Religious Intolerance*, 1780, and a *History of the Sorbonne*, 1790, but is best known by his *Life of Voltaire* (1787). In 1793 he wrote a letter to the Convention, in which he declares that he renounces the religion "born in a stable between an ox and an ass." Died in 1796.

Dyas (Richard H.), captain in the army. Author of *The Upas*. He resided long in Italy and translated several of the works of C. Voysey.

Eaton (Daniel Isaac), bookseller, b. about 1752, was educated at the Jesuits' College, St. Omer. Being advised to study the Bible, he did so, with the result of discarding it as a revelation. In 1792 he was prosecuted for publishing Paine's *Rights of Man*, but the prosecution fell through. He afterwards published *Politics for the People*, which was also prosecuted, 1793, as was his *Political Dictionary*, 1796. To escape punishment, he fled to America, and lived there for three years and a half. Upon returning to England, his person and property were seized. Books to the value of

£2,800 were burnt, and he was imprisoned for fifteen months. He translated from Helvetius and sold at his " Ratiocinato ry or Magazine for Truths and Good Sense," 8 Cornhill, in 1810, *The True Sense and Meaning of the System of Nature.* The *Law of Nature* had been previously translated by him. In '11 he issued the first and second parts of Paine's *Age of Reason,* and on 6 March, '12, was tried before Lord Ellenborough on a charge of blasphemy for issuing the third and last part. He was sentenced to eighteen months' imprisonment and to stand in the pillory. The sentence evoked Shelley's spirited *Letter to Lord Ellenborough.* Eaton translated and published Freret's *Preservative against Religious Prejudices,* 1812, and shortly before his death, at Deptford, 22 Aug. 1814, he was again prosecuted for publishing George Houston's *Ecce Homo.*

Eberhard (Johann August), German Deist, b. Halberstadt, 31 Aug. 1739, was brought up in the church, but persecuted for heresy in his *New Apology for Socrates,* 1772, was patronised by Frederick the Great, and appointed Professor of Philosophy at Halle, where he opposed the idealism of Kant and Fichte. He wrote a *History of Philosophy,* 1788. Died Halle, 7 Jan. 1809.

Eberty (Gustav), German Freethinker, b. 2 July, 1806. Author of some controversial works. Died Berlin, 10 Feb. 1887.

Echtermeyer (Ernst Theodor), German critic, b. Liebenwerda, 1805. He studied at Halle and Berlin, and founded, with A. Ruge, the *Hallische Jahrbücher,* which contained many Freethought articles, 1837–42. He taught at Halle and Dresden, where he died, 6 May, 1844.

Edelmann (Johann Christian), German Deist, b. Weissenfels, Saxony, 9 July, 1698; studied theology in Jena, joined the Moravians, but left them and every form of Christianity, becoming an adherent of Spinozism. His principal works are his *Unschuldige Wahrheiten,* 1735 (Innocent Truths), in which he argues that no religion is of importance, and *Moses mit Aufgedecktem Angesicht* (Moses Unmasked), 1740, an attack on the Old Testament, which, he believed, proceeded from Ezra ; *Die Gottlichkeit der Vernunft* (The Divinity of Reason), 1741, and *Christ and Belial.* His works excited much controversy, and were publicly burnt at Frankfort, 9 May, 1750. Edelmann was chased from Brunswick and Hamburgh, but was protected by

Frederick the Great, and died at Berlin, 15 Feb. 1767. Mira beau praised him, and Guizot calls him a " fameux esprit fort."

Edison (Thomas Alva), American inventor, b. Milan, Ohio, 10 Feb. 1847. As a boy he sold fruit and papers at the trains. He read, however, Gibbon, Hume and other important works before he was ten. He afterwards set up a paper of his own, then became telegraph operator, studied electricity, invented electric light, the electric pen, the telephone, microphone, phonograph, etc. Edison is known to be an Agnostic and to pay no attention to religion.

Eenens (Ferdinand), Belgian writer, b. Brussels, 7 Dec. 1811 Eenens was an officer in the Belgian army, and wrote many political and anti-clerical pamphlets. He also wrote *La Vérité*, a work on the Christian faith, 1859; *Le Paradis Terrestre*, '60, an examination of the legend of Eden, and *Du Dieu Thaumaturge*, '76. He used the pen names " Le Père Nicaise," " Nicodème Polycarpe " and " Timon III." Died at Brussels in 1883.

Effen (Justus van), Dutch writer, b. Utrecht, 11 Feb. 1684. Edited the *Misanthrope*, Amsterdam, 1712-16; translated *Robinson Crusoe*, Swift's *Tale of a Tub*, and Mandeville's *Thoughts on Religion*, 1722; published the *Dutch Spectator*, 1731-35. Died at Bois-le-Duc, 18 Sept. 1735.

Eichhorn (Johann Gottfried), German Orientalist and rationalist, b. 16 Oct. 1752, became Professor of Oriental Literature and afterwards Professor of Theology at Gottingen. He published *Introductions to the Old and New Testaments* and *A Commentary on the Apocalypse*, in which his criticism tends to uproot belief in the Bible as a divine revelation. He lectured every day for for fifty-two years. Died 25 June, 1827.

" Elborch (Conrad von)," the pseudonym of a living learned Dutch writer, whose position does not permit him to reveal his true name. Born 14 Jan. 1865, he has contributed to *De Dageraad* (The Daybreak), under various pen-names, as " Fra Diavolo," " Denis Bontemps," " J. Van den Ende," etc. He has given, in '88, a translation of the rare and famous Latin treatise, *De Tribus Impostoribus* (On Three Impostors) [Jesus, Moses, and Muhammad], with an important bibliographic and historical introduction.

"**Eliot** (George)," the pen-name of Mary Ann Lewes (*née* Evans) one of the greatest novelists of the century, b. at Arbury Farm, near Griff, Warwickshire, 22 Nov. 1819. In '41 the family removed to Foleshill, near Coventry. Here she made the friendship of the household of Charles Bray, and changed her views from Evangelical Christianity to philosophical scepticism. Influenced by *The Inquiry into the Origin of Christianity*, by C. C. Hennell (Bray's brother-in-law), she made an analysis of that work. Her first literary venture was translating Strauss' *Leben Jesu*, published in 1846. After the death of her father ('49) she travelled with the Brays upon the Continent, and upon her return assisted Dr. Chapman in the editorship of the *Westminster Review*, to which she contributed several articles. She translated Feuerbach's *Essence of Christianity*, '54, the only work published with her real name, and also translated from Spinoza's Ethics. Introduced by Herbert Spencer to George Henry Lewes, she linked her life with his in defiance of the conventions of society, July, '54. Both were poor, but by his advice she turned to fiction, in which she soon achieved success. Her *Scenes of Clerical Life*, *Adam Bede*, *Mill on the Floss*, *Silas Marner*, *Romola*, *Felix Holt*, *Middlemarch*, *Daniel Deronda*, and *Theophrastus Such* have become classics. As a poet, "George Eliot" does not rank so high, but her little piece, " Oh, may I join the choir invisible," well expresses the emotion of the Religion of Humanity, and her *Spanish Gipsy* she allowed was "a mass of Positivism." Lewes died in 1878, and within two years she married his friend, J. W. Cross. Her new happiness was short-lived. She died 22 Dec. 1880, and is buried with Lewes at Highgate.

Ellero (Pietro) Italian jurisconsult, b. Pordenone, 8 Oct. 1833, Counsellor of the High Court of Rome, has been Professor of Criminal Law in the University of Bologna. Author of many works on legal ,and social questions. His *Scritti Minori*, *Scritti Politici* and *La Question Sociale* have the honor of a place on the Roman I*ndex*.

Elliotson (John, M.D., F.R.S.), an eminent medical man, b. London, 1791. He became physician at St. Thomas's Hospital in 1822, and made many contributions to medical science. By new prescriptions of quinine, creasote, etc., he excited much hostility in the profession. He was the first in this country to advocate the use of the stethoscope. He was also the first physician to discard knee-breeches and silk stockings, and to wear a beard. In '31 he was chosen Prosessor at University College, but, becoming an advocate of curative mesmerism, he resigned his appointments, '38. He was founder and President of the London Phrenological Society, and, in addition to many medical works, edited the *Zoist* (thirteen vols.), translated Blumenbach's *Physiology*, and wrote an introduction to Engledue's *Cerebral Physiology*, defending materialism. Thackeray dedicated *Pendennis* to him, '50, and he received a tribute of praise from Dickens. Died at London, 29 July, 1868.

Eichthal (Gustave d'), French writer, b. of Jewish family, Nancy, 22 March, 1804. He became a follower of Saint Simon, was one of the founders of the Société d'Ethnologie, and published *Les Evangiles*, a critical analysis of the gospels, 2 vols, Paris, '63. This he followed by *The Three Great Mediterranean Nations and Christianity* and *Socrates and our Time*, '84. He died at Paris, April, 1886, and his son published his *Mélanges de Critique Biblique* (Miscellanies of Biblical Criticism), in which there is an able study on the name and character of " Jahveh."

Emerson (Ralph Waldo), American essayist, poet, and philosopher, b. Boston 25 May, 1803. He came of a line of ministers, and was brought up like his father, educated at Harvard College, and ordained as a Unitarian minister, 1829. Becoming too broad for the Church, he resigned in '32. In the next year he came to Europe, visiting Carlyle. On his return he settled at Concord, giving occasional lectures, most of which have been published. He wrote to the *Dial*, a transcendentalist paper. Tending to idealistic pantheism, but without systematic philosophy, all his writings are most suggestive, and he is always the champion of mental freedom, self-reliance, and the free pursuit of science. Died at Concord, 27 April, 1882. Matthew Arnold has pronounced his essays "the most important work done in prose " in this century.

Emerson (William), English mathematician, b. Hurworth, near Darlington, 14 May, 1701. He conducted a school and wrote numerous works on Mathematics. His vigorous, if eccentric, individuality attracted Carlyle, who said to Mrs.

121

Gilchrist, "Emerson was a Freethinker who looked on his neighbor, the parson, as a humbug. He seems to have defended himself in silence the best way he could against the noisy clamor and unreal stuff going on around him." Died 21 May, 1782. He compiled a list of Bible contradictions.

Emmet (Robert), Irish revolutionist, b. in Dublin 1778, was educated as a barrister. Expelled from Dublin University for his sympathy with the National Cause in 1798; he went to the Continent, but returned in 1802 to plan an ill-starred insurrection, for which he was executed 20 Sept. 1803. Emmet made a thrilling speech before receiving sentence, and on the scaffold refused the services of a priest. It is well known that his desire to see once more his sweetheart, the daughter of Curran, was the cause of his capture and execution.

Engledue (William Collins), M.D., b. Portsea 1813. After taking his degree at Edinburgh, he became assistant to Dr. Lizars and was elected President of the Royal Medical Society of Edinburgh. He returned to Portsmouth in 1835; originated the Royal Portsmouth Hospital and established public baths and washhouses. He contributed to the *Zoist* and published an exposition of materialism under the title of *Cerebral Physiology*, 1842, republished by J. Watson, 1857. Died Jan. 1859.

English (George Bethune), American writer and linguist, b. Cambridge, Mass., 7 March, 1787. He studied law and divinity. and graduated at Harvard, 1807, but becoming sceptical published *Grounds of Christianity Examined*, 1813. The work excited some controversy, and has been reprinted at Toronto. He joined the Egyptian service and became General of Artillery. He had a variable genius and a gift of languages. At Marseilles he passed for a Turk with a Turkish ambassador; and at Washington he surprised a delegation of Cherokees by disputing with them in their own tongue. He wrote a reply to his critics, entitled *Five Smooth Stones out of the Brook*, and two letters to Channing on his sermons against infidelity. Died at Washington, 20 Sept. 1828.

Ense (Varnhagen von). See Varnhagen.

Ensor (George), an Irish writer, b. Loughgall, 1769. Educated at Trinity College; he became B.A. 1790. He travelled largely, and was a friend of liberty in every country. Besides other political works he published, *The Independent Man*, 1806 ; *On National Government*, 1810 ; *A Review of the Miracles, Prophecies and Mysteries of the Old and New Testaments*, first printed as *Janus on Sion*, 1816, and republished 1835 ; and *Natural Theology Examined*, 1836, the last being republished in *The Library of Reason*. Bentham described him as clever but impracticable. Died Ardress, Co. Armagh, 3 Dec. 1843.

Epicurus, Greek philosopher, b. Samos, B.C. 342. He repaired to Athens, B.C. 323. Influenced by the works of Demokritos, he occupied himself with philosophy. He purchased a garden in Athens, in which he established his school. Although much culminated, he is now admitted to have been a man of blameless life. According to Cicero, he had no belief in the gods, but did not attack their existence, in order not to offend the prejudices of the Athenians. In physics he adopted the atomic theory, and denied immortality. He taught that pleasure is the sovereign good ; but by pleasure he meant no transient sensation, but permanent tranquility of mind. He wrote largely, but his works are lost. His principles are expounded in the great poem of Lucretius, *De Rerum Natura*. Died B.C. 270, leaving many followers.

" **Erdan** (Alexandre)," the pen-name of Alexandre Andre JACOB, a French writer, b Angles 1826. He was the natural son of a distinguished prelate. Educated at Saint Sulpice for the Church, he read Proudhon, and refused to take holy orders. He became a journalist and an advocate of phonography. His work, *La France Mystique* (1855), in which he gives an account of French religious eccentricities, was condemned for its scepticism which appears on every page. Sentenced to a year's imprisonment and a fine of three thousand francs, he took refuge in Italy. Died at Frascati, near Rome, 24 Sept. 1878·

Ernesti (Johann August), German critic, b. Tennstadt, 4 Aug. 1707. Studied at Wittenberg and Leipsic, where he was appointed professor of classical literature. Renowned as a philologist, he insisted that the Bible must be interpreted like any other book. Died Leipsic, 11 Sept. 1781.

Escherny (François Louis d') *Count*, Swiss litterateur, b. Neufchatel, 24 Nov. 1733. He spent much of his life in travel. At Paris he became the associate of Helvetius, Diderot, and particularly Rousseau, whom he much admired.   He wrote *Lacunes de la Philosophie* (Amsterdam, 1783) and a work on *Equality* (1795), in which he displays his Freethought.   Died at Paris, 15 July, 1815.

Espinas (Alfred), French philosopher, b. Saint-Florentin, 1844.   Has translated, with Th. Ribot, H. Spencer's *Principles of Psychology*, and has written studies on *Experimental Philosophy in Italy*, and on *Animal Societies* (1877).

Espronceda (José), popular Spanish poet, b. Almendralejo (Estremadura) in 1810.   After the War of Independence he went to Madrid and studied under Alberto Lista, the poet and mathematician.   He became so obnoxious to the government by his radical principles that he was imprisoned about the age of fifteen, and banished a few years later.   He passed several years in London and Paris, and was brought under the influence of Byron and Hugo.   He fought with the people in the Paris Revolution of July, 1830.   On the death of the Spanish King in '33 he returned to Madrid, but was again banished for too free expression of his opinions.   He returned and took part in the revolutionary contest of '35-36.   He was elected to the Cortes in '41, and appointed secretary of embassy to The Hague.   Died 23 May, 1842.   Among his works are lyrical poems, which often remind us of Heine ; an unfinished epic, *El Pelayo* ; and *El Diablo-Mundo* (the Devil-World), a fine poem, due to the inspiration of Faust and Don Juan.   Esproceda was a thorough sceptic.   In his *Song of the Pirate* he asks, "Who is my God ?—Liberty "; and in his concluding lines to a star he says :

> I unheedingly follow my path,
> At the mercy of winds and of waves.
> Wrapt thus within the arms of Fate,
> What care I if lost or saved.

Estienne (Henri), the ablest of a family of learned French printers, known in England as Stephens ; b. Paris, 1528.   At the age of eighteen he assisted his father in collating the MSS. of Dionysius and Halicarnassus.   In 1557 he established a printing office of his own, and issued many Greek authors ; and in 1572 the *Thesaurus Linguæ Græcæ*   His *Apologie pour Hérodote* (Englished as a World of Wonders) is designed as a satire on Christian legends, and directed against priests and priestcraft. He was driven from place to place. Sir Philip Sidney highly esteemed him, and "kindly entertained him in his travaile." Died 1598. Garasse classes him with Atheists.

Esteve (Pierre), French writer, b. Montpelier at the beginning of the eighteenth century. He wrote a History of Astronomy and an anonymous work on the *Origin of the Universe explained from a Principle of Matter :* Berlin, 1748.

Ettel (Konrad), Austrian Freethinker, b. 17 Jan. 1817, at Neuhof, Sternberg. Studied at the Gymnasium Kremsier, and at the wish of his parents at the Theological Seminary Olmütz, which he left to study philosophy at Vienna. He has written many poems and dramas. His *Grundzüge der Naturlichen Weltanschauung* (Sketch of a Natural View of the World), a Freethinker's catechism, 1886, has reached a fourth edition.

Evans (George Henry), b. at Bromyard, Herefordshire, 25 March, 1803. While a child, his parents emigrated to New York. He set up as a printer, and published the *Correspondent,* the first American Freethought paper. He also published the *Working Man's Advocate, Man, Young America,* and the *Radical.* He labored for the transportation of mails on Sundays, the limitation of the right to hold lands, the abolition of slavery, and other reforms. His brother became one of the chief elders of the Shakers. Died in Granville, New Jersey, 2 Feb. 1855.

Evans (William), b. Swansea, 1816, became a follower of Robert Owen. He established *The Potter's Examiner and Workman's Advocate,* '43, and wrote in the Co-operative journals under the anagram of " Millway Vanes." Died 14 March, 1887.

Evanson (Edward), theological critic, b. Warrington, Lancashire, 21 April, 1731. He graduated at Cambridge, became vicar of South Mimms, and afterwards rector of Tewkesbury. Entertaining doubts on the Trinity, he submitted them to the Archbishop of Canterbury without obtaining satisfaction. He made some changes in reading the Litany, and for expressing heretical opinions in a sermon in 1771, he was prosecuted, but escaped in consequence of some irregularity in the proceedings. In 1772 he published an anonymous tract on the Trinity. In 1797 he addressed a letter to the Bishop of Lichfield on the Prophecies of the New Testament, in which he tried to show that either Christianity was false or the orthodox churches. In

the following year he resigned both his livings and took pupils.
In 1792 he published his principal work, *The Dissonance of the
Four Generally-Received Evangelists*, in which he rejected all the
gospels, except Luke, as unauthentic.   This work involved him
in a controversy with Dr. Priestley, and brought a considerable
share of obliquy and persecution from the orthodox.   Died 25
Sept. 1805.

Eve'merus or **Euhemerus** (Ευημερος), a Sicilian author of
the time of Alexander the Great, who sought to rationalise
religion, and treated the gods as dead heroes.   He is usually
represented as an Atheist.

Eudes (Emile François Désiré), French Communist, b. Roncey,
1844.   He became a chemist, and was condemned, with
Régnard, to three months' imprisonment for writing in *La
Libre Pensée*, '67, of which he was director.   He joined the
ranks of the Commune and became a general.   When the
Versailles troops entered Paris he escaped to Switzerland.   On
his return after the Amnesty, he wrote with Blanqui.   Died at
a public meeting in Paris, 5 Aug. 1888.

Ewerbeck (August Hermann), Dr., b. Dantzic.   After the
events of 1848, he lived at Paris.   He translated into German
Cabet's *Voyage en Icarie*, and in an important work entitled
Qu'est ce que La Religion? (What is Religion), '50, translated into
French Feuerbach's "Essence of Religion," "Essence of
Christianity," and "Death and Immortality."   In a succeeding
volume *What is the Bible?* he translated from Daumer, Ghillany,
Luetzelberger and B. Bauer.   Ewerbeck also wrote in French
an historical work on Germany and the Germans; Paris, 1851.

Fabre D'Eglantine (Philippe François Nazaire), French
revolutionist and playwriter, b. Carcassonne, 28 Dec. 1755.
After some success as a poet and playwright he was chosen as
deputy to the National Convention.   He voted for the death of
Louis XVI., and proposed the substitution of the republican
for the Christian calendar, Sept. 1793.   He was executed with
his friend Danton, 5 April, 1794.

Fabricatore (Bruto), Italian writer, b. Sarno, Naples, 1824.
His father Antonio had the honor of having a political work
placed on the *Index*, 1821.   He took part in the anti-papal
Freethought Coucil of 1869, and has writen works on Dante, etc.

Farinata. See UBERTI (Farinata degli).

Fauche (Hippolyte), French Orientalist, b. Auxerre, 22 May, 1797. Translations of the Mahabharata, the Ramayana, and the plays of Kalidasa, attest his industry and erudition. He contributed to *La Liberté de Penser.* Died at Juilly, 28 Feb. 1869.

Fausto (Sebastiano), DA LONGIANO, Italian of the beginning of the 16th century, who is said to have projected a work *The Temple of Truth,* with the intention of overturning all religions. He translated the *Meditations of Antoninus,* also wrote observations on Cicero, 1566.

Feer (Henri Léon), French Orientalist, b. Rouen, 27 Nov. 1830, is chiefly known by his Buddhistic Studies, 1871-75.

Fellens (Jean Baptiste), Professor of History, b. Bar-sur-Aube, 1794. Author of a work on Pantheism, Paris, 1873.

Fellowes (Robert), LL.D., b. Norfolk 1771, educated at Oxford. He took orders in 1795, and wrote many books, but gradually quitted the doctrines of the Church and adopted the Deistic opinions maintained in his work entitled *The Religion of the Universe* (1836). Dr. Fellowes was proprietor of the *Examiner* and a great supporter of the London University. Died 5 Feb. 1847.

Fenzi (Sebastiano), Italian writer, b. Florence, 22 Oct. 1822. Educated by the Jesuits in Vienna, England and Paris. Founded in '49 the *Revista Britannica,* writer on the journal *L'Italiano,* and has written a credo which is a non-credo.

Feringa (Frederik), Dutch writer, b. Groningen, 16 April, 1840. Studied mathematics. A contributor to *De Dageraad* (The Daybreak) over the signature, " Muricatus "; he has written important studies, entitled *Democratie en Wetenschap* (Democracy and Science), 1871, also wrote in *De Vrye Gedachte* (Freethought).

Fernau (Rudolf), Dr , German author of *Christianity and Practical Life,* Leipsic, 1868; *The Alpha and Omega of Reason,* Leipsic, 1870; *Zoologica Humoristica,* 1882; and a recent work on *Religion as Ghost and God Worship.*

Feron (Emile), Belgian advocate, b. Brussels, 11 July, 1841. Councillor of the International Freethought Federation.

Ferrari (Giuseppe), Italian philosopher, b. Milan 7 March,

1811 A disciple of Romagnosi, a study of whose philosophical writings he published '35. He also published the works of Vico, and in '39 a work entitled *Vico and Italy*, and in the following year another on the *Religious Opinions of Campanella*. Attacked by the Catholic party, he was exiled, living in Paris, where he became a collaborator with Proudhon and a contributor to the *Revue de Deux Mondes*. In '42 he was made Professor of Philosophy at Strasbourg, but appointment was soon cancelled on account of his opinions. He wrote a *History of the Revolution of Italy*, '55, and a work on *China and Europe*. His history of the *Reason of the State*, '60, is his most pronounced work In '59, he was elected to the Italian Parliament, where he remained one of the most radical members until his death at Rome 1 July, 1876.

Ferri (Enrico), Member of the Italian Parliament, formerly professor of criminal law at the University of Siena, studied at Mantua under Professor Ardigo. Has written a large work on the Non-Existence of Free Will, and is with Professor Lombroso, leader of the new Italian school of criminal law reform.

Ferri (Luigi), Italian philosopher, b. Bologna, 15 June 1826 Studied in Paris and became licentiate of letters in 1850. Author of *History of Philosophy in Italy*, Paris 1868 ; *The Psychology of Pomponazzi.* etc.

Ferriere (Emile), French writer and licentiate of letters, b. Paris, 1830 ; author of *Literature and Philosophy*, 1865 ; *Darwinism*, 1872, which has gone through several editions ; *The Apostles*, a work challenging early Christian Morality, 1879 ; *The Soul the Function of the Brain*, a scientific work of popular character in two vols., 1883 ; and *Paganism of the Hebrews until the Babylonian Captivity*, 1884. All these are works of pronounced Freethought. M. Ferrière has also announced a work *Jesus bar Joseph*.

Feuerbach (Friedrich Heinrich), son of a famous German jurist, was b. at Ansbach 29 Sept. 1806. He studied philology, but set himself to preach what his brother Ludwig taught. He wrote *Theanthropos*, a series of Aphorisms (Zurich, '38), and an able work on the *Religion of the Future*, '43-47 ; and *Thoughts and Facts*, Hamburg, '62. Died Nurenberg, 24 Jan. 1880.

Feuerbach (Ludwig Andreas), brother of the preceding, b. Landshut, Bavaria, 28 July 1804. He studied theology with a view to the Church, but under the influence of Hegel abandoned it for philosophy. In '28 he was made professor at Erlangen, but was dismissed in consequence of his first published work, *Thoughts upon Death and Immortality*, '30, in which he limited immortality to personal influence on the human race. After a wandering life he married in '37, and settled near Anspach. He published there a history of modern philosophy from Bacon to Spinoza. This was followed by a work on Peter Bayle. In '38 he wrote on philosophy and Christianity, and in '41 his work called the *The Essence of Christianity*, in which he resolves theology into anthropology. This book was translated by Mary Ann Evans, '53. He also wrote *Principles of the Philosophy of the Future*. After the revolution of '48 he was invited to lecture by the students of Heidelberg, and gave his course on *The Essence of Religion*, published in '51. In '57 he published *Theogony from the Sources of Classical, Hebrew, and Christian Antiquity*, and in '66 *Theism, Freedom, and Immortality from the Standpoint of Anthropology*. Died at Rechenberg, near Nurenberg, 13 Sept. 1872. His complete works were published at Leipsic in 1876. He was a deep thinker and lucid writer.

Fichte (Johann Gottlieb), one of the greatest German thinkers, b. 19 May, 1762. He studied at the Universities of Jena, Leipsic, and Wittenberg, embraced "determinism," became acquainted with Kant, and published anonymously, *A Criticism of all Revelation*. He obtained a chair of philosophy at Jena, where he developed his doctrines of science, asserting that the problem of philosophy is to seek on what foundations knowledge rests. He gave moral discourses in the lecture-room on Sunday, and was accused of holding atheistical opinions. He was in consequence banished from Saxony, 1799. He appears to have held that God was not a personal being, but a system of intellectual, moral, and spiritual laws. Fichte took deep interest in the cause of German independence, and did much to rouse his countrymen against the domination of the French during the conquest which led to the fall of Napoleon. Besides many publications, in which he expounds his philosophy, he wrote eloquent treatises on *The Vocation of Man, The Nature* *and Vocation of the Scholar, The Way Towards the Blessed Life,* etc. Died Berlin 27 Jan. 1814.

"Figaro." See LARRA (Mariano José de).

Figuiera (Guillem), Provençal troubadour and precursor of the Renaissance, b. Toulouse about 1190. His poems were directed against the priests and Court of Rome.

Filangieri (Gaetano), an Italian writer on legislation, b. Naples, 18 Aug. 1752. He was professor at that city. His principal work is *La Scienza della Legislazione,* 1780. In the fifth volume he deals with pre-Christian religions. The work was put on the *Index.* Died 21 July, 1788.

Fiorentino (Francesco), Italian philosopher, b. Sambiasa, Nicastro, 1 May, 1834. In 1860 he became Professor of Philosophy at Spoletto, in '62 at Bologna, and in '71 at Naples. He was elected deputy to Parliament, Nov. '70. A disciple of Felice Tocco, he paid special attention to the early Italian Freethinkers, writing upon *The Pantheism of Giordano Bruno,* Naples, '61; Pietro Pomponazzi, Florence, '68; Bernardius Telesio, Florence, 2 vols., '72–74. He has also written on Strauss and Spinoza. In the *Nuova Antologia* he wrote on J. C. Vanini, and on Cæsalpinus, Campanella, and Bruno. A friend of Bertrando Spaventa, he succeeded to his chair at Naples in '83. Died 22 Dec. 1884.

Fischart (Johann), German satirist called *Mentzer,* b. Strasbourg about 1545. His satires in prose and verse remind one of Rabelais, whom he in part translated, and are often directed against the Church. Died at Forbach in 1614.

Fischer (J. C.), German materialist, author of a work on the freedom of the will 1858, a criticism of Hartmann's *Philosophy of the Unconscious,* '72; *Das Bewusstsein,* '74. Died 1888.

Fischer (Kuno), German philosopher, b. 23 July, 1824, at Sandewald, Silesia. Educated at Leipsic and Halle, in 1856 he was appointed Professor of Philosophy at Jena. His chief works are *History of Modern Philosophy,* '52-72; *Life and Character of Spinoza; Francis Bacon,* '56; and *Lessing,* '81.

Fiske (John), American author, b. Hartford, Connecticut, 30 March, 1842. Graduated at Harvard, '63. In '69-71 was Lecturer on Philosophy at that University, and from '72-9

Librarian.   Mr. Fiske has lectured largely, and has written *Myths and Mythmakers*, '72 ; *Outlines of Cosmic Philosophy*, 2 vols. '74 ; *Darwinism, and other essays*, '79 ; *Excursions of an Evolutionist*, '83 ; *The Idea of God as Affected by Modern Knowledge*, '85.

Flaubert (Gustave), French novelist, b. Rouen, 12 Dec. 1821. The son of a distinguished surgeon, he abandoned his father's profession for literature.   His masterpiece, *Madame Bovary*, published in '56 in the *Revue de Paris*, drew a prosecution upon that journal which ended in a triumph for the author.   For his next great work, *Salammbô*, '62, an epic of Carthage, he prepared himself by long antiquarian studies.   His intellectual tendencies are displayed in *The Temptation of Saint Anthony*. He stands eminent among the naturalist school for his artistic fidelity.   He was a friend of Théophile Gautier, Ivan Turgenev, Emile Zola and " George Sand."   His correspondence with the last of these has been published.   He distinctly states t'erein that on subjects like immortality men cheat themselves with words.   Died at Rouen, 9 May, 1880.

Flourens (Marie Jean Pierre), French scientist, b. near Béziers, 15 April, 1794.   In 1828 he was admitted into the Academy of Sciences, after having published a work on the nervous system of vertebrates ; he became perpetual secretary in '33.   A work on *Human Longevity and the Quantity of Life on the Globe* was very popular.   Died near Paris, 6 Dec. 1867.

Flourens (Gustave), eldest son of the preceding, b. Paris, 4 Aug. 1838.   In '63 he took his father's chair at the College of France, and his course on " Ethnography " attracted much attention.   In the following year he published his work on *The Science of Man*.   His bold heresy lost him his chair, and he collaborated on Larousse's *Grand Dictionnaire*.   In '65 he left France for Crete, where for three years he fought in the mountains against the Turkish troops.   Upon his return he was arrested for presiding at a political meeting.   He showed himself an ardent Revolutionist, and was killed in a skirmish near Nanterre, 3 April, 1871.

Fonblanque (Albany William), English journalist, b. London, 1793 ; the son of an eminent lawyer.   In 1820 he was on the staff of the *Times*, and contributed to the *Westminster Review*. In '30 he became editor of the *Examiner*, and retained his post until '47. His caustic wit and literary attainments did much to forward advanced liberal views. A selection of his editorials was published under the title, *England under Seven Administrations*. Died 13 Oct. 1872.

Fontanier (Jean), French writer, who was burnt at the Place de Grève, 1621, for blasphemies in a book entitled *Le Tresor Inestimable*. Garasse, with little reason, calls him an Atheist.

Fontenelle (Bernard LE BOVIER DE), nephew of Corneille. called by Voltaire the most universal genius of the reign of Louis XIV., b. Rouen. 11 Feb. 1657. Dedicated to the Virgin and St. Bernard, he was educated at the Jesuits' College. He went to Paris in 1671; wrote some plays and *Dialogues of the Dead*, 1683. In 1686 appeared his *Conversations on the Plurality of Worlds*, and in the following year his *History of Oracles*, based on the work of Van Dale, for which he was warmly attacked by the Jesuit Baltus, as impugning the Church Fathers. He was made secretary to the Academy of Sciences in 1699, a post he held forty-two years. He wrote *Doubts on the Physical System of Occasional Causes*, and is also credited with a letter on the *Resurrection of the Body*, a piece on *The Infinite*, and a *Treatise on Liberty*; "but, says l'Abbé Ladvocat, "as these books contain many things contrary to religion, it is to be hoped they are not his." Fontenelle nearly reached the age of one hundred. A short time before he died (9 Jan. 1757), being asked if he felt any pain, "I only feel,' he replied, "a difficulty of existing."

Foote (George William), writer and orator, b. Plymouth, 11 Jan. 1850. Was "converted" in youth, but became a Freethinker by reading and independent thought. Came to London in 1868, and was soon a leading member of the Young Men's Secular Association. He taught in the Hall of Science Sunday School, and became secretary of the Republican League. Devoting his time to propagating his principles, he wrote in the *Secular Chronicle* and *National Reformer*, and in '76 started the *Secularist* in conjunction with Mr. G. J. Holyoake, and after the ninth number conducting it alone. This afterwards merged in the *Secular Review*. In '79 Mr. Foote edited the *Liberal*, and in Sept. '81, started the *Freethinker*, which he still edits. In the following year a prosecution was commenced by the Public Prosecutor, who attempted to connect Mr. Bradlaugh with it. Undaunted, Mr. Foote issued a Christmas number with an illustrated "Comic Life of Christ." For this a prosecution was started by the City authorities against him and his publisher and printer, and the trial came on first in March, '83. The jury disagreed, but Judge North refused to discharge the prisoners, and they were tried again on the 5th March; Judge North directing that a verdict of guilty must be returned, and sentencing Mr. Foote to one year's imprisonment as an ordinary criminal subject to the same "discipline" as burglars. "I thank you, my lord; your sentence is worthy of your creed," he remarked. On 24 April, '83, Mr. Foote was brought from prison before Lord Coleridge and a special jury on the first charge, and after a splendid defence, upon which he was highly complimented by the judge, the jury disagreed. He has debated with Dr. McCann, Rev. A. J. Harrison, the Rev. W. Howard, the Rev. H. Chapman, and others. Mr. Foote has written much, and lectures continually. Among his works we mention *Heroes and Martyrs of Freethought* (1876); *God, the Soul, and a Future State; Secularism the True Philosophy of Life* (1879); *Atheism and Morality; The Futility of Prayer; Bible Romances; Death's Test*, afterwards enlarged into *Infidel Death-Beds; The God Christians Swear by; Was Jesus Insane? Blasphemy No Crime; Arrows of Freethought; Prisoner for Blasphemy* (1884); *Letters to Jesus Christ; What Was Christ? Bible Heroes :* and has edited *The Bible Hand-book* with Mr. W. P. Ball, and the *Jewish Life of Christ* with the present writer, in conjunction with whom he has written *The Crimes of Christianity.* From 1883-87 he edited *Progress*, in which appeared many important articles from his pen. Mr. Foote is President of the London Secular Federation, and a Vice-President of the National Secular Society.

Fouillee (Alfred), French philosopher, b. La Pouëze, near Angers, 18 Oct. 1838. Has been teacher at several lyceums, notably at Bordeaux. He was crowned by the Academy of Moral Sciences for two works on the Philosophy of Plato and Socrates. Elected Professor of Philosophy at the Superior Normal School, Paris, he sustained a thesis at the Sorbonne on *Liberty and Determinism*, which was violently attacked by

133

the Catholics. This work has gone through several editions. M. Fouillée has also written an able *History of Philosophy*, 1875, *Contemporary Social Science*, and an important *Critique of Contemporary Moral Systems* (1883). He has written much in the *Revue des Deux Mondes*, and is considered, with Taine, Ribot, and Renan, the principal representative of French philosophy. His system is known as that of *idées-forces*, as he holds that ideas are themselves forces. His latest work expounds the views of M. Guyau.

Forberg (Friedrich Karl), German philosopher, b. Meuselwitz, 30 Aug. 1770, studied theology at Leipsic, and became private docent at Jena. Becoming attached to Fichte's philosophy, he wrote with Fichte in Niethammer's *Philosophical Journal* on "The Development of Religious Ideas," and an article on "The Ground of our Faith in Divine Providence," which brought on them a charge of Atheism, and the journal was confiscated by the Electorate of Saxony. Forberg held religion to consist in devotion to morality, and wrote *An Apology for Alleged Atheism*, 1799. In 1807 he became librarian at Coburg, and devoted himself to the classics, issuing a *Manuel d'Erotologie Classique*. Died Hildburghausen 1 Jan. 1848.

Forder (Robert), b. Yarmouth, 14 Oct. 1844. Coming to to Woolwich, he became known as a political and Freethought lecturer. He took part in the movement to save Plumstead Common from the enclosers, and was sent to trial for riotous proceedings, but was acquitted. In '77 he was appointed paid secretary to the National Secular Society, a post he has ever since occupied. During the imprisonment of Messrs. Foote, Ramsey, and Kemp, in '83, Mr. Forder undertook charge of the publishing business. He has lectured largely, and written some pamphlets.

Forlong (James George Roche). Major General, H.B.A., b. Lanarkshire, Scotland, Nov. 1824. Educated as an engineer, joined the Indian army '43, fought in the S. Mahrata campaign '45-6, and in the second Barmese war. On the annexation of Barma he became head of the Survey, Roads and canal branches. In '58-9 he travelled extensively through Egypt, Palestine, Turkey, Greece, Italy, Spain, etc. From '61-71 was a superintending engineer of Calcutta, and in Upper Bengal,

North-west Provinces, and Rajputana, and '72-76 was Secretary and Chief Engineer to the Government of Oudh, He retired in '77 after an active service of 33 years, during which he frequently received the thanks of the Indian and Home Governments. In his youth he was an active Evangelical, preaching to the natives in their own tongues. He has, however, given his testimony that during his long experience he has known no one converted solely by force of reasoning or " Christian evidences." A great student of Eastern religions, archæology, and languages, he has written in various periodicals of the East and West, and has embodied the result of many years researches in two illustrated quarto volumes called *Rivers of Life*, setting forth the evolution of all religions from their radical objective basis to their present spiritualised developments. In an elaborate chart he shows by streams of color the movements of thought from 10,000 B.C. to the present time.

Fourier (François Marie Charles), French socialist, b. Besançon, 7 April, 1772. He passed some of the early years of his life as a common soldier. His numerous works amid much that is visionary have valuable criticisms upon society, and suggestions for its amelioration. He believed in the transmigration of souls. Died at Paris, 8 Oct. 1837.

Fox (William Johnson), orator and political writer, b. near Wrentham, Suffolk, 1786. Intended for the Congregational Ministry, he became a Unitarian, and for many years preached at South Place, Finsbury, where he introduced the plan of taking texts from other books besides the Bible. One of his first published sermons was on behalf of toleration for Deists at the time of the Carlile prosecutions 1819. He gradually advanced from the acceptance of miracles to their complete rejection. During the Anti-Corn Law agitation he was a frequent and able speaker. In 1847 he became M.P. for Oldham, and retained his seat until his retirement in '61. He was a prominent worker for Radicalism, contributing to the *Westminster Review*, *Weekly Dispatch*, and *Daily News*. For some years he edited the *Monthly Repository*. His works, which include spirited *Lectures to the Working Classes*, and a philosophical statement of *Religious Ideas*, were published in twelve volumes, '65–68. Died 3 June, 1864.

"**Franchi** (Ausonio)," the pen name of Francesco Cristoforo Bonavino, Italian ex-priest, b. Pegli, 24 Feb. 1821. Brought up in the Church and ordained priest in '44, the practice of the confessional made him sceptical and he quitted it for philosophy, having ceased to believe in its dogmas, '49. In '52 he published his principle work, entitled *The Philosophy of the Italian Schools*. The following year he published *The Religion of the Nineteenth Century*. He established *La Razione* (Reason) and *Il Libero Pensiero* at Turin, '51–57; wrote on the *Rationalism of the People*, Geneva, '56, and became an active organiser of anti-clerical societies. In '66 he published a criticism of Positivism, and has since written *Critical and Polemical Essays*, 3 vols. Milan, '70–72. In '68 was appointed Professor of Philosophy in the Academy of Milan by Terenzio Mamiani.

Francis (Samuel), M.D., author of *Watson Refuted*, published by Carlile, 1819.

Francois de Neufchateau (Nicolas Louis), *Count*, French statesman, poet, and academician b. Lorraine, 17 April, 1750. In his youth he became secretary to Voltaire, who regarded him as his successor. He favored the Revolution, and was elected to the Legislative Assembly in '91. As Member of the Directory, '97, he circulated d'Holbach's *Contagion Sacrée*. He became President of the Senate, '14–16. He wrote numerous pieces. Died at Paris 10 Jan. 1828.

Franklin (Benjamin), American patriot and philosopher, b. Boston 17 Jan. 1706. He was apprenticed to his uncle as a printer, came to England and worked at his trade '24–26; returned to Philadelphia, where he published a paper and became known by his *Poor Richard's Almanack*. He founded the public library at Philadelphia, and made the discovery of the identity of lightning with the electric fluid. He became member of the Provincial Assembly and was sent to England as agent. When examined before the House of Commons he spoke boldly against the Stamp Act. He was active during the war with this country, and was elected member of Congress. Became envoy to France, and effected the treaty of alliance with that country, 6 Feb. '78, which secured the independence of the American colonies. Turgot summed up his services in the fine line *Eripuit cœlo fulmen, sceptrumque tyrannis*. " He wrested the thunderbolt from heaven and the sceptre from kings." Died at Philadelphia, 17 April, 1790.

Fransham (John), a native of Norwich, b. 1730. Became a teacher of mathematics, renounced the Christian religion, and professed Paganism, writing several treatises in favor of disbelief. Died 1810.

Frauenstaedt (Christian Martin Julius), Dr., philosopher and disciple of Schopenhauer, b. 17 April, 1813, at Bojanowo, Posen. He studied philosophy and theology at Berlin, but meeting Schopenhauer at Frankfort in '47 he adopted the views of the pessimist, who made him his literary executor. Among Frauenstädt's works are *Letters on Natural Religion*, '58, *The Liberty of Men and the Personality of God*, '38; *Letters on the Philosophy of Schopenhauer*, '54, etc. Died at Berlin, 13 Jan. 1879.

Frederick II. (Emperor of Germany), the greatest man of the thirteenth century and founder of the Renaissance, b. 26 Dec. 1194. Was elected to the throne in 1210. He promoted learning, science, and art, founded the Universities of Vienna and Naples, had the works of Aristotle and Averroes translated, and was the patron of all the able men of his time. For his resistance to the tyranny of the Church he was twice excommunicated. He answered by a letter attacking the Pope (Gregory IX.), whom he expelled from Rome in '28. He made a treaty with the Sultan of Egypt, by which he became master of Jerusalem. For some heretical words in his letter, in which he associates the names of Christ, Moses, and Mohammed, he was reported author of the famous work *De Tribus Impostoribus*. He addressed a series of philosophical questions to Ibn Sabin, a Moslem doctor. He is said to have called the Eucharist *truffa ista*, and is credited also with the saying "Ignorance is the mother of devotion." Died at Florence, 13 Dec. 1250.

Frederick the Great (King of Prussia), b. 21 Jan. 1712, was educated in a very rigid fashion by his father, Frederick William I. He ascended the throne and soon displayed his political and military ability. By a war with Austria he acquired Silesia. He wrote several deistical pieces, and tolerated all religions and no religion saying "every man must get to heaven his own way." He attracted to his court

137

men like Lamettrie, D'Argens, Maupertuis, and Voltaire, who, says Carlyle, continued all his days Friedrich's chief thinker. In 1756 France, Austria, Sweden, and Russia united against him, but he held his own against "a world in arms." After a most active life Frederick died at Potsdam, 17 Aug. 1786. The *Philosophical Breviary* attributed to him was really written by Cérutti.

Fredin (Nils Edvard), Swedish writer, b. 1857. Has published translation of modern poets, and also of Col. Ingersoll's writings. In '80 he was awarded first prize by the Swedish Academy for an original poem.

Freeke (William), b. about 1663, wrote *A Brief but Clear Confutation of the Trinity*, which being brought before the notice of the House of Lords it was on 3 Jan. 1693 ordered to be burnt by the common hangman, and the author being prosecuted by the Attorney General was fined £500.

Freiligrath (Ferdinand) German poet, b, Detmold 17 June, 1810. In '35 he acquired notice by some poems. In '44 he published his profession of faith *Mein Glaubensbekenntniss*, and was forced to fly the country. In '48 he returned and joined Karl Marx on the *Neue Rheinische Zeitung*. Again prosecuted he took refuge in London, devoting his leisure to poetry and translation. Freiligrath holds a high place among the poets of his time. Died Kannstadt, near Stuttgart, 18 March 1876.

Freret (Nicolas), French historical critic, b. 15 Feb. 1688. He was a pupil of Rollin, and was patronised by Boulainvilliers. Distinguished by his attainments in ancient history, philosophy and chronology, he became member of the Academy of Inscriptions 1714. For a Discourse on the "Origin of the Franks," he was incarcerated for four months in the Bastille. While here he read Bayle so often that he could repeat much from memory. He was an unbeliever, and the author of the atheistic *Letters from Thrasybulus to Leucippe* on Natural and Revealed Religion, and perhaps of *La Moïsade*, a criticism of the Pentateuch, translated by D. I. Eaton, as *A Preservative against Religious Prejudices*. The *Letters to Eugenie*, attributed to Fréret, were written by D'Holbach, and the *Critical Examination of the Apologists of the Christian Religion* by J. Levesque de

138

Burigny. *A Critical Examination of the New Testament*, 1777
which long circulated in MS. has also been wrongly attributed
to Fréret. Died at Paris, 8 March, 1749.

Frey (William), the adopted name of a Russian Positivist
and philanthropist, b. of noble family, the son of a general,
1839. Educated at the higher military school, St. Petersburg,
he became teacher in a Government High School, and disgusted with the oppression and degradation of his country he
went to New York in 1866 where he established co-operative
communities and also Russian colonies in Kansas and Oregon.
In 1881 he came to London in order to influence his countrymen. In '87 he revisited Russia. Died 6 Nov. 1888.

Fries (Jacob Friedrich), German philosopher, b. Barby, 23
Aug. 1773. Brought up as a Moravian, he became a Deist.
Fries is of the Neo-Kantian rationalistic school. Among his
writings are a *System of Metaphysics*, 1824 ; a *Manual of the Philosophy of Religion and Philosophical Æsthetics*, Heidelberg '32 ; in
which he resolves religion into poetry. He criticised Kant's
proofs of God and immortality, and wrote a *History of Philosophy*.
Died Jena, 10 Aug. 1843.

Frothingham (Octavius Brooks), American author, b. Boston,
26 Nov. 1822. Graduated at Harvard, '43, and became Unitarian
minister. In '60 he became pastor of the most radical Unitarian
congregation in New York. In '67 he became first president of
the Free Religious Association, but, becoming too advanced,
resigned in '79 and came to Europe. Since his return to Boston,
'81, he has devoted himself to literature. He has published
The Religion of Humanity, N.Y., '73 ; *Life of Theodore Parker*,
'74 ; *The Cradle of the Christ*, '77 ; *Life of Gerrit Smith*, 78 ; and
numerous sermons.

Froude (James Anthony), man of letters and historian, the
son of an Archdeacon of Totnes, was b. Dartington, Devon, 23
April, 1818, and educated at Westminster and Oxford, where he
took his degree in '40, was elected fellow of Exeter College
and received deacon's orders. At first, under the influence of
the Romanising movement, he became a rationalist and
abandoned his fellowship and clerical life. His *Nemesis of Faith*,
'48, showed the nature of his objections. Mr. Froude devoted

his abilities to a literary career, and fell under the influence of Carlyle. For many years he edited *Fraser's Magazine*, in which he wrote largely. His essays are collected under the title of *Short Studies on Great Subjects*, '71-83. His largest work is the *History of England*, from the Fall of Wolsey to the Defeat of the Spanish Armada, '56-76. His *Life of Carlyle*, '82, and publication of *Carlyle's Reminiscenses* provoked much controversy. His magical translation of Lucian's most characteristic Dialogue of the Gods is done with too much *verve* to allow of the supposition that the translator is not in sympathy with his author.

Fry (John), a colonel in the Parliamentary army. In 1640 he was elected one of the burgesses of Shaftesbury, but his return was declared void. After serving with distinction in the army, he was called to the House of Commons by the Independents in 1618. He voted for Charles I. being put on trial; and sat in judgment when sentence was passed on him. He was charged with blasphemy and wrote *The Accuser Shamed*, 1649, which was ordered to be burnt for speaking against "that chaffie and absurd opinion of three persons in the Godhead." He also wrote *The Clergy in their Colors*, 1650.

Fuller (Sarah Margaret), American authoress, b. Cambridgeport, Massachusetts, 23 May, 1810. In '40-42 she edited the *Dial*. She also published *Woman in the Nineteenth Century*, '44. Among friends she counted Emerson, Hawthorne, Channing, and Mazzini. She visited Europe and married at Rome the Marquis D'Ossoli. Returning she was shipwrecked and drowned off the coast of New Jersey, 16 July, 1850.

Furnemont (Léon), Belgian advocate, b. Charleroi, 17 April, 1861. Entered the school of Mines Liége in '76, and founded the *Circle of Progressive Students*. Became president of International Congress of Students, '84, and represented Young Belgium at the funeral of Victor Hugo. Radical candidate at the Brussels municipal elections, he obtained 3,500 votes, but was not elected. He is a Councillor of the International Federation of Freethinkers and director of a monthly journal, *La Raison*, 1889.

Gabarro (Bartolomé) Dr., Spanish writer, b. Ygualade, Barcelona, 27 Sept. 1846, was educated in a clerical college with a view to taking the clerical habit, he refused and went to America. After travelling much, he established a day school in Barcelona and founded an Anti-clerical League of Free-thinkers pledged to live without priests. This induced much clerical whath, especially when Dr. Gabarro founded some 200 Anti-clerical groups and over 100 lay schools. For denouncing the assassins of a Freethinker he was pursued for libel, sentenced to four years' imprisonment, and forced to fly to Cerbere on the frontier, where he continues his anti-clerical journal *La Tronada*. He has written many anti-clerical brochures and an important work on Pius IX. and History.

Gabelli (Aristide), Italian writer, b. Belluno, 22 March, 1830. Author of *The Religious Question in Italy*, '64, *Man and the Moral Sciences*, '69, in which he rejects all metaphysics and super-naturalism, and *Thoughts*, 1886.

Gage (Matilda Joslyn), American reformer, b. Cicero, New York, 24 March, 1826. Her father, Dr. H. Joslyn, was an active abolitionist. Educated at De Peyster and Hamilton, N.Y., in '45 she married Henry H. Gage. From '52 till '61 she wrote and spoke against slavery. In '72 she was made President of the National Woman's Suffrage Association. She is joint author of *The History of Woman Suffrage* with Miss Anthony and Mrs. Stanton, and with them considers the Church the great obstacle to woman's progress.

Gagern (Carlos von), b. Rehdorf, Neumark, 12 Dec. 1826. Educated at Berlin, travelled in '47 to Paris where he became acquainted with Humboldt. He went to Spain and studied Basque life in the Pyrenees; served in the Prussian army, became a friend of Wislicenus and the free-religious movement. In '52 he went to Mexico; here he had an appointment under General Miramon. In the French-Mexican expedition he was taken prisoner in '63; released in '65 he went to New York. He was afterwards military attaché for Mexico at Berlin. His freethought appears in his memoirs entitled *Dead and Living*, 1884, and in his volume *Sword and Trowel*, 1888. Died Madrid 19 Dec. 1885.

Gall (Franz Joseph), founder of phrenology, b. Baden, 6 March, 1758. He practised as a physician in Vienna, devoting much time to the study of the brain, and began to lecture on craniology in that city. In 1802 he was prohibited from lecturing. He joined Dr. Spurzheim and they taught their system in various cities of Europe. Died at Paris, 22 Aug. 1828.

Galton (Francis), grandson of Erasmus Darwin, was born in 1822. Educated at Birmingham, he studied medicine at King's College, London, and graduated at Cambridge, '24. In '48 and '50 he travelled in Africa. He wrote a popular *Art of Travel*, and has distinguished himself by many writings bearing on heredity, of which we name *Hereditary Genius*, '69, *English Men of Science*, '70. In his *Inquiries into Human Faculty and Development*, '83, he gives statistical refutation of the theory of prayer. Mr. Galton was Secretary of the British Association from '63–68, President of the Geographical Section in '62 and '72, and of the Anthropological Section in '77 and '85. He is President of the Anthropological Institute.

Gambetta (Léon Michel), French orator and statesman, b. Cahors, 30 Oct. 1838. His uncle was a priest and his father wished him to become one. Educated at a clerical seminary, he decided to study for the law. In '59 he was enrolled at the bar. His defence of Delescluze (14 Nov. 1868), in which he vigorously attacked the Empire, made him famous. Elected to the Assembly by both Paris and Marseilles, he became the life and leader of the Opposition. After Sedan he proclaimed the Republic and organised the national defences, leaving Paris, then invested by the Germans, in a balloon. From Tours he invigorated every department, and was the inspiration of the few successes won by the French. Gambetta preserved the Republic against all machinations, and compelled Mac-Mahon to accept the second of the alternatives, "*Se soumettre ou se demettre.*" He founded the *Republique Française*, and became President of the Chamber. Gambetta was a professed disciple of Voltaire, an admirer of Comte, and an open opponent of clericalism. All the members of his Cabinet were Freethinkers. Died 31 Dec. 1882. His public secular funeral was one of the largest gatherings ever witnessed.

Gambon (Ferdinand Charles), French Communist, b. Bourges, 19 March, 1820. In 1839 he became an Advocate, and he founded the *Journal des Ecoles*. In '48 he was elected representative. The Empire drove him into exile, he returned at amnesty of '59. In '69 he refused to pay taxes. In '71 was elected deputy at Paris, and was one of the last defenders of the Commune. Imprisoned, he was released in '82. Formed a League for abolishing standing army. Died 17 Sept. 1887.

Garat (Dominique Joseph), Count, French revolutionist. orator and writer, b. near Bayonne, 8 September, 1749. He became a friend of d'Alembert, Diderot and Condercet, and in 1789 was elected to the Assembly, where he spoke in favor of the abolition of religion. As minister of justice he had to notify to Louis XVI his condemnation. He afterwards taught at the Normal School, and became a senator, count, and president of the Institute. Died at Urdains 9 December, 1833.

Garborg (Arne), b. Western Coast of Norway, 25 Jan. 1851, Brought up as a teacher at the public schools, he entered the University of Christiania in 1875. Founded a weekly paper *Fedraheimen*, written in the dialect of the peasantry. Held an appointment for some years in the Government Audit Office. In '81 he published a powerfully written tale, *A Freethinker*, which created a deal of attention. Since he has published *Peasant Students, Tales and Legends, Youth, Men*, etc, He is one of the wittiest and cleverest controversialists on the Norwegian press.

Garcia-Vao (Antonio Rodriguez), Spanish poet and miscellaneous writer, b. Manzanares, 1862. Educated at the institute of Cardinal Cisneros, where he made brilliant studies. He afterwards studied at the Madrid University and became a lawyer. After editing several papers, he attached himself to the staff of *Las Dominicales del Libre Pensiamento*. Among his numerous works are a volume of poems, *Echoes of a Free Mind, Love and the Monks*, a satire, a study of Greco-Roman philosophy, etc. This promising student was stabbed in the back at Madrid, 18 December, 1886.

Garde (Jehan de la), bookseller, burnt together with four little blasphemous books at Paris in 1537.

Garibaldi (Guiseppe), Italian patriot and general, b. Nice, 4 July, 1807. His father, a small shipmaster, hoped he would become a priest. Young Garibaldi objected, preferring a sailor's life. A trip to Rome made him long to free his country. He joined Mazzini's movement, "Young Italy," and being implicated in the Genoese revolt of '33, he fled at risk of his life to Marseilles, where he learnt he was sentenced to death. He went to South America and fought on behalf of the republic of Uruguay. Here he met Anita Rivera, his beautiful and brave wife, who accompanied him in numerous adventures. Returning to Italy he fought against the Austrians in '48, and next year was the soul of resistance to the French troops, who came to restore Papal authority. Garibaldi had to retire; his wife died, and he escaped with difficulty to Genoa, whence he went to New York, working for an Italian soap and candle-maker at Staten Island. In '54 he returned and bought a farm on the isle of Caprera. In '59 he again fought the Austrians, and in May, '60, landed at Marsala, Sicily, took Palermo, and drove Francis II. from Naples. Though a Republican he saluted Victor Emanuel as King of Italy. Vexed by the cessation of Nice to France, he marched to Rome, but was wounded by Victor Emanuel's troops, and taken prisoner to Varignaro. Here he wrote his *Rule of the Monk*, a work exhibiting his love of liberty and hatred of the priesthood. In '64 he visited England, and was enthusiastically received. In '67 he again took part in an attempt to free Rome from the Papal government. In '71 he placed his sword at the service of the French Republic, and the only standard taken from the Germans was captured by his men. Elected Member of the Italian Parliament in his later years he did much to improve the city of Rome. In one of his laconic letters of '80, he says "Dear Friend,—Man has created God, not God man,—Yours ever, Garibaldi." He died 2 June, '82, and directed in his will that he should be cremated without any religious ceremony.

Garrison (H. D.), Dr. of Chicago. Author of an able pamphlet on *The Absence of Design in Nature*, 1876.

Garth (Sir Samuel), English poet, wit, and physician, b. Yorkshire, 1672, and educated at Cambridge. He helped to establish dispensaries, and lashed the opposition in his poem *The Dispensary*. He was made physician to King George I Died 18 June 1719.

Gaston (H.), French author of a brochure with the title *Dieu, voila, l'ennemi*, God the enemy, 1882.

Gattina (F. P. della). See Petrucelli.

Gautama (called also GOTAMA, BUDDHA, and SAKYAMUNI), great Hindu reformer and founder of Buddhism, b. Kapilavastu, 624 B.C. Many legends are told of his birth and life. He is said to have been a prince, who, pained with human misery. left his home to dedicate himself to emancipation. His system was rather a moral discipline than a religion. Though he did not deny the Hindu gods he asserted that all beings were subject to "Karma," the result of previous actions. He said, 'If a man for a hundred years worship Agni in the forest, and if he but for one moment pay homage to a man whose soul is grounded in true knowledge, better is that homage than sacrifice for a hundred years." According to Ceylonese writers Gautama Buddha died at Kusinagara, B.C. 543.

Gautier (Théophile), exquisite French poet and prose writer, b. Tarbes, 31 Aug. 1811. He wrote no definite work against priestcraft or superstition, but the whole tendency of his writings is Pagan. His romanticism is not Christian, and he made merry with "sacred themes" as well as conventional morality. Baudelaire called him an impeccable master of French literature, and Balzac said that of the two men who could write French, one was Théophile Gautier. Died 22 Oct. 1872.

Geijer (Erik Gustaf), eminent Swedish historian, poet, and critic, b. Wermland, 12 Jan. 1783. At the age of 20 he was awarded the Swedish Academy s first prize for a patriotical poem. At first a Conservative in religious, philosophical, and political matters he became through his historical researches an ardent adherent of the principles of the French revolution. His historical work and indictment against "The Protestant creed" was published in 1820 in a philosophical treatise, *Thorild*, which was prosecuted. His acquittal by an enlightened jury stayed religious prosecutions in Sweden for over sixty years. He died 23 April 1847. A monument was erected to him last year at the University of Upsala, where he was professor of history. His works have been republished.

Geijerstam (Gustaf), Swedish novelist, b. 1858. Is one of the Freethinking group of *Young Sweden.*

Geismar (Martin von), editor of a Library of German Rationalists of the eighteenth century, in five parts, including some of the works of Bahrdt, Eberhardt, Knoblauch, etc, 1846-7. He also added pamphlets entitled *Germany in the Eighteenth Century.*

Gellion-Danglar (Eugène), French writer, b. Paris, 1829 Became Professor of Languages at Cairo, wrote in *La Pensée Nouvelle.* was made sous préfect of Compiègne, '71, wrote *History of the Revolution of* 1830, and *A Study of the Semites,* '82.

Gemistos (Georgios), surnamed Plethon, a philosophic reviver of Pagan learning, b. of noble parents at Byzantium about 1355. He early lost his faith in Christianity, and was attracted to the Moslem court at Brusa. He went to Italy in the train of John Palælogus in 1438, where he attracted much attention to the Platonic philosophy, by which he sought to reform the religious, political and moral life of the time. Gennadius, the patriarch of Constantinople, roundly accused him of Paganism. Died 1450.

Genard (François), French satirist, b. Paris about 1722. He wrote an irreligious work called *A Parallel of the Portraits of the Age, with the Pictures of the Holy Scriptures,* for which he was placed in the Bastille, where it is believed he finished his days.

Gendre (Barbe), Russian writer in French, b. Cronstadt, 15 Dec. 1842. She was well educated at Kief, where she obtained a gold medal. By reading the works of Büchner, Buckle, and Darwin she became a Freethinker. Settling in Paris, she contributed to the *Revue Internationale des Sciences,* to *La Justice* and the *Nouvelle Revue,* etc. Some of her pieces have been reprinted under the title *Etudes Sociales* (Social Studies. Paris, 1886), edited by Dr. C. Letourneau. Died Dec. 1884.

Gener (Pompeyo), Spanish philosopher, b. Barcelona, 1849, is a member of the Society of Anthropology, and author of a study of the evolution of ideas entitled *Death and the Devil,* Paris, '80. This able work is dedicated to Renan and has a preface by Littré. The author has since translated it into Spanish.

Genestet (Petrus Augustus de), Dutch poet and Agnostic, b. Amsterdam, 21 Nov. 1829. He studied theology, and for some years was a Protestant minister. His verses show him to be a Freethinker. Died at Rozendaal, 2 July, 1861.

Genin (François), French philologist, b. Amiens, 16 Feb. 1803. He became one of the editors of the *National*, of Paris, about '37, and wrote for it spirited articles against the Jesuits. He published works on *The Jesuits and the Universities, The Church or the State*, etc. In '45 the French Academy awarded a prize to his *Lexicon of the Language of Molière*. He edited Diderot, '47, and is known for his researches into the origin of the French language and literature. Died Paris, 20 Dec. 1856.

Genovesi (Antonio), Italian philosopher, b. Castiglione, 1 Nov. 1712. He read lectures in philosophy at Naples, but by his substitution of doubt for traditional belief he drew upon himself many attacks from the clergy. The book by which he is best known is his *Italian Morality*. Died at Naples, 20 Sept. 1769.

Gensonne (Armand), French lawyer and one of the leaders of the Girondists, b. Bordeaux, 10 Aug. 1758. He was, elected to the Legislative Assembly in 1791, and to the Convention in 1792. In the struggle with the Jacobins, Gensonné was one of the most active and eloquent champions of his party. He was executed with his colleagues 31 Oct. 1793.

Gentilis (Giovanni Valentino), Italian heretic, b. Consenza, Naples, about 1520. He fled to avoid persecution to Geneva, where in 1558 he was thrown into prison at the instigation of Calvin. Fear of sharing the fate of Servetus made him recant. He wandered to Poland, where he joined Alciati and Biandrata, but he was banished for his innovations. Upon the death of Calvin he returned to Switzerland, where he was arrested for heresy, 11 June, 1566. After a long trial he was condemned for attacking the Trinity, and beheaded at Berne, 26 (?) Sept. 1566. *Ludvocat* says "He died very impiously, saying he thought himself honored in being martyred for the glory of the Father, whereas the apostles and other martyrs only died for the glory of the Son."

147

Geoffrin (Marie Thérèse, neé RODET). a French lady distinguished as a patroness of learning and the fine arts, b. Paris, 2 June, 1699. She was a friend of Alembert, Voltaire, Marmontel, Montesquieu, Diderot, and the encyclopædists, and was noted for her benevolence. Died at Paris, 6 Oct. 1777.

Gerhard (H.), Dutch socialist, b. Delft, 11 June, 1829. Educated at an orphanage he became a tailor, travelled through France, Italy. and Switzerland, and in '61 returned to Amsterdam. He wrote for *De Dageraad*, and was correspondent of the *Internationale*. Died 5 July, 1886.

Gerhard (A. H.), son of foregoing, b. Lausanne, Switzerland, 7 April, 1858. Is headmaster of a public school, and one of the editors of *De Dageraad*.

Germond (J. B. L.), editor of Maréchal's *Dictionnaire des Athées*, Brussels, 1833.

Gertsen (Aleksandr Ivanovich). See Herzen.

Ghillany (Friedrich Wilhelm), German critic, b. at Erlangan, 18 April, 1807. In '35 he became Professor of History at Nurenberg. His principal work is on *Human Sacrifices among the Ancient Jews*, Nurnberg, '42. He also wrote on the Pagan and Christian writers of the first four centuries. Under the pseudonym of " Richard von der Alm " he wrote *Theological Letters*, 1862 ; *Jesus of Nazareth*, 1868 ; and a collection of the opinions of heathen and Jewish writers of the first four centuries upon Jesus and Christianity. Died 25 June, 1876.

Giannone (Pietro), Italian historian, b. Ischitella, Naples, 7 May, 1676. He devoted many years to a *History of the Kingdom of Naples*, in which he attacked the papal power. He was excommunicated and fled to Vienna, where he received a pension from the Emperor, which was removed on his avowal of heterdox opinions. He was driven from Austria and took refuge in Venice : here also was an Inquisition. Giannone was seized by night and cast before sunrise on the papal shore. He found means, however, of escaping to Geneva. Having been enticed into Savoy in 1736, he was arrested by order of the King of Sardinia, and confined in prison until his death, 7 March, 1748.

148

Gibbon (Edward), probably the greatest of historians, b. Putney, 27 April 1737. At Oxford he became a Romanist, but being sent to a Calvinist at Lausanne, was brought back to Protestantism. When visiting the ruins of the Capitol at Rome, he conceived the idea of writing the *Decline and Fall* of that empire. For twenty-two years before the appearance of his first volume he was a prodigy of arduous application, his investigations extending over the whole range of intellectual and political activity for nearly fifteen hundred years. His monumental work, bridging the old world and the new, is an historic exposure of the crimes and futility of Christianity. Gibbon was elected to Parliament in '74, but did not distinguish himself. He died of dropsy, in London, 16 Jan. 1794.

Gibson (Ellen Elvira), American lecturess, b. Winchenden, Mass. 8 May, 1821, and became a public school teacher. Study of the Bible brought her to the Freethought platform. At the outbreak of the American Civil War she organised Ladies' Soldiers' Aid Societies, and was elected chaplain to the 1st Wisconsin Volunteer Artillery. President Lincoln endorsed the appointment, which was questioned. She has written anonymously *Godly Women of the Bible*, and has contributed to the *Truthseeker, Boston Investigator*, and *Ironclad Age*, under her own signature and that of " Lilian."

Giessenburg (Rudolf Charles d'Ablaing van), one of the most notable of Dutch Freethinkers, b. of noble family, 26 April, 1826. An unbeliever in youth, in '47 he went to Batavia, and upon his return set up as a bookseller under the name of R. C. Meijer. With Junghuhn and Günst, he started *de Dageraad*, and from '56–68 was one of the contributors, usually under his name " Rudolf Charles." He is a man of great erudition, has written *Het verbond der vrije gedachte* (The Alliance of Freethought); *de Tydgenoot op het gebied der Rede* (The Contemporary in the Reign of Reason); *De Regtbank des Onderzoeks* (The Tribunal of Inquiry); *Zedekunde en Christendom* (Ethics and Christianity); *Curiosities van allerlei aard* (Curiosities of Various Kinds). He has also published the Religion and Philosophy of the Bible by W. J. Birch and Brooksbank's work on Revelation. He was the first who published a complete edition of the famous *Testament du Curé Jean Meslier* in three parts ('64), has published the works of Douwes Dekker and other writers, and also *Curieuse Gebruiken.*

Gilbert (Claude), French advocate, b. Dijon, 7 June, 1652. He had printed at Dijon, in 1700, *Histoire de Calejava, ou de l'isle des hommes raisonables, avec le paralelle de leur Morale et du Christianisme.* The book has neither the name of author or printer. It was suppressed, and only one copy escaped destruction, which was bought in 1784 by the Duc de La Vallière for 120 livres. It was in form of a dialogue (329 pp.), and attacked both Judaism and Christianity. Gilbert married in 1700, and died at Dijon 18 Feb. 1720.

Gill (Charles), b. Dublin, 8 Oct. 1824, was educated at the University of that city. In '83 he published anonymously a work on *The Evolution of Christianity.* It was quoted by Mr. Foote in his defences before Judge North and Lord Coleridge, and in the following year he put his name to a second edition. Mr. Gill has also written a pamphlet on the Blasphemy Laws, and has edited, with an introduction, Archbishop Laurence's *Book of Enoch,* 1883.

Giles (Rev. John Allen, D.Ph.), b. Mark, Somersetshire, 26 Oct. 1808. Educated at the Charterhouse and Oxford, where he graduated B.A. as a double first-class in '28. He was appointed head-master of the City of London School, which post he left for the Church. The author of over 150 volumes of educational works, including the *Keys to the Classics;* privately he was a confirmed Freethinker, intimate with Birch, Scott, etc. His works bearing on theology show his heresy, the principal being *Hebrew Records* 1850, *Christian Records* 1854. These two were published together in amended form in 1877. He also wrote *Codex Apocryphus Novi Testamenti* 1852, *Writings of the Early Christians of the Second Century* 1857, and *Apostolic Records,* published posthumously in 1886. Died 24 Sept 1884.

Ginguene (Pierre Louis), French historian b. Rennes, 25 April, 1748. Educated, with Parny, by Jesuits. At Paris he became a teacher, embraced the Revolution, wrote on Rousseau and Rabelais, and collaborated with Chamfort in the *Historic Pictures of the French Revolution.* Thrown into prison during the Terror, he escaped on the fall of Robespierre, and became Director of Public Instruction. His principal work is a *Literary History of Italy*. Died Paris, 11 Nov. 1816.

Gilliland (M. S.) Miss, b. Londonderry 1853, authoress of a little work on *The Future of Morality*, from the Agnostic standpoint, 1888.

Gioja (Melchiorre), Italian political economist, b. Piazenza, 20 Sept. 1767. He advocated republicanism, and was appointed head of a bureau of statistics. For his brochure *La Scienza del Povero Diavolo* he was expelled from Italy in 1809. He published works on *Merit and Rewards* and *The Philosophy of Statistics*. Died at Milan 2 Jan. 1829.

Girard (Stephen), American philanthropist, b. near Bordeaux France, 24 May, 1750. He sailed as cabin boy to the West Indies about 1760; rose to be master of a coasting vessel and earned enough to settle in business in Philadelphia in 1769. He became one of the richest merchants in America, and during the war of 1812 he took the whole of a Government loan of five million dollars. He called his vessels after the names of the philosophers Helvetius, Montesquieu, Voltaire, Rousseau, etc. He contributed liberally to all public improvements and radical movements. On his death he left large bequests to Philadelphia, the principal being a munificent endowment of a college for orphans. By a provision of his will, no ecclesiastic or minister of any sect whatever is to hold any connection with the college, or even be admitted to the premises as a visitor; but the officers of the institution are required to instruct the pupils in secular morality and leave them to adopt their own religious opinions. This will has been most shamefully perverted. Died Philadelphia, 26 Dec. 1831.

Glain (D. de Saint). See SAINT GLAIN.

Glennie (John Stuart Stuart), living English barrister and writer, author of *In the Morningland*, or the law of the origin and transformation of Christianity, 1873, the most important chapter of which was reprinted by Thomas Scott, under the title, *Christ and Osiris*. He has also written *Pilgrim Memories*, or travel and discussion in the birth-countries of Christianity with the late H. T. Buckle, 1875.

Glisson (Francis), English anatomist and physician, b.

Rampisham, Dorsetshire, 1597. He took his degree at Cambridge, and was there appointed Regius Professor of Physic, an office he held forty years. He discovered Glisson's capsule in the liver, and was the first to attribute irritability to muscular fibre. In his *Tractatus de natura substantiæ energetica,* 1672, he anticipates the natural school in considering matter endowed with native energy sufficient to account for the operations of nature. Dr. Glisson was eulogised by Harvey, and Boerhaave called him " the most accurate of all anatomists that ever lived." Died in 1677.

Godwin (Mary). See Wollstonecraft.

Godwin (William), English historian, political writer and novelist, b. Wisbeach, Cambridgeshire, 3 March, 1756. The son of a Dissenting minister, he was designed for the same calling. He studied at Hoxton College, and came out, as he entered, a Tory and Calvinist; but making the acquaintance of Holcroft, Paine, and the English Jacobins, his views developed from the Unitarianism of Priestley to the rejection of the supernatural. In '93 he published his republican work on *Political Justice.* In the following year he issued his powerful novel of *Caleb Williams.* He married Mary Wollstonecraft, '96; wrote, in addition to several novels and educational works, *On Population,* in answer to Malthus, 1820; a *History of the Commonwealth,* '24-28; *Thoughts on Man,* '31; *Lives of the Necromancers,* '34. Some Freethought essays, which he had intended to form into a book entitled *The Genius of Christianity Unveiled,* were first published in '73. They comprise papers on such subjects as future retribution, the atonement, miracles, and character of Jesus, and the history and effects of the Christian religion. Died 7 April, 1836.

Goethe (Johann Wolfgang von), Germany's greatest poet, b. Frankfort-on-Main, 28 Aug. 1749. He records that early in his seventh year (1 Nov. 1758) the great Lisbon earthquake filled his mind with religious doubt. Before he was nine he could write several languages. Educated at home until sixteen, he then went to Leipsic University. At Strasburg he became acquainted with Herder, who directed his attention to Shakespeare. He took the degree of doctor in 1771, and in the same year composed his drama " Goetz von Berlichingen." He went to Wetzlar, where he wrote *Sorrows of Werther*, 1774, which at once made him famous. He was invited to the court of the Duke of Saxe-Weimar and loaded with honors, becoming the centre of a galaxy of distinguished men. Here he brought out the works of Schiller and his own dramas, of which *Faust* is the greatest. His chief prose work is *Wilhelm Meister's Apprenticeship*. His works are voluminous. He declared himself "decidedly non-Christian," and said his objects of hate were "the cross and bugs." He was averse to abstractions and refused to recognise a Deity distinct from the world. In philosophy he followed Spinoza, and he disliked and discountenanced the popular creed. Writing to Lavater in 1772 he said: "You look upon the gospel as it stands as the divinest truth: but even a voice from heaven would not convince me that water burns and fire quenches, that a woman conceives without a man, and that a dead man can rise again. To you, nothing is more beautiful than the Gospel; to me, a thousand written pages of ancient and modern inspired men are equally beautiful." Goethe was opposed to asceticism, and Pfleiderer admits "stood in opposition to Christianity not merely on points of theological form, but to a certain extent on points of substance too." Goethe devoted much attention to science, and he attempted to explain the metamorphosis of plants on evolutionary principles in 1790. Died 22 March, 1832.

Goldstuecker (Theodor), Sanskrit scholar, of Jewish birth, bnt a Freethinker by conviction, b. Konigsberg 18 Jan. 1821; studied at Bonn under Schlegel and Lassen, and at Paris under Burnouf. Establishing himself at Berlin, he was engaged as tutor in the University and assisted Humboldt in the matter of Hindu philosophy in the *Cosmos*. A democrat in politics, he left Berlin at the reaction of '49 and came to England, where he assisted Professor Wilson in preparing his *Sanskrit-Engli h Dictionary*. He contributed important articles on Indian literature to the *Westminster Review*, the *Reader*, the *Athenæum* and *Chambers' Encyclopædia*. Died in London, 6 March, 1872.

Goldziher (Ignacz), Hungarian Orientalist, b. Stuhlweissenburg, 1850. Is since 1876 Doctor of Semitic Philology in Buda-pesth; is author of *Mythology Among the Hebrews*, which has been translated by Russell Martineau, '77, and has written many studies on Semitic theology and literature.

Gordon (Thomas), Scotch Deist and political reformer, was b. Kells, Kirkcudbright, about 1684, but settled early in London, where he supported himself as a teacher and writer. He first distinguished himself by two pamphlets in the Bangorian controversy, which recommended him to Trenchard, to whom he became amanuensis, and with whom he published *Cato's Letters* and a periodical entitled *The Independent Whig*, which he continued some years after Trenchard's death, marrying that writer's widow. He wrote many pamphlets, and translated from Barbeyrac *The Spirit of the Ecclesiastics of All Ages.* He also translated the histories of Tacitus and Sallust. He died 28 July, 1750, leaving behind him posthumous works entitled *A Cordial for Low Spirits* and *The Pillars of Priestcraft and Orthodoxy Shaken.*

Gorlæus (David), a Dutch philosopher, b. at Utrecht, towards the end of the sixteenth century, has been accused of Atheism on account of his speculations in a work published after his death entitled *Exercitationes Philosophicæ*, Leyden 1620.

Govea or GOUVEA [Latin Goveanus] (Antonio), Portugese jurist and poet, b. 1505, studied in France and gained great reputation by his legal writings. Calvin classes him with Dolet, Rabelais, and Des Periers. as an Atheist and mocker. He wrote elegant Latin poems. Died at Turin, 5 March, 1565.

Gratiolet (Louis-Pierre), French naturalist, b. Sainte Foy, 6 July 1815, noted for his researches on the comparative anatomy of the brain. Died at Paris 15 Feb. 1865.

Graves (Kersey), American, author of *The Biography of Satan* 1865, and *The World's Sixteen Crucified Saviors*, 1876. Works of some vogue, but little value.

Gray (Asa), American naturalist, b. 18 Nov. 1810, Paris, Oneida Co., New York. Studied at Fairfield and became physician 1831. Wrote *Elements of Botany*, 1836, became Professor of Nat. Hist. at Harvard, and was the first to introduce Darwinism to America. Wrote an *Examination of Darwin's Treatise* 1861. Succeeded Agassiz as Governor of Smithsonian Institute, and worked on *American Flora*. Died at Cambridge, Mass., 30 Jan. 1888.

Green (H. L.), American Freethinker, b. 18 Feb. 1828. Edits the *Freethinker's Magazine* published at Buffalo, New York.

Greg (William Rathbone), English Writer, b. Manchester 1809. Educated at Edinburgh university, he became attracted to economic studies and literary pursuits. He was one of the founders of the Manchester Statistical Society, a warm supporter of the Anti-Corn Law League, and author of one of its prize essays. In '40 he wrote on Efforts for the Extinction of the African Slave Trade. In '50 he published his *Creed of Christendom*, which has gone through eight editions, and in 1872 his *Enigmas of Life*, of which there were thirteen editions in his life. He published also Essays on Political and Social Science, and was a regular contributor to the *Pall Mall Gazette*. His works exhibit a careful yet bold thinker and close reasoner. Died at Wimbledon 15 Nov. 1881.

Grenier (Pierre Jules), French Positivist, b. Beaumont, Perigord, 1838, author of a medical examination of the doctrine of free will, '68, which drew out letter from Mgr. Dupanloup, Bishop of Orleans, imploring him to repudiate his impious doctrines. Also author of Aphorisms on the First Principles of Sociology, 1873.

"Grile (Dod),**"** pen name of Ambrose Bierce, American humorist, who wrote on the *San Francisco News-Letter*. His *Nuggets and Dust* and *Fiend's Delight*, were blasphemous; has also written in *Fun*, and published *Cobwebs from an Empty Skull*, 1873.

Grimm (Friedrich Melchior von), Baron. German philosophic writer in French, b. Ratisbon, 26 Dec. 1723. Going to France he became acquainted with D'Holbach and with Rousseau, who was at first his friend, but afterwards his enemy. He became secretary to the Duke of Orleans, and wrote in conjunction with Diderot and Raynal caustic literary bulletins containing criticisms on French literature and art. In 1776 he was envoy from the Duke of Saxe Gotha to the French Court, and after the French Revolution was appointed by Catherine of Russia her minister at Hamburg. Grimm died at Gotha, 19 Dec. 1807. He is chiefly known by his literary correspondence with Diderot published in seventeen vols. 1812—1813.

Gringore (Pierre), French poet and dramatist, b about 1475, satirised the pope and clergy as well as the early reformers. Died about 1544.

Grisebach (Eduard), German writer, b. Gottingen 9 Oct. 1845. Studied law, but entered the service of the State and became Consul at Bucharest, Petersburg, Milan and Hayti. Has written many poems, of which the best known is *The New Tan-häuser*, first published anonymously in '69, and followed by *Tanhäuser in Rome*, '75. Has also translated *Kin Ku Ki Kwan*, Chinese novels. Is a follower of Schopenhauer, whose bibliography he has compiled, 1888.

Grote (George), the historian of Greece, b. near Beckenham, Kent, 17 Nov. 1794. Descended from a Dutch family. He was educated for the employment of a banker and was put to business at the age of sixteen. He was however addicted to literary pursuits, and became a friend and disciple of James Mill and Jeremy Bentham. In 1820 he married a cultured lady, Harriet Lewin, and in '22 his *Analysis of the Influence of Natural Religion* was published by Carlile, under the pen name of Philip Beauchamp. He also wrote in the *Westminster Review*. In '33 he was elected as Radical M.P. for the City of London and retained his seat till '41. He was chiefly known in Parliament for his advocacy of the ballot. In '46—'56 he published his famous *History of Greece*, which cost him the best years of his life; this was followed by *Plato and the other Companions of Socrates*. His review of J. S. Mill's *Examination of Sir William Hamilton's Philosophy*, '61, showed he retained his Freethought until the end of his life. He died 18 June '71, and was buried in Westminster Abbey.

Grote (Harriet) nee LEWIN, wife of the above, b. 1792, shared in his opinions and wrote his life. Died 29 Dec. 1878.

Gruen (Karl) German author, b. 30 Sept. 1817, Lüdenschied, Westphalia, studied at Bonn and Berlin. In '44 he came to Paris, was a friend to Proudhon and translated his *Philosophy of Misery*, was arrested in '49 and condemned to exile, lived at Brussels till '62, when he was made professor at Frankfort. He became professor of English at the College of Colmar, established a Radical journal the *Mannheim Evening News* and he wrote Biograpical Studies of Schiller, '44, and Feuerbach, '71.

A Culture History of the 16th–17th *Centuries*, and *The Philosophy of the Present*, '76. Died at Vienna 17 February, 1887.

Gruet (Jacques), Swiss Freethinker, tortured and put to death for blasphemy by order of Calvin at Geneva, 26 July, 1547. After his death papers were found in his possession directed against religion. They were burnt by the common hangman, April, 1550.

Gruyer (Louis Auguste Jean François-Philippe), Belgian philosopher, b. Brussels, 15 Nov. 1778. He wrote an *Essay of Physical Philosophy*, 1828, *Tablettes Philosophiques*, '42. *Principles of Physical Philosophy*, '45, etc. He held the atomic doctrine, and that matter was eternal. Died Brussels 15 Oct. 1866.

Guadet (Marguerite Elie), Girondin, b. Saint Emilion (Gironde), 20 July, 1758. He studied at Bordeaux, and became an advocate in '81. He threw himself enthusiastically into the Revolution, and was elected Deputy for the Gironde. His vehement attacks on the Jacobins contributed to the destruction of his party, after which he took refuge, but was arrested and beheaded at Bordeaux, 15 June, 1794.

Gubernatis (Angelo de), see De Gubernatis.

Guepin (Ange), French physician, b. Pontivy, 30 Aug. 1805. He became M.D. in '28. After the revolution of July, '30, Dr. Guépin was made Professor at the School of Medicine at Nantes. He formed the first scientific and philosophical congress, held there in '33. In '48 he became Commissaire of the Republic at Nantes, and in '50 was deprived of his situation. In '54 he published his *Philosophy of the Nineteenth Century*. After the fall of the Empire, M. Guépin became Prefet of La Loire Inférieure, but had to resign from ill-health. Died at Nantes, 21 May, 1873, and was buried without any religious ceremony.

Gueroult (Adolphe), French author, b. Radepont (Eure), 29 Jan. 1810. Early in life he became a follower of Saint Simon. He wrote to the *Journal des Debats*, the *Republique*, *Credit* and *Industrie*, and founded *l'Opinion National*. He was elected to the Legislature in '63, when he advocated the separation of Church and State. Died at Vichy, 21 July, 1872.

Guerra Junqueiro. Portuguese poet, b. 1850. His principal work is a poem on *The Death of Don Juan*, but he has also written *The Death of Jehovah*, an assault upon the Catholic faith from the standpoint of Pantheism. Portuguese critics speak highly of his powers.

Guerrini (Olindo), Italian poet, b. Forli, 4 Oct. 1845. Educated at Ravenna, Turin, and Bologna University; he has written many fine poems under the name of Lorenzo Stecchetti. In the preface to *Nova Polemica* he declares " Primo di tutto dice, non credo in Dio " (" First of all I say do not believe in God.")

Gueudeville (Nicolas), French writer, b. Rouen, 1654. He became a Benedictine monk, and was distinguished as a preacher, but the boldness of his opinions drew on him the punishment of his superiors. He escaped to Holland, and publicly abjured Catholicism. He taught literature and philosophy at Rotterdam, wrote the Dialogue of the Baron de la Hontan with an American Savage Amst. 1704, appended to the Travels of La Honton, 1724, edited by Gueudeville. This dialogue is a bitter criticism of Christian usages. He translated Erasmus's *Praise of Folly* (1713), More's Utopia (1715), and C. Agrippa on the Uncertainty and Vanity of Sciences (1726). Died at the Hague, 1720.

Guichard (Victor), French writer, b. Paris, 15 Aug. 1803. He became Mayor of Sens, and was elected deputy for the Yonne department. He was exiled in '52, but again elected in '71. His principal work is *La Liberté de Penser, fin du Pouvoir Spirituel* (1868). Died at Paris, 11th Nov. 1884.

Guild (E. E.), b. in Connecticut, 6 May, 1811. In '35 he became a Christian minister, but after numerous debates became turned Universalist. In '44 he published *The Universalist Book of Reference*, which went through several editions. It was followed by *Pro and Con*, in which he gives the arguments for and against Christianity.

Guirlando (Giulio) di Treviso. Italian heretic, put to death at Venice for anti-trinitarian heresy, 19 Oct. 1562.

Gundling (Nicolaus Hieronymus), German scholar and Deistic philosopher, b. near Nuremberg, 25 Feb. 1671. He wrote a

History of the Philosophy of Morals, 1706, and *The Way to Truth*, 1713. One of the first German eclectics, he took much from Hobbes and Locke, with whom he derived all ideas from experience. Died at Halle, 16 Dec. 1729.

Gunning (William D.), American scientific professor, b. Bloomingburg, Ohio. Graduated at Oberlin and studied under Agassiz. He wrote *Life History of our Planet*, Chicago, 1876, and contributed to *The Open Court*. Died Greely, Colorado, 8 March, 1888.

Gunst (Dr. Frans Christiaan), Dutch writer and publisher, b Amsterdam, 19 Aug. 1823. He was intended for a Catholic clergyman; studied at Berne, where he was promoted '47. Returning to Holland he became bookseller and editor at Amsterdam. He was for many years secretary of the City Theatre. Günst contributed to many periodicals, and became a friend of Junghuhn, with whom he started *De Dageraad*, the organ of the Dutch Freethinkers, which he edited from '55 to '67. He usually contributed under pseudonyms as " Mephistho " or (∴). He was for many years President of the Independent Lodge of Freemasons, " Post Nubila Lux," and wrote on *Adon Hiram, the oldest legend of the Freemasons*. He also wrote *Wijwater voor Roomsch Katholieken* (Holy Water for the Roman Catholics); *De Bloedgetuigen der Spaanische Inquisitie* (The Martyrs of the Spanish Inquisition, '63,) ; and *Heidenen en Jezuieten, eene vergelijking van hunne zedeleer* (Pagans and Jesuits, a comparison of their morals, '67,). In his life and conversation he was a *frater gaudens*. Died 29 Dec. 1886.

Guyau (Marie Jean), French philosopher, b. 1854, was crowned at the age of 19 by the Institute of France for a monograph on Utilitarian morality. In the following year he had charge of a course of philosophy at the Condorcet lycée at Paris. Ill health, brought on by excess of work, obliged him to retire to Mentone, where he occupied himself with literature. His principal works are *La Morale d'Epicure* (the morality of Epicurus), in relation to present day doctrines, 1878, *La Morale Anglaise Contemporaine* (Contemporary English Ethics), '79, crowned by the Academy of Moral Sciences. Verses of a philosopher, '81. *Esquisse d'une morale sans obligation ni sanction* (Sketch of morality without obligation or sanction,) '84, and *L'Irreligion de l'Avenir* (the Irreligion of the Future) '87. M. Guyau was a follower of M. Fouillée, but all his works bear the impress of profound thought and originality. A chief doctrine is the expansion of life. Died Mentone, 31 March, 1888

Guyot (Yves), French writer and statesman, b. Dinan, 1843 He wrote with Sigismond Lacroix a *Study of the Social Doctrines of Christianity*, '73, and a work on morality in the *Bibliothèque Matérialiste*. Elected on the Municipal Council of Paris '74-78, he has since been a deputy to the Chamber, and is now a member of the government. He has written the *Principles of Social Economy*, '84, and many works on that topic ; has edited Diderot's *La Religieuse* and the journals *Droits de l'homme* and *le Bien public*.

Gwynne (George), Freethought writer in the *Reasoner* and *National Reformer*, under the pen-name of " Aliquis." His reply to J. H. Newman's *Grammar of Assent* shewed much acuteness. He served the cause both by pen and purse. Died 25 Sept. 1873.

Gyllenborg (Gustaf Fredrik), *Count*. Swedish poet, b 6 Dec. 1731, was one of the first members of the Academy of Stockholm and Chancellor of Upsala University. He published satires, fables, odes, etc., among which may be named *The Passage of the Belt*. His opinions were Deistic. Died 30 March, 1808.

Haeckel (Ernst Heinrich Philipp August), German scientist, b. Potsdam, 16 Feb. 1834 ; studied medicine and science at Würzburg, Berlin, and Vienna. In '59 he went to Italy and studied zoology at Naples, and two years later was made Professor of Zoology at Jena. Between 66 and '75 he travelled over Europe besides visiting Syria and Egypt, and later he visited India and Ceylon, writing an interesting account of his travels. He is the foremost German supporter of evolution ; his *Natural History of Creation*, '68, having gone through many editions, and been translated into English '76, as have also his *Evolution of Man*, 2 vols. '79, and *Pedigree of Man*, '83. Besides numerous monographs and an able work on *Cellular Psychology*, Professor Haeckel has published important *Popular Lectures on Evolution*, '78, and on *Freedom in Science and Teaching*, published with a prefatory note by Professor Huxley, '79.

Hagen (Benjamin Olive), Socialist, b. 25 June, 1791. About the year 1811 his attention was attracted to the Socialists by the abuse they received. Led thus to inquire, he embraced the views of Robert Owen, and was their chief upholder for many years in the town of Derby, where he lived to be upwards of seventy years of age. His wife also deserves mention as an able lady of Freethought views.

Halley (Edmund), eminent English astronomer, known in his lifetime as "the Infidel Mathematician," b. Haggerston, London, 29 Oct. 1656; educated at Oxford. At twenty he had made observations of the planets and of the spots on the sun. In Nov. '76 he went to St. Helena where he prepared his *Catalogue of Southern Stars*, '79 He also found how to take the sun's parallax by means of the transits of Mercury or Venus. In '78 he was elected a F.R.S. Two years later he made observation on "Halley's comet," and in '83 published his theory of the variation of the magnet. He became a friend of Sir Isaac Newton, whom he persuaded to publish his *Principia*. In '98 he commanded a scientific expedition to the South Atlantic. In 1713 he was made sec. of the Royal Society and in 1720 Astronomer-royal. He then undertook a task which required nineteen years to perform, viz: to observe the moon throughout an entire revolution of her nodes. He lived to finish this task. Died 14 Jan. 1742. Halley was the first who conceived that fixed stars had a proper motion in space. Chalmers in his *Biographical Dictionary* says. "It must be deeply regretted that he cannot be numbered with those illustrious characters who thought it not beneath them to be Christians."

Hammon (W.), pseudonym of TURNER William, *q. v.*

Hamond or Hamont (Matthew), English heretic, by trade a ploughwright, of Hethersett, Norfolk, burnt at Norwich, May 1579, for holding "that the New Testament and the Gospel of Christ were pure folly, a human invention, a mere fable." He had previously been set in the pillory and had both his ears cut off.

Hannotin (Emile), French Deist, b. Bar le Duc in 1812, and some time editor of the *Journal de la Meuse*. Author of *New Philosophical Theology*, '46; *Great Questions*, '67; *Ten Years of*

Philosophical Studies, '72 ; and an *Essay on Man,* in which he seeks to explain life by *sensibility.*

Hanson (Sir Richard Davies), Chief Justice of South Australia, b. London, 5 Dec. 1805. He practised as attorney for a short time in London, and wrote for the *Globe* and *Morning Chronicle.* In 1830 he took part in the attempt to found a colony in South Australia. In 1851 he became Advocate-General of the colony, and subsequently in 1861 Chief Justice. In 1869 he was knighted. He wrote on *Law in Nature* 1865, *The Jesus of History* 1869, and *St. Paul* 1875. Hanson wrote *Letters to and from Rome A.D.* 61, 62 and 63. *Selected and translated by C.V.S.* 1873. Died at Adelaide 10 Mar. 1876.

Hardwicke (Edward Arthur), M.D., eldest son of Junius Harwicke, F.R.C.S., of Rotherham, Yorks. In '75 he qualified as a surveyor, and in '86 as a physician. For twelve years he was Surgeon Superintendent of the Government Emigration Service. He is an Agnostic of the school of Herbert Spencer, and has contributed to Freethought and scientific periodicals.

Hardwicke (Herbert Junius), M.D., brother of above, b. Sheffield, 26 Jan. 1850. Studied at London, Edinburgh and Paris. In '78 he became a member of the Edinburgh College of Physicians. Next year he was the principal agent in establishing the Sheffield Public Hospital for Skin Diseases. Besides numerous medical works, Dr. Hardwicke set up a press of his own in order to print *The Popular Faith Unveiled,* the publishers requiring guarantee in consequence of the prosecution of Mr. Foote ('84), and *Evolution and Creation* ('87). He has contributed to the *Agnostic Annual,* and has recently written *Rambles in Spain, Italy and Morocco* ('89).

Harriot (Thomas), English mathematician, b. Oxford, 1560, accompanied Raleigh to Virginia and published an account of the expedition. He was noted for his skill in algebra, and A. Wood says " He was a Deist." Died 21 July 1621.

Harrison (Frederic), M.A., English Positivist b. London 18 Oct. 1831, educated at London and Oxford, when he was 1st class in classics. He was called to the bar in '58. He has since been appointed Professor of Jurisprudence and International Law. He has written many important articles in the

high-class reviews, and has published *The Meaning of History,
Order and Progress,* and on *The Choice of Books and Other Literary
Pieces,* '86, and has translated vol. ii of Comte's *Positive Polity.*
He was one of the founders of the Positivist school, '70, and of
Newton Hall in '81. A fine stylist, his addresses and magazine
articles bear the stamp of a cultured man of letters.

Hartmann (Karl Robert Eduard), German pantheistic pessimist philosopher, b. Berlin, 23 Feb. 1842. In '58 he entered
the Prussian army, but an affection of the knee made him
resign in '65. By the publication of his *Philosophy of the Unconscious* in '69, he became famous, though it was not translated
into English until '84. He has since written numerous works
of which we name *Self-Dissolution of Christianity and The Religion of the Future,* '75. *The Crisis of Christianity in Modern
Theology,* '80, *The Religious Consciousness of Mankind,* '81, and
Modern Problems, '86. Latterly Hartmann has turned his attention to the philosophy of politics.

Hartogh Heys Van Zouteveen (Dr. Herman), a learned Dutch
writer, b. Delft 13 Feb. 1841. He studied law and natural philosophy at Leyden, and graduated doctor of law in '64 and doctor
of natural philosophy in '66. In '66 he received a gold medal
from the king of Holland for a treatise on the synthesis of
organic bodies. Dr. Hartogh was some time professor of
chemistry and natural history at the Hague, but lived at Delft,
where he was made city councillor and in '69 and '70 travelled
through Egypt and Nubia as correspondent of *Het Vaderland*
and was the guest of the Khedive. He translated into Dutch
Darwin's *Descent of Man* and *Expressions of the Emotions,* both
with valuable annotations of his own. He has also translated
and annotated some of the works of Ludwig Büchner and
" Carus Sterne," from the German, and works from the
French, besides writing several original essays on anthropology, natural history, geology, and allied sciences, contributing largely to the spread of Darwinian ideas in Holland. In
'72 he visited the United States and the Pacific coast. Since
'73 he has resided at Assen, of which he was named member of
the city council, but could not take his seat because he refused
the oath. He is a director of the Provincial Archæological Museum
at Assen, and a member of the Dutch Literary Society the Royal

Institution of Netherlands, India, and other scientific associations. For a long while he was a member of the Dutch Freethinkers' Society, *De Dageraad*, of which he became president. To the organ *De Dageraad* he contributed important works, such as *Jewish Reports Concerning Jesus of Nazareth* and the *Origin of Religious Ideas*, the last of which has been published separately.

Haslam (Charles Junius), b. Widdington, Northumberland, 24 April, 1811. He spent most of his life near Manchester. where he became a Socialist and published *Letters to the Clergy of all Denominations*, showing the errors. absurdities, and irrationalities of their doctrines, '38. This work went through several editions, and the publishers were prosecuted for blasphemy. He followed it by *Letters to the Bishop of Exeter*, containing materials for deciding the question whether or not the Bible is the word of God, '41, and a pamphlet *Who are the Infidels?* In '61 he removed to Benton, where he has since lived. In '85 he issued a pamphlet entitled *The Suppression of War*.

Hassell (Richard), one of Carlile's shopmen, sentenced to two years imprisonment in Newgate for selling Paine's *Age of Reason*, 28 May, 1824. He died in October 1826.

Hattem (Pontiaam van), Dutch writer, b. Bergen 1641. He was a follower of Spinoza. inclined to Pantheistic mysticism, and had several followers. Died 1706.

Haureau (Jean Barthelemy), French historian, b. Paris 1812. At the age of twenty he showed his sympathy with the Revolution by a work on *The Mountain*. In turn journalist and librarian he has produced many important works, of which we name his *Manual of the Clergy*, '44, which drew on him attacks from the clericals, and his erudite *Critical Examination of the Scholastic Philosophy*, '50.

Hauy (Valentine), French philanthrophist, b. Saint-Just 13 Nov. 1745. He devoted much attention to enabling the blind to read and founded the institute for the young blind in 1784. He was one of the founders of Theophilantropy. In 1807 he went to Russia, where he stayed till 1817, devoting himself to the blind and to telegraphy. Died at Paris 18 March, 1822.

Havet (Ernest August Eugène), French scholar and critic, b. Paris, 11 April, 1813. In '40 he was appointed professor of Greek literature at the Normal School. In '55 he was made professor of Latin eloquence at the Collége de France. In '63 an article on Renan's *Vie de Jesus* in the *Revue des Deux Mondes* excited much attention, and was afterwards published separately. His work on *Christianity and its Origins*, 4 vols. 1872–84, is a masterpiece of rational criticism.

Hawkesworth (John), English essayist and novelist, b. in London about 1715. Became contributor to the *Gentleman's Magazine* and editor of the *Adventurer*. In '61 he edited Swift's works with a life of that author. He compiled an account of the voyages of Byron, Wallis, Carteret, and Cook for government, for which he received £6,000; but the work was censured as incidentally attacking the doctrine of Providence. His novel *Almoran and Hamet* was very popular. Died at Bromley, Kent, 17 Nov. 1773.

Hawley (Henry), a Scotch major-general, who died in 1765, and by the terms of his will prohibited Christian burial.

Hebert (Jacques René), French revolutionist, b. Alençon 15 Nov. 1757, published the notorious *Père Duchèsne*, and with Chaumette instituted the *Feasts of Reason*. He was denounced by Saint Just, and guillotined 2 March 1794. His widow, who had been a nun, was executed a few days later.

Hegel (Georg Wilhelm Friedrich), German metaphysician b. Stuttgart, 27 Aug. 1770. He studied theology at Tübingen, but, becoming acquainted with Schelling, devoted his attention to philosophy. His *Encyclopædia of the Philosophical Sciences* made a deep impression in Germany, and two schools sprang up, one claiming it as a philosophical statement of Christianity, the other as Pantheism hostile to revelation. Hegel said students of philosophy must begin with Spinozism. He is said to have remarked that of all his many disciples only one understood him, and he understood him falsely. He was professor at Jena, Heidelberg, and Berlin, in which last city he died 14 Nov. 1831, and was buried beside Fichte.

Heine (Heinrich), German poet and littérateur, b. of Jewish parents at Dusseldorf, 31 Dec. 1797. He studied law at Bonn,

Berlin, and Göttingen ; became acquainted with the philosophy of Spinoza and Hegel ; graduated LL.D., and in June 1825 renounced Judaism and was baptised. The change was only formal. He satirised all forms of religious faith. His fine *Pictures of Travel* was received with favor and translated by himself into French. His other principal works are the *Book of Songs, History of Recent Literature in Germany, The Romantic School, The Women of Shakespeare, Atta Troll* and other poems. In 1835 he married a French lady, having settled in Paris, where "the Voltaire of Germany" became more French than German. About 1848 he became paralysed and lost his eyesight, but he still employed himself in literary composition with the aid of an amanuensis. After an illness of eight years, mostly passed in extreme suffering on his "mattress grave," he died 17 Feb. 1856. Heine was the greatest and most influential German writer since Goethe. He called himself a Soldier of Freedom, and his far-flashing sword played havoc with the forces of reaction.

Heinzen (Karl Peter) German-American poet, orator and politician, b. near Dusseldorf, 22 Feb. 1809. He studied medicine at Bonn, and travelled to Batavia, an account of which he published (Cologne 1842). A staunch democrat, in 1845 he published at Darmstadt a work on the *Prussian Bureaucracy,* for which he was prosecuted and had to seek shelter in Switzerland. At Zurich he edited the *German Tribune* and the *Democrat.* At the beginning of '48 he visited New York but returned to participate in the attempted German Revolution. Again "the regicide" had to fly and in August '50 returned to New York. He wrote on many papers and established the *Pioneer* (now *Freidenker*), first in Louisville, then in Cincinnati, then in New York, and from '59 in Boston. He wrote many works, including *Letters on Atheism,* which appeared in *The Reasoner* 1856, *Poems, German Revolution, The Heroes of German Communism, The Rights of Women, Mankind the Criminal, Six Letters to a Pious Man* (Boston 1869), *Lessons of a Century,* and *What is Humanity ?* (1877.) Died Boston 12 Nov. 1880.

Hellwald (Friedrich von), German geographer, b. Padua 29 March 1842, and in addition to many works on various countries has written an able *Culture History,* 1875.

Helmholtz (Hermann Ludwig Ferdinand von) German scientist, b. Potsdam 31 Aug. 1821. Distinguished for his discoveries in acoustics, optics and electricity, he is of the foremost rank among natural philosophers in Europe. Among his works we mention *The Conservation of Force* (1847), and *Popular Scientific Lectures* (1865-76.) Professor Helmholtz rejects the design hypothesis.

Helvetius (Claude Adrien) French philosopher, b. Paris 18 Jan. 1715. Descended from a line of celebrated physicians, he had a large fortune which he dispensed in works of benevolence. Attracted by reading Locke he resigned a lucrative situation as farmer-general to devote himself to philosophy. In August 1758 he published a work *On the Mind* (De L'Esprit) which was condemned by Pope Clement XIII, 31 Jan. 1759, and burnt by the order of Parliament 6 Feb. 1759 for the hardihood of his materialistic opinions. Mme. Du Deffand said " he told everybody's secret." It was republished at Amsterdam and London. He also wrote a poem *On Happiness* and a work on *Man his Faculties and Education.* He visited England and Prussia and became an honored guest of Frederick the Great. Died 26 Dec. 1771. His wife, *née* Anne Catherine DE LING-VILLE, b. 1719, after his death retired to Auteuil, where her house was the rendezvous of Condillac, Turgot, d'Holbach, Morellet, Cabanis, Destutt de Tracy, etc. This re-union of Freethinkers was known as the Société d'Auteuil. Madame Helvetius died 12 August 1800.

Henault, or **Hesnault** (Jean), French Epicurean poet of the 17th century, son of a Paris baker, was a pupil of Gassendi, and went to Holland to see Spinoza. Bayle says he professed Atheism, and had composed three different systems of the mortality of the soul. His most famous sonnet is on *The Abortion.* Died Paris, 1682.

Henin de Cuvillers (Etienne Felix), *Baron*, French general and writer, b. Balloy, 27 April, 1755. He served as diplomatist in England, Venice, and Constantinople. Employed in the army of Italy, he was wounded at Arcola, 26 Sept. '96. He was made Chevalier of the Legion of Honor in 1811. He wrote much, particularly on magnetism. In the 8th vol. of his *Archives du Magnétisme Animal,* he suggests that the miracles of

Jesus were not supernatural, but wrought by means of magnetism learnt in Egypt. In other writings, especially in reflections on the crimes committed in the name of religion, '22, he shows himself the enemy of fanaticism and intolerance. Died **2 August, 1841.**

Hennell (Charles Christian), English Freethinker, b. 9 March, 1809, author of an able *Inquiry concerning the Origin of Christianity*, first published in '38, a work which powerfully influenced "George Eliot," and a translation of which was introduced to German readers by Dr. D. F. Strauss. It was Hennell who induced "George Eliot" to translate Strauss's *Life of Jesus*. He also wrote on *Christian Theism*. Hennell lived most of his time in Coventry. He was married at London in '39, and died 2 Sept. 1850.

Herault de Sechelles (Marie Jean), French revolutionist, b. of noble family, Paris, 1760. Brought up as a friend of Buffon and Mirabeau, he gained distinction as a lawyer and orator before the Revolution. Elected to the Legislative Assembly in '91, he was made President of the Convention, 2 Nov. 92. He edited the document known as the *Constitution of* 1793, and was president and chief speaker at the national festival, 10 Aug. '93. He drew on himself the enmity of Robespierre, and was executed with Danton and Camille Desmoulins, 5 April, 1794.

Herbart (Johann Friedrich), b. Oldenburg 4 May 1776. In 1805 he was made professor of philosophy at Göttingen, and in 1808 became Kant's successor at Königsberg and opposed his philosophy. Though religiously disposed, his philosophy has no room for the notion of a God. He was recalled to Göttingen, where he died 11 Aug. 1841.

Herbert (Edward), *Lord* of Cherbury, in Shropshire, b. Montgomery Castle, 1581. Educated at Oxford, after which he went on his travels. On his return he was made one of the king's counsellors, and soon after sent as ambassador to France to intercede for the Protestants. He served in the Netherlands, and distinguished himself by romantic bravery. In 1625 he was made a peer of Ireland, and in '31 an English peer. During the civil wars he espoused the side of Parliament. His principle work is entitled *De Veritate*, the object of which was to assert the sufficiency of natural religion apart from revelation.

He also wrote *Lay Religion*, his own *Memoirs*, a *History of Henry VIII.*, etc. Died 20 Aug. 1648.

Hertell (Thomas), judge of the Marine Court of New York, and for some years Member of the Legislature of his State. He wrote two or three small works criticising Christian Theology, and exerted his influence in favour of State secularization.

Hertzen or **Gertsen** (Aleksandr Ivanovich), Russian patriot, chief of the revolutionary party, b. Moscow, 25 March, 1812. He studied at Moscow University, where he obtained a high degree. In '34 he was arrested for Saint Simonian opinions and soon afterwards banished to Viatka, whence he was permitted to return in '37. He was expelled from Russia in '42, visited Italy, joined the "Reds" at Paris in '48, took refuge at Geneva, and soon after came to England. In '57 he set up in London a Russian printing press for the publication of works prohibited in Russia, and his publications passed into that country in large numbers. Among his writings are *Dilettantism in Science*, '42; *Letters on the Study of Nature*, '45–46; *Who's to Blame?* '57; *Memoirs of the Empress Catherine*, and *My Exile*, '55. In '57 Herzen started the magazine the *Kolokol* or *Bell*. Died at Paris, 21 Jan. 1870. His son, ALESSANDRO HERZEN, b. Wladimar, 1839, followed his father's fortunes, learnt most of the European languages and settled at Florence. where he did much to popularise physiological science. He has translated Maudsley's *Physiology of Mind*, and published a physiological analysis of human free will.

Herwegh (Georg), German Radical and poet, b. Stuttgart, 31 May, 1817. Intended for the Church, he left that business for Literature. His *Gedichte eines Lebendigen* (Poems of a Living Man) aroused attention by their boldness. In '48 he raised a troop and invaded Baden, but failed, and took refuge in Switzerland and Paris. Died at Baden-Baden, 7 April, 1875.

Hetherington (Henry), English upholder of a free press, b. Soho, London, 1792. He became a printer, and was one of the most energetic of working men engaged in the foundation of mechanics' institutes. He also founded the Metropolitan Political Union in March, 1830, which was the germ both of trades' unionism and of the Chartist movement. He resisted the " taxes upon knowledge " by issuing unstamped *The Poor Man's Guardian*, a weekly newspaper for the people, established, contrary to " law," to try the power of " might " against " right," '31–35. For this he twice suffered sentences of six months' imprisonment. He afterwards published *The Unstamped*, and his persistency had much to do in removing the taxes. While in prison he wrote his *Cheap Salvation* in consequence of conversation with the chaplain of Clerkenwell Gaol. On Dec. 8, '40, he was tried for " blasphemous libel " for publishing Haslam's *Letters to the Clergy*, and received four month's imprisonment. Hetherington published *A Few Hundred Bible Contradictions*, and other Freethought works. Much of his life was devoted to the propaganda of Chartism. He died 21 Aug. 1849, leaving a will declaring himself an Atheist.

Hetzer (Ludwig), anti-Trinitarian martyr, b. Bischopzell, Switzerland; was an Anabaptist minister at Zurich. He openly denied the doctrine of the Trinity, and was condemned to death by the magistrates of Constance on a charge of blasphemy. The sentence was carried out 4 Feb. 1529.

Heusden (C. J. van), Dutch writer in *De Dageraad*. Has written several works, *Thoughts on a Coming More Universal Doctrine*, by a Believer, etc.

Hibbert (Julian), Freethought philanthropist, b. 1801. During the imprisonment of Richard Carlile he was active in sustaining his publications. Learning that a distinguished political prisoner had received a gift of £1,000, he remarked that a Freethinking prisoner should not want equal friends, and gave Carlile a cheque for the same amount. Julian Hibbert spent nearly £1,000 in fitting up Carlile's shop in Fleet Street. He contributed " Theological Dialogues " to the *Republican*, and also contributed to the *Poor Man's Guardian*. Hibbert set up a private press and printed in uncial Greek the *Orphic Hymns*, '27, and also *Plutarch and Theophrastus on Superstition*, to which he wrote a life of Plutarch and appended valuable essays " on the supposed necessity of deceiving the vulgar "; " various definitions of an important word " [God], and a catalogue of the principal modern works against Atheism. He also commenced a *Dictionary of Anti-Superstitionists*, and

Chronological Tables of British Freethinkers. He wrote a short life of Holbach, published by James Watson, to whom, and to Henry Hetherington, he left £500 each. Died December 1834.

Hidenin (Sven Adolph), Swedish member of the "Andra Kammaren" [House of Commons], b. 1834. Studied at Upsala and became philosophical candidate, '61. Edited the *Afton-bladet*, '74-76. Has written many radical works.

Higgins (Godfrey), English archæologist, b. Skellow Grange, near Doncaster, 1771. Educated at Cambridge and studied for the bar, but never practised. Being the only son he inherited his father's property, married, and acted as magistrate, in which capacity he reformed the treatment of lunatics in York Asylum. His first work was entitled *Horæ Sabbaticæ*, 1813, a manual on the Sunday Question. In '29 he published *An Apology for the Life and Character of Mohammed* and *Celtic Druids*, which occasioned some stir on account of the exposure of priestcraft. He died 9 Aug. 1833, leaving behind a work on the origin of religions, to the study of which he devoted ten hours daily for about twenty years. The work was published in two volumes in 1826, under the title of "*Anacalypsis*, an attempt to draw aside the veil of the Saitic Isis; or an Inquiry into the Origin of Languages, Nations, and Religions."

Hillebrand (Karl), cosmopolitan writer, b. 17 Sept. 1829, at Giessen. His father, Joseph Hillebrand, succeeded Hegel as professor at Heidelberg. Involved in the revolutionary movement in Germany, Karl was imprisoned in the fortress of Rastadt, whence he escaped to France. He taught at Strasbourg and Paris, where he became secretary to Heine. On the poet's death he removed to Bordeaux, where he became a naturalised Frenchman. He became professor of letters at Douay. During the Franco-Prussian war he was correspondent to the *Times*, and was taken for a Prussian spy. In 1871 he settled at Florence, where he translated the poems of Carducci. Hillebrand was a contributor to the *Fortnightly Review, Nineteenth Century, Revue des deux Mondes, North American Review,* etc. His best known work is on France and the French in the second half of the nineteenth century. Died at Florence, 18 Oct. 1884.

Hins (Eugène), Belgian writer, Dr. of Philosophy, Professor at Royal Athenæum, Charleroi, b. St. Trond, 1842. As general secretary of the International, he edited *L'Internationale*, in which he laid stress on anti-religious teaching. He contributed to *La Liberté*, and was one of the prominent lecturers of the Societies *Les Solidaires*, and *La Libre-pensée* of Brussels. He has written *La Russie dé voilée au moyen de sa littérature populaire*, 1883, and other works.

Hippel (Theodor Gottlieb von). German humoristic poet, b. Gerdauen, Prussia, 31 Jan. 1711. He studied theology, but resigned it for law, and became in 1780 burgomaster of Königsberg. His writings, which were published anonymously, betray his advanced opinions. Died Bromberg, 23 April, 1796.

Hittell (John S.), American Freethinker, author of the *Evidences against Christianity* (New York, 1857): has also written *A Plea for Pantheism*, *A New System of Phrenology*, *The Resources of California*, a *History of San Francisco*, *A Brief History of Culture* (New York, 1875), and *St. Peter's Catechism* (Geneva, 1883).

Hoadley (George), American jurist, b. New Haven, Conn., 31 July, 1836. He studied at Harvard, and in '47 was admitted to the bar, and in '51 was elected judge of the superior court of Cincinnati. He afterwards resigned his place and established a law firm. He was one of the counsel that successfully opposed compulsory Bible reading in the public schools.

Hobbes (Thomas), English philosopher, b. Malmesbury, 5 April, 1588. In 1608 he beame tutor to a son of the Earl of Devonshire, with whom he made the tour of Europe. At Pisa in 1628 he made the acquaintance of Galileo. In 1642 he printed his work *De Cive*. In 1650 appeared in English his work on *Human Nature*, and in the following year his famous *Leviathan*. At the Restoration he received a pension, but in 1666 Parliament, in a Bill against Atheism and profaneness, passed a censure on his writings, which much alarmed him. The latter years of his life were spent at the seat of the Duke of Devonshire, Chatsworth, where he died 4 Dec. 1679.

Hodgson (William, M.D.), English Jacobin, translator of d'Holbach's *System of Nature* (1795). In 1794 he was confined in Newgate for two years for drinking to the success of the French Republic. In prison he wrote *The Commonwealth of Reason*.

Hoelderlin (Johann Christian Friedrich), German pantheistic poet, b. Laufen, 20 March, 1770. Entered as a theological student at Tübingen, but never took to the business. He wrote *Hyperion*, a fine romance (1797-99), and *Lyric Poems*, admired for their depth of thought. Died Tübingen, 7 June, 1843.

Hoijer (Benjamin Carl Henrik), Swedish philosopher, b. Great Skedvi, Delecarlia, 1 June, 1767. Was student at Upsala University '83, and teacher of philosophy '98. His promotion was hindered by his liberal opinions. By his personal influence and published treatises he contributed much to Swedish emancipation. In 1808 he became Professor of Philosophy at Upsala. Died 8 June, 1812.

Holbach (Paul Heinrich Dietrich von) *Baron*, b. Heidelsheim Jan. 1723. Brought up at Paris where he spent most of his life. Rich and generous he was the patron of the Encyclopædists. Buffon, Diderot, d'Alembert, Helvetius, Rousseau, Grimm, Raynal, Marmontel, Condillac, and other authors often met at his table. Hume, Garrick, Franklin, and Priestley were also among his visitors. He translated from the German several works on chemistry and mineralogy, and from the English, Mark Akenside's *Pleasures of the Imagination*. He contributed many articles to the *Encyclopédie*. In 1765 he visited England, and from this time was untiring in his issue of Freethought works, usually put out under pseudonyms. Thus he wrote and had published at Amsterdam *Christianity Unveiled*, attributed to Boulanger. The *Spirit of the Clergy*, translated, from the English of Trenchard and Gordon, was partly rewritten by d'Holbach, 1767. His *Sacred Contagion or Natural History of Superstition*, was also wrongly attributed to Trenchard and Gordon. This work was condemned to be burnt by a decree of the French parliament, 8 Aug. 1770. D'Holbach also wrote and published *The History of David*, 1768, *The Critical History of Jesus Christ, Letters to Eugenia*, attributed to Freret, *Portable Theology*, attributed to Bernier, an *Essay on Prejudices*, attributed to M. Du M [arsais], *Religious Cruelty, Hell Destroyed*, and other works, said to be from the English. He also translated the *Philosophical Letters* of Toland, and Collins's *Discourses on Prophecy*, and attributed to the latter a work with the title *The Spirit of Judaism*. These works were mostly conveyed to the printer, M. Rey, at Amsterdam, by Naigeon, and the secret of their authorship was carefully preserved. Hence d'Holbach escaped persecution. In 1770 he published his principal work *The System of Nature, or The Laws of the Physical and Moral World*. This text-book of atheistic philosophy, in which d'Holbach was assisted by Diderot, professed to be the posthumous work of Mirabaud. It made a great sensation. Within two years he published a sort of summary under the title of *Good Sense*, attributed to the curé Meslier. In 1773 he wrote on *Natural Politics* and the *Social System*. His last important work was *Universal Morality; or the Duties of Man founded upon Nature*. D'Holbach, whose personal good qualities were testified to by many, was depicted in Rousseau's *Nourelle Héloise* as the benevolent Atheist Wolmar. Died 21 Jan. 1789.

Holcroft (Thomas), English author, b. 10 Dec. 1745, was successively a groom, shoemaker, schoolmaster, actor and author. His comedies "Duplicity," 1781, and "The Road to Ruin," 1792, were very successful. He translated the *Posthumous Works of Frederick the Great*, 1789. For his active sympathy with the French Republicans he was indicted for high treason with Hardy and Horne Tooke in 1794, but was discharged without a trial. Died 23 March, 1809.

Holland (Frederic May), American author, b. Boston, 2 May, 1836 graduated at Harvard in '49, and in '63 was ordained Unitarian minister at Rockford, Ill. Becoming broader in his views, he resigned, and has since written in the *Truthseeker*, the *Freethinkers' Magazine*, etc. His principal work is entitled *The Rise of Intellectual Liberty*, 1885.

Hollick (Dr. Frederick), Socialist, b. Birmingham, 22 Dec 1813. He was educated at the Mechanics' Institute of that town, and became one of the Socialist lecturers under Robert Owen. He held a public discussion with J. Brindley at Liverpool, in 1840, on "What is Christianity?" On the failure of Owenism he went to America. where some of his works popularising medical science have had a large circulation.

Hollis (John), English sceptic, b. 1757. Author of *Sober and Serious Reasons for Scepticism*, 1796; *An Apology for Disbelief in Revealed Religion*, 1799; and *Free Thoughts*, 1812. Died at High Wycombe, Bucks 26 Nov. 1824. Hollis, who came of an oppulent dissenting family, was distinguished by his love of truth, his zeal in the cause of freedom, and by his beneficence.

Holmes (William Vamplew), one of Carlile's brave shopmen who came up from Leeds to uphold the right of free publication. He was sentenced to two years' imprisonment, 1 March, '22, for selling blasphemous and seditious libels in *An Address to the Reformers of Great Britain*, and when in prison was told that "if hard labor was not expressed in his sentence, it was implied." On his release Holmes went to Sheffield and commenced the open sale of all the prohibited publications.

Holwell (John Zephaniah), noted as one of the survivors of the Black Hole of Calcutta, b. Dublin, 7 Sept. 1711. He practised as a surgeon, went to India as a clerk, defended a fort at Calcutta against Surajah Dowlah, was imprisoned with one hundred and forty-five others in the " Black Hole," 20th June, 1756, of which he published a *Narrative*. He succeeded Clive as governor of Bengal. On returning to England he published a dissertation directed against belief in a special providence, and advocating the application of church endowments to the exigencies of the State (Bath, 1786). Died 5 Nov. 1798.

Holyoake (Austin), English Freethinker, b. Birmingham, 27 Oct. 1826. His mental emancipation came from hearing the lectures of Robert Owen and his disciples. He took part in the agitation for the abolition of the newspaper stamp—assisting when risk and danger had to be met—and he co-operated with his brother in the production of the *Reasoner* and other publications from '45 till '62. Soon after this he printed and sub-edited the *National Reformer*, in which many of his Freethought articles appeared. Among his pamphlets may be mentioned *Heaven and Hell*, *Ludicrous Aspects of Christianity*, *Thoughts on Atheism*, the *Book of Esther*, and *Daniel the Dreamer*. He also composed a Secular Burial Service. Austin Holyoake took pride in the character of Freethought, and was ever zealous in promoting its welfare. His amiable spirit endeared him to all who knew him. He died 10 April, 1874, leaving behind thoughts written on his deathbed, in which he repudiated all belief in theology.

Holyoake (George Jacob), b. Birmingham, 13 April 1817. Became mathematical teacher of the Mechanics' Institution. Influenced by Combe and Owen he became a Freethinker, and in '40 a Socialist missionary. In '42, when Southwell was imprisoned for writing in the *Oracle of Reason*, Mr. Holyoake took charge of that journal, and wrote *The Spirit of Bonner in the Disciples of Jesus*. He was soon arrested for a speech at Cheltenham, having said, in answer to a question, that he would put the Deity on half-pay. Tried Aug. '42, he was sentenced to six months imprisonment, of which he gave a full account in his *Last Trial by Jury for Atheism in England*. In Dec. '43 he edited with M. Q. Ryall the *Movement*, bearing the motto from Bentham, "Maximise morals, minimise religion." The same policy was pursued in *The Reasoner*, which he edited from 1816 till 1861. Among his many pamphlets we must notice the *Logic of Death*, '50, which went through numerous editions, and was included in his most important Freethought work, *The Trial of Theism*. In '19 he published a brief memoir of R. Carlile. In '51 he first used the term "Secularist," and in Oct. '52 the first Secular Conference was held at Manchester Mr. Holyoake presiding. In Jan. '53 he held a six nights discussion with the Rev. Brewin Grant, and again in Oct. '54. He purchased the business of James Watson, and issued many Freethought works, notably *The Library of Reason*—a series, *The Cabinet of Reason*, his own *Secularism; The Philosophy of the People*, etc. In '60 he was Secretary to the British Legion sent out to Garibaldi. Mr. Holyoake did much to remove the taxes upon knowledge, and has devoted much attention to Co-operation, having written a history of the movement and contributed to most of its journals.

Home (Henry), Scottish judge, was b. 1696. His legal ability was made known by his publication of *Remarkable Decisions of the Court of Session*, 1728. In 1752 he was raised to the bench as Lord Kames. He published *Essays on the Principles of Morality and Natural Religion* (1751), *Elements of Criticism* (1762), and *Sketches of the History of Man*, in which he proved himself in advance of his age. Died 27 Dec. 1782.

Hon, Le (Henri). See Le Hon.

Hooker (Sir Joseph Dalton), English naturalist, b. 1817. He studied medicine at Glasgow, graduating M.D ’39. In ’55 he became assistant-director of Kew Gardens, and from ’65—85 sole director. Renowned as a botanist, he was the first eminent man of science to proclaim his adoption of Darwinism.

Hope (Thomas), novelist and antiquarian, b. 1770. Famous for his anonymous *Anastasius*, or Memories of a Modern Greek, he also wrote an original work on *The Origin and Prospects of Man* ’31. Died at London 3 Feb. 1831.

Houten (Samuel van), Dutch Freethinker, b. Groningen. 17 Feb. 1837; he studied law and became a lawyer in that city, In ’69 he was chosen member of the Dutch Parliament. Has published many writings on political economy. In ’88 he wrote a book entitled *Das Causalitatgesatz* (The Law of Causality).

Houston (George). Was the translator of d’Holbach’s *Ecce Homo*, first published in Edinburgh in 1799, and sometimes ascribed to Joseph Webb. A second edition was issued in 1813. Houston was prosecuted and was imprisoned two years in Newgate, with a fine of £200. He afterwards went to New York, where he edited the *Minerva* (1822). In Jan. 1827, he started *The Correspondence*, which, we believe, was the first weekly Freethought journal published in America. It lasted till July 1828. He also republished *Ecce Homo*. Houston helped to establish in America a “ Free Press Association ” and a Society of Free Inquirers.

Hovelacque (Abel), French scientist, b. Paris 14 Nov. 1843. He studied law and made part of the groupe of *la Pensée Nouvelle*, with Asseline, Letourneau, Lefevre, etc. He also studied anthropology under Broca and published many articles in the *Revue d’Anthropologie*. He founded with Letourneau, Thulié, Asseline, etc. The “ Bibliothèque des sciences contemporains ” and published therein *La Linguistique*. He also founded with the same the library of anthropological science and published in collaboration with G. Hervé a *précis* of Anthropology and a study of the *Negroes of Africa*. He has also contributed to the Dictionary of Anthropology. For the " Bibliothèque Materialiste " he wrote a work on Primitive man He has also published choice extracts from the works of Voltaire, Diderot and Rousseau, a grammar of the Zend language, and a work on the *Avesta Zoroaster and Mazdaism*. In '78 he was made a member of the municipal council of Paris, and in '81 was elected deputy to the chamber where he sits with the autonomist socialist group.

Howdon (John), author of *A Rational Investigation of the Principles of Natural Philosophy, Physical and Moral*, printed at Haddington, 1810, in which he attacks belief in the Bible.

Huber (Marie), Swiss Deist, b. of Protestant parents, Geneva, 1694. In a work on the *System of Theologians*, 1731, she opposed the dogma of eternal punishment. In '38 published *Letters on the Religion essential to Man*. This was translated into English in the same year. Other works show English reading. She translated selections from the *Spectator*. Died at Lyons, 13 June, 1753.

Hudail (Abul). See Muhammad ibn Hudail (*Al Allaf.*)

Huet (Coenraad Busken), Dutch writer, b. the Hague, 28 Dec. 1826. He became minister of the Walloon Church at Haarlem, but through his Freethought left the church in '63, and became editor of various newspapers, afterwards living in Paris. He wrote many works of literary value, and published *Letters on the Bible*, '57, etc. Died 1887.

Hugo (Victor Marie), French poet and novelist, b. Besançon, 26 Feb. 1802. Was first noted for his *Odes*, published in '21. His dramas, " Hernani," '30, and " Marion Delorme," '31, were highly successful. He was admitted into the French Academy in '41, and made a peer in '45. He gave his cordial adhesion to the Republic of '48, and was elected to the Assembly by the voters of Paris. He attacked Louis Napoleon, and after the *coup d'état* was proscribed. He first went to Brussels, where he published *Napoleon the Little*, a biting satire. He afterwards settled at Guernsey, where he remained until the fall of the Empire, producing *The Legend of the Ages*, '59, *Les Misérables*, '62, *Toilers of the Sea*, '69, and other works. After his return to Paris he produced a new series of the *Legend of the Ages*, *The Pope, Religions and Religion, Torquemada*, and other poems.

He died 22 May, 1885, and it being decided he should have a national funeral, the Pantheon was secularised for that purpose, the cross being removed. Since his death a poem entitled *The End of Satan* has been published.

Hugues (Clovis), French Socialist, poet, and deputy, b. Menerbes, 3 Nov. 1850. In youth he desired to become a priest, but under the influence of Hugo left the black business. In '71 he became head of the Communist movement at Marseilles He was sentenced to three years' imprisonment. In '81 he was elected deputy, and sits on the extreme left.

Humboldt (Friedrich Heinrich Alexander von), illustrious German naturalist and traveller, b. Berlin, 14 Sept. 1769. He studied under Heyne and Blumenbach, travelled in Holland, France and England with George Forster, the naturalist, and became director-general of mines. In 1799 he set out to explore South America and Mexico, and in 1804 returned with rich collection of animals, plants and minerals. Humboldt became a resident of Paris, where he enjoyed the friendship of Lalande, Delambre, Arago, and all the living distinguished French scientists. After numerous important contributions to scientific knowledge, at the age of seventy-four he composed his celebrated *Cosmos*, the first volume of which appeared in '45 and the fourth in '58. To Varnhagen von Ense he wrote in 1841 : " Bruno Bauer has found me pre-adamatically converted. Many years ago I wrote, ' Toutes les réligions positives offrent trois parties distinctes ; un traité de mœurs partout le même et très pur, un rêve géologique, et un mythe ou petit roman historique ; le dernier élément obtient le plus d'importance.' " Later on he says that Strauss disposes of "the Christian myths." Humboldt was an unwearied student of science, paying no attention to religion, and opposed his brother in regard to his essay *On the Province of the Historian*, because he considered it to acknowledge the belief in the divine government of the world, which seemed to him as complete a delusion as the hypothesis of a principle of life. He died in Berlin, 6 May, 1859, in his ninetieth year.

Humboldt (Karl Wilhelm von), Prussian statesman and philosopher, b. Potsdam, 22 June. 1767. He was educated by Campe. Went to Paris in 1789, and hailed the revolution with

179

enthusiasm. In '92 he published *Ideas on the Organisation of the State.* He became a friend of Schiller and Goethe, and in 1809 was Minister of Public Instruction. He took part in founding the University of Berlin. He represented Prussia at the Congress of Vienna. '14. He advocated a liberal constitution, but finding the King averse, retired at the end of '19, and devoted himself to the study of comparative philology. He said there were three things he could not comprehend—orthodox piety, romantic love, and music. He died 8 April, 1835. His works were collected and edited by his brother.

Hume (David), philosopher and historian, b. Edinburgh, 26 April, 1711. In 1735 he went to France to study, and there wrote his *Treatise on Human Nature*, published in 1739. This work then excited no interest friendly or hostile. Hume's *Essays Moral and Political* appeared in 1742, and in 1752 his *Inquiry Concerning the Principles of Morals* which of all his writings he considered the best. In 1755 he published his *Natural History of Religion*, which was furiously attacked by Warburton in an anonymous tract. In 1754 he published the first volume of his *History of England*, which he did not complete till 1761. He became secretary to the Earl of Hertford, ambassador at Paris, where he was cordially welcomed by the philosophers. He returned in 1766, bringing Rousseau with him. Hume became Under Secretary of State in 1767, and in 1769 retired to Edinburgh, where he died 25 Aug. 1776. After his death his *Dialogues on Natural Religion* were published, and also some unpublished essays on Suicide, the Immortality of the Soul, etc. Hume's last days were singularly cheerful. His friend, the famous Dr. Adam Smith, considered him " as approaching as nearly to the idea of a perfectly wise and virtuous man as perhaps the nature of human frailty will permit."

Hunt (James), Ph.D., physiologist, b. 1833, was the founder of the Anthropological Society, of which he was the first president, '63. He was the author of the *Negro's Place in Nature*, a work on Stammering, etc. Died 28 Aug. 1869.

Hunt (James Henry Leigh), poet, essayist and critic, b. Southgate, Middlesex, 19 Oct. 1784, was educated with Lamb and Coleridge at Christ's Hospital, London. He joined his brother John in editing first the *Sunday News*, 1805, and then the *Examiner*, 1808. They were condemned to pay a fine, each of £500, and to be imprisoned for two years, 1812–14, for a satirical article, in which the prince regent was called an "Adonis of fifty." This imprisonment procured him the friendship of Shelley and Byron, with whom, after editing the *Indicator* he was associated in editing the *Liberal*. He wrote many choice books of poems and criticisms, and in his *Religion of the Heart*, '53, repudiates orthodoxy. Died 28 Aug. 1859.

Hutten (Ulrich von), German poet and reformer, b. of noble family Steckelberg, Hesse Cassel, 22 April 1488. He was sent to Fulda to become a monk, but fled in 1501 to Erfurt, where he studied *humaniora*. After some wild adventures he went to Wittenberg in 1510, and Vienna 1512, and also studied at Pavia and Bologna. He returned to Germany in 1517 as a common soldier in the army of Maximilian. His great object was to free his country from sacerdotalism, and most of his writings are satires against the Pope, monks and clergy. Persecution drove him to Switzerland, but the Council of Zurich drove him him out of their territory and he died on the isle of Ufnau, Lake Zürich, 29 Aug. 1523.

Hutton (James), Scotch geologist and philosopher, b. at Edinburgh 3 June, 1736. He graduated as M.D. at Leyden in 1749, and investigated the strata of the north of Scotland. He published a dissertation on *Light, Heat, and Fire*, and in his *Theory of the World*, 1795, attributes geological phenomena to the action of fire. He also wrote a work entitled *An Investigation of the Principles of Knowledge*, the opinions of which, says Chalmers, "abound in sceptical boldness and philosophical infidelity." Died 26 March 1797.

Huxley (Thomas Henry), LL.D., Ph.D., F.R.S., b. Ealing, 4 May, 1825. He studied medicine, and in '46 took M.R.C.S., and was appointed assistant naval surgeon. His cruises afforded opportunities for his studies of natural history. In '51 he was elected Fellow of the Royal Society, and in '54 was made Professor at the School of Mines. In '60 he lectured on "The Relation of Man to the Lower Animals," and afterwards published *Evidence as to Man's Place in Nature* (1863). In addition to numerous scientific works, Professor Huxley has written numerous forcible articles, addresses, etc , collected in *Lay Sermons,* '70 ; *Critiques and Addresses,* '73 ; and *American Addresses,* '79. A vigorous writer, his *Hume* in the " English Men of Letters " series is a model of clear exposition. In his controversies with Mr. Gladstone, in his articles on the *Evolution of Theology,* and in his recent polemic with the Rev. Mr. Wace in the *Nineteenth Century.* Professor Huxley shows all his freshness, and proves himself as ready in demolishing theological fictions as in demonstrating scientific facts. He states as his own life aims " The popularising of science and untiring opposition to that ecclesiastical spirit, that clericalism, which in England, as everywhere else, and to whatever denomination it may belong, is the deadly enemy of science."

Hypatia, Pagan philosopher and martyr, b. Alexandria early in the second half of the fourth century. She became a distinguished lecturer and head of the Neo-Platonic school (c. 400). The charms of her eloquence brought many disciples. By a Christian mob, incited by St. Cyril, she was in Lent 415 torn from her chariot, stripped naked, cut with oyster-shells and finally burnt piecemeal. This true story of Christian persecution has been disguised into a legend related of St. Catherine in the Roman breviary (Nov. 25).

Ibn Bajjat. See Avenpace.

Ibn Massara. See Massara.

Ibn Rushd. See Averroes.

Ibn Sabîn. See Sabin.

Ibn Sina. See Avicenna.

Ibn Tofail. See Abu Bakr.

Ibsen (Henrik), an eminent Norwegian dramatist and poet, b. Skien, 20 March, 1828. At first he studied medicine, but he turned his attention to literature. In '52, through the influence of Ole Bull, he became director of the theatre at Bergen, for which he wrote a great deal. From '57 to '63 he directed the theatre at Christiania. In the following year he went to Rome. The Storthing accorded him an annual pension for his services to literature. His dramas, *Brand, (Peer Gynt),* *Kejser og Galilær* (Cæsar [Julian] and the Galilean), *Nora,* and *Samfundets Stotler* (the Pillars of Society), and *Ghosts* exhibit his unconventional spirit. Ibsen is an open unbeliever in Christianity. He looks forward to social regeneration through liberty, individuality, and education without superstition.

Ilive (Jacob), English printer and letter founder, b. Bristol about 1710. He published a pretended translation of the Book of Jasher, 1751, and some other curious works. He was prosecuted for blasphemy in *Some Modest Remarks on the late Bishop Sherlock's Sermons*, and sentenced to two years' imprisonment, 15 June, 1756—10 June, 1758. He was confined in the Clerkenwell House of Correction and published some pamphlets exposing the bad condition of the prison and suggesting means for its improvement. He died in 1768.

Imray (I. W.), author, b. 1802. Wrote in Carlile's *Republican* and *Lion*, and published "Altamont," an atheistic drama, in 1828.

Ingersoll (Robert Green), American orator, b. Dresden, New York, 11 Aug. 1833. His father was a Congregationalist clergyman. He studied law, and opened an office in Shawneetown, Illinois. In '62 he became colonel of the 11th Illinois Cavalry, and served in the war, being taken prisoner. In '66 he was appointed attorney-general for Illinois. At the National Republican Convention, '76, he proposed Blaine for President in a speech that attracted much attention. In '77 he refused the post of Minister to Germany. He has conducted many important cases, and defended C. B. Reynolds when tried for blasphemy in '86. Col. Ingersoll is the most popular speaker in America. Eloquence, humor, and pathos are alike at his command. He is well known by his books, pamphlets, and speeches directed against Christianity. He had published the *Gods, Ghosts, Some Mistakes of Moses*, and a collection of his Lectures, '83, and *Prose Poems and Extracts*, '84. Most of his lectures have been republished in England. We mention *What must I do to be Saved? Hell, The Dying Creed, Myth and Miracle, Do I Blaspheme? Real Blasphemy*. In the pages of the *North American Review* Col. Ingersoll has defended Freethought against Judge Black, the Rev. H. Field, Mr. Gladstone, and Cardinal Manning.

Inman (Thomas), B.A., physician and archæologist, b. 1820. Educated at London University, he settled at Liverpool, being

connected with the well-known shipping family of that port.
He is chiefly known by his work on *Ancient Faiths Embodied in
Ancient Names*, in which he deals with the evidences of phallic
worship amongst Jews and other nations. It was first published
in '69. A second edition appeared in '73. He also wrote
*Ancient Pagan and Modern Christian Symbolism Exposed and
Explained*, '69, and a controversial Freethought work, entitled
Ancient Faiths and Modern, published at New York '76. Dr.
Inman was for some time President of the Liverpool Literary
and Philosophical Society, and was physician to the Royal
Infirmary of that city. His professional life was one of
untiring industry. He wrote several medical works, including
two volumes on the *Preservation and Restoration of Health*.
Died at Clifton, 3 May. 1876.

Iron (Ralph), pseudonym of Olive Schreiner, *q.v*

Isnard (Felix), French physician, b. Grasse 1829. Author
of a work on *Spiritualism and Materialism*, 1879.

Isnard (Maximin), Girondin revolutionist, b. Grasse 16 Feb.
1751. He was made a member of the Assembly, in which he
declared, " The Law, behold my God. I know no other." He
voted for the death of the King, and was nominated president
of the Convention. On the fall of the Girondins he made his
escape, and reappeared after the fall of Robespierre. In 1796
he was one of the Council of Ffve Hundred. Died 1830.

Isoard (Eric Michel Antoine), French writer, b. Paris, 1826.
Was naval officer in '48 but arrested as socialist in '49. In '70
he was made sous-prefet of Cambrai and wrote *Guerre aux
Jésuites*.

Isoard Delisle (Jean Baptiste Claude), called also Delisle de
Sales, French man of letters, b. Lyons 1743. When young he
entered the Congregation of the Oratory, but left theology for
literature. In 1769 he published the *Philosophy of Nature*,
which in 1771 was discovered to be irreligious, and he was
condemned to perpetual banishment. While in prison he was
visited by many of the philosophers, and a subscription was
opened for him, to which Voltaire gave five hundred francs.
He went to the court of Frederick the Great, and subsequently
published many works of little importance. Died at Paris 22
Sept. 1816.

Jacob (Andre Alexandre). See Erdan (A.)

Jacobson (Augustus), American, author of *Why I do not Believe*, Chicago 1881, and *The Bible Inquirer*.

" **Jacobus** (Dom) " Pseudonym of POTVIN (Charles) *q.v.*

Jacoby (Leopold) German author of *The Idea of Development.* 2 vols. Berlin 1874–76.

Jacolliot (Louis), French orientalist, b. Saint Etienne, 1806. Brought up to the law, in '43 he was made judge at Pondichery. He first aroused attention by his work, *The Bible in India*, '70. He also has written on *Genesis of Humanity*, '76. *The Religious Legislators, Moses, Manu and Muhammad*, '80, and *The Natural and Social History of Humanity*, '84, and several works of travel.

Jantet (Charles and Hector), two doctors of Lyons. b. the first in 1826, the second in '28, have published together able *Aperçus Philosophiques* on Renan's Life of Jesus, '64, and *Doctrine Medicale Matérialiste*, 1866.

Jaucourt (Louis de), Chevalier, French scholar and member of the Royal Society of London and of the academies of Berlin and Stockholm, b. Paris 27 Sept. 1704. He studied at Geneva, Cambridge, and Leyden, furnished the *Encyclopédie* with many articles, and conducted the *Bibliothèque Raisonnée.* Died at Compiègne, 3 Feb. 1779.

Jefferies (Richard), English writer, b. 1848, famous for his descriptions of nature in *The Gamekeeper at Home, Wild Life in a Southern Country*, etc. In his autobiographical *Story of My Heart* (1883) Mr. Jefferies shows himself a thorough Freethinker. Died Goring-on-Thames, 14 Aug. 1887.

Jefferson (Thomas), American statesman, b. Shadwell, Virginia, 2 April 1743. He studied law and was admitted to the bar in 1767. He became a member of the House of Burgesses, 1769–75. In 1774 he published his *Summary Views of the Rights of British-Americans*. He drafted and reported to Congress the "Declaration of Independence" which was unanimously adopted, 4 July 1766. He was Governor of Virginia from 1719 to 1781, and originated a system of education in the State. He was Ambassador to Paris from 1785–89, secretary of state from 1789–93, vice-president 1791–1801 and third president of the United States 1801–9. In '19 he founded the University of Virginia, of which he was rector till his death, 4 July 1826. Dr. J. Thomas in his *Dictionary of Biography* says "In religion he was what is denominated a freethinker." He spoke in old age of " the hocus-pocus phanton of God, which like another Cerberus had one body and three heads." See his life by J. Parton.

Johnson (Richard Mentor), Colonel, American soldier and statesman, b. Bryant's Station, Kentucky, 17 Oct. 1781. Was educated at Lexington, studied law, and practiced with success. Became member of the Kentucky Legislature in 1805, and raised a regiment of cavalry '12. Fought with distinction against British and Indians. Was member of Congress from 1807-19, and from '29-37 ; a United States Senator from '19-29, and Vice-President of the United States, '37-40. Is remembered by his report against the suspension of Sunday mails and his speeches in favor of rights of conscience. Died at Frankfort, Kentucky, 19 Nov. 1850.

Johnson (Samuel), American author, b. Salem, Massachusetts, 10 Oct. 1822. He was educated at Harvard, and became pastor of a " Free Church " at Lynn in '53. He never attached himself to any denomination, although in some points his views were like those of the Unitarians and Universalists. About '46 he published, in conjunction with S. Longfellow, brother of the poet, *Hymns of the Spirit, Oriental Religions in relation to Universal Religion*, of which the volume on India appeared in '72, China '77, and Persia '84. Died Andover, 19 Feb. 1882.

Jones (Ernest Charles), barrister and political orator, b. Berlin, 25 Jan. 1819. His father was in the service of the King of Hanover, who became his godfather. Called to the bar in '44 in the following year he joined the Chartist movement, editing the *People's Paper, Notes to the People*, and other Chartist periodicals. In '48 he was tried for making a seditious speech, and condemned to two years' imprisonment, during which he wrote *Beldagon Church* and other poems. He stood for Halifax in '47, and Nottingham in '53 and '57, without success. He was much esteemed by the working classes in Manchester, where he died 26 Jan. 1869.

Jones (John Gale), Political orator, b. 1771. At the time of the French Revolution he became a leading member of the

London Corresponding Society. Arrested at Birmingham for sedition, he obtained a verdict of acquittal. He was subsequently committed to Newgate in Feb. 1810, for impugning the proceedings of the House of Commons, and there remained till his liberation was effected by the prorogation of Parliament, June 21. On 26 Dec. '11 he was again convicted for " a seditious and blasphemous libel." He was a resolute advocate of the rights of free publication during the trials of Carlile and his shopmen. Died Somers Town, 4 April, 1838.

Jones (Lloyd), Socialist, b. of Catholic parents at Brandon, co. Cork, Ireland, in March, 1811. In '27 he came over to Manchester, and in '32 joined the followers of Robert Owen. He became " a social missionary," and had numerous debates with ministers, notably one on " The Influence of Christianity " with J. Barker, then a Methodist, at Manchester, in '39. Lloyd Jones was an active supporter of co-operation and trades-unionism, and frequently acted as arbitrator in disputes between masters and men. He contributed to the *New Moral World, Spirit of the Age, Glasgow Sentinel, Leeds Express, North British Daily Mail, Newcastle Chronicle*, and *Co-operative News.* Died at Stockwell, 22 May, 1886, leaving behind a *Life of Robert Owen.*

Joseph II., Emperor of Germany, son of Francis I. and Maria Theresa, b. Vienna 13 March 1741. In 1764 he was elected king of the Romans, and in the following year succeeded to the throne of Germany. He wrought many reforms, suppressed the Jesuits 1773, travelled in France as Count Falkenstein, saw d'Alembert but did not visit Voltaire. He abolished serfdom, allowed liberty of conscience, suppressed several convents, regulated others, abridged the power of the pope and the clergy, and mitigated the condition of the Jews. Carlyle says "a mighty reformer he had been, the greatest of his day. Austria gazed on him, its admiration not unmixed with terror. He rushed incessantly about, hardy as a Charles Twelfth ; slept on his bearskin on the floor of any inn or hut ;—flew at the throat of every absurdity, however broad and based or dangerously armed. 'Disappear I say.' A most prompt, severe, and yet beneficent and charitable kind of man. Immensely ambitious, that must be said withal. A great admirer of Friedrich ; bent to imitate him with profit. ' Very clever indeed ' says Friedrich, ' but has the fault ' (a terribly grave one!) of generally taking the second step without having taken the first.' " Died Vienna 20 Feb. 1790.

Jouy (Victor Joseph ETIENNE DE), French author b. Jouy near Versailles 1764. He served as soldier in India and afterwards in the wars of the Republic. A disciple of Voltaire to whom he erected a temple, he was a prolific writer, his plays being much esteemed in his own day. Died 4 Sept. 1846.

Julianus (Flavius Claudius), Roman Emperor, b. Constantinople 17 Nov. 331. In the massacre of his family by the sons of Constantine he escaped. He was educated in the tenets of Christianity but returned to an eclectic Paganism. In 354 he was declared Cæsar. He made successful campaigns against the Germans who had overrun Gaul and in 361 was made Emperor. He proclaimed liberty of conscience and sought to uproot the Christian superstition by his writings, of which only fragments remain. As Emperor he exhibited great talent tact, industry, and skill. He was one of the most gifted and learned of the Roman Emperors, and his short reign (Dec. 361—26 June, 363), comprehended the plans of a life-long administration. He died while seeking to repel a Persian invasion, and his death was followed by the triumph of Christianity and the long night of the dark ages.

Junghuhn (Franz Wilhelm), traveller and naturalist, b. Mansfeld, Prussia 29 Oct 1812. His father was a barber and surgeon. Franz studied at Halle and Berlin. He distinguished himself by love for botany and geology. In a duel with another student he killed him and was sentenced to imprisonment at Ehrenbreitster for 20 years. There he simulated madness and was removed to the asylum at Coblentz, whence he escaped to Algiers. In '34 he joined the Dutch Army in the Malay Archipelago. He travelled through the island of Java making a botanical and geological survey. In '54 he published his *Licht en Schaduwbulden uit de binnenlanden van Java* (Light and Shadow pictures from the interior of Java), which contains his ideas of God, religion and science, together with sketches of nature and of the manners of the inhabitants. This book aroused much indignation from the pious, but also much agreement among freethinkers, and led to the establishment of *De Dageraad* (The Daybreak,) the organ of the Dutch Freethinkers Union. Junghuhn afterwards returned to Java and died 21 April, '64 at Lemberg, Preanges, Regentsch. His *Light and Shadow pictures* have been several times reprinted.

Kalisch (Moritz Marcus), Ph.D., b. of Jewish parents in Pomerania, 16 May, 1828. Educated at the University of Berlin, where he studied under Vatke and others. Early in '49 he came to England as a political refugee, and found employment as tutor to the Rothschild family. His critical *Commentary on the Pentateuch* commenced with a volume on Exodus, '55, Genesis '58, Leviticus in two vols. in '67 and '72 respectively. His rational criticism anticipated the school of Wellhausen. He published *Bible Studies* on Balaam and Jonah '77, and discussions on philosophy and religion in a very able and learned work entitled *Path and Goal.* '80. Kalisch also contributed to Scott's series of Freethought tracts. Died at Baslow, Derbyshire, 23 Aug. 1885.

Kames (Lord). See Home (Henry).

Kant (Immanuel), German critical philosopher, b. Königsberg, 22 April, 1724. He became professor of mathematics in 1770. In 1781 he published his great work, *The Critick of Pure Reason*, which denied all knowledge of the " Thing itself," and overthrew the dogmatism of earlier metaphysics. In 1792 the philosopher fell under the royal censorship for his *Religion within the Limits of Pure Reason.* Kant effected a complete revolution in philosophy, and his immediate influence is not yet exhausted. Died at Königsberg, 12 Feb. 1804.

Kapila. One of the earliest Hindu thinkers. His system is known as the Atheistic philosophy. It is expounded in the Sankhya Karika, an important relic of bold rationalistic Indian thought. His aphorisms have been translated by J. R. Ballantyne.

Karneades. See Carneades.

Keeler (Bronson C.) American author of an able *Short History of the Bible*, being a popular account of the formation and development of the canon, published at Chicago 1881.

Keim (Karl Theodor), German rationalist, b. Stuttgart, 17 Dec. 1825. Was educated at Tübingen, and became professor of theology at Zürich. Is chiefly known by his *History of Jesus of Nazara* ('67—'72). He also wrote a striking work on *Primitive Christianity* ('78), and endeavored to reproduce the lost work of Celsus. His rationalism hindered his promotion, and he was an invalid most of his days. Died at Giessen, where he was professor, 17 Nov. 1878.

Keith (George), Lord Marshall, Scotch soldier, b. Kincardine 1685, was appointed by Queen Anne captain of Guard. His property being confiscated for aiding the Pretender, he went to the Continent, and like his brother, was in high favor with Frederick the Great. Died Berlin, 25 May, 1778.

Keith (James Francis Edward), eminent military commander, b. Inverugie, Scotland, 11 June, 696. Joined the army of the Pretender and was wounded at Sheriffmuir, 1715. He afterwards served with distinction in Spain and in Russia, where he rose to high favor under the Empress Elizabeth. In 1647 he took service with Frederick the Great as field-marshal, and became Governor of Berlin. Carlyle calls him " a very clear-eyed, sound observer of men and things. Frederick, the more he knows him, likes him the better." From their correspondence it is evident Keith shared the sceptical opinions of Frederick. After brilliant exploits in the seven years' war at Prague, Rossbach, and Olmutz, Marshal Keith fell in the battle of Hochkirch, 14 Oct. 1758.

Kenrick (William), LL.D., English author, b. near Watford, Herts, about 1720. In 1751 he published, at Dublin, under the pen-name of Ontologos, an essay to prove that the soul is not immortal. His first poetic production was a volume of *Epistles, Philosophical and Moral* (1759), addressed to Lorenzo; an avowed defence of scepticism. In 1775 he commenced the *London Review*, and the following year attacked Soame Jenyns's work on Christianity. He translated some of the works of Buffon, Rousseau, and Voltaire. Died 10 June 1779.

Kerr (Michael Crawford) American statesman, b. Titusville, Western Pennsylvania. 15 March 1871. He was member of the Indiana Legislature '56, and elected to Congress in '74 and endeavoured to revise the tariff in the direction of free-trade. Died Rockbridge, Virginia, 19 Aug. 1876, a confirmed Freethinker and Materialist.

190

Ket, Kett, or **Knight** (Francis), of Norfolk, a relative of
the rebellious tanner. He was of Windham and was an M.A.
He was prosecuted for heresy and burnt in the castle ditch,
Norwich, 14 Jan. 1588. Stowe says he was burnt for "divers
detestable opinions against Christ our Saviour."

Khayyam (Omar) or UMAR KHAIYAM, Persian astronomer,
poet, b. Naishapur Khorassan, iu the second half of the eleventh
century, and was distinguished by his reformation of the calendar as well as by his verses (Rubiyat), which E. Fitzgerald
has so finely rendered in English. He alarmed his contempo-
raries and made himself obnoxious to the Sufis. Died about
1123. Omar laughed at the prophets and priests, and told men
to be happy instead of worrying themselves about God and the
Hereafter. He makes his soul say, " I myself am Heaven and
Hell."

Kielland (Alexander Lange), Norwegian novelist, b. Sta-
vanger, 18 Feb. 1849. He studied law at Christiania, but never
practised. His stories, *Workpeople, Skipper Worsē, Poison*, and
Snow exhibit his bold opinions.

Kleanthes. See Cleanthes.

Klinger (Friedrich Maximilian von), German writer, b.
Frankfort, 19 Feb. 1753. Went to Russia in 1780, and became
reader to the Grand Duke Paul. Published poems, dramas,
and romances, exhibiting the revolt of nature against conven-
tionality. Goethe called him "a true apostle of the Gospel of
nature." Died at Petersburg, 25 Feb. 1831.

Kneeland (Abner), American writer, b. Gardner, Mass.,
7 April, 1774, became a Baptist and afterwards a Universalist
minister. He invented a new system of orthography, published
a translation of the New Testament, 1823, *The Deist* (2 Vols.),
'22, edited the *Olive Branch* and the *Christian Inquirer*. He wrote
The Fourth Epistle of Peter, '29, and a *Review of the Evidences of
Christianity*, being a series of lectures delivered in New York in
'29. In that year he removed to Boston, and in April '31
commenced the *Boston Investigator*, the oldest Freethought
journal. In '33 he was indicted and tried for blasphemy for
saying that he "did not believe in the God which Universalists
did." He was sentenced 21 Jan. '34, to two months' imprison-

ment and a fine of five hundred dollars. The verdict was confirmed in the Courts of Appeal in '36, and he received two months' imprisonment. Kneeland was a Pantheist. He took Frances Wright as an associate editor, and soon after left the *Boston Investigator* in the hands of P. Mendum and Seaver, and retired to a farm at Salubria, where he died 27 August, 1844. His edition, with notes, of Voltaire's *Philosophical Dictionary*, was published in two volumes in 1852.

Knoblauch (Karl von), German author, b. Dillenburg, 3 Nov· 1757. He was a friend of Mauvillon and published several works directed against supernaturalism and superstition. Died at Bernburg, 6 Sept. 1794.

Knowlton (Charles) Dr., American physician and author, b. Templeton, Mass., 10 May, 1800. He published the *Fruits of Philosophy*, for which he was imprisoned in '32. He was a frequent correspondent of the *Boston Investigator*, and held a discussion on the Bible and Christianity with the Rev. Mr. Thacher of Harley. About '29 he published *The Elements of Modern Materialism*. Died in Winchester, Mass., 20 Feb. 1850.

Knutzen (Matthias), b. Oldensworth, in Holstein, 1645. He early lost his parents, and was brought to an uncle at Königsberg, where he studied philosophy. He took to the adventurous life of a wandering scholar and propagated his principles in many places. In 1674 he preached Atheism publicly at Jena, in Germany, and had followers who were called " Gewissener," from their acknowledging no other authority but conscience. It is said there were seven hundred in Jena alone. What became of him and them is unknown. A letter dated from Rome gives his principles. He denied the existence of either God or Devil, deemed churches and priests useless, and held that there is no life beyond the present, for which conscience is a sufficient guide, taking the place of the Bible, which contains great contradictions. He also wrote two dialogues.

Koerbagh (Adriaan), Dutch martyr, b. Amsterdam, 1632 or 1633. He became a doctor of law and medicine. In 1668 he published *A Flower Garden of all Loveliness*, a dictionary of definitions in which he gave bold explanations. The work was rigidly suppressed, and the writer fled to Culenborg. There he translated a book *De Trinitate*, and began a work entitled

A Light Shining in Dark Places, to illuminate the chief things of theology and religion by Vrederijk Waarmond, inquisitor of truth. Betrayed for a sum of money, Koerbagh was tried for blasphemy, heavily fined and sentenced to be imprisoned for ten years, to be followed by ten years banishment. He died in prison, Oct. 1669.

Kolb (Georg Friedrich), German statistician and author, b. Spires 14 Sept. 1808, author of an able *History of Culture*, 1869-70. Died at Munich 15 May. 1884.

Koornhert (Theodore). See Coornhert (Dirk Volkertszoon.)

Korn (Selig), learned German Orientalist of Jewish birth, b. Prague, 26 April, 1804. A convert to Freethought, under the name of "F. Nork," he wrote many works on mythology which may still be consulted with profit. A list is given in Fuerst's *Bibliotheca Judaica*. We mention *Christmas and Easter Explained by Oriental Sun Worship*, Leipsic, '36; *Brahmins and Rabbins*, Weissen, '36; *The Prophet Elijah as a Sun Myth*, '37; *The Gods of the Syrians*, '42; *Biblical Mythology of the Old and New Testament*, 2 vols. Stuttgart, '42—'43. Died at Teplitz, Bohemia, 16 Oct. 1850.

Krause (Ernst H. Ludwig), German scientific writer, b. Zielenzig 22 Nov. 1839. He studied science and contributed to the *Vossische Zeitung* and *Gartenlaube*. In '63 he published, under the pen-name of "Carus Sterne," a work on *The Natural History of Ghosts*, and in '76 a work on *Growth and Decay*, a history of evolution. In '77 he established with Hæckel, Dr. Otto Caspari, and Professor Gustav Jaeger, the monthly magazine *Kosmos*, devoted to the spread of Darwinism. This he conducted till '82. In *Kosmos* appeared the germ of his little book on *Erasmus Darwin*, '79, to which Charles Darwin wrote a preliminary notice. As "Carus Sterne" he has also written essays entitled *Prattle from Paradise*, *The Crown of Creation*, '84, and an illustrated work in parts on *Ancient and Modern Ideas of the World*, '87, etc.

Krekel (Arnold), American judge, b. Langenfield, Prussia 14 March, 1815. Went with parents to America in '32 and settled in Missouri. In '42 he was elected Justice of the Peace and afterwards county attorney. In '52 he was elected to the Missouri State Legislature. He served in the civil war being elected colonel, was president of the constitutional convention of '65 and signed the ordinance of emancipation by which the slaves of Missouri were set free. He was appointed judge by President Lincoln 9 March, '65. A pronounced Agnostic, when he realized he was about to die he requested his wife not to wear mourning, saying that death was as natural as birth. Died at Kansas 14 July, 1888.

Krekel (Mattie H. Hulett), b. of freethinking parents, Elkhart Indiana 13 April, 1840. Educated at Rockford, Illinois, in her 16th year became a teacher. Married Judge Krekel, after whose death, she devoted her services to the Freethought platform.

Kropotkin (Petr Aleksyeevich) *Prince.* Russian anarchist, b. Moscow 9 Dec 1842. After studying at the Royal College of Pages he went to Siberia for five years to pursue geological researches. In '71 he went to Belgium and Switzerland and joined the International. Arrested in Russia, he was condemned to three years imprisonment, escaped '76 and came to England. In '79 he founded at Geneva, *Le Révolté* was expelled. Accused in France in '83 of complicity in the outrage at Lyons. he was condemned to five years imprisonment, but was released in '86, since which he has lived in England. A brother who translated Herbert Spencer's " Biology" into Russian, died in Siberia in the autumn of 1886.

Laas (Ernst) German writer, b. Furstenwalde, 16 June, 1837. He has written three volumes on *Idealism and Positivism,* 1879–'84, and also on *Kant's Place in the History of the Conflict between Faith and Science,* Berlin, 1882. He was professor of philosophy at Strassburg, where he died 25 July, 1885.

Labanca (Baldassarre), professor of moral philosophy in the University of Pisa, b. Agnone, 1829. He took part in the national movement of '48, and in '51 was imprisoned and afterwards expelled from Naples. He has written on progress in philosophy and also a study on primitive Christianity, dedicated to Giordano Bruno, the martyr of Freethought, '86.

Lachatre (Maurice), French writer, b. Issoudun 1814, edits a " Library of Progress," in which has appeared his own *History of the Inquisition,* and *History of the Popes,* '83.

194

Lacroix (Sigismund), the pen name of Sigismund Julien Adolph KRZYZANOWSKI, b. Warsaw 26 May, 1845. His father was a refugee. He wrote with Yves Guyot *The Social Doctrines of Christianity.* In '71 he was elected a municipal councillor of Paris. In '77 he was sentenced to three months' imprisonment for calling Jesus "*enfant adulterin*" in *Le Radical.* In Feb. '81 he was elected president of the municipal council, and in '83 deputy to the French parliament.

Laffitte (Pierre), French Positivist philosopher, b. 21 Feb. 1823 at Beguey (Gironde), became a disciple of Comte and one of his executors. He was professor of mathematics, but since the death of his master has given a weekly course of instruction in the former appartment of Comte. M. Laffitte has published discourses on *The General History of Humanity,* '59, and *The Great Types of Humanity,* '75-6. In '78 he founded *La Revue Occidentale.*

Lagrange (Joseph Louis), Count, eminent mathematician, b. Turin, 25 Jan. 1736. He published in 1788 his *Analytical Mechanics,* which is considered one of the masterpieces of the human intellect. He became a friend of D'Alembert, Diderot, Condorcet, and Delambre. He said he believed it impossible to prove there was a God. Died 10 April 1813.

La Hontan (Jean), early French traveller in Canada, b. 1666. In his account of *Dialogues with an American Savage,* 1704, which was translated into English, he states objections to religion. Died in Hanover, 1715.

Lainez (Alexandre), French poet, b. Chimay, Hainault, 1650, of the same family with the general of the Jesuits. He lived a wandering Bohemian life and went to Holland to see Bayle. Died at Paris 18 April, 1710.

Laing (Samuel), politician and writer, b. Edinburgh 1812, the son of S. Laing of Orkney. Educated at Cambridge, where he took his degree '32; called to the bar '42; became secretary of the railway department of the Board of Trade; returned as Liberal M.P. for Kirkwall '52; helped repeal duty on advertisements in newspapers. In '60 he became finance minister for India. His *Modern Science and Modern Thought,* '85, is a plain exposition of the incompatibility of the old and new

view of the universe. In the *Modern Zoroastrian*, '87, he gives
the philosophy of polarity, in which, however, he was anticipated by Mr. Crozier, who in turn was anticipated by Emerson.
In '88 he entered into a friendly correspondence with Mr.
Gladstone on the subject of Agnosticism his portion of which
has been published.

Lakanal (Joseph), French educator, b. Serres, 14 July, 1762·
Studied for priesthood, but gave up that career. He entered
with ardor into the Revolution, was a member of the Convention 1792-5, and there protected the interests of science. At
the restoration in 1814 he retired to America, and was
welcomed by Jefferson and became president of the University
of Louisana. He returned to France after the Revolution of '30,
and died in Paris 14 Feb. 1845.

Lalande (Joseph Jérome LE FRANCAIS de), distinguished
French astronomer, b. Bourg en Bresse, 11 July 1732. Educated by the Jesuits, he was made a member of the
Academy of Sciences in his 20th year. In 1762 he became
Professor of Astronomy at the College of France. In 1764 he
published his *Treatise of Astronomy*, to which Dupuis subjoined
a memoir, which formed the basis of his *Origin of all Religions*,
the idea of which he had taken from Lalande, In Aug 1793
Lalande hazarded his own life to save Dupont de Nemours, and
some priests whom he concealed in the observatory of Mazarin
college. It was upon Lalande's observations that the Republican
calender was drawn up. At Lalande's instigation Sylvain
Maréchal published his *Dictionary of Atheists*, to which the
astronomer contributed supplements after Maréchal's death.
Lalande professed himself prouder of being an Atheist than of
being an astronomer. His *Bibliographie Astronomique* is called
by Prof. de Morgan " a perfect model of scientific bibliography." It was said that never did a young man address
himself to Lalande without receiving proof of his generosity.
He died at Paris 4 April, 1807.

Lamarck (Jean Baptiste Pierre Antoine de MONET) French
naturalist, b. Picardy 1 Aug. 1744, educated for the Church,
but entered the army in 1761, and fought with distinction.
Having been disabled, he went to Paris, studied Botany, and
published *French Flora* in 1788, which opened to him the

196

Academy of Sciences. He became assistant at the Museum of Natural History, and in 1809 propounded, in his *Zoological Philosophy*, a theory of transmutation of species His *Natural History of Invertebrate Animals* (1815—22) was justly celebrated. He became blind several years before his death, 18 Dec. 1829.

Lamborelle (Louis). Belgian author of books on *The Good Old Times*, Brussells, 1874 ; *The Apostles and Martyrs of Liberty of Conscience*, Antwerp, 1882, and other anti-clerical works. Lamborelle lost a post under government through his anti-clerical views, and is one of the council of the Belgian Free-thought party.

Lamettrie (Julian Offray de). French physician and philosopher, b. St. Malo, 25 Dec. 1709. Destined for the Church, he was educated under the Jesuits at Caen. He, however, became a physician, studying under Boerhaave, at Leyden. Returning to France, he became surgeon to the French Guard, and served at the battles of Fontenoy and Dettingen. Falling ill, he noticed that his faculties fluctuated with his physical state, and drew therefrom materialistic conclusions. The boldness with which he made his ideas known lost him his place, and he took refuge in Holland. Here he published *The Natural History of the Soul*, under the pretence of its being a translation from the English of Charp [Sharp], 1745. This was fellowed by *Man a Machine* (1748), a work which was publicly burnt at Leyden, and orders given for the author's arrest. It was translated into English, and reached a second edition (London, 1750). It was often attri-. buted to D'Argens. Lamettrie held that the senses are the only avenues to knowledge, and that it is absurd to assume a god to explain motion. Only under Atheism will religious strife cease. Lamettrie found an asylum with Frederick the Great, to whom he became physician and reader (Feb. 1748). Here he published *Philosophical Reflections on the Origin of Animals* (1750), translated Seneca on Happiness, etc. He died 11 Nov. 1751, and desired by his will to be buried in the garden of Lord Tyrconnel. The great king thought so well of him that he composed his funeral eulogy.

La Mothe Le Vayer (François de). French sceptical philosopher, b. Paris, 1588, was patronised by Louis XIV., and was

197

preceptor to the Duke of Anjou. Published *The Virtue of Pagans* and *Dialogues after the Manner of the Ancients*, in which he gave scope to his scepticism. Two editions of his collected works appeared, but neither of these contains *The Dialogues of Orasius Tubero* (Frankfort 1606, probably a false date). Died 1672.

Lancelin (Pierre F.), French materialist, b. about 1770. Became a constructive engineer in the French navy, wrote an able *Introduction to the Analysis of Science*, 3 vols. 1801–3, and a physico-mathematical theory of the organisation of worlds, 1805. Died Paris, 1809.

Land (Jan Pieter Nicolaus), Dutch writer, b. Delft, 23 April, 1834. Has written critical studies on Spinoza, and brought out an edition of the philosopher's works in conjunction with J. van Vloten.

Landesmann (Heinrich). See Lorm.

Landor (Walter Savage), English poet, b. Ipsley Court, Warwickshire, 30 Jan. 1775. He was educated at Rugby and Oxford, and, inheriting a fortune, could indulge his tastes as an author. He published a volume of poems in 1795, and *Gebir* in 1798. An ardent Republican, he served as a volunteer colonel in the Spanish Army against Napoleon from 1808 to 1814, besides devoting a considerable sum of money to the Spanish cause. He became a resident of Florence about 1816. His reputation chiefly rests on his great *Imaginary Conversations*, in which many bold ideas are presented in beautiful language. Landor was unquestionably the greatest English writer of his age. While nominally a Christian, he has scattered many Freethought sentiments over his various works. Died at Florence, 17 Sept. 1864.

Lanessan (Jean Louis de), French naturalist, b. at Saint André de Cubzac (Gironde), 13 July, 1843. At 19 he became a naval physician, and M.D. in '68. He was elected in '79 as Radical member of the Muncipal Council of Paris, and re-elected in '81. In August of the same year he was elected Deputy for the Department of the Seine. He founded *Le Reveil*, edited the *Marseillaise*, and started the International Biological Library, to which he contributed a study on the doctrine of Darwin. He has written a standard work on botany, and has written vol. iii. of the " Materialists' Library," on the *Evolution of Matter*.

Lanfrey (Pierre), French author and senator, b. Chambéry' 26 Oct. 1828, became known by a book on *The Church and the Philosophers of the Eighteenth Century*, '55, and celebrated by his *History of Napoleon I.* '67–75. M. Lanfrey also wrote *The Political History of the Popes*, a work placed on the *Index*. Died at Pau, 15 Nov. 1877.

Lang (Andrew), man of letters, b. Selkirk, 31 March, 1844. Educated at St. Andrews and Oxford. Mr. Lang made his name by his translation of the *Odyssey* with Mr. Butcher, and by his graceful poems and ballads. He has written *In the Wrong Paradise*, and many other pleasant sketches. More serious work is shown in *Custom and Myth*, '84, and *Myth, Ritual and Religion*, '87. A disciple of E. B. Tylor, Mr. Lang successfully upholds the evolutionary view of mythology.

Lang (Heinrich), German Rationalist, b. 14 Nov. 1826. Studied theology under Baur at Tübingen, and became teacher at Zürich, where he died, 13 Jan. 1876.

Lange (Friedrich Albert), German philosopher and writer, b. Wald, near Solix, 28 Sept. 1828. He studied at Bonn, and became teacher in the gymnasium of Cologne, '52. In '53 he returned to Bonn as teacher of philosophy, and there enjoyed the friendship of Ueberweg. He became proprietor and editor of the democratic *Landbote*, and filled various municipal offices. In '70 he was called to the chair of philosophy at Zürich, but resigned in '72 and accepted a similar post at Marburg, where he died 21 Nov. 1875. His fame rests on his important *History of Materialism*, which has been translated into English.

Langsdorf (Karl Christian), German Deist, b. 18 May, 1757, author of *God and Nature*, a work on the immortality of the soul, and some mathematical books. Died Heidelberg, 10 June, 1834.

Lankester (Edwin Ray), F.R.S., LL.D., English scientist, b. London, 15 May, 1847, and educated at St. Paul's School and Oxford. Has published many scientific memoirs, revised the translation of Haeckel's *History of Creation*, and has done much to forward evolutionary ideas. In 1876 he exposed the spiritist medium Slade, and procured his conviction.- He is Professor of Zoology and Natural History in the University of London.

La Place (Pierre Simon). One of the greatest astronomers, b. Beaumont-en-Auge, 23 March, 1749. His father was a poor peasant. Through the influence of D'Alembert, La Place became professor of mathematics in the military school, 1768. By his extraordinary abilities he became in 1785 member of the Academy of Science, which he enriched with many memoirs. In 1796 he published his *Exposition of the System of the Universe*, a popularisation of his greater work on *Celestial Mechanics*, 1799-1825. Among his sayings were, " What we know is but little, what we know not is immense." " There is no need for the hypothesis of a God." Died Paris, 5 March, 1827.

Larevelliere-Lepaux (Louis Marie DE), French politician, b. Montaigu 25 Aug. 1753. Attached from youth to the ideas of Rousseau, he was elected with Volney to represent Angers in the national assembly. He was a moderate Republican, defended the proscribed Girondins, was doomed himself but escaped by concealment, and distinguished himself by seeking to replace Catholicism with theophilanthropy or natural religion. He wrote *Reflections on Worship and the National Fêtes.* He became President of the Directory, and after the 18 Brumaire retired, refusing to swear fealty to the empire though offered a pension by Napoleon. Died Paris, 27 March, 1824.

Larousse (Pierre Athanase), French lexicographer, b. of poor parents, 23 Oct. 1817, at Toucy, Yonne, where he became teacher. He edited many school books and founded the *Grand Dictionnaire Universel du XIXe. Siecle*, 1864-77. This is a collection of dictionaries, and may be called the Encyclopedie of this century. Most of M. Larousse's colleagues were also Freethinkers. Died at Paris, 3 Jan. 1875.

Larra (Mariano José de), distinguished Spanish author, b. Madrid, 4 March, 1809. He went with his family to France and completed his education. He returned to Spain in '22. At eighteen he published a collection of poems, which was followed by *El Duende Satirico* (The Satirical Goblin). In '31 appeared his *Pobrecito Hablador* (Poor Gossip), a paper in which he unmercifully satirised the public affairs and men of Spain. It was suppressed after its fourteenth number. He edited in the following year the *Revista Espanola*, signing his articles "Figaro." He travelled through Europe, and on his return to Madrid edited *El Mundo*. Larra wrote also some dramas and translated Lamennais' *Paroles d'un Croyant*. Being disappointed in love he shot himself, 13 April, 1837. Ch. de Mazade, after speaking of Larra's scepticism, adds, " Larra could see too deep to possess any faith whatever. All the truths of this world, he was wont to say, can be wrapped in a cigarette paper!"

Larroque (Patrice), French philosopher, b. Beaume, 27 March, 1801. He became a teacher and was inspector of the academy of Toulouse, 1830–36, and rector of the academies of Cahors, Limoges, and Lyons, 1836–49. In the latter year he was denounced for his opposition to clerical ideas and lost his place. Among his numerous works we mention *De l'Esclavage chez les Nations Chrétiennes*, '57, in which he proves that Christianity did not abolish slavery. This was followed by an *Critical Examnation of the Christian Religion*, '59, and a work on *Religious Renovation*, '59, which proposes a moral system founded upon pure deism. Both were for a while prohibited in France. M. Larroque also wrote on *Religion and Politics*, '78. Died at Paris, 15 June, 1879.

Lassalle (Ferdinand Johann Gottlieb), founder of German Social Democratic party, b. of Jewish parents, 11 April, 1825, in Breslau, studied philosophy and law at Breslau and Berlin. He became a follower of Hegel and Feuerbach. Heine, at Paris, '46, was charmed with him. Humboldt called him "Wunderkind." In 1858 he published a profound work on the philosophy of Heraclitus. For planning an insurrection against the Prussian Government he was arrested, but won his acquittal. Died through a duel, 31 Aug. 1864.

Lastarria (José Victorino), Chilian statesman and Positivist, b. Rancagua, 1812. From youth he applied himself to teaching and journalism, and in '38 was appointed teacher of civil law and literature in the National Institute. He has founded several journals and literary societies. From '43 he has been at different times deputy to the legislature and secretary to the republic of Chili. He has also served as minister to Peru and Brazil. In '73 he founded the Santiago Academy of Science and Literature; has written many works, and his *Lecciones de Politicia Positiva* has been translated into French by E. de Rivière and others, 1879.

Lau (Theodor Ludwig), German philosopher, b. at Königsberg, 15 June 1670, studied at Königsberg and Halle, and about 1695 travelled through Holland, England, and France. In 1717 he published in Latin, at Frankfort, *Philosophical Meditations on God, the World, and Man*, which excited an outcry for its materialistic tendency and was supressed. He was a follower of Spinoza, and held several official positions from which he was deposed on account of his presumed atheism. Died at Altona, 8 Feb. 1740.

Laurent (François), Belgian jurisconsult, b. Luxembourg, 8 July, 1810. Studied law and became an advocate. In '35 he was made Professor of Civil Law in the University of Ghent, a post he held, despite clerical protests, till his retirement in '80. A voluminous author on civil and international law, his principal work is entitled *Studies in the History of Humanity*. He was a strong advocate of the separation of Church and State, upon which he wrote, 1858-60. He also wrote *Letters on the Jesuits*, '65. Died in 1887.

Law (Harriet), English lecturess, who for many years occupied the secular platform, and engaged in numerous debates. She edited the *Secular Chronicle*, 1876-1879.

Lawrence (James), Knight of Malta, b. Fairfield, Jamaica, 1773, of good Lancashire family. Educated at Eton and Goltingen; became acquainted with Schiller and Goethe at Stuttgartt and Weimar, was detained with English prisoners at Verdun. In 1807 he published his *The Empire of the Nairs, or the Rights of Women*, a free-love romance which he wrote in German, French, and English. He also wrote in French and English, a curious booklet *The Children of God*, London, 1853. He addressed a poem on Tolerance to Mr. Owen, on the occasion of his denouncing the religions of the world. It appears in *The Etonian Out of Bounds*. Died at London 26 Sept. 1841.

Lawrence (Sir William), surgeon, b. Cirencester, 1783. Admitted M.R.C.S., 1805, in '13 he was chosen, F.R.S., and two years later was named Professor of Anatomy and Surgery at the Royal College of Surgeons. While he held that chair he delivered his *Lectures on Man*, which on their publication in 1819 roused a storm of bigotry. In his early manhood. Lawrence was an earnest advocate of radical reform ; but notwithstanding his early unpopularity, he acquired a lucrative practice. Died London, 5 July, 1867.

Layton (Henry), educated at Oxford, and studied at Gray's Inn, being called to the bar. He wrote anonymously observations on Dr. Bentley's *Confutation of Atheism* (1693), and a *Search After Souls, and Spiritual Observations in Man* (1700).

Leblais (Alphonse), French professor of mathematics, b. Mans, 1820. Author of a study in Positivist philosophy entitled *Materialism and Spiritualism* (1865), to which Littré contributed a preface.

Le Bovier de Fontenelle. See Fontenelle.

Lecky (William Edward Hartpole), historian, b. near Dublin, 26 March, 1838. Educated at Trinity College, Dublin. His works, which are characterised by great boldness and originality of thought, are *A History of the Rise and Spirit of Rationalism in Europe* ('65), *A History of European Morals from Augustus to Charlemagne* ('69), and *A History of England in the Eighteenth Century* (1878-87).

Leclerc (Georges Louis). See Buffon.

Leclerc de Septchenes (N.), b. at Paris. Became secretary to Louis XVI., translated the first three vols. of Gibbon, and wrote an essay on the religion of the ancient Greeks (1787). A friend of Lalande, he prepared an edition of Freret, published after his death. Died at Plombieres, 9 June, 1788.

Leconte de Lisle (Charles Marie René), French poet, b. Isle of Bourbon, 23 Oct. 1818. After travelling in India, returned to Paris, and took part in the revolution of '48, but has since devoted himself mainly to poetry, though he has written also *A Republican Catechism* and *A Popular History of Christianity* ('71). One of his finest poems is *Kain*. On being elevated to the seat of Victor Hugo at the Academy in '87, he gave umbrage to

Jews and Catholics by incidentally speaking of Moses as "the chief of a horde of ferocious nomads."

Lecount (Peter), lieutenant in the French navy. He was engaged in the battle of Navarino. Came to England as a mathematician in the construction of the London and Birmingham Railway, of which he wrote a history (1839). He wrote a curious book in three volumes entitled *A Few Hundred Bible Contradictions; A Hunt After the Devil and other Old Matters*, by John P. Y., M.D.; published by H. Hetherington ('43). The author's name occurs on p. 141, vol i., as "the Rev. Peter Lecount."

Leenhof (Frederick van), b. Middelburg (Zealand), Aug. 1647. Became a minister of Zwolle, where he published a work entitled *Heaven on Earth* (1703), which subjected him to accusations of Atheism. It was translated into German in 1706.

Lefevre (André), French writer, b. Provins, 9 Nov. 1834 He became, at the age of twenty-three, one of the editors of the *Magasin Pittoresque*. He wrote much in *La Libre Pensée* and *La Pensée Nouvelle;* has translated *Lucretius* in verse ('76), and written *Religions and Mythologies Compared* ('77); contributed a sketchy *History of Philosophy* to the Library of Contemporary Science ('78); has written *Man Across the Ages* ('80) and the *Renaissance of Materialism* ('81). He has also edited the *Lettres Persanes* of Montesquieu, some *Dialogues* of Voltaire, and Diderot's *La Religieuse* ('86).

Lefort (César), disciple of Comte. Has published a work on the method of modern science (Paris, 1864).

Lefrancais de Lalande. See Lalande.

Legate (Bartholomew), Antitrinitarian native of Essex, b. about 1572, was thrown into prison on a charge of heresy, 1611. King James had many personal interviews with him. On one occasion the king asked him if he did not pray to Jesus Christ. He replied that he had done so in the days of his ignorance, but not for the last seven years. "Away, base fellow!" said His Majesty, "It shall never be said that one stayeth in my presence who hath never prayed to the Savior for seven years together." He was burnt at Smithfield by the

King's writ, *De Hæretico Comburendo*, 18 March, 1612, being one of the last persons so punished in England.

Leguay de Premontval. See Premontval.

Le Hon (Henri) Belgian scientist, b. Ville-Pommerœul (Hainault) 1809, was captain in the Belgian army, professor at the military school of Brussels, and Chevalier of the Order of Leopold. Author of *L'Homme Fossile en Europe*, '66. Translated Professor Omboni's exposition of Darwinism. Died at San Remo, 1872.

Leidy (Joseph), M.D., American naturalist, b. Philadelphia, 9 Sept. 1823. He became professor of biology at the University of Philadelphia, and is eminent for his contributions to American palæontology.

Leigh (Henry Stone), English author of a Deistic work on the *Religions of the World*, 1869.

Leland (Theron C.), American journalist, b. 9 April, 1821. He edited with Wakeman the journal *Man*. Died 2 June, 1885.

Lemaire (Charles), member of the Academical Society of Saint Quentin, author of an atheistic philosophical work, in two vols., entitled *Initiation to the Philosophy of Liberty*, Paris, 1842.

Lemonnier (Camille), Belgian writer, b. Ixel les Bruxelles, 1845, author of stories and works on Hysteria, Death, etc., in which he evinces his freethought sentiments.

Lenau (Nicolaus), *i.e.* Nicolaus Franz Niembsch von STREHLENAU, Hungarian poet, b. Czatad, 15 Aug. 1802. His poems, written in German, are pessimistic, and his constitutional melancholy deepened into insanity. Died Ober-Döbling, near Vienna, 22 Aug. 1850.

Lennstrand (Viktor E.), Swedish writer and orator, b. Gefle, 30 Jan. 1861. Educated at Upsala University. Founded the Swedish Utilitarian Society, March '88, and in May was sentenced to a fine of 250 crowns for denial of the Christian religion. On the 29th Nov. he was imprisoned for three months for the same offence. Has written several pamphlets and has incurred several fresh prosecutions. In company with

A. Lindkvist he has founded the *Fritankaren* as the organ of Swedish freethought.

Leontium, Athenian Hetæra, disciple and mistress of Epicurus (q.v.) She acquired distinction as a philosopher, and wrote a treatise against Theophrastus, which is praised by Cicero as written in a skilful and elegant manner.

Leopardi (Giacomo), count, Italian pessimist poet, b. Recanati (Ancona), 29 June, 1798. In 1818 he won a high place among poets by his lines addressed *To Italy*. His *Canti*, '31, are distinguished by eloquence and pathos, while his prose essays, *Operette Morali*, '27, are esteemed the finest models of Italian prose of this century. Leopardi's short life was one long disease, but it was full of work of the highest character. As a poet, philologist, and philosopher, he is among the greatest of modern Italians. Died at Naples, 14 July, 1837.

Lequinio (Joseph Marie), French writer and Conventionnel, b. Sarzeau, 1740. Elected Mayor of Rennes, 1790, and Deputy from Morbihar to the Legislative Assembly. He then professed Atheism. He voted the death of Louis XVI. "regretting that the safety of the state did not permit his being condemned to penal servitude for life." In 1792 he published *Prejudices Destroyed*, signed "Citizen of the World," in which he considered religion as a political chain. He took part in the Feasts of Reason, and wrote *Philosophy of the People*, 1796. Died 1813.

Lermina (Jules Hippolyte), French writer, b. 27 March, 1839. Founded the *Corsair* and *Satan*, and has published an illustrated biographical dictionary of contemporary France, 1884-5.

Lermontov (Mikhail Yur'evich), Russian poet and novelist, b. Moscow, 3 Oct. 1814. Said to have come of a Scotch family, he studied at Moscow University, from which he was expelled. In '32 he entered the Military Academy at St. Petersburg, and afterwards joined the Hussars. In '37 some verses on the death of Pushkin occasioned his being sent to the Caucasus, which he describes in a work translated into English, '53. His poems are much admired. *The Demon*, exhibiting Satan in love, has been translated into English, and so has his romance entitled *A Hero of Our Times*. He fell in a duel in the Caucasus, 15 July, 1840.

Leroux (Pierre), French Socialist and philosophic writer, b. Bercy, near Paris, 6 April, 1797. At first a mason, then a typographer, he invented an early composing machine which he called the pianotype. In 1824 he became editor of the *Globe*. Becoming a Saint Simonian, he made this paper the organ of the sect. He started with Reynaud *L'Encyclopédie Nouvelle*, and afterwards with L. Viardot and Mme. George Sand the *Revue Indépendante* ('41), which became noted for its pungent attacks on Catholicism. His principal work is *De l'Humanité* ('40). In June '48 M. Leroux was elected to the Assembly. After the *coup d'état* he returned to London and Jersey. Died at Paris, 12 April, 1871.

Leroy (Charles Georges), lieutenant ranger of the park of Versailles, b, 1723, one of the writers on the *Encyclopédie* He defended the work of Helvetius on the Mind against Voltaire, and wrote *Philosophical Letters on the Intelligence and Perfectibility of Animals* (1768), a work translated into English in 1870. Died at Paris 1789.

Lespinasse (Adolf Frederik Henri de). Dutch writer, b. Delft, 14 May, 1819. Studied medicine, and established himself first at Deventer and afterwards at Zwartsluis, Vaassen, and Hasselt. In the *Dageraad* he wrote many interesting studies under the pen-name of " Titus," and translated the work of Dupuis into Dutch. In 1870 he emigrated to America and became director of a large farm in Iowa. Died in Orange City (Iowa) 1881,

L'Espinasse (Julie Jeanne Eléonore de). French beauty and wit, b. Lyons, 9 Nov. 1732. She became the protégé of Madame du Deffand, and gained the favor of D'Alembert. Her letters are models of sensibility and spirit. Died Paris, 23 May, 1776.

Lessing (Gotthold Ephraim). German critic and dramatic poet, b. Kamenz, 22 Jan. 1729. He studied at Leipsic, and at Berlin became acquainted with Voltaire and Mendelssohn. Made librarian at Wolfenbüttel he published *Fragments of an Unknown* (1777), really the *Vindication of Rational Worshippers of God*, by Reimarus, in which it was contended that Christian evidences are so clad in superstition as to be unworthy credence. Among his writings were *The Freethinker* and *Nathan the Wise*, his noblest play, in which he enforces lessons of toleration and charity to all faiths. The effect of his writings was decidedly sceptical. Heine calls Lessing, after Luther, the greatest German emancipator. Died at Brunswick 15 Feb. 1781.

Lessona (Michele). Italian naturalist, b. 20 Sept., 1823; has translated some of the works of Darwin.

Leucippus. Greek founder of the atomic philosophy.

L'Estrange (Thomas), writer, b. 17 Jan. 1822. With a view to entering the Church he graduated at Trinity College, Dublin, 26 Feb. '44, but became an attorney. Having read F. A. Paley's Introduction to the Iliad, he became convinced that the "cooking" process there described, has been undergone by all sacred books now extant. He wrote for Thomas Scott's series valuable tracts on *Our First Century, Primitive Church History, Irenæus, Order, The Eucharist.* He also edited Hume's *Dialogues on Natural Religion,* and wrote *The First Ten Alleged Persecutions.*

Levallois (Jules). French writer, b. Rouen 18 May, 1829. In '55 he became secretary to Sainte Beuve. Wrote *Deisme et Christianisme,* 1866.

Lewes (George Henry), English man of letters, b. in London, 18 April, 1817, he became a journalist and dramatic critic. In 1845-6 appeared his *Biographical History of Philosophy,* which showed higher power. This has been republished as *History of Philosophy from Thales to Comte.* Lewes was one of the first to introduce English readers to Comte in his account of *Comte's Philosophy of the Sciences,* '47. In '49 he became one of the founders of the *Leader,* for which he wrote till '54. In that year he began his association with "George Eliot" (*q.v.*). His *Life of Goethe* appeared in '55, and from this time he began to give his attention to scientific, especially biological, studies. In '64 he published an important essay on Aristotle. On the foundation of the *Fortnightly Review,* '65, Lewes was appointed editor. His last work, *Problems of Life and Mind,* 5 vols. '74-79, was never completed owing to his death, 28 Nov. 1878. He bequeathed his books to Dr. Williams's library.

Lichtenberg (Georg Christoph), German satirical writer and scientist, b. Ober-Ramstädt, 1 July, 1742; a friend of G. Forster, he left many thoughts showing his advanced opinions.   Died Göttingen, 21 Feb. 1799.

Lick (James), American philanthropist, b. Fredericksburg, Pa., 25 Aug. 1796.   In 1847 he settled in California and made a large fortune by investing in real estate.   He was a Materialist and bequeathed large sums to the Lick Observatory, Mount Hamilton, and for other philanthropic purposes.   Died San Francisco, 1 Oct. 1876.

Lilja (Nicolai), Swedish writer, b. Rostanga, 18 Oct. 1808. Studied at Lund and became parish clerk in the Lund diocese. He wrote on *Man; his Life and Destiny.*   Died Lund 1870.

Lincoln (Abraham), sixteenth President of the United States, b. Kentucky, 12 Feb. 1809.   An uncompromising opponent of slavery, his election (Nov. '60) led to the civil war and the emancipation of slaves.   Ward H. Lamon, who knew him well, says he " read Volney and Paine and then wrote a deliberate and labored essay, wherein he reached conclusions similar to theirs.   The essay was burnt, but he never denied or regretted its composition."   Mrs. Lincoln said, " Mr. Lincoln had no hope and no faith in the usual acceptance of those words."   Assassinated 14 April, 1865, he expired the following morning.

Lindet (Robert [Thomas), "apostate" French bishop, b. Bernay, 1743.   Was elected to the States-General by the clergy of his district.   He embraced Republican principles, and in March, 1791, was made Bishop of L'Eure.   In Nov. 1792 he publicly married.   On 7 Nov. 1793, renounced his bishopric. He proposed that civil festivals should take the place of religious ones.   He became member of the *Conseil des Anciens.* Died Bernay, 10 Aug. 1823, and was buried without religious service.

Lindh (Theodor Anders), b. Borgo (Finland), 13 Jan. 1833. Studied at Helsingfors University, '51–57 ; became lawyer in '71, and is now a member of the Muncipal Council of Borgo. He has written many poems in Swedish, and also translated from the English poets, and has published Freethought essays, which have brought him into controversy with the clergy.

Lindkvist (Alfred), Swedish writer, b. Gefle, 21 Oct. 1860, of pious parents. At the University of Upsala he studied European literature, and became acquainted with the works of Mill, Darwin, and Spencer. He has published two volumes of poems, *Snow Drops* and *April Days*, and lost a stipend at the University by translating from the Danish a rationalistic life of Jesus entitled *The Reformer from Galilee*. Mr. Lindkvist has visited Paris, and collaborated on a Stockholm daily paper. In '88 he joined his friend Lennstrand in propagating Freethought, and in Nov. received a month's imprisonment for having translated one of J. Symes's anti-Christian pamphlets. He now edits *Fritankaren* in conjunction with Mr. Lennstrand.

Lindner (Ernst Otto Timotheus), German physician, b. Breslau, 28 Nov. 1820. A friend of Schopenhauer, whose philosophy he maintained in several works on music. He edited the *Vossische Zeitung* from '63. Died at Berlin, 7 Aug. 1867.

Liniere (François PAYOT de), French satiric poet, b. Paris, 1628; known as the Atheist of Senlis. Boileau says the only act of piety he ever did was drinking holy water because his mistress dipped her finger in it. Wrote many songs and smart epigrams, and is said to have undertaken a criticism of the New Testament. Died at Paris in 1701

Linton (Eliza, née LYNN) novelist and journalist, daughter of vicar of Crosthwaite, Cumberland, b. Keswick, 1822. Has contributed largely to the leading Radical journals, and has written numerous works of fiction, of which we must mention *Under which Lord?* and *The Rebel of the Family*. In '72 she published *The True History of Joshua Davidson, Christian and Communist*, and in '85 the Autobiography of Christopher Kirkland. She has also written on the woman question, and contributed largely to periodical literature.

Linton (William James), poet, engraver, and author, b. at London, 1812. A Chartist in early life, he was intimately associated with the chief political refugees. He contributed to the democratic press, and also, we believe, to the *Oracle of Reason*. He wrote the *Reasoner* tract on " The Worth of Christianity." He was one of the founders of the *Leader*, has edited the *Truthseeker*, the *National* and the *English Republic*, and has published *Famine a Masque*, a *Life of Paine*, and a memoir of

James Watson and some volumes of poems. In '67 he went to America, but has recently returned.

Liscow (Christian Ludwig), one of the greatest German satirists, b. Wittenberg, 29 April, 1701. He studied law in Jena, and became acquainted with Hagedorn in Hamburg. In 1745 he was Councillor of War at Dresden. This post he abandoned, occupying himself with literature until his death, 30 Oct. 1760. Liscow's principal satires are *The Uselessness of Good Works for our Salvation* and *The Excellence and Utility of Bad Writers*. He has been called the German Swift, and his works show him to have been an outspoken Freethinker.

Lisle (Lionel), author of *The Two Tests: the Supernatural Claims of Christianity Tried by Two of its own Rules* (London, 1877).

Liszinski (Casimir), Polish martyr of noble birth. Denounced as an Atheist in 1688 by the Bishop of Wilna and Posnovia, he was decapitated and burnt at Grodno 30 March, 1689. His ashes were placed in a cannon and scattered abroad. Among the statements in Liszinski's papers was that man was the creator of God, whom he had formed out of nothing.

Littre (Maximilian Paul Emile), French philologist and philosopher, b. Paris, 1 Feb. 1801. He studied medicine, literature and most of the sciences. An advanced Republican, he was one of the editors of the *National*. His edition of the works of Hippocrates (1839-61) proved the thoroughness of his learning. He embraced the doctrines of Comte, and in '45 published a lucid analysis of the Positive Philosophy. He translated the *Life of Jesus*, by Strauss, and wrote the *Literary History of France*. His *Dictionary of the French Language*, in which he applied the historical method to philology, is one of the most colossal works ever performed by one man. He wrote on *Comte and Positive Philosophy, Comte and Mill*, etc., but refused to follow Comte in his later vagaries. From '67 till his death he conducted *La Philosophie Positive*. Littré also wrote *Science from the Standpoint of Philosophy*, '73; *Literature and History*, '75; *Fragments of Positive Philosophy and Contemporary Sociology*, '76. He was proposed for the Academy in '63, but was bitterly opposed by Bishop Dupanloup, and was elected in '71. In the same year he was elected to the National Assembly, and in '75 was chosen senator. Under the Empire he twice refused the Legion of Honor. After a long life of incessant labor, he died at Paris, 2 June 1881.

Lloyd (John William), American poet and writer, b. of Welsh-English stock at Westfield, New Jersey, 4 June, 1857. Is mostly self-educated. After serving apprenticeship as a carpenter, became assistant to Dr. Trall. Brought up as an orthodox Christian he became an Agnostic and Anarchist, and has written much in *Liberty* and *Lucifer*.

Lohmann (Hartwic), a native of Holstein, who in 1616 occupied a good position in Flensburg. He was accused of Atheism. In 1635 he practised medicine at Copenhagen. He wrote a work called the *Mirror of Faith*. Died 1642.

Lollard (Walter), heretic and martyr, b. England, towards end of thirteenth century, began to preach in Germany in 1315. He rejected the sacraments and ceremonies of the Church. It is said he chose twelve apostles to propagate his doctrines and that he had many followers. Arrested at Cologne in 1322, he was burnt to death, dying with great courage.

Loman (Abraham Dirk), Dutch rationalist, b. The Hague 16 Sep. 1823. He holds the entire New Testament to be un-historical, and the Pauline Epistles to belong to the second century, and has written many critical works.

Lombroso (Cesare). Italian writer and scientist, b. Nov. 1836, has been a soldier and military physician. Introduced Darwinism to Italy. Has written several works, mostly in relation to the physiology of criminals.

Longet (François Achille), French physiologist, b. St. Germain-en-Laye, 1811, published a *Treatise on Physiology* in 3 vols. and several medical works. Died Bordeaux, 20 April, 1871.

Longiano (Sebastiano). See FAUSTO.

Longue (Louis Pierre de), French Deist, writer in the service of the house of Conti ; wrote *Les Princesses de Malabares*, Adrianople, 1734, in which he satirised religion. It was con-demned to be burnt 31 Dec. 1734, and a new edition published in Holland with the imprint Tranquebar, 1735.

Lorand (Georges), Belgian journalist, b. Namur, 1851, studied law at Bologna (Italy) and soon became an active propagator of Atheistic doctrines among the youth of the University and in workmen associations. He edits *La Réforme* at Brussels, the ablest daily exponent of Freethought and Democratic doctrines in Belgium. He has lately headed an association for the suppression of the standing army.

"**Lorm** (Hieronymus)," the pen name of Heinrich LANDES MANN. German pessimistic poet, b. Nikolsberg, 9 Aug. 1821. In addition to many philosophical poems, he has written essays entitled *Nature and Spirit*, Vienna, '84.

Lozano (Fernando), Spanish writer in *Las Dominicales dal Libre Pensamiento*, where he uses the signature "Demofilo." He has written *Batttes of Freethought*, *Possessed by the Devil*, *The Church and Galeote*, etc.

Lubbock (Sir John), banker, archæologist, scientist and statesman, b. in London, 30 April, 1834. Educated at Eton, he was taken into his father's bank at the age of fourteen, and became a partner in '56. By his archæological works he has most distinguished himself. He has written *Prehistoric Times as Illustrated by Ancient Remains, and the Manners and Customs of Modern Savages* ('65), and *The Origin of Civilisation and the Primitive Condition of Man* ('70).

Lucretius Carus (Titus). Roman philosophical poet, b. about B.C. 99. Little is known of his life, but his name is immortalised by his atheistic work, *De Rerum Natura*, in six books, which is the finest didactic poem in any language. Lucretius has been said to have believed in one god, Epicurus, whose system he expounds. Full of animation, dignity, and sublimity, he invests philosophy with the grace of genius. Is said to have died by his own hand B.C. 55.

Luetzelberger (Ernst Karl Julius), German controversialist b. Ditterswind, 19 Oct. 1802. He was a friend of the Feuerbachs. He wrote on *The Church Tradition of the Apostle John*. He also wrote a work on Jesus, translated in Ewerbeck's *Qu'est ce que la Religion*. In '56 he was appointed town librarian at Nuremberg.

Lunn (Edwin), Owenite lecturer. Published pamphlets *On Prayer, its Folly, Inutility, etc.* 1839, and *Divine Revelation Examined*, 1841.

213

Luys (Jules Bernard), French alienist, b. Paris, 1828. Is physician at l'Hopital de la Charité, Paris, and author of a work on *The Brain and its Functions* in the " International Scientific Series."

Lyell (Sir Charles), geologist, b. Kinnordy, Forfarshire, 14 Nov. 1797. Was educated at Exeter College, Oxford, and devoted himself to geology. In 1830-33 appeared his great work, *The Principles of Geology*, which went through numerous editions. His last important work was *Geological Evidences of the Antiquity of Man*, in which he accepts the Darwinian theory. Died 22 Feb. 1875.

Maccall (William), writer, b. Largs. Scotland, 1812. Educated at Glasgow, he found his way to the Unitarian Church which he left as insufficiently broad. He wrote *Elements of Individualism* ('47), translated Spinoza's Treatise on Politics ('54), wrote to the *Critic* as " Atticus," contributed to the *National Reformer*, *Secular Review*, etc., published *Foreign Biographies* ('73), and translated Dr. Letourneau's *Biology* and other works. Maccall was an idealistic Pantheist of strong individual character. Died at Bexley, 19 Nov. 1888.

Macchi (Mauro), Italian writer, b. Milan, 1 July, 1818. Became professor of rhetoric at the age of twenty-four, when, becoming obnoxious to the Austrians by the liberty of his opinions, he was deprived of his position. He betook himself to radical journalism, founded *l'Italia*, a Republican journal, for which he was exiled. He was associated with Ausonio Franchi and Luigi Stefanoni in the *Libero Pensiero* and the *Libero Pensatore*, and founded an Italian Association of Freethinkers. In '61 he was elected deputy to Parliament for Cremona, and in '79 was elevated to the Senate. Died at Rome, 24 Dec. 1880. One of his principal works is on the *Council of Ten*.

Macdonald (Eugene Montague), editor of the New York *Truthseeker*, b. Chelsea, Maine, 4 Feb. 1855. He learned the printer's trade in New York, where he became foreman to D. M. Bennett, and contributed to the paper, which he has conducted since Mr. Bennett's death.

Macdonald (George), brother of the preceding. Wrote on

the *Truthseeker*, and now conducts *Freethought*, of San Francisco, in company with S. P. Putnam. George Macdonald is a genuine humorist and a sound Freethinker.

McDonnell (William), American novelist, b 15 Sept. 1824. Author of *The Heathens of the Heath* and *Exeter Hall*, '73, both Freethought romances.

Mackay (Robert William), author of *The Progress of the Intellect*, 1850, *Sketch of the Rise and Progress of Christianity*, '53, and *The Tubingen School*, '63.

Mackey (Sampson Arnold), astronomer and shoemaker, of Norwich, who is said to have constructed an orrery out of leather. He wrote *The Mythological Astronomy of the Ancients*, Norwich, 1822-24, *Pious Frauds*, '26, A Lecture on Astronomy and Geology, edited by W. D. Saull, '32, *Urania's Key* to the Revelation, '33, and *The Age of Mental Emancipation*, '36-39. Mackey also wrote the *Sphinxiad*, a rare book. Died 1846.

Mackintosh (Thomas Simmons), author of *The Electrical Theory of the Universe*, 1848, and *An Inquiry into the Nature of Responsibility*. Died 1850.

MacSweeney (Myles), mythologist, b. at Enniskillen 1811. He came to London, and hearing Robert Taylor at the Rotunda in 1830, adopted his views. He held that Jesus never existed, and wrote in the *National Reformer*, *Secular Chronicle*, and other papers. He published a pamphlet on *Moses and Bacchus* in 1874. Died Jan. 1881.

Madach (Imré), Hungarian patriot and poet, b. 21 Jan. 1823, at Sztregova, studied at the University of Buda Pesth, and afterwards lived at Cseszlova. He was in '52 incarcerated for a year for having given asylum at his castle to a political refugee. He became in '61 delegate at Pesth. In this year he published his fine poem *Az Ember Tragédiaja* (The Human Tragedy), in which mankind is personified as Adam, with Lucifer in his company. Many Freethought views occur in this poem. Died 5 Oct. 1864. His works were published in 3 vols., 1880.

Maier (Lodewyk). See Meyer.

Maillet (Benôit de). French author, b. Saint Michiel, 12 April, 1656. He was successively consul in Egypt and at

Leghorn ; and died at Marseilles, 30 Jan. 1738. After his death was published "Telliamed" (the anagram of his name), in which he maintained that all land was originally covered with water and that every species of animal, man included, owes its origin to the sea.

"**Mainlaender**" (Philipp), pseudonym of Philipp BATZ, German pessimist, author of a profound work entitled the *Philosophy of Redemption*, the first part of which was published in 1876. It was said that "Mainländer" committed suicide in that year, but the second part of his work has come out 1882-86. He holds that Polytheism gives place to Monotheism and Pantheism, and these again to Atheism. "God is dead, and his death was the life of the world."

Malherbe (François de). French poet, b. Caen, 1555. He served in the civil wars of the League, and enjoyed the patronage of Henry IV. He was called the prince of poets and the poet of princes. Many stories are told illustrating his sceptical raillery. When told upon his death-bed of paradise and hell he said he had lived like others and would go where others went. Died Paris, 16 Oct. 1628.

Mallet (Mme. Josephine). French authoress of a work on *The Bible*, its origin, errors and contradictions (1882).

Malon (Benoît). French Socialist, b. near St. Etienne, 1841. One of the founders of the *International*; he has written a work on that organisation, its history and principles (Lyons, 1872). He is editor on *L'Intransigeant*, conducted the *Revue Socialiste,* and has written on the religion and morality of the Socialists and other works.

Malvezin (Pierre). French journalist, b. Junhac, 26 June 1841. Author of *La Bible Farce* (Brussels, 1879.) This work was condemned and suppressed, 1880, and the author sentenced to three month's imprisonment. He conducts the review *La Fraternité.*

Mandeville (Bernhard), b. Dort. 1670. He studied medicine, was made a doctor in Holland, and emigrated to London. In 1705 he published a poetical satire, *The Grumbling Hive*, or Knaves Turned Honest. In 1709, he published *The Virgin Unmasked,* and in 1723, *Free Thoughts on Religion the Church and*

National Happiness. In the same year appeared his *Fables of the Bees or Private Vices, Public Benefits.* This work was presented by the grand jury of Middlesex, 1723 and 1728. It was attacked by Law, Berkeley, and others. Mandeville replied to Berkeley in *A Letter to Dion,* occasioned by a book called Alciphron, or the Minute Philosopher, 1732. He also wrote *An Inquiry of Honor.* and *Usefulness of Christianity in War,* 1731. Died, London, 19 Jan. 1733.

Mantegazza (Paolo), Italian anthropologist, b. Monza, 31 Oct. 1831. Studied medicine at Milan, Pisa, and Paria, and travelled considerably through Europe, and produced at Paris in 1854 his first book *The Physiology of Pleasure.* He has also written on the physiology of pain, spontaneous generation, anthropological works on Ecstacy, Love and other topics, and a fine romance *Il Dio Ignoto,* the unknown god (1876). Mantegazza is one of the most popular and able of Italian writers.

Manzoni (Romeo), Dr. Italian physician, b. Arogno, 1847, studied philosophy at Milan, and graduated at Naples. He has written on the doctrine of love of Bruno and Schopenhauer *A Life of Jesus,* also *Il Prete,* a work translated into German with the title Religion as a Pathological Phenomenon, etc.

Marchena (José), Spanish writer, b. Utrera, Andalusia, 1768. Brought up for the church, reading the writings of the French philosophers brought on him the Inquisition. He fled to France where he became a friend of Brissot and the Girondins. He wrote a pronounced *Essai de Théologie,* 1797, and translated into Spanish Molière's *Tartufe,* and some works of Voltaire. He translated Dupins' *Origine de tous les Cultes,* became secretary to Murat, and died 10 Jan. 1821.

Marechal (Pierre Sylvain), French author, b. Paris, 15 Aug. 1750; was brought up to the Bar, which he quitted for the pursuit of literature. He was librarian to the Mazarin College, but lost his place by his *Book Escaped from the Deluge,* Psalms, by S. Ar. Lamech (anagram), 1784. This was a parody of the style of the prophets. In 1781 he wrote *Le Nouveau Lucrece.* In 1788 appeared his *Almanack of Honest People,* in which the name of Jesus Christ was found beside that of Epicurus. The work was denounced to Parliament, burnt at the hands of the hangman, and Maréchal imprisoned for four months. He welcomed the Revolution, and published a republican almanack, 1793. In 1797 and 1798 he published his *Code of a Society of Men without God*, and *Free Thoughts on the Priests*. In 1799 appeared his most learned work, *Travels of Pythagoras* in Egypt, Chaldea, India, Rome, Carthage, Gaul, etc. 6 vols. Into this fiction Maréchal puts a host of bold philosophical, political, and social doctrines. In 1800 he published his famous *Dictionary of Atheists*, which the Government prohibited and interdicted journals from noticing. In the following year appeared his *For and Against the Bible*. Died at Montrouge, 18 Jan. 1803. His beneficence is highly spoken of by Lalande.

Maret (Henry), French journalist and deputy, b. Santerre, 4 March, 1838. He ably combatted against the Empire, and edits *Le Radical*; was elected deputy in '81.

Marguerite, of Valois, Queen of Navarre, sister to Francis I. b. at Angouleme, 11 April, 1492. Deserves place for her protection to religious reformers. Died 21 Dec. 1549.

Marguetel de Saint Denis. See Saint Evremond (C.)

Mario (Alberto), Italian patriot, b. 3 June, 1825. He edited the *Tribune* and *Free Italy*, became *aide-de-camp* to Garibaldi and married Jessie White, an English lady. In '60 he wrote a polemic against the papacy entitled *Slavery and Thought*. Died 2 June, 1883.

Marlow (Christopher), English poet and dramatist, b. Canterbury, 8 Feb. 1564. Educated at Benet College, Cambridge, where he took his degree in 1587. He devoted himself to dramatic writing and according to some became an actor. He was killed in a brawl at Deptford, 1 June, 1593, in time to escape being tried on an information laid against him for Atheism and blasphemy. The audacity of his genius is displayed in *Tamburlaine* and *Dr. Faustus*. Of the latter, Goethe said " How greatly is it all planned." Swinburne says " He is the greatest discoverer, the most daring and inspired pioneer in all our poetic literature."

Marr (Wilhelm), German socialist, author of *Religious Excursions*, 1876, and several anti-Semitic tracts.

Marsais (Cesar Chesneau du). See Du Marsais.

Marselli (Niccola), Italian writer, b. Naples, 5 Nov. 1832. Author of advanced works on the Science of History, *Nature and Civilisation*, the Origin *of Humanity*, the *Great Races of Humanity*, etc.

Marston (Philip Bourke), English poet, b. London, 13 Aug. 1850. He became blind in childhood, and devoted to poetry. A friend of D. G. Rossetti, Swinburne, and Thomson, his poems are sad and sincere. Died 14 Feb. 1887, and was buried in accordance with his own wishes in unconsecrated ground at Highgate, and without religious service.

Marsy (François Marie de), b. Paris, 1714, educated as a Jesuit. He brought out an analysis of Bayle, 1755, for which he was confined in the Bastile. Died 16 Dec. 1763.

Marten (Henry), regicide, b. Oxford, 1602. Educated at Oxford, where he proceeded B.A., 1619. He was elected to Parliament in 1640, and expelled for his republican sentiments in 1643. He resumed his seat 6 Jan. 1646, took part in the civil war, sat as one of King Charles's judges, and became one of the Council of State. He proposed the repeal of the statute of banishment against the Jews, and when it was sought to expel all profane persons, proposed to add the words " and all fools." Tried for regicide 10 Oct. 1660, he was kept in Chepstow Castle till his death, Sep. 1680. Carlyle calls him " sworn foe of Cant in all its figures; an indomitable little Pagan if no better."

Martin (Emma), English writer and lecturess, b. Bristol, 1812. Brought up as a Baptist, she, for a time, edited the *Bristol Magazine*. She wrote the *Exiles of Piedmont* and translated from the Italian the Maxims of Guicciardini. The trials of Holyoake and Southwell for blasphemy led her to inquire and embrace the Freethought cause. While Holyoake and Paterson were in gaol, Mrs. Martin went about committing the " crime " for which they were imprisoned. In '43 she published *Baptism A Pagan Rite*. This was followed by *Tracts for the People* on the Bible no Revelation, Religion Superseded, Prayer, God's Gifts and Men's Duties, a conversation on the being of God, etc. She also lectured and wrote on the *Punishment of Death*, to which she was earnestly opposed. Died Oct. 1851.

Martin (Bon Louis Henri), French historian, b. St. Quentin. 20 Feb. 1810. He was sent to Paris to study law, but abandoned it for history. His *History of France*, in nineteen vols. (1838—53), is a monumental work of erudition, A confirmed Republican, he warmly opposed the Second Empire and after its fall became member of the National Assembly, '71. and senator, '76. He was elected member of the Academy, '78. In addition to his historical works he contributed to *le Siecle, la Liberte de penser*, and *l'Encyclopédie Nouvelle*, etc. Died 14 Dec. 1883.

Martin (Louis), author of *Les Evangiles Sans Dieu* (called by Victor Hugo *cette-noble page*), Paris, 1887, describes himself as an Atheist Socialist.

Martin (Louis Auguste). French writer, b. Paris, 25 April, 1811, editor of the *Morale Independante* and member of the Institute of Geneva. For his *True and False Catholics* ('58), he was fined three thousand francs and imprisoned for six months He published the *Annuaire Philosophique*. Several of his works are placed on the Roman *Index*. Died Paris, 6 April, 1875.

Martinaud (M.), an ex-abbé who refused ordination, and wrote Letters of a young priest, who is an Atheist and Materialist, to his bishop, Paris, 1868, in which he says, "Religion is the infancy of peoples, Atheism their maturity."

Martineau (Harriet), b. Norwich 12 June, 1803, descended from a Huguenot family. Brought up as a Unitarian, she began writing Devotional Exercises for Young Persons, and, taking to literature as a means of living, distinguished herself by popularisations of political economy. The *Letters on the Laws of Man's Nature and Development*, which passed between her and H. G. Atkinson, appeared in '51, and disclosed her advance to the Positivist school of Thought. In '53 she issued a condensed account of Comte's philosophy. She wrote a *History of England during the Thirty Years' Peace*, and numerous other works. Died at Ambleside 27 June, 1876. Her *Autobiography*, published after her death, shows the full extent of her unbelief.

Masquerier (Lewis), American land reformer of Huguenot descent, b. 1 March, 1802. Wrote *The Sataniad*, established

Greenpoint Gazette, and contributed to the *Boston Investigator*. Died 7 Jan. 1888.

Massenet (Jules Emile Fréderic), French musical composer, b. Montard, 12 May, 1842. Has written a daring and popular oratorio on *Marie Magdeleine*, and an opera, *Herodiade*.

Massey (Gerald), poet and archæologist, b. of poor parents at Tring, in Herts, 29 May, 1828. At eight years of age he was sent to a factory to earn a miserable pittance. At the age of fifteen he came to London as an errand boy, read all that came in his way, and became a Freethinker and political reformer. Inspired by the men of '48, he started *The Spirit of Freedom*, '49. It cost him five situations in eleven months. In '53 his *Ballad of Babe Christabel, with other Lyrical Poems* at once gave him position as a poet of fine taste and sensibility. Mr. Massey devoted himself to the study of Egyptology, the result of which is seen in his *Book of Beginnings* and *Natural Genesis*, '81-83, in which he shows the mythical nature of Christianity. Mr. Massey has also lectured widely on such subjects as Why Don't God Kill the Devil? The Historical Jesus and the Mythical Christ, The Devil of Darkness in the Light of Evolution, The Coming Religion, etc. His poems are being re-published under the title *My Lyrical Life*.

Massey (James). See Tyssot. (S.)

Massol (Marie Alexandre), French writer, b. Beziers, 18 March, 1805. He studied under Raspail, went to Paris in '30 and became a Saint Simonian. In '48 he wrote on Lamennais' *La Réforme*, and on the *Voix du Peuple* with his friend Proudhon, to whom he became executor. In '65 he established *La Morale Independante* with the object of showing morality had nothing to do with theology. Died at Paris 20 April, 1875.

Maubert de Gouvest (Jean Henri), French writer, b. Rouen, 20 Nov. 1721. Brought up as a monk, he fled and took service in the Saxon army. He was thrown into prison by the King of Poland, but the Papal nuncio procured his release on condition of retaking his habit. This he did and went to Rome to be relieved of his vows. Failing this he went to Switzerland and England, where he was well received by Lord

Bolingbroke. He published *Lettres Iroquoises*, Irocopolis, 1752, and other anonymous works. At Frankfort in 1764 he was arrested as a fugitive monk and vagabond, and was imprisoned eleven months. Died at Altona, 21 Nov. 1767.

Maudsley (Henry), M.D., b. near Giggleswick, Yorkshire, 5 Feb. 1835. Educated at London University, where he graduated M D. in 1857. Taking mental pathology as his speciality, he soon reached eminence in his profession. From '69–'79 he was professor of medical jurisprudence at University College, London His works on *The Physiology and Pathology of the Mind* ('67), *Body and Mind* ('70), *Responsibility in Mental Disease* ('73), and Body and Will ('83) have attracted much attention. His *Natural Laws and Supernatural Seemings* ('80) is a powerful exposure of the essence of all superstition.

Mauvillon (Jakob von), b. Leipzig, 8 March, 1743. Though feeble in body, he had a penchant for the army, and joined the engineer corps of Hanover, and afterwards became lieutenant-colonel in the service of the Duke of Brunswick. A friend and admirer of Mirabeau, he defended the French Revolution in Germany. He wrote anonymously *Paradoxes Moraux* (Amsterdam, 1768) and *The Only True System of the Christian Religion* (Berlin, 1787), at first composed under the title of *False Reasonings of the Christian Religion*. Died in Brunswick, 11 Jan. 1794.

Mazzini (Giuseppe), Italian patriot, b. Genoa, 28 June 1808. In '26 he graduated LL.D., in the University of Genoa, and plunged into politics, becoming the leader of Young Italy, with the object of uniting the nation. Condemned to death in '33, he went to Switzerland and was expelled, then came to England in '37. In '48 he returned, and in March '49 was made triumvir of Rome with Saffi and Armellini. Compelled, after a desperate resistance, to retire, he returned to London. He wrote in the *Westminster Review* and other periodicals and and his works are numerous though mostly of a political character. They are distinguished by highmindedness, love of toleration and eloquence. Carlyle called Mazzini "a man of genius and virtue, a man of sterling veracity, humanity and nobleness of mind." Died at Pisa 10 March, 1872. He was a Deist.

Meissner (Alfred), German poet, b. Teplitz, 15 Oct. 1822. Has written Ziska, an epic poem, *The Son of Atta Troll*, *Recollections of Heine*, etc. Died Teplitz, 20 May, 1885.

Meister (Jacques Henri), Swiss writer, b. Bückeburg, 6 Aug. 1744. Intended for a religious career, he went to France, and became acquainted with D'Holbach and Diderot, of whom he wrote a short life, and was secretary to Grimm. He wrote the *Origin of Religious Principles*, 1762, and *Natural Morality*, 1787.

Menard (Louis), French author and painter, b. Paris, 1822. In '48–'49 he wrote *Prologue of a Revolution*, for which he was obliged to leave France. Has written on *Morality before the Philosophers*, '60, *Studies on the Origin of Christianity*, '67, and *Freethinkers' Religious Catechism*, '75.

Mendoza (Diego Hurtado de), famous and learned Spanish author, b. of distinguished family, Granada, 1503. Intended for the church, he studied Latin, Greek, Arabic, and Hebrew, but on leaving the university he joined the army. At school he wrote his well known comic novel, *Lazarillo de Tormes*, which was condemned by the Inquisition. Sent on an embassy to Pope Paul III., the latter was greatly shocked at his audacity and vehemence of speech. His chief work is his *History of the Moorish Wars*, which remained unprinted thirty years, through the intolerant policy of Philip II. Mendoza's satires and burlesques were also prohibited by the Inquisition. He commented Aristotle and translated his Mechanics. Died at Valladolid, April, 1575.

Mendum (Josiah P.), publisher and proprietor of the *Boston Investigator*, b. Kennebunk, Maine, 7 July, 1811. He became a printer, and in 1833 became acquainted with Abner Kneeland and after his imprisonment engaged to print the *Investigator*, and when Kneeland left Boston for the West to recruit his health, he carried on the paper together with Mr. Horace Seaver. Mr. Mendum was one of the founders of the Paine Memorial Hall, Boston, and a chief support of Freethought in hat city.

Mentelle (Edme), French geographer and historian, b. Paris, 11 Oct. 1730. Studied at the College de Beauvais under Crévier. His *Précis de l'Histoire des Hébreux* (1798), and *Précis* *de l'Histoire Universelle* are thoroughly anti-Christian. He doubted if Jesus ever existed. He was a member of the Institute and Chevalier of the Legion of Honor. Died at Paris, 28 Dec. 1815.

Mercier (L. A.), author of *La Libre Pensee*, Brussels, 1879.

Meredith (Evan Powell), Welsh writer, author of *The Prophet of Nazareth* (1864), an able work exposing the prophecies of Jesus, and *Amphilogia*, a reply in to the Bishop of Landaff and the Rev. J. F. Francklin, '67.

Meredith (George), philosophical poet and novelist, b. Hampshire, 1828, and educated partly on the Continent. Intended for the law, he adopted literature in preference. He first appeared as a poet with *Poems* ('51). Of his powerful novels we mention the *Ordeal of Richard Feveril* ('59), *Emilia in England* ('64), now *Sandra Belloni*, with *Vittoria* ('66) for a sequel. *Rhoda Fleming*, *Beauchamp's Career* ('76), *The Egoist* ('79), *The Tragic Comedians* ('81) and *Diana of the Crossways* ('85). Deep thought and fine grace characterise his writings. As a poet Mr. Meredith is not popular, but his volumes of verse are marked by the highest qualities, and give him a place apart from the throng of contemporary singers.

Merimee (Prosper), learned French writer, b. Paris, 28 Sept. 1808, author of numerous essays and romances. Was made Inspector General of Historic Monuments and was admitted to the Academy in '44. In his anonymous brochure on H(enri) B(eyle), Eleutheropolis (Brussels), '64, there is an open profession of Atheism. Died at Cannes, 23 Sept. 1870.

Merritt (Henry), English painter and writer, b. Oxford, 8 June, 1822. On coming to London he lived with Mr. Holyoake, and contributed to the *Reasoner*, using the signature "Christopher." He wrote on *Dirt and Pictures* and *Robert Dalby and his World of Troubles*. etc. Died in London, 10 July, 1877.

Meslier or **Mellier** (Jean), curé of Etrepigny, Champagne, b. Mazerny, Rethelois, 15 June, 1664. Died in 1729. After his death a will was discovered of which he had made three copies, in which he repudiated Christianity and requested to be buried in his own garden. His property he left to his parishoners. Voltaire published it under the title of Extract from the sentiments of Jean Meslier. To Meslier has been attributed the work entitled *Le Bon Sens*, written by Baron D'Holbach. *Le Testament de Jean Meslier* has been published in three volumes at Amsterdam, 1864, preceded by a study by Rudolf Charles (R. C. d'Ablaing van Giessenburg). It calls in question all the dogmas of Christianity. Anacharsis Clootz proposed to the National Convention to erect a statue to this " honest priest."

Metchnikov (Léon), Russian writer in French ; author of a work on Japan and of able articles, notably one on Christian Communion in the *Revue Internationale des Sciences Biologiques*, tome 12.

Metrodorus of Lampsacus.   Greek philosopher, b. 330 B.C., a disciple and intimate friend of Epicurus.   He wrote numerous works, the titles of which are preserved by Diogenes Laertius.   Died B.C. 277.

Mettrie, see La Mettrie

Meunier (Amédée Victor), French writer, b. Paris, 2 May, 1817.   Has done much to popularise science by his *Scientific Essays*, 1851-58, the *Ancestors of Adam*, '75, etc.

Meyer (Lodewijk), a Dutch physician, a friend and follower of Spinoza, who published *Exercitatio Paradoxa* on the philosophical interpretation of scripture, Eleutheropoli (Amst.), 1666. This has been wrongly attributed to Spinoza. It was translated into Dutch in 1667.   He is also credited with Lucii Antistic Constantes, de jure ecclesiasticorum. Alethopoli (Amst.), 1665. This work is also attributed to another writer, viz. P. de la Court.

Mialhe (Hippolyte), French writer, b. Roquecourbe (Tarn) 1834.   From '60–62 he was with the French army of occupation at Rome.   He has organised federations of Freethinkers in France, edited *L'Union des Libres-Penseurs*, and has written *Mémoires d'un libre Penseur* (Nevers, 1888).

Michelet (Jules), French historian, b. Paris, 21 Aug. 1798. Became a Professor of History in 1821.   Has written a *History of France* and of the *French Revolution; The Jesuits*, with his friend Quinet, '13 ; *The Priest, Woman and the Family*, '44 ; *The Sorceress*, dealing with witchcraft in the Middle Ages, '62 ; *The Bible of Humanity*, '64.   His lectures were interdicted by the Government of Louis Phillippe, and after the *coup d'état* he was deprived of his chair. All Michelet's works glow with eloquence and imagination. He never forgot that he was a republican and Freethinker of the nineteenth century. Died at Hyères, 9 Feb. 1874.

Michelet (Karl Ludwig), German philosopher of French family, b. Berlin, 4 Dec. 1801. In '29 he became Professor of Philosophy. A disciple of Hegel, he edited his master's works, '32. His principle work is *A System of Philsophy as an Exact Science*, '76–81, He has also written on the relation of Herbert Spencer to German philosophy.

Middleton (Conyers), Freethinking clergyman, b. York 1683. His *Letters from Rome*, 1729, showed how much Roman Christianity had borrowed from Paganism, and his *Free Inquiry into the Miraculous Powers supposed to have subsisted in the Christian Church*, 1749, was a severe blow to hitherto received " Christian Evidences." He also wrote a classic *Life of Cicero*. Died at Hildersham near Cambridge, 28 July, 1750.

Mignardi (G.), Italian writer, who in 1881 published *Memorie di un Nuovo Credente* (Memoirs of a New Believer).

Milelli (Domenico), Italian poet, b. Catanzaro, Feb. 1841. His family intended to make him a priest, but he turned out a rank Pagan, as may be seen in his *Odi Pagane*, '79, *Canzonieri*, '84, and other works.

Mill (James), philosopher and historian, b. Northwaterbridge, Montrose, 6 April. 1773. Studied at Edinburgh, and distinguished himself by his attainments in Greek and moral philosophy. He was licensed as preacher in the Scotch Church, but removed to London in 1800, and became editor of the *Literary Review*, and contributed to the reviews. He published, '17–'19, his *History of British India*. He contributed many articles to the fifth edition of the *Encyclopædia Britannica*. A friend of Bentham, he wrote largely in the *Westminster Review*, and did much to forward the views of Philosophic Radicalism. His *Analysis of the Human Mind*, '39, is a profound work. In religion he was a complete sceptic. Reading Bishop Butler's *Analogy* made him an Atheist. Died 23 June, 1836.

Mill (John Stuart), eminent English writer, son of the preceding, b. London, 20 May, 1806. Educated by his father without religion, he became clerk in the East India House, and early in life contributed to the *Westminster* and *Edinburgh Reviews*. Of the first he became joint editor in '35. His *System of Logic*, '43, first made him generally known. This was followed by his *Principles of Political Economy*. In '59 appeared his small but valuable treatise *On Liberty*, in which he defends the unrestricted free discussion of religion. Among subsequent works were *Utilitarianism*, '63; *Auguste Comte and Positivism*, '67; *Examination of Sir William Hamilton's Philosophy* '65; *Dissertations and Discussions*, '59–'75; and the *Subjection of Women*, '69. In '65 he was elected to Parliament for Westminster, but lost his seat in '68. In '67 he was chosen Rector of St. Andrews, and delivered the students an able address. Prof. Bain says " in everything characteristic of the creed of Christendom he was a thorough-going negationist. He admitted neither its truth nor its utility." Died at Avignon, 8 May, 1873, leaving behind his interesting *Autobiography* and three essays on " Nature," " Theism," and " Religion."

Mille (Constantin), Roumanian writer, b. at Bucharest, educated at Paris. He lectured at Jassy and Bucharest on the History of Philosophy, from a Materialistic point of view. He was also active with Codreano, and after the latter's death ('77), in spreading Socialism. Millé contributes to the Rivista Sociala and the Vütorul, edited by C. Pilitis.

Milliere (Jean Baptiste), Socialist, b. of poor parents, Lamarche (Côte d'Or), 13 Dec. 1817. He became an advocate, and founded the *Proletaire* at Clermont Ferrand. For writing *Revolutionary Studies* he was, after the *coup d'état*, banished to Algeria until the amnesty of '59. In '69 Millière started, with Rochefort, the *Marseillaise*, of which he became one of the principal directors. At the election for the National Assembly he was elected for Paris by 73,000 votes. Although he took no part in the Commune, but sought to act as an intermediary, he was arrested and summarily shot near the Pantheon, Paris, 26 May, 1871. He died crying " *Vive l'Humanité.*"

Mirabaud (Jean Baptiste de), French writer, b. Paris, 1675. He translated Tasso and Ariosto, and became perpetual secretary to the French Academy. He wrote *Opinions of the Ancients on the Jews*, a *Critical Examination of the New Testament*, (published under the name of Fréret), *The World: its Origin and Antiquity*, 1751, *Sentiments of a Philosopher on the Nature of the Soul* inserted in the collection entitled Nouvelle libertés de Penser, Amst. (Paris) 1743. The *System of Nature*, attributed to Mirabaud, was written by d'Holbach. Mirabaud died 24 June, 1760.

Mirabeau (Honoré Gabriel RIQUETTI Comte de), French statesman and orator, b. at the Chateau de Bignon (Loiret) 9 March, 1749. He inherited a passionate nature, a frank strong will, generous temper, and a mind of prodigious activity. He entered the army in 1767, but by an amorous intrigue provoked the ire of his father, by whom he was more than once imprisoned. In 1776 he went to Amsterdam and employed himself in literary work. In 1783 appeared anonymously his *Erotika Biblion*, dealing with the obscenity of the Bible. In 1786 he was sent to Berlin, where he met Frederick and collected materials for his work on *The Prussian Monarchy*. He returned to the opening of the States General and soon became leader of the Revolution, being in Jan. 1791 chosen President of the National Assembly. He advocated the abolition of the double aristocracy of Lords and bishops, the spoliation of the Church and the National Guard. Carlyle calls him "far the strongest, best practical intellect of that time." He died 2 April, 1791, Among his last words were, "Envelop me with perfumes and crown me with flowers that I may pass away into everlasting sleep."

Miranda (Don Francisco). South American patriot and general, b. Caracas 1750, aided the Americans in their War of Independence, tried to free Guatimalans from the Spanish, allied himself to the Girondins and became second in command in the army of Dumouriez. He was a friend of Thomas Paine. In 1806—11 he was engaged seeking to free Peru from the Spaniards, by whom he was made prisoner, and died in a dungeon at Cadiz, 16 Jan. 1816. It was said General Miranda made a sceptic of James Mill.

Miron. See MORIN (André Saturnin.)

Mitchell (J. Barr), Dr., anonymous author of *Dates and Data* (1876) and *Chrestos; a Religious Epithet* (1880). Dr. Mitchell has also written in the *National Reformer*, using his initials only.

Mitchell (Logan), author of Lectures published as *The Christian Mythology Unveiled*. This work was also issued under the title *Superstition Besieged*. It is said that Mitchell committed suicide in Nov. 1841. He left by his will a sum of £500 to any bookseller who had the courage to publish his book. It was first published by B. Cousens, and was republished in '81.

Mittermaier (Karl Josef Anton von), German jurisconsult, b. Munich, 5 Aug. 1787. Studied law and medicine at Landshut, where he became professor. His works on Law gained him a high reputation. He obtained a chair at the Heidelberg University. In 1831 he represented Baden in Parliament. He advocated the unity of Germany and took an active part in the Radical movement of '48. His writings are all in the direction of freedom. Died 28 Aug. 1867.

Mittie (Stanilas), in 1789 proposed the taking of church bells to make money and cannon, and during the revolution distinguished himself by other anti-clerical suggestions. Died 1816.

Mocenicus (Philippus), Archbishop of Nicosia, Cyprus, a Venetian philosopher, whose heretical *Contemplations* were printed at Geneva, 1588, with the *Peripatetic Question of Cæsal_pinus* and the books of Telesio on *The Nature of Things* in the volume entitled *Tractationum Philosophicarum.*

Moleschott (Jacob), scientific Materialist, b. of Dutch parents at Herzogenbusch, 9 Aug. 1822 ; studied at Heidelburg where he graduated M.D. Became Professor of Physiology at Zurich and afterwards at Turin. Becoming a naturalised Italian he was in '76 made a senator, and in '78 Professor of Physiology at the University of Rome. He has written *Circulation of Life, Light and Life, Physiological Sketches*, and other medical and scientific works. Lange calls him "the father of the modern Materialistic movement."

Molesworth (Sir William), statesman and man of letters, the eighth baronet of his family, b. Cornwall, 23 May, 1810. In '32 he was returned M.P. for East Cornwall, and from '37–41 sat for Leeds. In '53 he was First Commissioner of Public Works, and in '55 was Secretary for the Colonies. He was for some time proprietor and conductor of the *Westminster Review*, in which he wrote many articles. A noble edition of Hobbes was produced at his expense, '39-45, and he contributed to the support of Auguste Comte. Died 22 Oct. 1855.

Mommsen (Theodor), historian, b. Garding (Schleswig), 30 Nov. 1817. Studied at Kiel, and travelled from '44 to 47. He became Professor of Law of Leipsic, Zürich and Berlin. Is best known by his *History of Rome*, '53-85, a work of great research and suggestiveness in which he expresses the opinion that it is doubtful if the world was improved by Christianity.

Monboddo (Lord). See Burnett (James).

Monge (Gaspard), French scientist, b. at Beaume, 10 May 1746. Taught physics and mathematics at the military school of Mezieres, became a member of the Academy of Sciences in 1780, and through the influence of Condorcet was made Minister of the Marine in 1792. He was one of the founders of the Polytechnic School. Napoleon made him a senator, created him Count of Pelusuin, and gave him an estate for his many services to the French nation. On the return of the Bourbons he was deprived of all his emoluments. Died 28 July, 1818. Maréchal and Lalande insert his name in their list of Atheists.

Mongez (Antoine), French archaeologist, b. Lyons, 30 June 1747. Distinguished by his studies, he became a member of the Academy of Inscriptions and of the Institute, before which he said "he had the honor to be an Atheist." He was one of the most ardent members of the Convention, and wrote many memoirs. Died at Paris, 30 July, 1835.

Monroe (J. R.), Dr., editor and proprietor of the *Ironclad Age*, b. Monmouth, co. New Jersey, about 1825. In '50 he went to Rochford, where he had a good practice as a doctor. In '55 he started the *Rochford Herald*, and in July, '57, the *Seymour Times*. During the Civil War he was appointed surgeon to the 150th regiment, and after some hard service his own health broke down. In '75 Dr. Monroe published his dramas and poems in a volume. From this time his paper became more Freethought and less political. In April, '82, he removed to Indianopolis, Indiana, and changed the name to *The Age*, afterwards Monroe's Ironclad Age. Dr. Monroe is a clever writer and a modest man, with a remarkable fund of natural humor. Among his publications are poems on *The Origin of Man*, etc., *Genesis Revised*, and *Holy Bible Stories*.

Montaigne (Michel de), French philosophic essayist, b. at the family castle in Perigord, 28 Feb. 1533. He studied law and became a judge at Bordeaux about 1554. In 1580 he produced his famous "Essays," which indicate a sprightly humor allied to a most independent spirit. The Essays, Hallam says, make in several respects an epoch in literature. Emerson says, "Montaigne is the frankest and honestest of all writers." Montaigne took as his motto: Que scais je? [What know I?] and said that all religious opinions are the result of custom. Buckle says, "Under the guise of a mere man of the world, expressing natural thoughts in common language, Montaigne concealed a spirit of lofty and audacious inquiry." Montaigne seems to have been the first man in Europe who doubted the sense and justice of burning people for a difference of opinion. His denunciation of the conduct of the Christians in America does him infinite honor. Died 13 Sept. 1592.

Monteil (Charles François Louis Edgar), French journalist, b. Vire, 26 Jan. 1845. Fought against the Empire, writing in *Le Rappel*. During the Commune he was secretary to Delescluze. For his *Histoire d'un Frère Ignorantin*, '74, he was prosecuted by the Christian Brothers, and condemned to one year's imprisonment, 2,000 francs fine, and 10,000 francs damages. In '77 he wrote a *Freethinker's Catechism*, published at Antwerp, and in '79 an edition of *La République Française*. In '80 he was made a member of the Municipal Council of Paris, and re-elected in '84. In '83 he was made Chevalier of the Legion of Honor. He has compiled an excellent secular *Manual of Instruction* for schools.

Montesquieu (Charles de SECONDAT), *Baron*, eminent French writer, b. near Bordeaux, 18 Jan. 1689. His first literary performance was entitled *Persian Letters*, 1721. In 1728 he was admitted a member of the French Academy, though opposed by Cardinal Fleury on the ground that his writings were dangerous to religion. His chief work is the *Spirit of Laws*, 1748. This work was one of the first-fruits of the positive spirit in history and jurisprudence. The chapters on Slavery are written in a vein of masterly irony, which

Voltaire pronounced to be worthy of Molière.   Died 10 Feb. 1755.

Montgomery (Edmund), Dr. philosopher, b. of Scotch parents, Edinburgh 1835.   In youth he lived at Frankfort, where he saw Schopenhauer, and afterwards attended at Heidelburg the lectures of Moleschott and Kuno Fischer. He became a friend of Feuerbach.   He wrote in German and published at Munich in '71, *The Kantian Theory of Knowledge refuted from the Empirical Standpoint.*   In '67 he published a small book On the Formation of so-called Cells in Animal Bodies,   In '71 he went to Texas and prosecuted his scientific studies on life.   He has written in the *Popular Science Monthly, The Index,* and *The Open Court* and *Mind.*   Dr. Montgomery holds not only that there is no evidence of a God, but that there is evidence to the contrary.

Montgolfier (Michel Joseph), aeronaut. b. Aug. 1740.   He was the first to ascend in an air balloon, 5 June 1783.   A friend of Delambre and La Lalande, he was on the testimony of this last an atheist.   Died 26 June 1810.

Mook (Friedrich) German writer, b. Bergzabern, 29 Sept. 1844, studied philosophy and theology at Tübingen, but gave up the latter to study medicine.   He lived as a writer at Heidelberg and became lecturer to a free congregation at Nürenburg, and wrote a popular *Life of Jesus,* published at Zürich, '72–3.   He travelled abroad and was drowned in the river Jordan, 13 Dec. 1880.   His brother Kurt, b. 12 Feb. 1847, is a physician who has published some poems.

Moor (Edmund), Major in the East Indian Company, author of the *Hindu Pantheon,* 1810 and *Oriental Fragments,* '34. Died 1840.

Moreau (Hégésippe), French poet, b. Paris 9, April 1810. A radical and freethinker, he fought in the barricades in '30. Wrote songs and satires of considerable merit, and a prose work entitled *The Miseltoe and the Oak.*   His life, which was a continual struggle with misery, terminated in a hospital, 20 Dec. 1838.   His works have been collected, with an introduction by Sainte-Beuve.

Moreau (Jacques Joseph), Dr. of Tours, b. Montresor, 1804.

He became a distinguished alienist of the materialist school, and wrote on Moral Faculties from a medical point of view, '36, and many physiological works.

Morelly, French socialist of the eighteenth century, b. Vitry-le-Français, author of a work called *Code de la Nature,* sometimes attributed to Diderot. It was published in 1755' and urges that man should find circumstances in which depravity is minimised.

Morgan (Thomas), Welsh Deist, known by the title of his book as *The Moral Philosopher,* 1737. Was a Presbyterian, but was deposed for Arianism about 1723, and practised medicine at Bristol. He edited Radicati's Dissertation on Death, 1731. His *Moral Philosopher* seeks to substitute morality for religion. He calls Moses " a more fabulous romantic writer than Homer or Ovid," and attacks the evidence of miracles and prophecy. This was supplemented by *A Further Vindication of Moral Truth and Reason,* 1739, and Superstition and Tyranny Inconsistent with Theocracy, 1710. He replied to his opponents over the signature " Philalethes." His last work was on Physico-Theology, 1741. Lechler calls Morgan " the modern Marcion." Died at London, 14 Jan. 1743.

Morgan (Sir Thomas Charles), M.D., b. 1783. Educated at Cambridge. In 1811 he was made a baronet, and married Miss Sidney Owenson. A warm friend of civil and religious liberty and a sceptic, he is author of *Sketches of the Philosophy of Life,* '18, and the *Philosophy of Morals,* '19. The *Examiner* says, " He was never at a loss for a witty or wise passage from Rabelais or Bayle." Died 28 Aug. 1843.

Morin (André Saturnin), French writer, b. Chatres, 28 Nov. 1807. Brought up to the law, and became an advocate. In '30 he wrote defending the revolution against the restoration. In '48 he was made sous-prefet of Nogent. During the Empire he combated vigorously for Republicanism and Freethought, writing under the signature " Miron," in the *Rationaliste* of Geneva, the *Libre Pensée* of Paris, the *Libero-pensiero* of Milan, and other papers. He was intimately associated with Ausonio Franchi, Trezza, Stefanoni, and the Italian Freethinkers. His principal work is an *Examination of Christianity,* in three volumes, '62. His *Jesus Reduced to his True Value* has gone

233

through several editions. His *Essai de Critique Religieuse*, '85, is an able work. M. Morin was one of the founders of the *Bibliothèqne Démocratique*, to which he contributed several anti-clerical volumes, the one on *Confession* being translated into English by Dr. J. R. Beard. In '76 he was elected on the Municipal Council of Paris, where he brought forward the question of establishing a crematorium. Died at Paris, 5 July, 1888, and was cremated at Milan.

Morison (James Augustus Cotter), English Positivist and man of letters, b. London, 1831. Graduated at Lincoln Coll. Oxford, M.A., '59. In '63 he published the *Life and Times of Saint Bernard*. He was one of the founders of the *Fortnightly Review*, in which he wrote, as well as in the *Athenæum*. He contributed monographs on Gibbon and Macaulay to Morley's " Men of Letters " Series. In '86 he published his striking work *The Service of Man*, an Essay towards the Religion of the Future, which shows that the benefits of Christianity have been much exaggerated and its evils palpable. All his writings are earnest and thoughtful. He collected books and studied to write a History of France, which would have been a noble contribution to literature; but the possession of a competence seems to have weakened his industry, and he never did justice to his powers. Even the *Service of Man* was postponed until he was no longer able to complete it as he intended. Morison was a brilliant talker, and the centre of a wide circle of friends. George Meredith dedicated to him a volume of poems. Died at Hampstead, 26 Feb. 1888.

Morley (John), English writer and statesman, b. Blackburn, 24 Dec. 1838, educated at Oxford. Among his fellow students was J. C. Morison. He contributed to *The Leader* and the *Saturday Review*, edited the *Morning Star*, and the *Fortnightly Review*, '67-82, in which appeared the germs of most of his works, such as *On Compromise*, *Voltaire*, '72; *Rousseau*, '73; *Diderot and the Encyclopædists* '78. During his editorship important Freethought papers appeared in that review. From May, '80 till Aug. '83 he edited the *Pall Mall Gazette*. Upon the death of Ashton Dilke, M.P., he was elected to Parliament for Newcastle, and in Feb. '86 was appointed by Mr. Gladstone Chief Secretary for Ireland.

Morselli (Enrico Agostino), Italian doctor and scientist, b. Modena, 1852. Has written many anthropological works, notably one on *Suicide* in the International Scientific Series, and a study on " The Religion of Mazzini." He edits the *Rivista di Filosofia Scientifica*, and has translated Herbert Spencer on the past and future of religion.

Mortillet (Louis Laurent Gabriel de), French scientist, b. Meylan (Isère), 29 Aug. 1821, and was educated by Jesuits. Condemned in '49 for his political writings he took refuge in Switzerland. He has done much to promote prehistoric studies in France. Has written *Materials to serve for the positive and philosophical history of man*, '64. *The Sign of the Cross before Christianity*, '66, *Contribution to the History of Superstition*, and *Prehistoric Antiquity of Man*, '82. He contributed to the *Revue Irdépendante, Pensée Nouvelle*, etc. M. de Mortillet is curator of the Museum of St. Germain and was elected Deputy in 1885.

Moss (Arthur B.), lecturer and writer, b. 8 May, 1855. Has written numerous pamphlets, a number of which are collected in *Waves of Freethought*, '85. Others are *Nature and the Gods, Man and the Lower Animals, Two Revelations*, etc. Mr. Moss has been a contributor to the *Secular Chronicle, Secular Review, Freethinker, Truthseeker*, and other journals, and has had a written debate on " Was Jesus God or Man." A School Board officer, he was for a time prohibited from lecturing on Sunday. A collection of his *Lectures and Essays* has been published, 1889.

Mothe Le Vayer. See La Mothe Le Vayer.

Mott (Lucretia), American reformer, *nee* Coffin, b. Nantucket, 3 Jan. 1793. She was a Quakeress, but on the division of the Society in 1827 went with the party who preferred conscience to revelation. A strong opponent of slavery, she took an active part in the abolitionist movement. She was delegated to the World's Anti-slavery Convention in London in 1840, but excluded on account of her sex. A friend of Mrs. Rose and Mrs. Stanton. Took an active part in Women's Rights conventions. Died at Philadelphia, 11 Nov. 1880.

Muhammad ibn al Hudail *al Basri*, philosopher of Asia Minor, founder of the Muhammadan Freethinking sect of Mutazilah, b. about 757. Died about 819.

Muhammad Ibn Muhammad Ibn Tarkhan (Abu Nasr.) See Alpharabius.

Muhammad Ibn Yahya Ibn Bajjat. See Avempace.

Muhammad Jalal ed din. See Akbar.

Muller (Dr. H. C.) Dutch writer, b. 31 Oct. 1855. Has contributed good articles to *de Dageraad* (the Daybreak), and is now teacher of modern Greek at the University of Amsterdam.

Murger (Henri), French author, b. Paris, 1822, contributed to the *Revue des Deux Mondes*, tales poems and dramas. In his poem *Le Testament* in " Winter Nights " he says in answer to the inquiring priest "Reponds lui que j'ai lu Voltaire." His most popular work is entitled *Scenes of Bohemian Life*. Died Paris, 28 Jan. 1861.

Musset (Louis Charles Alfred de), French poet, b. Paris, 11 Nov. 1810. Before the age of twenty he became one of the leaders of the Romantic school. His prose romance, *Confession d'un Enfant du Siècle*, '36, exhibits his intellectual development and pessimistic moods. Among his finest works are four poems entitled *Nuits*, He contributed to the *Revue des Deux Mondes*, and was admitted into the Academy in '52. Died at Paris 1 May, 1857.

Naber (Samuel Adriaan), learned Dutch writer, b. Gravenhage, 16 July, 1828. Studied at Leyden and became rector of the Haarlem gymnasium, and head teacher at the Amsterdam Athenæum. He has edited a journal of literature, and is joint author with Dr. A. Pierson of Verisimilia (1886), a Latin work showing the fragmentary and disjointed character of the Epistles attributed to Paul.

Nachtigal (Gustav.), Dr., German traveller, b. Eichstadt, 23 Feb. 1834. He studied medicine, went to Algiers and Tunis, became private physician to the Bey of Tunis, explored North Africa, and wrote an account thereof, *Sahara und Sudan*. He became German Consul General at Tunis, and died 20 April, 1885.

Naigeon (Jacques André), French atheist, b. Dijon 1728 At first an art student, he became a disciple and imitator of Diderot. He became copyist to and collaborator with Holbach and conveyed his works to Amsterdam to be printed. He

contributed to the Encyclopédie, notably the articles AME and
UNITAIRES and composed the *Militaire Philosophe*, or difficulties
on religion proposed to Father Malebranche, 1768.   This was
his first work, the last chapter being written by Holbach.   He
took some share in several of the works of that writer, notably
in the *Theologie Portative*.   He published the *Recuéil Philosophique*, 2 vols., Londres (Amst.), 1770; edited Holbach's Essay on
Prejudices and his *Morale Universelle*. He also edited the
works of Diderot, the essays of Montaigne and a translation of
Toland's philosophical letters.   His principal work is the
Dictionary of Ancient and Modern Philosophy in the *Encyclopédie
Méthodique* (Paris 1791-94.)   He addressed the National
Assembly on Liberty of Opinion, 1790, and asked them to with-
hold the name of God and religion from their declaration of the
rights of man.   Naigeon was of estimable character.   Died
at Paris, 28 Feb. 1810.

Naquet (Joseph Alfred).   French materialist, b. Carpentras,
6 Oct. 1834, became M D. in '59.   In '67 he received fifteen
months imprisonment for belonging to a secret society.   He
founded, with M. Regnard, the *Revue Encyclopédique*, which was
suppressed at once for containing an attack on theism.   In
'69 he issued a work on *Religion, Property, and Family*, which
was seized and the author condemned to four months imprisonment, a fine of five hundred francs, and the perpetual interdict
of civil rights.   He represented Vaucluse in the National
Assembly, where he has voted with the extreme left.   He was
re-elected in '81.   The new law of divorce in France has been
passed chiefly through M. Naquet's energetic advocacy.   In
'83 he was elected to the Senate, and of late has distinguished
himself by his advocacy of General Boulanger.

Nascimento (Francisco Manuel do).   Portugese poet, b.
Lisbon, 23 Dec, 1734.   He entered the Church, but having
translated Molière's *Tartuffe*, was accused of heresy (1778), and
had to fly for his life from the Inquisition.   He wrote many
poems and satires under the name of " Filinto Elysio."   Died
25 Feb. 1819.

Navez (Napoleon), Belgian Freethinker, president of *La
Libre Pensée*, of Antwerp, and active member of the Council of
the International Federation of Freethinkers.

Nelson (Gustave), a writer in the New York *Truthseeker*, conjectured to be the author of *Bible Myths and their Parallels in other Religions*, a large and learned work, showing how much of Christianity has been taken from Paganism.

Newcomb (Simon), LL.D., American astronomer, b. Wallace, (Nova Scotia), 12 March, 1835. Went to the United States in '53, and was appointed computor on the *Nautical Almanack*. In '77 he became senior professor of mathematics in the U. S. navy. He has been associated with the equipment of the Lick observatory, and has written many works on mathematics and astronomy, as well as *Principles of Political Economy*, 1885.

Newman (Francis William) brother of Cardinal Newman, b. London 1805. Educated at Oxford, he was elected to a fellowship at Balliol College '26, but resigned in '30, being unable conscientiously to comply with the regulations of the Test Act then in force. He then went to Bagdad with the object of assisting in a Christian mission, but his further studies convinced him he could not conscientiously undertake the work. He returned to England and became classical teacher in Bristol College, and subsequently Latin Professor at London University. In *The Soul: its Sorrows and Aspirations*, '49, he states his Theistic position, and in *Phases of Faith*, '50, he explains how he came to give up Christianity. He has also written *A History of the Hebrew Monarchy*, '47, *Theism: Doctrinal and Practical*, '58, and a number of Scott's tracts on the Defective Morality of the New Testament, the Historical Depravation of Christianity, the Religious Weakness of Protestantism, etc. Also *Religion not History*, '77; *What is Christianity without Christ?* '81; *Christianity in its Cradle*, '84; and *Life after Death*, '86.

Neymann (Clara), German American Freethought lecturess, friend and colleague of Frau Hedwig Henrich Wilhelmi.

Nicholson (William), English writer on chemistry and natural philosophy, b. London 1753. He went to India at an early age, and upon returning settled at London as a Mathematical teacher. He published useful introductions to chemistry and natural philosophy. Conducted the British Encyclopedia, and the Journal of Natural Philosophy. He also wrote *The Doubts of the Infidels*, submitted to the Bench of

Bishops by a weak Christian, 1781, a work republished by Carlile and also by Watson. He died in poor circumstances 21 May, 1815.

Nicolai (Christoph Friedrich), German writer, b. Berlin, 18 March, 1733. A friend of Lessing, and Moses Mendelssohn; he was noted for founding " The Universal German Library." He wrote anecdotes of Friedrich II., and many other works. Died at Berlin, 8 Jan. 1811.

Nietzsche (Friedrich Wilhelm), German writer, b. Lutzen, 15 Oct. 1844, author of sketches of Strauss, Schopenhauer, and Wagner, and of *Morgenröthe*, and other philosophical works. Died 1889.

Nieuwenhuis (Ferdinand Jakob Domela), Dutch publicist, b. Utrecht, 3 May, 1848. At first a minister of the Lutheran church, on Nov. 25, '77, he told his congregation that he had ceased to believe in Christianity, and as an honest man resigned. He then contributed to *De Banier* (Banner) *de Dageraad* (Dawn) and *de Vragen des Tijds* (Questions of the time.) On 1st March, '79 he started a Socialist paper *Recht voor Allen*, now an important daily organ of Socialism and Freethought. His principle writings are— *With Jesus, For or against Socialism, The Religious Oath Question, The Religion of Reason, The Religion of Humanity.* On Jan. 19, '87, he was sentenced to one years' solitary confinement for an article he had not written, and was harshly treated till upon pressure of public opinion, he was liberated 30 Aug. 1887. He is now member of the Dutch Parliament.

Noeldeke (Theodor), German Orientalist, b. Harburg, 2 March, 1836. Studied at Gottingen, Vienna, Leyden, and Berlin, and has been professor of oriental studies at Gottingen, Kiel, and Strasburg. He has written a *History of the Koran*, '56; a *Life of Mahomet*, '63; and a *Literary History of the Old Testament*, which has been translated into French by MM. Derembourg and J. Soury, '73.

Noire (Ludwig), German monist, b. 26 March, 1829. Studied at Geissen, and became a teacher at Mainz. His works show the influence of Spinoza and Schopenhauer. He is the author of Aphorisms on the Monist philosophy, '77, and a work on the Origin of Speech, '77. He contends that language originates in

instinctive sounds accompanying will in associative actions.
Died 26 March, 1889.

Noorthouck (John), author of a *History of London*, 1773,
and an Historical and Classical Dictionary, 1776. Has been
credited with the *Life of the Man After God's Own Heart*. See
Annet.

Nordau (Max Simon), b. of Jewish parents at Pesth, 29 July,
1849. He became a physician in '73. He has written several
books of travels and made some noise by his trenchant work
on *Convential Lies of our Civilisation*. He has since written on
The Sickness of the Century.

Nork (Felix). See Korn (Selig).

Nott (Josiah Clark), Dr., American ethnologist, b. Columbia,
South Carolina, 24 March, 1804. He wrote *The Physical
History of the Jewish Race*, *Types of Mankind*, '54, and *Indigenous
Races of the Earth*, '55; the last two conjointly with G. R.
Gliddon, and with the object of disproving the theory of the
unity of the human race. Died at Mobile, 31 March, 1873.

Noun (Paul), French author of *The Scientific Errors of the
Bible*, 1881.

Noyes (Thomas Herbert), author of *Hymns of Modern Man*,
1870.

Nunez (Rafael), President of Columbia, b. Carthagena,
28 Sept. 1825. He has written many poems and political
articles, and in philosophy is a follower of Mill and Spencer.

Nuytz (Louis André). See Andre-Nuytz.

Nystrom (Anton Christen), Dr. Swedish Positivist, b. 15
Feb. 1842. Studied at Upsala and became a medical doctor in
Lund, '68. He served as assistant and field doctor in the
Dano-Prussian war of '67, and now practises as alienist in
Stockholm, where he has established a Positivist Society and
Workmen's Institute. Has written a *History of Civilisation*.

Ocellus Lucanus, early Greek philosopher, who maintained
the eternity of the cosmos. An edition of his work was
published with a translation by the Marquis d'Argens, and
Thomas Taylor published an English version.

Ochino (Bernardino Tommasini), Italian reformer, b. Sienna,
1487. A popular preacher, he was chosen general of the
Capuchins. Converted to the Reformation by Jean Valdez, he

had to fly to Geneva, 1542. Invited to England by Cranmer, he became prebend of Canterbury and preached in London until the accession of Mary, when he was expelled and went to Zurich. Here he became an Antitrinitarian, and was banished about 1562 for *Thirty Dialogues*, in one of which he shows that neither in the Bible nor the Fathers is there any express prohibition of polygamy. He went to Poland and joined the Socinians, was banished thence also, and died Slankau, Moravia, in 1564. Beza ascribes the misfortunes of Ochinus, and particularly the accidental death of his wife, to the special interposition of God on account of his erroneous opinions.

O'Connor (Arthur, afterwards Condorcet), General, b. Mitchells, near Bandon (Cork), 4 July, 1768. Joined the United Irishmen and went to France to negotiate for military aid. In May 1798 he was tried for treason and acquitted. He entered the French service and rose to distinction. In 1807 he married Elisa, the only daughter of Condorcet, whose name he took, and whose works he edited. He also edited the *Journal of Religious Freedom*. Died at Bignon, 25 April, 1852.

O'Donoghue (Alfred H.) Irish American counsellor at law, b. about 1840. Educated for the Episcopal ministry at Trinity College, Dublin, but became a sceptic and published *Theology and Mythology,* an inquiry into the claims of Biblical inspiration and the supernatural element in religion, at New York, 1880.

Oest (Johann Heinrich) German poet, b. Cassel 1727. Wrote poems published at Hamburg, 1751, and was accused of materialism.

Offen (Benjamin), American Freethinker, b. in England, 1772. He emigrated to New York, where he became lecturer to the Society of Moral Philantropists at Tammany Hall. He wrote *Biblical Criticism* and *A Legacy to the Friends of Free Discussion,* and supported the *Correspondent, Free Inquirer,* and *Boston Investigator.* Died New York, 12 May, 1848.

Offray de la Mettrie (Julian). See Lamettrie.

O'Keefe (J. A), M.D. Educated in Germany; author of an essay *On the Progress of the Human Understanding,* 1795, in which he speaks disparagingly of Christianity. He was a follower of Kant, and was classed with *Living Authors of Great Britain* in 1816.

O'Kelly (Edmund de Pentheny), a descendant of the O'Kelly's; author of *Consciousness, or the Age of Reason*, 1853; *Theological Papers*, published by Holyoake; and *Theology for the People*, '55, a series of short papers suggestive of religious Theism.

Oken (Lorenz), German morphologist and philosopher, b. Offenburg, 2 Aug. 1779. He studied at Göttingen and became a privat-docent in that university. In a remarkable *Sketch of Natural Philosophy*, 1802, he advanced a scheme of evolution. He developed his system in a work on *Generation*, 1805, and a *Manual of Natural Philosophy*, 1809. He was professor at Jena, but dismissed for his liberal views. From '17 till '48 he edited the scientific journal *Isis*. In '32 he became a professor at Zürich, where he died, 11 Aug. 1851.

Oliver (William), M.D., of Bath, who was accused of Atheism. Died 1764.

Omar Khayyam. See Khayyam.

Omboni (Giovanni), Lombard naturalist, b. Abbiategrasso, 29 June, 1829. Is professor of geology at Padua, and author of many scientific works.

Onimus (Ernest Nicolas Joseph), Dr., French Positivist, b. near Mulhouse, 6 Dec. 1840. Studied medicine at Strasburg and Paris, and wrote a treatise on *The Dynamical Theory of Heat in Biological Sciences*, 1866. In '73 he was one of the jury of the Vienna Exhibi tion, and obtained the Cross of the Legion of Honor. Is author of the *Psychology in the Plays of Shakespere*, '78, and has written in the *Revue Positive* and other periodicals.

Oort (Henricus), Dutch rationalist, b. Eemnes, 27 Dec. 1836. Studied theology at Leyden, and became teacher at Amsterdam. Has written many works, of which we mention *The Worship of Baalim in Israel*, translated by Bp. Colenso, 1865, and *The Bible for Young People*, written with Drs. Hooykaas and Kuenen, and translated by P. H. Wickstead, 1873-79.

Orelli (Johann Kaspar von), learned Swiss critic, b. Zürich, 13 Feb. 1789. Edited many classics, and wrote a letter in

favor of Strauss at the time when there was an outcry at his
being appointed Professor at Zürich.   Died 6 Jan. 1849.

Osborne (Francis), English writer, b. Clucksand, Beds. 1589
Was an adherent of Cromwell in the Civil War.   His *Advice to
a Son*, 1656, was popular though much censured by the Puritans
who drew up a complaint against his works and proposed to
have them burnt, and an order was passed 27 July, 1658, for-
bidding them to be sold.   Died 1659.

Oscar (L.), Swiss writer, author of *Religion Traced Back to
its Source*, Basel, 1874.   He considers religion "a belief in
conflict with experience and resting on exaggerated fancies" of
animism and mythology.   One of his chapters is entitled "The
Crucifixion of the Son of God as Christian mythology."

Ossoli (Countess d').   See Fuller (Margaret).

Oswald (Eugen), German teacher in England.   Author of
many popular school books, and a Study of Positivism in
England, 1881.

Oswald (Felix Leopold), American writer, b. Belgium, 1845.
Educated as a physician, he has devoted his attention to
natural history, and in pursuit of his studies has travelled
extensively.   He has contributed to the *Popular Science Monthly,
The Truthseeker* and other journals, and has published *Summer-
land Sketches*, or Rambles in the Backwoods of Mexico and
Central America, '81; Physical Education, '82; *The Secrets of
the East*, '83, which argues that Christianity is derived from
Buddhism, and *The Bible of Nature* or the Principles of
Secularism, '88.   Dr. Oswald is now employed as Curator of
Natural History in Brazil.

O'Toole (Adam Duff), Irish Freethought martyr, burnt to
death at Hogging (now College) Green, Dublin, in 1327.
Holinshed says he "denied obstinatelie the incarnation of our
savior. the trinitie of persons in the vnitie of the Godhead
and the resurrection of the flesh; as for the Holie Scripture,
he said it was but a fable; the Virgin Marie he affirmed to be a
woman of dissolute life, and the Apostolike see erronious."

"Ouida," See Ramée (Louise de la).

Ouvry (Henry Aimé), Col., translator of Feuchterslebens,
Dietetics of the Soul and Rau's *Unsectarian Catechism*, and author
of several works on the land question.

Overton (Richard), English Republican, who wrote a satire on relics, 1642, and a treatise on *Man's Mortality* (London, 1643, Amsterdam, 1644) a work designed to show man is naturally mortal.

Owen (Robert), social reformer, b. Newton, Montgomeryshire, Wales, 14 March, 1771. At 18 he was so distinguished by his business talents that he became partner in a cotton mill. In 1797 he married the daughter of David Dale, and soon afterwards became partner and sole manager at New Lanark Mills, where he built the first infant schools and improved the dwellings of the workmen. From 1810-15 he published *New Views on Society*, or, Essays on the Formation of Character. In '17 he caused much excitement by proclaiming that the religions of the world were all false, and that man was the creature of circumstances. In '24 he went to America and purchased New Harmony, Indiana, from the Rappists to found a new community, but the experiment was a failure, as were also others at Orbiston, Laner, and Queenswood, Hants. In '28 he debated at Cincinatti with Alex. Campbell on the Evidences of Christianity. He published a numerous series of tracts, *Robert Owen's Journal*, and *The New Moral World*, '35. He debated on his Social System with the Rev. J. H. Roebuck, R. Brindley, etc. As his mind began to fail he accepted the teachings of Spiritism. Died Newton, 17 Nov. 1858. Owen profoundly influenced the thought of his time in the direction of social amelioration, and he is justly respected for his energy, integrity and disinterested philanthropy.

Owen (Robert Dale), son of the above, b. Glasgow 9 Nov. 1800. Was educated by his father till 1820, when he was sent to Fellenberg's school, near Berne, Switzerland. In '25 he went to America to aid in the efforts to found a colony at New Harmony, Indiana. On the failure of that experiment he began with Frances Wright, in Nov. '28, the publication of the *Free Inquirer*, which was continued till '32. In that year he had a written discussion with O. Bachelor on the existence of God, and the authenticity of the Bible, in which he ably championed the Freethought cause. He wrote a number of tracts of which we mention *Situations*, 1839; *Address on Free Inquiry*, 1840; *Prossimo's Experience, Consistency, Galileo and the Inquisition.*

He was elected to Congress in '43. After fifteen years of labor he secured the women of Indiana independent rights of property. He became charge d'affaires at Naples in '53. During the civil war he strongly advocated slave emancipation. Like his father he became a Spiritualist. Died at Lake George, 17 June, 1877.

Paalzow (Christian Ludwig), German jurist, b. Osterburg (Altmark), 26 Nov. 1753, translated Voltaire's commentaries on *The Spirit of the Laws* and Burigny's *Examination of the Apologists of Christianity* (Leipzic, 1793), and wrote a *History of Religious Cruelty* (Mainz, 1800). Died 20 May, 1824.

Paepe (Cesar de). See De Paepe.

Pagano (Francisco Mario Saverio Antonio Carlo Pasquale). Italian jurist, philosopher and patriot, b. Brienza, 1748. He studied at Naples, and became the friend of Filangieri. Was made professor of criminal law in 1787. For his *Political Essays* in three volumes (1783-92) he was accused of Atheism and impiety. He wrote on *Criminal Process* and a work on *God and Nature*. Taking part in the Provisional Government of the Neapolitan Republic in 1791, he was taken prisoner by the royalists and executed 6 Oct. 1800.

Page (David). Scotch geologist, b. 29 Aug. 1814. Author of introductory and advanced text-books of geology. which went through many editions. He gave advanced lectures in Edinburgh. and edited *Life Lights of Song*, '64. His *Man Where, Whence, and Whither?*, '67, advocating Darwinian views, made some stir in Scotland. He became professor of geology at Durham University. A friend of Robert Chambers, he was for some time credited with that writer's *Vestiges of Creation*, in the scientific details of which he assisted. Died at New-castle on-Tyne, 9 March, 1879.

Paget (Violet). English authoress, who, under the pen-name of " Vernon Lee," has written *Studies of the Eighteenth Century in Italy* and *Baldwin*, dialogues on views and aspirations 1886. Since '71 she has lived chiefly in Florence, and contributes to the principal reviews, an article in the *Contemporary* (May '83) on " Responsibilities of Unbelief " being particularly noticeable. Miss Paget's writings show a cultivated mind and true literary instinct.

Pageze (L.) French Socialist; has written on the Concordat and the Budget des Cultes, '86, Separation of Church and State, '87, etc.

Paine (Thomas), Deist, b. Thetford, Norfolk, 29 Jan., 1737 His father was a Quaker and staymaker, and Paine was brought up to the trade. He left home while still young, went to London and Sandwich, where he married the daughter of a an exciseman, and entered the excise. He was selected by his official associates to embody their wants in a paper, and on this work he displayed such talent that Franklin, then in London, suggested America as a good field for his abilities. Paine went in 1774, and soon found work for his pen. He became editor of the *Pennsylvanian Magazine* and contributed to the Pennsylvanian journal a strong anti-slavery essay. *Common Sense,* published early in 1776, advocating absolute independence for America, did more than anything else to precipitate the great events of that year. Each number of the *Crisis*, which appeared during the war, was read by Washington's order to each regiment in the service. Paine subscribed largely to the army, and served for a short time himself. After peace was declared, congress voted him three thousand dollars, and the state of New York gave him a large farm. Paine turned his attention to mechanics, and invented the tubular iron bridge. which he endeavored to introduce in Europe. Reaching France during the Revolution, he published a pamphlet advocating the abolition of royalty. In 1791 he published his *Rights of Man*, in reply to Burke. For this he was outlawed. Escaping from England, he went to France, where he was elected to the Convention. He stoutly opposed the execution of the king, and was thrown by Robespierre into the Luxembourg prison, where for nearly a year he awaited the guillotine. During this time he wrote the first part of the *Age of Reason*, which he completed on his release. This famous book, though vulnerable in some minor points of criticism, throws a flood of light on Christian dogmas, and has had a more extended sale than any other Freethought work. As a natural consequence, Paine has been an object of incessant slander by the clergy. Paine died at New York 8 June, 1809, and, by his own direction was buried on his farm at New

Rochelle. Cobbett is said to have disinterred him and brought his bones to England.

Pajot (François). See LINIERE.

Paleario (Aonio), *i e.*, Antonio, della Paglia, Italian humanist and martyr, b. about 1500 at Véroli in the Roman Campagna. In 1520 he went to Rome and took place among the brilliant men of letters of court of Leo X. After the taking of Rome by Charles V. he retired to Sienna. In 1536 he published at Lyons an elegant Latin poem on the Mortality of the Soul—modeled on Lucretius. He was Professor of Eloquence at Milan for ten years, but was accused of heresy. He had called the Inquisition a poignard directed against all men of letters. On 3 July, 1570, he was hung and his body thrown into the flames. A work on the Benefit of Christ's Death has been attributed to him on insufficient grounds. It is attributed to Benedetto da Mantova.

Pallas (Peter Simon), German naturalist and traveller, b. Berlin, 22 Sept. 1741. Educated as a physician at Gottingen and Leyden, he was invited by Catherine II. to become Professor of Natural History at St. Petersburg. He travelled through Siberia and settled in the Crimea. In 1810 he returned to Berlin, where he died 8 Sept. 1811. Lalande spoke highly of him, and Cuvier considered him the founder of modern geology.

Pallavicino (Ferrante), Italian poet and wit, b. Piacenza 1616. He became a canon of the Lateran congregation, but for composing some satirical pieces against Pope Urban VIII. had a price set on his head. He fled to Venice, but a false friend betrayed him to the Inquisition, and he was beheaded at Avignon, 5 March, 1644.

Palmer (Courtlandt), American reformer, b. New York, 25 March, 1843, graduated at the Columbia law-school in '69 He was brought up in the Dutch Reformed Church, but became a Freethinker while still young. Mr. Palmer did much to promote Liberal ideas. In '80 he established and became President of the Nineteenth Century Club, for the utmost liberty of public discussion. He contributed to the *Freethinker's Maga_zine, Truthseeker*, etc. A sister married Prof. Draper with whom he was intimate. Died at New York, 23 July, 1888, and was

247

cremated at Fresh Pond, his friend Col. R. G. Ingersoll delivering an eulogium.

Palmer (Elihu), American author, b. Canterbury, Connecticut, 1764. He graduated at Dartmouth in 1787, and studied divinity but became a deist in 1791. In 1793 he became totally blind from an attack of yellow fever. In 1797 he lectured to a Deistical Society in New York. After this he dictated his *Principles of Nature*, 1802, a powerful anti-Christian work, reprinted by Carlile in '19. He also wrote *Prospect or View of the Moral World from the year* 1804. Palmer was the head of the Society of Columbian Illuminati founded in New York in 1801. He died in Philadelphia, 7 April, 1806

Panaetius (Παναιτιος), Stoic philosopher, b. Rhodes, a pupil of Diogenes the Stoic, and perhaps of Carneades. About 150 B.C. he visited Rome and taught a moderate stoicism, denying the doctrine of the conflagration of the world, and placing physics before dialectics. He wrote a work *On Duties*, to which Cicero expresses his indebtedness in his *De Officiis*. Died in Athens 111 B.C.

Pancoucke (Charles Joseph), eminent French publisher, b. Lille, 26 Nov. 1736. He settled at Paris and became acquainted with d'Alembert, Garat, etc., and was a correspondent of Rousseau, Buffon and Voltaire, whose works he brought out. He translated Lucretius, 1768, brought out the *Mercure de France*, projected in 1781 the important *Encyclopédie Méthodique*, of which there are 166 vols., and founded the *Moniteur*, 1789. Died at Paris, 19 Dec. 1798.

Pantano (Eduardo), Italian author of a little book on the Sicilian Vespers and the Commune, Catania, 1882.

Papillon (J. Henri Fernand), French philosophic writer, b. Belfort, 5 June, 1847. He wrote an *Introduction to Chemical Philosophy*, '65; contributed to the *Revue de Philosophie Positive* and the *Revue des Deux Mondes*. His principle work is entitled *Nature and Life*, '73. Died at Paris 31 Dec. 1873.

Paquet (Henri Remi René), French writer, b. Charleville, 29 Sep. 1845. After studying under the Jesuits he went to Paris, where he became an advocate, but devoted his main

attention to literature. Under the anagram of " Nérée Quépat "
he has published *La Lorgnette Philosophique*, '72. a dictionary of
the great and little philosophers of our time, a study of La
Mettrie entitled *Materialist Philosophy in the Eighteenth Century*
and other works.

Pare (William), Owenite Social reformer, b. Birmingham
1805. Wrote an abridgment of Thompson's *Distribution of
Wealth*, also works on *Capital and Labor* '54, *Co-operative
Agriculture*, at Rahaline, '70, etc. He compiled vol. 1 of the
Biography of Robert Owen. Died at Croydon, 18 June, 1873.

Parfait (Noel), French writer and politician, b. Chartres,
30 Nov. 1814. Took part in the revolution of '30, and wrote
many radical brochures. After the coup d'état he took refuge
in Belgium. In '71 was elected deputy and sat on the extreme
left.

Parfait (Paul), son of the foregoing, b. Paris, 1841. Author
of *L'Arsenal de la Dévotion*, '76, Notes to serve for a history of
superstition, and a supplement *Le Dossier des Pèlerinages*, '77,
and other pieces. Died 1881.

Parisot (Jean Patrocle), a Frenchman who wrote *La Foy
devoilée par la raison*, 1681 [Faith Unveiled by Reason], a work
whose title seems to have occasioned its suppression.

Parker (Theodore), American rationalist, b. Lexington,
Mass., 24 Aug. 1810. From his father—a Unitarian—he inherited independence of mind, courage, and love of speculation.
Brought up in poverty he studied hard, and acquired a University education while laboring on the farm. In March, '31, he
became an assistant teacher at Boston. In June, '37, he was
ordained Unitarian minister. Parker gradually became known
as an iconoclast, and study of the German critics made him a
complete rationalist, so that even the Unitarian body rejected
him. A society was established to give him a hearing in
Boston, and soon his fame was established. His *Discourse on
Matters Pertaining to Religion*, '47, exhibited his fundamental
views. He translated and enlarged De Wette's Critical Introduction to the Old Testament. A fearless opponent of the
Fugitive Slave Law, he sheltered slaves in his own house.
Early in '59 failing health compelled him to relinquish his

duties. Died at Florence, 10 May, 1860. He bequeathed his library of 13,000 volumes to the Boston Public Library.

Parmenides, a Greek philosopher, b. Elea, Italy, 518 B.C. Is said to have been a disciple of Xenophanes. He developed his philosophy about 470 B.C. in a didactic poem *On Nature*, fragments of which are preserved by Sextus Empiricus. He held to Reason as our guide, and considered nature eternal.

Parny (Evariste Désiré DE FORGES de), *Viscount.* French poet, b. St. Paul, Isle of Bourbon, 6 Feb. 1753. Educated in France, he chose the military profession. A disappointed passion for a creole inspired his " Amatory Poems," and he afterwards wrote the audacious *War of the Gods, Paradise Lost,* and *The Gallantries of the Bible.* His poems, though erotic, are full of elegant charm, and he has been named the French Tibullus. He was admitted into the French Academy in 1803. Died at Paris, 5 Dec. 1814.

Parton (James), author, b. Canterbury, England, 9 Feb. 1822. Was taken to the United States when a child and educated at New York. He married Miss Willis, " Fannie Fern," and has written many biographies, including Lives of Thomas Jefferson, '74, and of Voltaire, '81. He has also written on *Topics of the Time*, '71, and *Church Taxation.* He resided in New York till '75 when he removed to Newburyport, Massachusetts.

Parvish (Samuel), Deistic author of *An Inquiry into the Jewish and Christian Revelation* (London, 1739), of which a second edition was issued in 1746.

Pasquier (Etienne). French journalist, b. 7 April, 1529, at Paris, Brought up to the bar he became a successful pleader. He defended the Universities against the Jesuits, whom he also attacked in a bitter satire, *Catéchisme des Jesuites.* Died Paris, 30 Aug. 1615.

Passerano (Alberto RADICATI di) *count.* Italian philosopher of last century, attached to the court of Victor Amedée II. For some pamphlets written against the Papal power he was pursued by the Inquisition and his goods seized. He lived in England and made the acquaintance of Collins, also in France and Holland, where he died about 1736, leaving his goods to the poor. In that year he published at Rotterdam *Recueil de Pièces* *curieuses sur les matieres les plus intéressantes*, etc., which contains a *Parallel between Mahomet and Sosem* (anagram of Moses), *an abridged history of the Sacerdotal Profession*, and a *Faithful and comic recital of the religion of modern cannibals*, by Zelin Moslem; also a *Dissertation upon Death*, which was published separately in 1733. The *Recueil* was republished at London in 1719. He also wrote a pretended translation from an Arabic work on Mohammedanism, satirising the Bible, and a pretended sermon by Elwall the Quaker.

Pasteur (Louis). French scientist b. Dôle, 27 Dec 1822, became doctor in '47 and professor of physic at Strassburg in '48. He received the Rumford medal of the Royal Society in '56 for his discoveries in polarisation and molecular chemistry. Decorated with the Legion of honor in '53, he was made commander '68 and grand officer '78. His researches into innoculation have been much contested, but his admirers have raised a large institute for the prosecution of his treatment. He was elected to the Academy as successor of Littré. He gave his name as Vice-President of the British Secular Union.

Pastoret (Claude Emmanuel Joseph Pierre de), *Marquis*, French statesman and writer, b. of noble family at Marseilles, 25 Oct. 1756. Educated by the Oratorians at Lyons, in 1779 he published an *Eloge de Voltaire*. By his works on *Zoroaster, Confucius and Mahomet* (1787) and on *Moses Considered as Legislator and Moralist* (1788) he did something for the infant science of comparative religion. His principal work is a learned *History of Legislation*, in 11 vols. (1817—37), in which he passes in review all the ancient codes. He embraced the Revolution, and became President of the Legislative Assembly (3 Oct. 1791). He proposed the erection of the Column of July on the Place of the Bastille, and the conversion of the church of Ste Geneviève into the Pantheon. On the 19th June, 1792, he presented a motion for the complete separation of the state from religion. He fled during the Terror, but returned as deputy in 1795. In 1820 he succeeded his friend Volney as member of the French Academy, in '23 received the cross of the Legion of Honor, and in '29 became Chancellor of France. Died at Paris, 28 Sept. 1840.

Pater (Walter Horatio), English writer, b. London, 4 Aug.
251

1839. B.A. at Oxford in '62, M.A. in '65. Has written charming essays in the *Westminster Review*, *Macmillan*, and the *Fortnightly Review*. In '73 he published *The Renaissance*, and in '85 *Marius the Epicurean, His Sensations and Ideas.*

Paterson (Thomas), b. near Lanark early in this century. After the imprisonment of Southwell and Holyoake he edited the *Oracle of Reason*. For exhibiting profane placards he was arrested and sentenced 27 Jan. 1843 to three months' imprisonment. His trial was reported under the title *God v. Paterson* ('43.) He insisted on considering God as the plaintiff and in quoting from "the Jew book" to show the plaintiff's bad character. When released he went to Scotland to uphold the right of free publication, and was sentenced 8 Nov. '43 to fifteen months' imprisonment for selling "blasphemous" publications at Edinburgh. On his release he was presented with a testimonial 6 April, 1845, H. Hetherington presiding. Paterson went to America.

Patin (Gui), French physician, writer, and wit, b. near Beauvais 31 Aug. 1602. He became professor at the college of France. His reputation is chiefly founded on his *Letters*, in which he attacked superstition. Laroussa says "C'etait un libre penseur de la famille de Rabelais." Died at Paris 30 Aug. 1672.

Patot. See Tyssot de Patot (S.)

Pauw (Cornelius), learned Dutch writer, b. Amsterdam, 1739. He wrote philosophical researches on the Americans, and also on the Egyptians, Chinese, and Greeks. Was esteemed by Frederick the Great for his ingenuity and penetration. Died at Xanten, 7 July, 1799. He was the uncle of Anacharsis Clootz.

Peacock (John Macleay), Scotch poet, b. 21 March, 1817 He wrote many poems in the *National Reformer*, and in '67 published *Hours of Reverie*. Died 4 May, 1 77.

Peacock or **Pecock** (Reginald), the father of English rationalism, b. about 1390, and educated at Oriel College Oxford, of which he was chosen fellow in 1417. Was successively Bishop of St Asaph, 1444, and Chichester, 1450, by the favor of Humphrey, the good Duke of Gloster. He declared that Scripture must in all cases be accommodated to "the doom of reason." He questioned the genuineness of the Apostles' Creed. In 1457 he was accused of heresy, recanted from fear of martyrdom, was deprived of his bishopric, and imprisoned in a monastery at Canterbury, where he used to repeat to those who visited him,

> " Wit hath wonder, that reason cannot skan,
> How a Moder is Mayd, and God is Man."

His books were publicly burnt at Oxford. He died in 1460. His influence doubtless contributed to the Reformation.

Pearson (Karl), author of a volume of essays entitled *The Ethic of Freethought*, 1888. Educated at Cambridge; B.A. '79, M.A. '82.

Pechmeja (Jean de), French writer. A friend of Raynal, he wrote a socialistic romance in 12 books in the style of Telemachus, called Télèphe, 1784. Died 1785.

Peck (John), American writer in the *Truthseeker*. Has published *Miracles and Miracle Workers*, etc.

Pecqueur (A.), contributor to the *Rationaliste* of Geneva, 1864.

Pelin (Gabriel), French author of works on *Spiritism Explained and Destroyed*, 1864, and *God or Science*, '67.

Pelletan (Charles Camille), French journalist and deputy, son of the following; b. Paris, 23 June, 1846. Studied at the Lycée Louis le Grand. He wrote in *La Tribune Française*, and *Le Rappel*, and since '80 has conducted *La Justice* with his friend Clémenceau, of whom he has written a sketch.

Pelletan (Pierre Clement Eugène), French writer, b. Saint-Palais-sur-Meir, 20 Oct. 1813. As a journalist he wrote in *La Presse*, under the name of " Un Inconnu," articles distinguished by their love of liberty and progress. He also contributed to the *Revue des Deux Mondes*. In '52 he published his *Profession of Faith of the Nineteenth Century*, and in '57 *The Law of Progress* and *The Philosophical Kings*. From '53-'55 he opposed Napoleon in the Siècle, and afterwards established *La Tribune Française*. In '83 he was elected deputy, but his election being annulled, he was re-elected in '64. He took distinguished rank among the democratic opposition. After the battle of Sedan he was made member of the Committee of

National Defence, and in '76 of the Senate, of which he became vice-president in '79. In '78 he wrote a study on Frederick the Great entitled *Un Roi Philosophe*, and in '83 *Is God Dead?* Died at Paris, 14 Dec. 1884.

Pemberton (Charles Reece), English actor and author. b. Pontypool, S. Wales, 23 Jan. 1790. He travelled over most of the world and wrote *The Autobiography of Pel Verjuice*, which with other remains was published in 1843. Died 3 March, 1840.

Pennetier (Georges), Dr., b. Rouen, 1836, Director of the Museum of Natural History at Rouen. Author of a work on the *Orgin of Life*, '68, in which he contends for spontaneous generation. To this work F. A. Pouchet contributed a preface.

Perfitt (Philip William), Theist, b. 1820, edited the *Pathfinder*, '59–61. Preached at South Place Chapel. Wrote *Life and Teachings of Jesus of Nazareth*, '61.

Periers (Bonaventure des). See Desperiers.

Perot (Jean Marie Albert), French banker, author of a work on *Man and God*, which has been translated into English, 1881, and *Moral and Philosophical Allegories* (Paris, 1883).

Perrier (Edmond), French zoologist, Curator at Museum of Natural History, Paris, b. Tulle, 1844. Author of numerous works on Natural History, and one on *Transformisme*, '88.

Perrin (Raymond S.), American author of a bulky work on *The Religion of Philosophy*, or the Unification of Knowledge: a comparison of the chief philosophical and religious systems of the world, 1885.

Perry (Thomas Ryley), one of Carlile's shopmen, sentenced 1824 to three years' imprisonment in Newgate for selling Palmer's *Principles of Nature*. He became a chemist at Leicester and in 1844 petitioned Parliament for the prisoners for blasphemy, Paterson and Roalfe, stating that his own imprisonment had not fulfilled the judge's hope of his recantation.

Petit (Claude), French poet, burnt on the Place de Grève in 1665 as the author of some impious pieces.

Petronius, called Arbiter (Titus), Roman Epicurean poet at the Court of Nero, in order to avoid whose resentment he opened his veins and bled to death in A.D. 66, conversing meanwhile with his friends on the gossip of the day. To him we owe the lines on superstition, beginning " Primus in orbe Deos fecit timor." Petronius is famous for his " pure Latinity." He is as plain-spoken as Juvenal, and with the same excuse, his romance being a satire on Nero and his court.

Petruccelli della Gattina (Ferdinando) Italian writer, b. Naples, 1816, has travelled much and written many works. He was deputy to the Naples Parliament in '48, and exiled after the reaction.

Petrus de Abano. A learned Italian physician, b. Abano 1250. He studied at Paris and became professor of medicine at Padua. He wrote many works and had a great reputation. He is said to have denied the existence of spirits, and to have ascribed all miracles to natural causes. Cited before the Inquisition in 1306 as a heretic, a magician and an Atheist, he ably defended himself and was acquitted. He was accused a second time but dying (1320) while the trial was preparing, he was condemned after death, his body disinterred and burnt, and he was also burnt in effigy in the public square of Padua.

Peypers (II. F. A.), Dutch writer, b. De Dijp, 2 Jan. 1856, studied medicine, and is now M.D. at Amsterdam. He is a man of erudition and good natured though satirical turn of mind. He has contributed much to *De Dageraad*, and is at present one of the five editors of that Freethought monthly.

Peyrard (François), French mathematician, b. Vial (Haute Loire) 1760. A warm partisan of the revolution, he was one of those who (7 Nov. 1793) incited Bishop Gobel to abjure his religion. An intimate friend of Sylvian Maréchal, Peyrard furnished him with notes for his *Dictionnaire des Athées*. He wrote a work on *Nature and its Laws*, 1793-4, and proposed the piercing of the Isthmus of Suez. He translated the works of Euclid and Archimedes. Died at Paris 3 Oct. 1822.

Peyrat (Alphonse), French writer, b. Toulouse, 21 June, 1812. He wrote in the *National* and *la Presse*, and combated against the Second Empire. In '65 he founded *l'Avenir National*, which was several times condemned. In Feb. '71, he was elected deputy of the Seine, and proposed the proclamation of the Republic. In '76 he was chosen senator.

He wrote a History of the Dogma of the Immaculate Conception, '55; *History and Religion*, '58; *Historical and Religious Studies*, '58; and an able and scholarly *Elementary and Critical History of Jesus*, '64.

Peyrere (Isaac de la), French writer, b. Bordeaux, 1594, and brought up as a Protestant. He entered into the service of the house of Condé, and became intimate with La Mothe de Vayer and Gassendi. His work entitled *Præadamitæ*, 1653, in which he maintained that men lived before Adam, made a great sensation, and was burnt by the hangman at Paris. The bishop of Namur censured it, and la Peyrère was arrested at Brussels, 1656, by order of the Archbishop of Malines, but escaped by favor of the Prince of Condé on condition of retracting his book at Rome. The following epitaph was nevertheless made on him :

> La Peyrere ici gît, ce bon Israelite,
> Huguenot, Catholique, enfin Pre-adamite :
> Quatre religions lui plurent à la fois:
> Et son indifférence était si peu commune
> Qu'après 80 ans qu'il eut à faire un choix
> Le bon homme partit, et n'en choisit pas une.

Died near Paris, 30 Jan. 1676.

Pfeiff (Johan Gustaf Viktor), Swedish baron, b. Upland, 1829. Editor of the free religious periodical, *The Truthseeker*, since 1882. He has also translated into Swedish some of the writings of Herbert Spencer.

Pharmacopulo (A.P.) Greek translator of Büchner's *Force and Matter*, and corresponding member of the International Federation of Freethinkers.

Phillips (Sir Richard), industrious English writer, b. London, 1767. He was hosier, bookseller, printer, publisher, republican, Sheriff of London (1807-8), and Knight. He compiled many schoolbooks, chiefly under pseudonyms, of which the most popular were the Rev. J. Goldsmith and Rev. D. Blair. His own opinions are seen most in his *Million of Facts*. Died at Brighton 2 April, 1840.

Phillippo (William Skinner), farmer, of Wood Norton, near Thetford, Norfolk. A deist who wrote an *Essay on Political and Religious Meditations*, 1868.

Pi-y Margall (Francisco), Spanish philosopher and Republican statesman, b. Barcelona, 1820. The first book he learnt to read was the *Ruins* of Volney. Studied law and became an advocate. He has written many political works, and translated Proudhon, for whom he has much admiration, into Spanish. He has also introduced the writings and philosophy of Comte into his own country. He was associated with Castelar and Figueras in the attempt to establish a Spanish Republic, being Minister of the Interior, and afterwards President in 1873.

Pichard (Prosper). French Positivist, author of *Doctrine of Reality*, " a catechism for the use of people who do not pay themselves with words," to which Littré wrote a preface, 1873.

Pierson (Allard). Dutch rationalist critic, b. Amsterdam 8 April, 1831. Educated in theology, he was minister to the Evangelical congregation at Leuven, afterwards at Rotterdam and finally professor at Heidelberg. He resigned his connection with the Church in '64. He has written many works of theological and literary value of which we mention his *Poems* '82, *New Studies on Calvin*, '83, and *Verisimilia*, written in conjunction with S. A. Naber, '86.

Pigault-Lebrun (Guillaume Charles Antoine), witty French author, b. Calais, 8 April, 1753. He studied under the Oratorians of Boulogne. He wrote numerous comedies and romances, and *Le Citateur*, 1803, a collection of objections to Christianity, borrowed in part from Voltaire, whose spirit he largely shared. In 1811 Napoleon threatened the priests he would issue this work wholesale. It was suppressed under the Restoration, but has been frequently reprinted. Pigault-Lebrun. He became secretary to King Jerome Napoleon, and died at La Celle-Saint-Cloud, 24 July, 1835.

Pike (J. W.) American lecturer, b. Concord (Ohio), 27 June, 1826, wrote *My Religious Experience* and *What I found in the Bible*, 1867.

Pillsbury (Parker), American reformer, b. Hamilton, Mass., 22 Sep. 1809. Was employed in farm work till '35, when he entered Gilmerton theological seminary. He graduated in '38 studied a year at Andover, was congregational minister for one year, and then, perceiving the churches were the bulwark of slavery, abandoned the ministry. He became an abolitionist lecturer, edited the *Herald of Freedom, National Anti-Slavery Standard*, and the *Revolution*. He also preached for free religious societies, wrote *Pious Frauds*, and contributed to the *Boston Investigator* and *Freethinkers' Magazine*. His principal work is *Acts of the Anti-Slavery Apostles*, 1883.

Piron (Alexis), French comic poet, b. Dijon, 9 July, 1689. His pieces were full of wit and gaiety, and many anecdotes are told of his profanity. Among his sallies was his reply to a reproof for being drunk on Good Friday, that failing must be excused on a day when even deity succumbed. Being blind in his old age he affected piety. Worried by his confessor about a Bible in the margin of which he had written parodies and epigrams us the best commentary, he threw the whole book in the fire. Asked on his death-bed if he believed in God he answered "Parbleu, I believe even in the Virgin." Died at Paris, 21 Jan. 1773.

Pisarev (Dmitri Ivanovich) Russian critic, journalist, and materialist, b. 1840. He first became known by his criticism on the Scholastics of the nineteenth century. Died Baden, near Riga, July 1868. His works are published in ten vols. Petersburg, 1870.

Pitt (William). Earl of Chatham, an illustrious English statesman and orator, b. Boconnoc, Cornwall, 15 Nov. 1808. The services to his country of "the Great Commoner," as he was called, are well known, but it is not so generally recognised that his *Letter on Superstition*, first printed in the *London Journal* in 1733, entitles him to be ranked with the Deists. He says that "the more superstitious people are, always the more vicious; and the more they *believe*, the less they practice." Atheism furnishes no man with arguments to be vicious ; but superstition, or what the world made by religion, is the greatest possible encouragement to vice, by setting up something as religion, which shall atone and commute for the want of virtue. This remarkable letter ends with the words "Remember that the only true divinity is humanity."

Place (Francis), English Radical reformer and tailor ; b. 1770 at Charing Cross. He early became a member of the London,

Corresponding Society. He wrote to Carlile's *Republican* and *Lion*. A friend of T. Hardy, H. Tooke, James Mill, Bentham, Roebuck, Hetherington, and Hibbert (who puts him in his list of English Freethinkers). He was connected with all the advanced movements of his time and has left many manuscripts illustrating the politics of that period, which are now in the British Museum. He always professed to be an Atheist —see *Reasoner*, 26 March, '51. Died at Kensington, 1 Jan. 1854.

Platt (James), F.S.S., a woolen merchant and Deistic author of popular works on *Business*, '75; *Morality*, '78; *Progress*, '80; *Life*, '81; *God and Mammon*, etc.

Pliny (Caius Plinius Secundus), the elder, Roman naturalist, b. Verona, A.D. 22. He distinguished himself in the army, was admitted into the college of Augurs, appointed procurator in Spain, and honored with the esteem of Vespasian and Titus. He wrote the history of his own time in 31 books, now lost, and a *National History* in 37 books, one of the most precious monuments of antiquity, in which his Epicurean Atheism appears. Being with the fleet at Misenum, 24 Aug. A.D. 79, he observed the erruption of Mount Vesuvius, and landing to assist the inhabitants was himself suffocated by the noxious vapors.

Plumacher (Olga), German pessimist, follower of Hartmann, and authoress of a work on *Pessimism in the Past and Future*, Heidelberg, 1884. She has also defended her views in *Mind*.

Plumer (William) American senator, b. Newburyport, Mass. 25 June, 1759. In 1780 he became a Baptist preacher, but resigned on account of scepticism. He remained a deist. He served in the Legislature eight terms, during two of which he was Speaker. He was governor of New Hampshire, 1812-18, wrote to the press over the signature "Cincinnatus," and published an *Address to the Clergy*, '11. He lived till 22 June, 1850.

Plutarch. Greek philosopher and historian, b. Cheronæa in Bœtia, about A.D 50. He visited Delphi and Rome, where he lived in the reign of Trajan. His *Parallel Lives* of forty-six Greeks and Romans have made him immortal. He wrote numerous other anecdotal and ethical works, including a treatise on Superstition. He condemned the vulgar notions of Deity, and remarked, in connection with the deeds popularly ascribed to the gods, that he would rather men said there was no Plutarch than traduce his character. In other words, superstition is more impious than Atheism. Died about A.D. 120.

Poe (Edgar Allan), American poet, grandson of General Poe, who figured in the war of independence, b. Boston, 19 Jan. 1809. His mother was an actress. Early left an orphan. After publishing *Tamerlane and other Poems*, '27, he enlisted in the United States Army, but was cashiered in '31. He then took to literary employment in Baltimore and wrote many stories, collected as the *Tales of Mystery, Imagination, and Humor*. In '45 appeared *The Raven and other Poems*, which proved him the most musical and dextrous of American poets. In '48 he published *Eureka, a Prose Poem*, which, though comparatively little known, he esteemed his greatest work. It indicates pantheistic views of the universe. His personal appearance was striking and one of his portraits is not unlike that of James Thomson. Died in Baltimore, 7 Oct. 1849.

Poey (Andrés), Cuban meteorologist and Positivist of French and Spanish descent, b. Havana, 1826. Wrote in the *Modern Thinker*, and is author of many scientific memoirs and a popular exposition of Positivism (Paris, 1876), in which he has a chapter on Darwinism and Comtism.

Pompery (Edouard), French publicist, b. Courcelles, 1812. A follower of Fourier, he has written on Blanquism and opportunism, '79, and a Life of Voltaire, '80.

Pomponazzi (Pietro) [Lat. Pomponatius], Italian philosopher, b. Mantua, of noble family, 16 Sept. 1462. He studied at Padua, where he graduated 1487 as laureate of medicine. Next year he was appointed professor of philosophy at Padua, teaching in concurrence with Achillini. He afterwards taught the doctrines of Aristotle at Ferrara and Bologna. His treatise *De Immortalitate Animæ*, 1516, gave great offence by denying the philosophical foundation of the doctrine of the immortality of the soul. The work was burnt by the hangman at Venice, and it is said Cardinal Bembo's intercession with Pope Leo X. only saved Pomponazzi from ecclesiastical procedure. Among his works is a treatise on Fate, Free Will, etc. Pomponazzi was a diminutive man, and was nicknamed "Peretto." He held that doubt was necessary for the development of knowledge, and left an unsullied reputation for upright conduct and sweet temper. Died at Bologna, 18 May, 1525, and was buried at Mantua, where a monument was erected to his memory.

Ponnat (de), *Baron*, French writer, b. about 1810. Educated by Jesuits, he became a thorough Freethinker and democrat and a friend of A. S. Morin, with whom he collaborated on the *Rationaliste* of Geneva. He wrote many notable articles in *La Libre Pensée*, *Le Critique*, and *Le Candide*, for writing in which last he was sentenced to one year's imprisonment. He published, under the anagram of De Pontan, *The Cross or Death*, a discourse to the bishops who assisted at the Ecumenical Council at Rome (Brussels, '62). His principal work is a history of the variations and contradictions of the Roman Church (Paris, '82). Died in 1884.

Porphyry (Πορφύριος), Greek philosoper of the New Platonic school, b. Sinia, 233 A.D. His original name was MALCHUS or MELECH—a "King." He was a pupil of Longinus and perhaps of Origen. Some have supposed that he was of Jewish faith, and first embraced and then afterwards rejected Christianity. It is certain he was a man of learning and intelligence; the friend as well as the disciple of Plotinus. He wrote (in Greek) a famous work in fifteen books against the Christians, some fragments of which alone remain in the writings of his opponents. It is certain he showed acquaintance with the Jewish and Christian writings, exposed their contradictions, pointed out the dispute between Peter and Paul, and referred Daniel to the time of Antiochus Epiphanes. He wrote many other works, among which are lives of Plotinus and Pythagorus. Died at Rome about 305.

Porzio (Simone), a disciple of Pomponazzi, to whom, when lecturing at Pisa, the students cried "What of the soul?" He frankly professed his belief that the human soul differed in no essential point from the soul of a lion or plant, and that those who thought otherwise were prompted by pity for our mean estate. These assertions are in his treatise *De Mente Humanâ*.

"**Posos** (Juan de)," an undiscovered author using this pen-name, expressed atheistic opinions in a book of imaginary travels, published in Dutch at Amsterdam in 1708, and translated into German at Leipsic, 1721.

Post (Amy), American reformer. b. 1803. From '28 she was a leading advocate of slavery abolition, temperance, woman's suffrage and religious reform. Died Rochester, New York, 29 Jan. 1889.

Potter (Agathon Louis de.) See De Potter (A. L.)

Potter (Louis Antoine Joseph de). See De Potter (L. A. J.)

Potvin (Charles), Belgian writer b. Mons. 2 Dec. 1818, is member of the Royal Academy of Letters, and professor of the history of literature at Brussels. He wrote anonymously *Poesie et Amour* '58, and *Rome and the Family*. Under the name of "Dom Jacobus" he has written an able work in two volumes on *The Church and Morality*, and also *Tablets of a Freethinker*. He was president of " La Libre Pensée " of Brussels from '78 to '83, is director of the Revue de Belgique and has collaborated on the *National* and other papers.

Pouchet (Felix Archimède), French naturalist, b. Rouen 26 Aug. 1800. Studied medicine under Dr. Flaubert, father of the author of *Mme. Bovary*, and became doctor in '27. He was made professor of natural history at the Museum of Rouen, and by his experiments enriched science with many discoveries. He defended spontaneous generation and wrote many monographs and books of which the principal is entitled *The Universe*, '65. Died at Rouen, 6 Dec. 1872.

Pouchet (Henri Charles George), French naturalist, son of the preceeding, b. Rouen, 1833, made M.D. in '64, and in '79 professor of comparative anatomy in the museum of Natural History at Paris. In '80 he was decorated with the Legion of Honor. He has written on *The Plurality of the Human Race*, '58, and collaborated on the *Siècle*, and the *Revue des Deux Mondes* and to *la Philosophie Positive*.

Pouchkine (A.), see Pushkin.

Pougens (Marie Charles Joseph de), French author, a natural son of the Prince de Conti, b. Paris, 15 Aug. 1755. About the age of 24 he was blinded by small pox. He became an intimate friend of the philosophers, and, sharing their views, embraced the revolution with ardor, though it ruined his fortunes. He wrote *Philosophical Researches*, 1786, edited the posthumous works of D'Alembert, 1799, and worked at a dictionary of the French language. His *Jocko*, a tale of a monkey, exhibits his keen sympathy with animal intelligence, and in his *Philosophical Letters*, 1826, he gives anecdotes of Voltaire, Rousseau, D'Alembert, Pechmeja, Franklin, etc. Died at Vauxbuin, near Soissons, 19 Dec. 1833.

Poulin (Paul), Belgian follower of Baron Colins and author of *What is God? What is Man?* a scientific solution of the religious problem (Brussels, 1865), and re-issued as *God According to Science*, '75, in which he maintains that man and God exclude each other, and that the only divinity is moral harmony.

Poultier D'Elmolte (François Martin), b. Montreuil-sur-Mer, 31 Oct. 1753. Became a Benedictine monk, but cast aside his frock at the Revolution, married, and became chief of a battalion of volunteers. Elected to the Convention he voted for the death of the King. He conducted the journal, *L'Ami des lois*, and became one of the Council of Ancients. Exiled in 1816, he died at Tournay in Belgium, 16 Feb. 1827. He wrote *Morceau Philosophiques* in the *Journal Encyclopédique*; *Victoire*, or the Confessions of a Benedictine; *Discours Décadaires*, for the use of Theophilantropists, and *Conjectures on the Nature and Origin of Things*, Tournay, 1821.

Powell (B. F.), compiler of the *Bible of Reason*, or Scriptures of Ancient Moralists; published by Hetherington in 1837.

Prades (Jean Martin de), French theologian b. Castel-Sarrasin, about 1720. Brought up for the church, he nevertheless became intimate with Diderot and contributed the article CERTITUDE to the Encyclopédie. On the 18th Nov. 1751 he presented to the Sorbonne a thesis for the doctorate, remarkable as the first open attack on Christianity by a French theologian. He maintained many propositions on the soul, the origin of society, the laws of Moses, miracles, etc., contrary to the dogmas of the Church, and compared the cures recorded in the Gospels to those attributed to Esculapius. The thesis made a great scandal. His opinions were condemned by Pope

Benedict XIV., and he fled to Holland for safety. Recommended to Frederick the Great by d'Alembert he was received with favor at Berlin, and became reader to that monarch, who wrote a very anti-Christian preface to de Prades' work on ecclesiastical history, published as *Abrége de l'Histoire ecclesiastique de Fleury*, Berne (Berlin) 1766. He retired to a benefice at Glogau (Silesia), given him by Frederick, and died there in 1782.

Prater (Horatio), a gentleman of some fortune who devoted himself to the propagation of Freethought ideas. Born early in the century, he wrote on the *Physiology of the Blood*, 1832. He published *Letters to the American People*, and *Literary Essays*, '56. Died 20 July, 1835. He left the bulk of his money to benevolent objects, and ordered a deep wound to be made in his arm to insure that he was dead.

¶**Preda** (Pietro), Italian writer of Milan, author of a work on *Revelation and Reason*, published at Geneva, 1865, under the pseudonym of " Padre Pietro."

Premontval (Andre Pierre Le Guay de), French writer, b. Charenton, 16 Feb. 1716. At nineteen years of age, while in the college of Plessis Sorbonne, he composed a work against the dogma of the Eucharist. He studied mathematics and became member of the Academy of Sciences at Berlin. He wrote *Le Diogene de D'Alembert*, or Freethoughts on Man, 1754, *Panangiana Panurgica*, or the false Evangelist, and *Vues Philosophiques*, Amst., 2 vols., 1757. He also wrote *De la Théologie de L'Etre*, in which he denies many of the ordinary proofs of the existence of a God. Died Berlin, 1767.

Priestley (Joseph), LL.D., English philosopher, b. Fieldhead, near Leeds, 18 March, 1733. Brought up as a Calvinist, he found his way to broad Unitarianism. Famous as a pneumatic chemist, he defended the doctrine of philosophical necessity, and in a dissertation annexed to his edition of Hartley expressed doubts of the immateriality of the sentient principal in man. This doctrine he forcibly supported in his *Disquisitions on Matter and Spirit*, 1777. Through the obloquy these works produced, he lost his position as librarian to Lord Shelburne. He then removed to Birmingham, and became minister of an independent Unitarian congregation, and occupied himself on his

History of the Corruptions of Christianity and *History of the Early Opinions Concerning Jesus Christ*, which involved him in controversy with Bishop Horsley and others. In consequence of his sympathy with the French Revolution, his house was burnt and sacked in a riot, 14 July, 1791. After this he removed to Hackney, and was finally goaded to seek an asylum in the United States, which he reached in 1794. Even in America he endured some uneasiness on account of his opinions until Jefferson became president. Died 6 Feb. 1804.

Pringle (Allen), Canadian Freethinker, author of *Ingersoll in Canada*, 1880.

Proctor (Richard Anthony), English astronomer, b. Chelsea, 23 March, 1837. Educated at King's College, London, and at St. John's, Cambridge, where he became B.A. in '60. In '66 he became Fellow of the Royal Astronomical Society, of which he afterwards became hon. sec. He maintained in '69 the since-established theory of the solar corona. He wrote, lectured, and edited, far and wide, and left nearly fifty volumes, chiefly popularising science. Attracted by Newman, he was for a while a Catholic, but thought out the question of Catholicism and science, and in a letter to the *New York Tribune*, Nov. '75, formally renounced that religion as irreconcilable with scientific facts. His remarks on the so-called Star of Bethlehem in *The Universe of Suns, and other Science Gleanings,* and his Sunday lectures, indicated his heresy. In '81 he started *Knowledge*, in which appeared many valuable papers, notably one (Jan. '87), "The Beginning of Christianity." He entirely rejected the miraculous elements of the gospels, which he considered largely a *rechauffé* of solar myths. In other articles in the *Freethinkers' Magazine* and the *Open Court* he pointed out the coincidence between the Christian stories and solar myths, and also with stories found in Josephus. The very last article he published before his untimely death was a vindication of Colonel Ingersoll in his controversy with Gladstone in the *North American Review*. In '84 he settled at St. Josephs, Mobille, where he contracted yellow fever and died at New York, 12 Sep. 1888.

Proudhon (Pierre Joseph), French anarchist and political thinker, b. Besançon, 15 Jan. 1809. Self-educated he became a printer, and won a prize of 1,500 francs for the person "best fitted for a literary or scientific career." In '40 appears his memoir, What is Property? in which he made the celebrated answer "*C'est le vol.*" In '43 the *Creation of Order in Humanity* appeared, treating of religion, philosophy and logic. In '46 he published his *System of Economical Contradictions*, in which appeared his famous aphorism, "*Dieu, c'est le mal.*" In '48 he introduced his scheme of the organisation of credit in a Bank of the People, which failed, though Proudhon saw that no one lost anything. He attacked Louis Bonaparte when President, and was sentenced to three years' imprisonment and a fine of 10,000 francs. On 2 Jan. '50 he married by private contract while in prison. For his work on *Justice in the Revolution and in the Church* he was condemned to three years' imprisonment and 4,000 francs fine in '58. He took refuge in Belgium and returned in '63. Died at Passy, 19 Jan. 1865. Among his posthumous works was *The Gospels Annotated*, '66. Proudhon was a bold and profound thinker of noble aspirations, but he lacked the sense of art and practicability. His complete works have been published in 26 vols.

Protagoras, Greek philosopher, b. Abdera, about 480 B.C. Is said to have been a disciple of Democritus, and to have been a porter before he studied philosophy. He was the first to call himself a sophist. He wrote in a book on the gods, "Respecting the gods, I am unable to know whether they exist or do not exist." For this he was impeached and banished, and his book burnt. He went to Epirus and the Greek Islands, and died about 411. He believed all things were in flux, and summed up his conclusions in the proposition that "man is the measure of all things, both of that which exists and that which does not exist." Grote, who defends the Sophists, says his philosophy "had the merit of bringing into forcible relief the essentially relative nature of cognition."

Prudhomme (Sully). See Sully Prudhomme.

Pueckler Muskau (Hermann Ludwig Heinrich), Prince, a German writer, b. Muskau, 30 Oct. 1785. He travelled widely and wrote his observations in a work entitled *Letters of a Defunct*, 1830; this was followed by *Tutti Frutti*, '32; *Semilasso in Africa*, '36, and other works. Died 4 Feb. 1871.

Pushkin (Aleksandr Sergyeevich), eminent Russian poet, often called the Russian Byron, b. Pskow, 26 May, 1799. From youth he was remarkable for his turbulent spirit, and his first work, which circulated only in manuscript, was founded on Parny's *Guerre des Dieux*, and entitled the Gabrielade, the archangel being the hero. He was exiled by the Emperor, but, inspired largely by reading Voltaire and Byron, put forward numerous poems and romances, of which the most popular is Eugene Onéguine, an imitation of Don Juan. He also wrote some histories and founded the *Sovremennik* (Contemporary), 1836. In Jan. 1837 he was mortally wounded in a duel.

Putnam (Samuel P.), American writer and lecturer, brought up as a minister. He left that profession for Freethought, and became secretary to the American Secular Union, of which he was elected president in Oct. 1887. In '88 he started *Freethought* at San Francisco in company with G. Macdonald. Has written poems, *Prometheus, Ingersoll and Jesus, Adami and Heva*; romances entitled *Golden Throne, Waifs and Wanderings*, and *Gottlieb*, and pamphlets on the *Problem of the Universe, The New God*, and *The Glory of Infidelity*.

Putsage (Jules), Belgian follower of Baron Colins, founder of the Colins Philosophical Society at Mons; has written on *Determinism and Rational Science*, Brussels 1885, besides many essays in *La Philosophie de L'Avenir* of Paris and *La Societe Nouvelle* of Brussels.

Pyat (Felix) French socialist, writer and orator, b. Vierzon, 4 Oct. 1810. His father was religious and sent him to a Jesuit college at Bourges, but he here secretly read the writings of Beranger and Courier. He studied law, but abandoned it for literature, writing in many papers. He also wrote popular dramas, as *The Rag-picker of Paris*, '47. After '52 he lived in England, where he wrote an apology for the attempt of Orsini, published by Truelove, '58. In '71 he founded the journal *le Combat*. Elected to the National Assembly he protested against the treaty of peace, was named member of the Commune and condemned to death in '73. He returned to France after the armistice, and has sat as deputy for Marseilles. Died, Saint Gerainte near Nice, 3 Aug. 1889.

Pyrrho (Πυρρον). Greek philosopher, a native of Elis, in

Peloponesus, founder of a sceptical school about the time of Epicurus; is said to have been attracted to philosophy by the books of Democritus. He attached himself to Anaxarchus, and joined her in the expedition of Alexander the Great, and became acquainted with the philosophy of the Magi and the Indian Gymnosophists. He taught the wisdom of doubt, the uncertainty of all things, and the rejection of speculation. His disciples extolled his equanimity and independence of externals. It is related that he kept house with his sister, and shared with her in all domestic duties. He reached the age of ninety years, and after his death the Athenians honored him with a statue. He left no writings, but the tenets of his school, which were much misrepresented, may be gathered from Sextus and Empiricus.

Quental. See Anthero de Quental.

"Quepat (Nérée.") See Paquet (René.)

Quesnay (François), French economist, b. Mérey, 4 June 1694. Self educated he became a physician, but is chiefly noted for his *Tableau Economique*, 1708, and his doctrine of *Laissez Faire*. He derived moral and social rules from physical laws. Died Versailles, 16 Dec. 1774.

Quinet (Edgar), French writer, b. Bourgen Bresse, 17 Feb. 1803. He attracted the notice of Cousin by a translation of Herder's *The Philosophy of History*. With his friend Michelet he made many attacks on Catholicism, the *Jesuits* being their joint work. He fought in the Revolution of '48, and opposed the Second Empire. His work on *The Genius of Religion*, '42, is profound, though mystical, and his historical work on *The Revolution*, '65 is a masterpiece. Died at Versailles, 27 March, 1875.

Quintin (Jean), Heretic of Picardy, and alleged founder of the Libertines. He is said to have preached in Holland and Brabant in 1525, that religion was a human invention. Quintin was arrested and burnt at Tournay in 1530.

Quris (Charles), French advocate of Angers, who has published some works on law and *La Défense Catholique et la Critique*, Paris, 1864.

Rabelais (François), famous and witty French satirist and philosopher, b. Chinon, Touraine, 7 Jan. 1495. At an early age he joined the order of Franciscans, but finding monastic life incompatible with his genial temper, quitted the convent without the leave of his superior. He studied medicine at Montpelier about 1530, after which he practised at Lyons. His great humorous work, published anonymously in 1535, was denounced as heretical by the clergy for its satires, not only on their order but their creed. The author was protected by Francis I. and was appointed curé of Meudon. Died at Paris, 9 April, 1553. His writings show surprising fertility of mind, and Coleridge says, " Beyond a doubt he was among the deepest as well as boldest thinkers of his age."

Radenhausen (Christian), German philosopher, b. Friedrichstadt, 3 Dec. 1813. At first a merchant and then a lithographer, he resided at Hamburg, where he published *Isis, Mankind and the World* (4 vols.), '70-72 ; *Osiris*, '74 ; *The New Faith*, '77 ; *Christianity is Heathenism*, '81 ; *The True Bible and the False*, '87 ; *Esther*, '87.

Radicati (Alberto di), *Count.* See Passerano.

Ragon (Jean Marie de), French Freemason, b. Bray-sur-Seine, 1781. By profession a civil engineer at Nancy, afterwards Chief of Bureau to the Minister of the Interior. Author of many works on Freemasonry, and *The Mass and its Mysteries Compared with the Ancient Mysteries*, 1844. Died at Paris, 1862.

Ram (Joachim Gerhard), Holstein philosopher of the seventeenth century, who was accused of Atheism.

Ramaer (Anton Gerard Willem), Dutch writer b. Jever, East Friesland, 2 Aug. 1812. From '29 he served as officer in the Dutch army. He afterwards became a tax collector, and in '60 was pensioned. He wrote on Schopenhauer and other able works, and also contributed largely to *De Dageraad*, often under the pseudonym of " Laghmé." He had a noble mind and sacrificed much for his friends and the good cause. Died 16 Feb. 1867.

Ramee (Louise de la), English novelist, b., of French extraction, Bury St. Edmunds, 1840. Under the name of " Ouida," a little sister's mispronunciation of Louisa, she has published many popular novels, exhibiting her free and pessimistic opinions. We mention *Tricotin, Folle Farine, Signa, Moths* and

A Village Commune. She has lived much in Italy, where the scenes of several novels are placed.

Ramee (Pierre de la) called Ramus, French humanist, b. Cuth (Vermandois) 1515. He attacked the doctrines of Aristotle, was accused of impiety, and his work suppressed 1543. He lost his life in the massacre of St. Bartholomew, 26 Aug. 1572.

Ramsey (William James), b. London, 8 June, 1844. Becoming a Freethinker early in life, he for some time sold literature at the Hall of Science and became manager of the Freethought Publishing Co. Starting in business for himself he published the *Freethinker,* for which in '82 he was prosecuted with Mr. Foote and Mr. Kemp. Tried in March '83, after a good defence, he was sentenced to nine months' imprisonment, and on Mr. Foote's release acted as printer of the paper.

Ranc (Arthur), French writer and deputy, b. Poitiers, 10 Dec. 1831, and was brought up a Freethinker and Republican by his parents. He took the prize for philosophy at the College of Poitiers, and studied law at Paris. He conspired with C. Delescluze against the Second Empire and was imprisoned, but escaped to Geneva. He collaborated on *La Marseillaise,* was elected on the Municipal Council of Paris in '71, and Deputy, '73. Has written *Under the Empire* and many other political works.

Randello (Cosimo), Italia author of *The Simple Story of a Great Fraud,* being a criticism of the origin of Christianity, directed against Pauline theology, published at Milan, 1882.

Rapisardi (Mario), Italian poet, b. Catania, Sicily, 1843. Has translated Lucretius, '80, and published poems on *Lucifer,* and *The Last Prayer of Pius IX.,* '71, etc.

Raspail (François Vincent), French chemist and politician b. Carpentras 24 Jan. 1794, was brought up by ecclesiastics and intended for the Church. He became, while quite young, professor of philosophy at the theological seminary of Avignon but an examination of theological dogmas led to their rejection. He went to Paris, and from 1815—24 gave lessons, and afterwards became a scientific lecturer. He took part in the Revolution of '30. Louis Philippe offered him the Legion of Honor but he refused. Taking part in all the revolutionary outbreaks he was frequently imprisoned. Elected to the chamber in '69 and sat on the extreme left. Died at Arcueil 6 Jan. 1878.

Rau (Herbert), German rationalist b. Frankfort 11 Feb. 1813. He studied theology and became preacher to free congregations in Stuttgart and Mannheim. He wrote *Gospel of Nature, A Catechism of the Religion of the Future,* and other works. Died Frankfort 26 Sept. 1876.

Rawson (Albert Leighton) LL.D. American traveller and author, b. Chester, Vermont 15 Oct. 1829. After studying law, theology, and art, he made four visits to the East, and made in '51–2 a pilgrimage from Cairo to Mecca, disguised as a Mohammedan student of medicine. He has published many maps and typographical and philological works, and illustrated Beecher's *Life of Jesus.* Has also written on the *Antiquities of the Orient,* New York, '70, and Chorography of Palestine, London, '80. Has written in the *Freethinkers' Magazine,* maintaining that the Bible account of the twelve tribes of Israel is non-historical.

Raynal (Guillaume Thomas François) *l'abbe,* French historian and philosopher, b. Saint Geniez, 12 April, 1713. He was brought up as a priest but renounced that profession soon after his removal to Paris, 1747, where he became intimate with Helvetius, Holbach, etc. With the assistance of these, and Diderot, Pechmeja, etc., he compiled a philosophical History of European establishments in the two Indies (4 vols. 1770 and 1780), a work full of reflections on the religious and political institutions of France. It made a great outcry, was censured by the Sorbonne, and was burnt by order of Parliament 29 May, 1781. Raynal escaped and passed about six years in exile. Died near Paris, 6 March, 1796.

Reade (William Winwood), English traveller and writer, nephew of Charles Reade the novelist, b. Murrayfield, near Crieff, Scotland, 26 Dec. 1824. He studied at Oxford, then travelled much in the heart of Africa, and wrote *Savage Africa,* 63, *The African Sketch Book,* and in '73, *The Story of the Ashantee Campaign;* which he accompanied as *Times* correspondent. In the *Martrydom of Man* ('72), he rejects the doctrine of a personal creator. It went through several editions and is still worth reading. He also wrote *Liberty Hall,* a novel, '60; *The*

Veil of Isis, '61, and *See Saw*, a novel, '65.   He wrote his last work *The Outcast*, a Freethought novel, with the hand of death upon him.   Died 24 April, 1875.

Reber (George), American author of *The Christ of Paul*, or the Enigmas of Christianity (New York, 1876), a work in which he exposes the frauds and follies of the early fathers.

Reclus (Jean Jacques Elisée), French geographer and socialist, the son of a Protestant minister, b. Sainte-Foy-la-Grande (Gironde), 15 March, 1830, and educated by the Moravian brethren, and afterwards at Berlin.   He early distinguished himself by his love for liberty, and left France after the *coup d'état* of 2 Dec. '51, and travelled till '57 in England, Ireland, and the North and South America, devoting himself to studying the social and political as well as physical condition of the countries he visited, the results being published in the *Tour du monde*, and *Revue des Deux Mondes*, in which he upheld the cause of the North during the American war.   In '71 he supported the Commune and was taken prisoner and sentenced to transportation for life.   Many eminent men in England and America interceded and his sentence was commuted to banishment.   At the amnesty of March '79, he returned to Paris, and has devoted himself to the publication of a standard *Universal Geography* in 13 vols.   In '82 he gave two of his daughters in marriage without either religious or civil ceremony.   He has written a preface to Bakounin's *God and the State*, and many other works.

Reddalls (George Holland), English Secularist, b. Birmingham, Nov. 1846.   He became a compositor on the Birmingham *Daily Post*, but wishing to conduct a Freethought paper started in business for himself, and issued the *Secular Chronicle*, '73, which was contributed to by Francis Neale, H. V. Mayer, G. Standring, etc.   He died 13 Oct. 1875.

Reghillini de Schio (M.), Professor of Chemistry and Mathematics, b. of Venetian parents at Schio in 1760.   He wrote in French an able exposition of *Masonry*, 1833, which he traced to Egypt; and an *Examination of Mosaism and Christianity*, '34.   He was mixed in the troubles of Venice in '48, and fled to Belgium, dying in poverty at Brussels Aug. 1853.

Regnard (Albert Adrien), French doctor and publicist, b. Lachante (Nièvre), 20 March, 1836, author of *Essais d'Histoire et de Critique Scientifique* (Paris, '65)—a work for which he could find no publisher, and had to issue himself—in which he proclaimed scientific materialism. Losing his situation, he started, with Naquet and Clemenceau, the *Revue Encyclopédique*, which being suppressed on its first number, he started *La Libre Pensée* with Asseline, Condereau, etc. His articles in this journal drew on him and Eudes a condemnation of four months' imprisonment. He wrote *New Researches on Cerebral Congestion*, '68, and was one of the French delegates to the anti-Council of Naples, '69. Has published *Atheism*, studies of political science, dated Londres, '78; a *History of England since* 1815; and has translated Büchner's *Force and Matter*, '84. He was delegate to the Freethinkers' International Congress at Antwerp, '85.

Regnard (Jean François), French comic poet, b. Paris, 8 Feb. 1655. He went to Italy about 1676, and on returning home was captured by an Algerian corsair and sold as a slave. Being caught in an intrigue with one of the women, he was required to turn Muhammadan. The French consul paid his ransom and he returned to France about 1681. He wrote a number of successful comedies and poems, and was made a treasurer of France. He died as an Epicurean, 4 Sept. 1709.

Regnier (Mathurin), French satirical poet, b. Chartres, 21 Dec. 1573. Brought up for the Church, he showed little inclination for its austerities, and was in fact a complete Pagan, though he obtained a canonry in the cathedral of his native place. Died at Rouen, 22 Oct. 1613.

Reich (Eduard) Dr., German physician and anthropologist of Sclav descent on his father's side, b. Olmütz, 6 March 1839. He studied at Jena and has travelled much, and published over thirty volumes besides editing the *Athenæum* of Jena '75, and *Universities* of Grossenbain, '83. Of his works we mention *Man and the Soul*, '72; *The Church of Humanity*, 74; *Life of Man as an Individual*, '81; *History of the Soul*, '84; *The Emancipation of Women*, 84.

Reil (Johann Christian), German physician, b. Rauden, East Friesland, 20 Feb. 1758. Intended for the Church, he took instead to medicine; after practising some years in his native town he went in 1787 to Halle, and in 1810 he was made Professor of Medicine at Berlin University. He wrote many medical works, and much advanced medical science, displacing the old ideas in a way which brought on him the accusation of pantheism. Attending a case of typhus fever at Halle he was attacked by the malady, and succumbed 22 Nov. 1813.

Reimarus (Hermann Samuel), German philologist, b. Hamburg, 22 Dec. 1694. He was a son-in-law of J. A. Fabricus. Studied at Jena and Wittenberg; travelled in Holland and England; and was appointed rector of the gymnasium in Weimar, 1723, and in Hamburg, 1729. He was one of the most radical among German rationalists. He published a work on *The Principle Truths of Natural Religion*, 1754, and left behind the *Wolfenbüttel Fragments*, published by Lessing in 1777. Died at Hamburg, 1 March, 1768. Strauss has written an account of his services, 1862.

Reitzel (Robert), German American revolutionary, b. Baden, 1849. Named after Blum, studied theology, went to America, walked from New York to Baltimore, and was minister to an independent Protestant church. Studied biology and resigned as a minister, and became speaker of a Freethought congregation at Washington for seven years. Is now editor of *Der Arme Teufel* of Detroit, and says he " shall be a poor man and a Revolutionaire all my life."

Remsburg (John E.), American lecturer and writer, b. 1848. Has written a series of pamphlets entitled *The Image Breaker*, *False Claims of the Christian Church*, '83, *Sabbath Breaking*, *Thomas Paine*, and a vigorous onslaught on *Bible Morals*, instancing twenty crimes and vices sanctioned by scripture, '85.

Renan (Joseph Ernest), learned French writer, b. Tréguier (Brittany) 27 Feb. 1823. Was intended for the Church and went to Paris to study. He became noted for his linguistic attainment, but his studies and independence of thought did not accord with his intended profession. My faith, he says was destroyed not by metaphysics nor philosophy but by historical criticism. In '45 he gave up all thoughts of an ecclesiastic career and became a teacher. In '48 he gained the Volney prize, for a memoir on the Semitic Languages, afterwards amplified into a work on that subject. In '52 he published his work on Averroës and Averroïsm. In '56 was elected member of the Academy of Inscriptions, and in '60 sent on a mission to Syria; having in the meantime published a translation of *Job* and *Song of Songs*. Here he wrote his long contemplated *Vie de Jesus*, '63. In '61 he had been appointed Professor of Hebrew in the Institute of France, but denounced by bishops and clergy he was deprived of his chair, which was, however, restored in '70. The Pope did not disdain to attack him personally as a "French blasphemer." The *Vie de Jesus* is part of a comprehensive *History of the Origin of Christianity*, in 8 vols., '63—83, which includes *The Apostles, St Paul, Anti-Christ, The Gospels, The Christian Church*, and *Marcus Aurelius, and the end of the Antique World*. Among his other works we must mention Studies on Religious History ('58). *Philosophical Dialogues and Fragments* ('76), *Spinoza* ('77), *Caliban*, a satirical drama ('80), the Hibbert Lecture on the Influence of Rome on Christians, *Souvenirs*, '81; *New Studies of Religious History*, '84; *The Abbess of Jouarre*, a drama which made a great sensation in '86; and *The History of the People of Israel*, '87—89.

Renand (Paul), Belgian author of a work entitled *Nouvelle Symbolique*, on the identity of Christianity and Paganism, published at Brussels in 1861.

Rengart (Karl Fr.), of Berlin, b. 1803, democrat and free-thought friend of C. Deubler. Died about 1879.

Renard (Georges), French professor of the Academie of Lausanne; author of *Man, is he Free?* 1881, and a *Life of Voltaire*, '83.

Renouvier (Charles Bernard), French philosopher, b. Montpellier, 1815. An ardent Radical and follower of the critical philosophy. Among his works are *Manual of Ancient Philosophy* (2 vols., '44); *Republican Manual,* '48; *Essays of General Criticism*, '54; *Science of Morals*, '69; a translation, made with F. Pillon, of Hume's *Psychology*, '78; and *A Sketch of a Systematic Classification of Philosophical Doctrines*, '85.

Renton (William), English writer, b. Edinburgh, 1852. Educated in Germany. Wrote poems entitled *Oil and Water Colors*, and a work on *The Logic of Style*, '74. At Keswick he published *Jesus*, a psychological estimate of that hero, '76.

Has since published a romance of the last generation called *Bishopspool*, '83.

Rethore (François), French professor of philosophy at the Lyceum of Marseilles, b. Amiens, 1822. Author of a work entitled *Condillac, or Empiricism and Rationalism*, '64. Has translated H. Spencer's *Classification of Sciences*.

Reuschle (Karl Gustav), German geographer, b. Mehrstetten, 12 Dec. 1812. He wrote on Kepler and Astronomy, '71, and Philosophy and Natural Science, '71, dedicated to the memory of D. F. Strauss. Died at Stuttgart, 22 May, 1875.

Revillon (Antoine, called Tony), French journalist and deputy, b. Saint-Laurent-les Mâcon (Ain), 29 Dec. 1832. At first a lawyer in '57, he went to Paris, where he has written on many journals, and published many romances and brochures. In '81 he was elected deputy.

Rey (Marc Michel), printer and bookseller of Amsterdam. He printed all the works of d'Holbach and Rousseau and some of Voltaire's, and conducted the *Journal des Savans*.

Reynaud (Antoine Andre Louis), *Baron*, French mathematician, b. Paris, 12 Sept. 1777. In 1790 he became one of the National Guard of Paris. He was teacher and examiner for about thirty years in the Polytechnic School. A friend of Lalande. Died Paris, 24 Feb. 1844.

Reynaud (Jean Ernest), French philosopher, b. Lyons, 14 Feb. 1806. For a time he was a Saint Simonian. In '36 he edited with P. Leroux the *Encyclopédie Nouvelle*. He was a moderate Democrat in the Assembly of '48. His chief work, entitled *Earth and Heaven*, '54, had great success. It was formally condemned by a clerical council held at Périgueux. Died Paris, 28 June, 1863.

Reynolds (Charles B.), American lecturer, b. 4 Aug. 1832. Was brought up religiously, and became a Seventh Day Baptist preacher, but was converted to Freethought. He was prosecuted for blasphemy at Morristown, New Jersey, May 19, 20, 1887, and was defended by Col. Ingersoll The verdict was. one of guilty, and the sentence was a paltry fine of 25 dollars Has written in the *Boston Investigator, Truthseeker*, and *Ironc lad Age*.

Reynolds (George William MacArthur), English writer: author of many novels. Wrote *Errors of the Christian Religion*, 1832.

Rialle (J. GIRARD de), French anthropologist, b. Paris 1841. He wrote in *La Pensée Nouvelle*, conducted the *Revue de Linguistique et de Philologie comparée*, and has written on *Comparative Mythology*, dealing with fetishism, etc., '78, and works on Ethnology.

Ribelt (Léonce), French publicist, b. Bordeaux 1824, author of several political works and collaborator on *La Morale Indépendante*.

Ribeyrolles (Charles de), French politician, b. near Martel (Lot) 1812. Intended for the Church, he became a social democrat; edited the *Emancipation* of Toulouse, and *La Réforme* in '48. A friend of V. Hugo, he shared in his exile at Jersey. Died at Rio-Janeiro, 13 June, 1861.

Ribot (Théodule), French philosopher, b. Guingamp (Côtes du-Nord) 1839; has written *Contemporary English Psychology* '70, a resume of the views of Mill, Bain, and Spencer, whose *Principles of Psychology* he has translated. Has also written on *Heredity*, '73; *The Philosophy of Schopenhauer*, '74; The maladies of Memory, personality and Will, 3 vols.; and Contemporary German Psychology. He conducts the *Revue Philosophique*.

Ricciardi (Guiseppe Napoleone), Count, Italian patriot, b. Capodimonte (Naples), 19 July, 1808, son of Francesco Ricciardi, Count of Camaldoli, 1758-1842. Early in life he published patriotic poems. He says that never after he was nineteen did he kneel before a priest. In '32 he founded at Naples *Il Progresso*, a review of science, literature, and art. Arrested in '34 as a Republican conspirator, he was imprisoned eight months and then lived in exile in France until '48. Here he wrote in the *Revue Indépendante*, pointing out that the Papacy from its very essence was incompatible with liberty. Elected deputy to the Neapolitan Parliament, he sat on the extreme left. He wrote a *History of the Revolution of Italy in* '48 (Paris '49). Condemned to death in '53, his fortune was seized. He wrote an *Italian Martyrology from* 1792-1847 (Turin '56), and *The Pope and Italy*, '62. At the time of the Eucumenical Council he called an Anti-council of Freethinkers at Naples, '69. This was dissolved by the Italian government, but it led to the International Federation of Freethinkers. Count Ricciardi published an account of the congress. His last work was a life of his friend Mauro Macchi, '82. Died 1884.

Richepin (Jean), French poet, novelist, and dramatist, b. Médéah (Algeria) in 1849. He began life as a doctor, and during the Franco-German war took to journalism. In '76 he published the *Song of the Beggars*, which was suppressed. In '84 appeared *Les Blasphèmes*, which has gone through several editions.

Richer (Leon), French Deist and journalist, b. Laigh, 1824. He was with A. Guéroult editor of *l'Opinion Nationale*, and in '69 founded and edits *L'Avenir des Femmes*. In '68 he published *Letters of a Freethinker to a Village Priest*, and has written many volumes in favor of the emancipation of women, collaborating with Mdlle. Desraismes in the Women's Rights congresses he ld in Paris.

Rickman (Thomas Clio), English Radical. He published several volumes of poems and a life of his friend Thomas Paine, 1819, of whom he also published an excellent portrai t painted by Romney and engraved by Sharpe.

Riem (Andreas), German rationalist b. Frankenthal 1749. He became a preacher, and was appointed by Frederick the Great chaplain of a hospital at Berlin. This he quitted in order to become secretary of the Academy of Painting. He wrote anonymously on the *Aufklaring*. Died 1807.

Ritter (Charles), Swiss writer b. Geneva 1838, and has translated into French Strauss's Essay of Religious History, George Eliot's *Fragments and Thoughts*, and Zeller's *Christian Baur and the Tübingen School*.

Roalfe (Matilda), a brave woman, b. 1813. At the time of the blasphemy prosecutions in 1843, she went from London to Edinburgh to uphold the right of free publication. She opened a shop and circulated a manifesto setting forth her determination to sell works she deemed useful "whether they did or did not bring into contempt the Holy Scriptures and the Christian Religion." When prosecuted for selling *The Age of Reason, The*

Oracle of Reason, etc., she expressed her intention of continuing her offence as soon as liberated. She was sentenced to two months imprisonment 23 Jan. '44, and on her liberation continued the sale of the prosecuted works. She afterwards married Mr. Walter Sanderson and settled at Galashiels, where she died 29 Nov. 1880.

Robert (Pierre François Joseph), French conventionnel and friend of Brissot and Danton, b. Gimnée (Ardennes) 21 Jan. 1763. Brought up to the law he became professor of public law to the philosophical society. He was nominated deputy for Paris, and wrote *Republicanism adapted to France*, 1790, became secretary to Danton, and voted for the death of the king. He wrote in Prudhomme's *Révolutions de Paris*. Died at Brussels 1826.

Robertson (A. D.), editor of the *Free Enquirer*, published at New York, 1835.

Robertson (John Mackinnon), Scotch critic, b. Arran, 14 Nov. 1856. He became journalist on the *Edinburgh Evening News*, and afterwards on the *National Reformer*. Mr. Robertson has published a study of Walt Whitman in the " Round Table Series." *Essays towards a Critical Method*, '89, and has contributed to *Our Corner*, *Time*, notably an article on Mithraism, March, '89, *The Westminster Review*, etc. He has also issued pamphlets on *Socialism and Malthusiasm*. and *Toryism and Barbarism*, '85, and edited Hume's *Essay on Natural Religion* '89.

Roberty (Eugène de), French positivist writer, of Russian birth, b. Podolia (Russia), 1843; author of works on Sociology, Paris, '81, and *The Old and the New Philosophy*, an essay on the general laws of philosophic development, '87. He has recently written a work entitled *The Unknowable*, '89.

Robin (Charles Philippe), French physician, senator member of the Institute and of the Academy of Medecine, b. Jasseron (Aix), 4 June, 1821. Became M.D. in '46, and D.Sc. '47. In company with Littré he refounded Nysten's *Dictionary of Medicine*, and he has written many important medical works, and one on *Instruction*. In '72 his name was struck out of the list of jurors on the ground of his unbelief in God, and it thus remained despite many protests until '76. In the same year he was elected Senator, and sits with the Republican Left. He has been decorated with the Legion of Honor.

Robinet (Jean Baptiste René), French philosopher, b. Rennes, 23 June, 1735. He became a Jesuit, but gave it up and went to Holland to publish his curious work, *De la Nature*, 1776, by some attributed to Toussaint and to Diderot. He continued Marsy's *Analysis of Bayle*, edited the *Secret Letters* of Voltaire, translated Hume's *Moral Essays*, and took part in the *Recueil Philosophique*, published by J. L. Castilhon. Died at Rennes, 24 March, 1820.

Robinet (Jean Eugène François), French physician and publicist, b. Vic-sur-Seille, 1825. He early attached himself to the person and doctrine of Auguste Comte, and became his physician and one of his executors. During the war of '70 he was made Mayor of the Sixth Arrondissement of Paris. He has written a *Notice of the Work and Life of A. Comte*, '60, a memoir of the private life of *Danton*, '65, *The Trial of the Dantonists*, '79, and contributed an account of the *Positive Philosophy of A. Comte and P. Lafitte* to the " Bibliotheque Utile," vol. 66, '81.

Roell (Hermann Alexander), German theologian, b. 1653, author of a Deistic dissertation on natural religion, published at Frankfort in 1700. Died Amsterdam, 12 July, 1718.

Rogeard (Louis Auguste), French publicist, b. Chartres, 25 April, 1820. Became a teacher but was dismissed for refusing to attend mass. In '49 he moved to Paris and took part in the revolutionary movement. He was several times imprisoned under the Empire, and in '65 was sentenced to five years' imprisonment for writing *Les Propos de Labienus* (London, *i.e.* Zürich), '65. He fled to Belgium and wrote some excellent criticism on the Bible in the *Rive Gauche*. In '71 he assisted Pyat on *Le Vengeur*, and was elected on the Commune but declined to sit. An incisive writer, he signed himself " Atheist." Is still living in Paris.

Rokitansky (Karl), German physician and scientist, founder of the Vienese school in medicine, b. Königgrätz (Bohemia) 11 Feb. 1804. studied medicine at Prague and Vienna, and received his degree of Doctor in '28. His principal work is a *Manual of Practical Anatomy*, '42-6. Died Vienna, 23 July, 1878.

Roland (Marie Jeanne), *née* PHLIPON, French patriot, b. Paris, 17 March, 1754. Fond of reading, *Plutarch's Lives* influenced her greatly. At a convent she noted the names of sceptics attached and read their writings, being, she says, in turn Jansenist, stoic, sceptic, atheist, and deist. The last she remained, though Miss Blind classes her with Agnostics. After her marriage in 1779 with Jean Marie Roland de la Platiêrè (b. Lyons, 1732), Madame Roland shared the tasks and studies of her husband, and the Revolution found her an ardent consort. On the appointment of her husband to the ministry, she became the centre of a Girondist circle. Carlyle calls her " the creature of Simplicity and Nature, in an age of Artificiality, Pollution, and Cant," and " the noblest of all living French-women." On the fall of her party she was imprisoned, and finally executed, 8 Nov. 1793. Her husband, then in hiding, hearing of her death, deliberately stabbed himself, 15 Nov. 1793.

Rolph (William Henry), German philosopher, b. of English father, Berlin, 26 Aug. 1847. He became *privat-docent* of Zoology in the University of Leipsic, and wrote an able work on *Biological Problems*, '81, in which he accepts evolution, discards theology, and places ethics on a natural basis. Died 1 Aug. 1883.

Romagnosi (Giovanni Domenico), Italian philosopher and jurist, b. Salso Maggiore, 13 Dec. 1761. He published in 1791 an able work on penal legislation, *Genesis of Penal Law*, many pages of which are borrowed from d'Holbach's *System of Nature* He became Professor of Law in Parma, Milan, and Pavia. A member of the Italian Academy, he was named professor at Corfu, where he died 8 June, 1835. In '21 he wrote *Elements of Philosophy*, followed by *What is a Sound Mind?* ('27) and *Ancient Moral Philosophy*, '32. A somewhat obscure writer, he nevertheless contributed to the positive study of sociology.

Romiti (Guglielmo), Italian Positivist. Professor of Anatomy in the University of Siena. Has published *Anatomical Notes*, and a Discourse which excited some commotion among the theologians.

Romme (Gilbert), French Mathematician, b. Riou, 1750, became deputy to the Legislative Assembly in 1791, and to the

Convention in 1792. In Sept. 1793 he introduced the new Republican Calendar, the plan of which was drawn by Laland, and the names assigned by Fabre d'Eglantine. He advocated the Fêtes of Reason. Being condemned to death, he committed suicide, 18 June, 1795. His brother Charles, b. 1744, was also an eminent geometrician, and a friend of Laland. He died 15 June, 1805.

Ronge (Johannes), German religious reformer, b. Bischopwalde (Silesia), 16 Oct. 1813. He entered the seminary of Breslau, and became a Catholic priest in '40. His liberal views and bold preaching soon led to his suspension. In '44 his letter denouncing the worship of " the holy coat," exhibited by Arnoldi, Bishop of Treves, made much clamor. Excommunicated by the Church, he found many free congregations, but was proscribed after the revolution of '49 and took refuge in England. In '51 he issued a revolutionary manifesto. In '61 he returned to Frankfort, and in '73 settled at Darmstadt. Died at Vienna, 25 Oct. 1887.

Ronsard (Pierre), French poet, b. of noble family 11 Sept. 1524. He became page to the Duke of Orleans, and afterwards to James V. of Scotland. Returning to France, he was a great favorite at the French Court. Died 27 Dec. 1585.

Roorda van Eysinga (Sicco Ernst Willem), Dutch positivist, b. Batavia (Java), 8 Aug. 1825. He served as engineer at Java, and was expelled about '64 for writing on behalf of the Javanese. He contributed to the *De Dageraad* and *Revue Positive.* Died Clarens (Switzerland), 23 Oct. 1887.

Roquetaillade (Jean de la), also known as RUPESCINA, early French reformer of Auvillac (Auvergne), who entered the order of the Franciscans. His bold discourses led to his imprisonment at Avignon 1356, by order of Innocent VI., when he wrote an apology. Accused of Magic, Nostradamus says he was burnt at Avignon in 1362, but this has been disputed.

Rose (Charles H.), formerly of Adelaide, Australia, author of *A Light to Lighten the Gentiles,* 1881.

Rose (Ernestine Louise) née Süsmond Potowsky, Radical reformer and orator, b. Peterkov (Poland), 13 Jan. 1810. Her father was a Jewish Rabbi. From early life she was of a bold and inquiring disposition. At the age of 17 she went to Berlin. She was in Paris during the Revolution of '30. Soon after she came to England where she embraced the views of Robert Owen, who called her his daughter. Here she married Mr. William E. Rose, a gentleman of broad Liberal views. In May '36, they went to the United States and became citizens of the Republic. Mrs. Rose lectured in all the states on the social system, the formation of character, priestcraft, etc. She lectured against slavery in the slave-owning states and sent in '38 the first petition to give married women the right to hold real estate. She was one of the inaugurators of the Woman's Rights Movement, and a constant champion of Freethought. An eloquent speaker, some of her addresses have been published. *Defence of Atheism, Women's Rights* and *Speech at the Hartford Bible Convention in '54.* About '73 she returned to England where she still lives. One of her last appearances at public was at the Conference of Liberal Thinkers at South Place Chapel in '76, where she delivered a pointed speech. Mrs. Rose has a fine face and head, and though aged and suffering, retains the utmost interest in the Freethought cause.

Roskoff (Georg Gustav), German rationalist, b. Presburg, Hungary, 30 Aug. 1814. He studied theology and philosophy at Halle, and has written works on *Hebrew Antiquity,* '57. The Samson legend and Herakles myth, '60, and a standard *History of the Devil* in 2 vols., Leipzig, '69.

Ross (William Stewart), Scotch writer, b. 20 Mar. 1844. Author of poems and educational works, and editor of *Secular Review,* now *The Agnostic Journal.* Wrote *God and his Book,* '87, and several brochures published under the pen name of " Saladin."

Rosseau (Leon), French writer in the Rationalist of Geneva under the name of L. Russelli. He published separately the *Female Followers of Jesus,* founded the *Horizon,* contributed to *la Libre Pensée,* and was editor of *l'Athée.* Died 1870.

Rossetti (Dante Gabriel), poet and painter, b. of Italian parents, London, 12 May, 1828. Educated at King's College, he became a student at the Royal Academy and joined the pre-Raphaelites. As a poet artist he exhibited the richest gifts of orignality, earnestness, and splendour of expression. Died at Westgate on Sea, 9 April, 1882.

Rossetti (William Michael) critic and man of letters, brother of the preceding, b. London, 25 Sep. 1829. Educated at King's College, he became assistant secretary in the Inland Revenue Office. He has acted as critic for many papers and edited many works, the chief being an edition of Shelley, '70, with a memoir and numerous notes. He is Chairman of the Commitee of the Shelley Society.

Rossmaessler (Emil Adolf), German naturalist b. Leipsic 3 March, 1806. Studied theology, but abandoned it for science, and wrote many scientific works of repute. In '48 he was elected to Parliament. Among his writings are *Man in the Mirror of Nature.* '49—55. *The History of the Earth,* '68. Died as a philosopher 8 April, 1867.

Roth (Julius), Dr., German author of Religion and Priest-craft, Leipzig, 1869 ; *Jesuitism,* '71.

Rothenbuecher (Adolph), Dr., German author of an able little *Handbook of Morals,* written from the Secular standpoint, Cottbus, 1884.

Rotteck (Karl Wenceslaus von), German historian and statesman b. Freiburg 18 July, 1775. Studied in his native town, where in 1798 he became Professor of History. In 1819 he represented his University in the States of Baden, where he distinguished himself by his liberal views. He was forbidden by government to edit any paper and was deprived of his chair. This persecution hastened his death, which occurred 26 Nov 1840. Rotteck's *General History of the World* (9 vols., 1827) was very popular and gave one of the broadest views of history which had then appeared.

Rousseau (Jean Jacques), Swiss philosopher, b. Geneva, 28 June, 1712. After a varied career he went to Paris in 1741 and supported himself. In 1715 he obtained a prize from the academy of Dijon for negative answer to the question " whether the re-establishment of the arts and sciences has conduced to the purity of morals." This success prompted further literary efforts. He published a dictionary of music, the *New Heloise* (1759), a love stories in the form of letters, which had great success, and *Emilius* (May 1762), a moral romance, in which he condemns other education than that of following nature. In this work occurs his *Confession of Faith of a Savoyard Vicar*, discarding the supernatural element in Christianity. The French parliament condemned the book 9 June, 1762, and prosecuted the writer, who fled to Switzerland, Pope Clement XVIII fulminated against Emile, and Rousseau received so many insults on account of his principles that he returned to Paris. and on the invitation of Hume came to England in Jan. 1766. He knew little English and soon took offence with Hume, and asked permission to return to Paris, which he obtained on condition of never publishing anything more. He however completed his *Confessions*, of which he had previously composed the first six books in England. Rousseau was a sincere sentimentalist, an independent and eloquent, but not deep thinker. His captious temper spoiled his own life, but his influence has been profound and far-reaching. Died near Paris, 2 July, 1778.

Rouzade (Leonie) Madame, French Freethought lecturess. Has written several brochures and novels, notably *Le Monde Renversé*, 1872, and *Ci et ca, ca et la*, ideas upon moral philosophy and social progress. Writes in Malon's *Revue Sociuliste*, and is one of the editors of *Les Droits des Femmes*.

Roy (Joseph), French translator of Feuerbach's *Essence of Christianity*, 1864, and *Religion, Death, Immortality*, '66. Has also translated Marx's *Capital*.

Royer (Clemence Auguste), French authoress, b. Nantes, 21 April, 1830, of Catholic royalist family. Visiting England in '54, she studied our language and literature. Going to Switzerland, in '59 she opened at Lausanne a course of logic and philosophy for women. In '60 she shared with Proudhon in a prize competition on the subject of taxation. In '62 she translated Darwin's *Origin of Species*, with a bold preface and notes. In '64 her philosophical romance *The Twins of Hellas* appeared at Brussels, and was interdicted in France. Her ablest work is on *The Origin of Man and of Societies*, '69. In this she states the scientific view of human evolution, and challenges the Christian creed. This was followed by many memoirs, *Pre-historic Funeral Rites*, '76; *Two Hypotheses of Heredity*, '77;

The Good and the Moral Law, '81. Mdlle. Royer has contributed to the *Revue Moderne, Revue de Philosophie, Positive, Revue d'Anthropologie,* etc., and has assisted and spoken at many political, social, and scientific meetings.

Ruedt (P. A.), Ph. D., German lecturer and "apostle of unbelief," b. Mannheim, 8 Dec. 1844. Educated at Mannheim and Carlsruhe, he studied philosophy, philology, and jurisprudence at Heidelberg University, '65-69. Dr. Rüdt became acquainted with Lassalle, and started a paper, *Die Waffe,* and in '70 was imprisoned for participation in social democratic agitation. From '74 to '86 he lived in St. Petersburg as teacher, and has since devoted himself to Freethought propaganda. Several of his addresses have been published.

Ruelle (Charles Claude), French writer, b. Savigny, 1810. Author of *The History of Christianity,* '66, and *La Schmita,* '69.

Ruge (Arnold), German reformer, b. Bergen (Isle Rügen), 13 Sept. 1802. Studied at Halle, Jena, and Heidelberg, and as a member of the Tugenbund was imprisoned for six years. After his liberation in '30 he became professor at Halle, and with Echtermeyer founded the Hallische Jahrbücher, '38, which opposed Church and State. In '48 he started *Die Reform.* Elected to the Frankfort Assembly, he sat on the Extreme Left. When compelled to fly he came to England, where he wrote *New Germany* in "Cabinet of Reason" series, and translated Buckle's *History of Civilisation.* He acted as visiting tutor at Brighton, where he died 30 Dec. 1880.

Ruggieri (Cosmo), Florentine philosopher and astrologer, patronised by Catherine de Medicis. He began to publish *Almanachs* in 1604, which he issued annually. He died at Paris in 1615, declaring himself an Atheist, and his corpse was in consequence denied Christian burial.

Rumpf (Johann Wilhelm), Swiss author of Church, Faith, and Progress, and *The Bible and Christ,* a criticism (Strasburg, 1858). Edited *Das Freire Wort* (Basle, '56).

Russell (John). See Amberley.

Ryall (Malthus Questell), was secretary of the Anti-Persecution Union, 1842, and assisted his friend Mr. Holyoake on *The Oracle of Reason* and *The Movement.* Died 1846.

Rydberg (Abraham Viktor), Swedish man of Letters, b. Jönköping, 18 Dec. 1829. He has written many works of which we mention *The Last Athenian Roman Days*, and *The Magic of the Middle Ages*, which have been translated into English.

Rystwick (Herman van), early Dutch heretic who denied hell and taught that the soul was not immortal, but the elements of all matter eternal. He was sent to prison in 1499, and set at liberty upon abjuring his opinion, but having published them a second time, he was arrested at the Hague, and burnt to death in 1511.

Sabin (Ibn), *Al Mursi*, Spanish Arabian philosopher, b. Murcia about 1218 of noble family. About 1249 he corresponded with Frederick II., replying to his philosophical questions. Committed suicide about 1271.

Sadoc, a learned Jewish doctor in the third centnry B.C. He denied the resurrection, the existence of angels, and the doctrine of predestination, and opposed the idea of future rewards and punishments. His followers were named after him, Sadducees.

Saga (Francesco) de Rovigo, Italian heretic, put to death for Anti-Trinitarianism at Venice, 25 Feb. 1566.

Saigey (Emile), French inspector of telegraph wires. Wrote *Modern Physics*, 1867, and *The Sciences in the Eighteenth Century: Physics of Voltaire*, '74. Died 1875.

Saillard (F.), French author of *The Revolution and the Church* (Paris, '69), and *The Organisation of the Republic*, '83.

Sainte Beuve (Charles Augustin), French critic and man of letters b. Boulogne, 23 Dec. 1804. Educated in Paris, he studied medicine, which he practised several years. A favorable review of V. Hugo's *Odes and Ballades* gained him the intimacy of the Romantic school. As a critic he made his mark in '28 with his *Historical and Critical* Picture of French Poetry in the Sixteenth Century. His other principal works are his *History of Port Royal*, '40—62; *Literary Portraits*, '32—39; and *Causeries du Lundi*, '51—57. In '45 he was elected to the Academy, and in '65 was made a senator. As a critic he was penetrative, comprehensive, and impartial.

Saint Evremond (Charles de Marguetel de Saint Denis) seigneur de, French man of letters, b. St. Denys-le-Guast (Normandy), 1 April, 1713. He studied law, but subsequently entered the army and became major-general. He was confined in the Bastile for satirising Cardinal Mazarin. In England he was well received at the court of Charles II. He died in London, 20 Sept. 1703, and was buried in Westminster Abbey. Asked on his death-bed if he wished to reconcile himself to God, he replied, he desired to reconcile himself to appetite. His works, consisting of essays, letters, poems, and dramas, were published in 3 vols. 1705.

Saint-Glain (Dominique de), French Spinozist, b. Limoges, about 1620. He went into Holland that he might profess the Protestant religion more freely; was captain in the service of the States, and assisted on the Rotterdam *Gazette*. Reading Spinoza, he espoused his system, and translated the Tractatus Theologico-Politicus into French, under the title of *La Clef du Sanctuaire*, 1678. This making much noise, and being in danger of prosecution, he changed the title to *Ceremonies Superstitieuses des Juifs*, and also to *Réflexions Curieuses d'un Esprit Désintéressé*, 1678.

Saint-Hyacinthe (Themiseul de CORDONNIER de), French writer, b. Orleans, 24 Sept. 1684. Author of *Philosophical Researches*, published at Rotterdam, 1743. Died near Breda (Holland), 1746. Voltaire published his *Diner Du Comte de Boulainvilliers* under the name of St. Hyacinthe.

Saint John (Henry). See Bolingbroke, *Lord*.

Saint Lambert (Charles, or rather Jean François de), French writer, b. Nancy, 16 Dec. 1717. After being educated among the Jesuits he entered the army, and was admired for his wit and gallantry. He became a devoted adherent of Voltaire and an admirer of Madame du Chatelet. He wrote some articles in the *Encyclopédie*, and many fugitive pieces and poems in the literary journals. His poem, the Seasons, 1769 procured him admission to the Academy. He published essays on Helvetius and Bolingbroke, and *Le Catéchisme Universel*. His *Philosophical Works* were published in 1801. Died Paris, 9 Feb. 1803.

Sale (George), English Oriental scholar, b. Kent, 1680, educated at Canterbury. He was one of a society which undertook to publish a *Universal History*, and was, also one of the compilers of the *General Dictionary*. His most important work was a translation of the *Koran*, with a preliminary discourse and explanatory notes, 1734. He was one of the founders of the Society for the Encouragement of Learning. Died 14 Nov. 1736.

Salieres (A.), contributor to *l'Athée*, 1870. Has written a work on *Patriotism*, 1881.

Sallet (Friedrich von), German pantheist poet of French descent, b. Neisse (Silesia), 20 April, 1812. An officer in the army, he was imprisoned for writing a satire on the life of a trooper. In '34 he attended Hegel's lectures at Berlin, and in '38 quitted the army. He wrote a curious long poem entitled the Layman's Gospel, in which he takes New Testament texts and expounds them pantheistically—the God who is made flesh is replaced by the man who becomes God. Died Reichau (Silesia), 21 Feb. 1843.

Salmeron y Alonso (Nicolas), Spanish statesman, b. Alhama lo Seco, 1838. Studied law, and became a Democratic journalist; a deputy to the Cortes in 1871, and became President thereof during the Republic of '73. He wrote a prologue to the work of Giner on *Philosophy and Arts*, '78, and his own works were issued in 1881.

Salt (Henry Stephens), English writer, b. India, 20 Sept 1821; educated at Eton, where he bacame assistant master A contributor to *Progress*, he has written *Literary Sketches*, '88. A monograph on Shelley, and a *Life of James Thomson, "B.V."* 889.

Saltus (Edgar Evertson), American author, b. New York 8 June 1858. Studied at Concord, Paris, Heidelberg and Munich. In '84 he published a sketch of *Balzac*. Next year appeared *The Philosophy of Disenchantment*, appreciative and well written views of Schopenhauer and Hartmann. This was followed by *The Anatomy of Negation*, a sketchy account of some atheists and sceptics from Kapila to Leconte de Lisle, '86. Has also written several novels, and *Eden*, an episode, '89. His brother Francis is the author of *Honey and Gall*, a book of poems (Philadelphia, '73.)

Salverte (Anne Joseph Eusèbe BACONNIERE DE), French philosopher, b. Paris, 18 July, 1771. He studied among the Oratorians. Wrote *Epistle to a Reasonable Woman*, an Essay on *What should be Believed*, 1793, contributed to Maréchal's *Dictionnaire des Athées*, published an eloge on Diderot, 1801, and many brochures, among others a tragedy on the Death of Jesus Christ. Elected deputy in '28, he was one of the warm partisans of liberty, and in '30, demanded that Catholicism should not be recognised as the state religion. He is chiefly remembered by his work on *The Occult Sciences*, '29, which was translated into English, '46. To the French edition of '56 Littré wrote a Preface. He died 27 Oct. 1839. On his death bed he refused religious offices.

Sand (George), the pen name of Amandine Lucile Aurore DUPIN, afterwards baroness DUDNEVANT, French novelist, b. Paris, 1 July, 1804, and brought up by her grandmother at the Château de Nohant. Reading Rousseau and the philosophers divorced her from Catholicism. She remained a Humanitarian. Married Sept. 1822, Baron Dudnevant, an elderly man who both neglected and ill-treated her, and from whom after some years she was glad to separate at the sacrifice of her whole fortune. Her novels are too many to enumerate. The Revolution of '48 drew her into politics, and she started a journal and translated Mazzini's *Republic and Royalty in Italy*, Died at her Chateau of Nohant, 8 June, 1876. Her name was long obnoxious in England, where she was thought of as an assailant of marriage and religion, but a better appreciation of her work and genius is making way.

Sarcey (Franscique), French critic, b. Dourdan, 8 Oct. 1828, editor of *Le XIXe. Siècle*, has written plays, novels, and many anti-clerical articles.

"Sarrasi," pseudonym of A. de C.........; French Orientalist b. Department of Tarn, 1837, author of *L'Orient Devoilé*, '80, in which he shows the mythical elements in Christianity.

Saull (William Devonshire), English geologist, b. 1783. He established a free geological museum, contributed to the erection of the John Street Institute, and was principally instrumental in opening the old Hall of Science, City Road. He wrote on the connection between astronomy, geology, etc. He died 26 April, 1855, and is buried in Kensal Green, near his friends, Allen Davenport and Henry Hetherington.

Saunderson (Nicholas), English mathematican, b. Thurleston (Yorkshire), 2 Jan. 1682. He lost both his eyes and his sight by small pox when but a year old, yet he became conversant with Euclid, Archimedes, and Diophantus, when read to him in Greek. He lectured at Cambridge University, explaining Newton's Mathematical Principles of Natural Philosophy, and even his works on light and color. It was said, " They have turned out Whiston for believing in but one God, and put in Saunderson, who believes in no God at all." Saunderson said that to believe in God he must first touch him. Died 19 April, 1739.

Sauvestre (Charles), French journalist, b. Mans. 1818, one of the editors of *L'Opinion Nationale*. Has written on *The Clergy and Education* ('61), *Monita Secreta Societatis Jesu; Secret Instructions of the Jesuits* ('65), *On the Knees of the Church* ('68), *Religious Congregations Unveiled* ('70), and other anti-clerical works. He died at Paris in 1883.

Saville (Sir George), Marquis of Halifax, English statesman, b. Yorkshire, 1630. He became President of the Council in the reign of James II., but was dismissed for opposing the repeal of the Test Acts. He wrote several pieces and memoirs. Burnet gives a curious account of his opinions, which he probably tones down.

Sawtelle (C. M.), American author of *Reflections on the Science of Ignorance*, or the art of teaching others what you don't know yourself, Salem, Oregon, 1868.

Sbarbaro (Pietro), Italian publicist and reformer, b. Savona, 1838; studied jurisprudence. He published a work on *The Philosophy of Research*, '66. In '70 he dedicated to Mauro Macchi a book on *The Task of the Nineteenth Century*, and presided at a congress of Freethinkers held at Loreto. Has written popular works on the Conditions of Human Progress, the Ideal of Democracy, and an essay entitled *From Socino to Mazzini*, '86.

Schade (Georg), German Deist, b. Apenrade, 1712. He believed in the immortality of brutes. In 1770 he was impri-

soned for his opinions on the Isle of Christiansoe.   He settled
at Kiel, Holstein, in 1775, where he died in 1795.

Scherer (Edmond), French critic and publicist, b. Paris
8 April, 1815.   Of Protestant family, he became professor of
exegesis at Geneva, but his views becoming too free, he
resigned his chair and went to Strasburg, where he became
chief of the School of Liberal Protestants, and in the *Revue de
Théologie et de Philosophie Chrétienne*, '50-60, put forward views
which drew down a tempest from the orthodox.   He also wrote
in the *Bibliotheque Universelle* and *Revue des Deux-Mondes*.   Some
of his articles have been collected as *Mélanges de Critique
Religieuse*, '60 ; and *Mélanges d'Histoire Religieuse*, '64.   He
was elected deputy in '71, and sat with the Republicans of the
Left.   Died 1889.

Scherr (Johannes), German author, b. Hohenrechberg,
3 Oct. 1817.   Educated at Zürich and Tübingen, he wrote in
'43 with his brother Thomas a *Popular History of Religious and
Philosophical Ideas*, and in '57 a *History of Religion*, in three
parts.   In '60 he became Professor of History and Literature
at Zürich, and has written many able literary studies, including histories of German and English literature.   Died at
Zürich, 21 Nov. 1887.

Schiff (Johan Moriz), German physiologist, b. Frankfort,
1823.   Educated at Berlin and Gottingen, he became Professor
of Comparative Anatomy at Berne, '51-63 ; of Physiology at
Florence, '63-76, and at Genoa. Has written many physiological
treatises, which have been attacked as materialistic.

Schiller (Johann Christoph Friedrich von), eminent German
poet and historian, b. Marbech, 10 Nov. 1759.   His mother
wished him to become a minister, but his tastes led him in a
different direction.   A friend of Goethe, he enriched German
literature with numerous plays and poems, a History of the
Netherlands Revolt, and of the Thirty Years' War.   He died in
the prime of mental life at Weimar, 9 May, 1805.

Schmidt (Eduard Oskar), German zoologist, b. Torgau,
21 Feb. 1823.   He travelled widely, and became professor of
natural history at Jena.   Among the first of Germans to accept
Darwinism, he has illustrated its application in many direc-

tions, and published an able work on *The Doctrine of Descent and Darwinism* in the "International Scientific Series." Died at Strasburg, 17 Jan. 1886.

Schmidt (Kaspar), German philosopher, b. Bayreuth, 25 Oct. 1806. Studied at Berlin, Erlangen, and Königsberg, first theology, then philosophy. Under the pseudonym of "Max Stirner" he wrote a system of individualism *The Only One, and His Possession* (Der Einzige und sein Eigenthum), '45. He also wrote a *History of Reaction* in two parts (Berlin, '52), and translated Smith's *Wealth of Nations* and Say's *Text-book of Political Economy*. Died at Berlin, 25 June, 1856.

Schneeberger (F. J.), Austrian writer, b. Vienna, 7 Sept, 1827. Has written some popular novels under the name of "Arthur Storch," and was one of the founders of the German Freethinkers' Union.

Schœlcher Victor), French philosophist, b. Paris, 21 July 1804 While still young he joined the secret society *Aide-toi, le ciel t'aidera*, and studied social questions. He devoted himself from about '26 to advocating the abolition of slavery, and wrote many works on the subject. On 3 March, '48, he was made Under Secretary of the Navy, and caused a decree to be issued by the Provisional Government enfranchising all slaves on French territory. He was elected Deputy for Martinique '48 and '49. After 2 Dec. '51, he came to London, where he wrote occasionally in the *Reasoner* and *National Reformer*. He returned to France during the war, and took part in the defence of Paris. In '71 he was again returned for Martinique, and in '75 he was elected a life senator.

Scholl (Aurélien), French journalist, b. Bordeaux, 14 July, 1833. He began life as a writer on the *Corsaire*, founded *Satan, Le Nain Jaune*, etc., and writes on *l'Evénement*. Has written several novels, and *le Procès de Jésus Christ*, '77.

Scholl (Karl), German writer and preacher to the Free religious bodies of Mannheim and Heidelberg, b. Karlsruhe, 17 Aug. 1820. He became a minister '44, but was suspended for his free opinions in '45. His first important work was on *the Messiah Legend of the East* (Hamburg, '52), and in '61 he published a volume on *Free Speech*, a collection of extracts from French,

English, and American Freethinkers. In '70 he started a monthly journal of the Religion of Humanity, *Es Werde Licht!* which continued for many years. Has published many discourses, and written *Truth from Ruins*, '73, and on *Judaism and the Religion of Humanity*, '79.

Schopenhauer (Arthur), German pessimist philosopher, b· Danzig, 22 Feb. 1788. The son of a wealthy and well-educated merchant and a vivacious lady, he was educated in French and English, and studied at Göttingen science, history, and the religions and philosophies of the East. After two visits to Italy, and an unsuccessful attempt to obtain pupils at Berlin, he took up his abode at Frankfort. In 1815 he wrote his chief work, *The World as Will and Idea*, translated into English in '83. His philosophy is expressed in the title, will is the one reality, all else appearance. He also wrote *The Two Ground Problems of Ethics*, '61, *On the Freedom of Will*, and a collection of essays entitled *Parega and Paralipomena* (51). Died at Frankfort, 21 Sept. 1860. Schopenhauer was a pronounced Atheist, and an enemy of every form of superstition. He said that religions are like glow-worms; they require darkness to shine in.

Schroeter (Eduard), German American writer, b. Hannover, 4 June, 1810, studied theology at Jena; entered the Free-religious communion in '45. In '50, he went to America, living since '53 in Sauk City, and frequently lecturing there· In '81, he attended the International Conference of Freethinkers at Brussels. He was a constant contributor to the *Freidenker*, of Milwaukee, until his death 2 April, 1888.

Schroot (A), German author of *Visions and Ideas* (Berlin, 1865), *Natural Law and Human Will; Creation and Man*, and *Science and Life* (Hamburg, 1873).

Schuenemann Pott (Friedrich), German American, b. Hamburg, 3 April, 1826. He joined the " Freie Gemeinde," and was expelled from Prussia in '48. After the Revolution he returned to Berlin and took part in democratic agitation, for which he was tried for high treason, but acquitted. In '54 he removed to America, where he made lecturing tours over the States settling at San Francisco.

Schultze (Karl August, Julius Fritz), German writer, b. Celle, 7 May, 1846, studied at Jena, Göttingen and Münich, has written an able study on *Fetishism*, Leipzig '71, a pamphlet on Religion in German Schools, '72, a *History of the Philosophy of the Renaissance*, '74, and *Kant and Darwin*, '75. In '76, he was appointed Professor of Philosophy in Jena, since which he has written *The Elements of Materialism*, '80, *Philosophy of the Natural Sciences*, 2 vols. '81-82, and *Elements of Spiritualism*, 1883.

Schumann (Robert Alexander), German musical composer, b. Nekau, 8 July, 1810. He studied law at Leipsic, but forsook it for music. He started a musical journal '34, which he edited for some years. His lyrical compositions are unsurpassed, and he also composed a " profane " oratorio, *Paradise and the Peri* ('40). His character and opinions are illustrated by his *Letters*. Died 29 July, 1856.

Schweichel (Georg Julius Robert), German writer, b. Königsberg, 12 July, 1821. He studied jurisprudence, but took to literature. Taking part in the events of '48, after the reaction he went to Switzerland. Has written several novels dealing with Swiss life, also a *Life of Auerbach*. He wrote the preface to Dulk's *Irrgang des Leben's Jesu*, 1884.

Schweitzer (Jean Baptista von), German Socialist poet, b. Frankfort, 12 July, 1833. He studied law in Berlin and Heidelberg ; became after Lassalle's death president of the German Workmen's Union, and was sent to Parliament in '67. He wrote the *Zeitgeist and Christianity*, '62, *The Darwinians*, '75, and several other works. Died 28 July, 1875.

Scot (Reginald), English rationalist, author of *The Discoverie of Witchcraft*, 1584, the first English work to question the existence of witches. It was burnt by order of King James I, and was republished in 1886. Scot died in 1599.

Scott (Thomas), English scholar, b. 28 April 1808. In early life he travelled widely, lived with Indians and had been page to Chas. X, of France. Having investigated Christianity, he in later life devoted himself to Freethought propaganda by sending scholarly pamphlets among the clergy and cultured classes. From '62-77, he issued from Mount Pleasant, Ramsgate, over a hundred different pamphlets by Bp. Hinds, F. W. Newman, Kalisch, Lestrange, Willis, Strange, etc., most of which were given away. He issued a challenge to the

Christian Evidence Society, and wrote with Sir G. W. Cox. *The English Life of Jesus* '71. Altogether his publications extend to twenty volumes. Little known outside his own circle, Thomas Scott did a work which should secure him lasting honor. Died at Norwood, 30 Dec. 1878.

Seaver (Horace Holley), American journalist, b. Boston, 25 Aug. 1810. In '37 he became a compositor on the *Boston Investigator*, and during Kneeland's imprisonment took the editorship, which he continued for upwards of fifty years during which he battled strenuously for Freethought in America. His articles were always very plain and to the point. A selection of them has been published with the title *Occasional Thoughts* (Boston, '88). With Mr. Mendum, he helped the erection of the Paine Memorial Hall, and won the esteem of all Freethinkers in America. Died, 21 Aug. 1889. His funeral oration was delivered by Colonel Ingersoll.

Sebille (Adolphe), French writer, who, under the pseudonym of "Dr. Fabricus," published *God, Man, and his latter end*, a medico-psychological study, 1868, and *Letters from a Materialist to Mgr. Dupanloup*, 1868–9.

Sechenov or **Setchenoff** (Ivan), Russian philosopher, who, in 1863, published *Psychological Studies*, explaining the mind by physiology. The work made a great impression in Russia, and has been translated into French by Victor Derély, and published in '84 with an introduction by M. G. Wyrouboff.

Secondat (Charles de). See Montesquieu.

Seeley (John Robert), English historian and man of letters b. London, 1834, educated at City of London School and Cambridge, where he graduated in '57. In '63, he was appointed Professor of Latin in London University. In '66, appeared his *Ecce Homo*, a survey of the Life and Work of Jesus Christ, published anonymously, and which Lord Shaftesbury denounced in unmeasured terms as vomitted from the pit of hell. In '69, he became professor of modern history at Cambridge, and has since written some important historical works as well as *Natural Religion* ('82). Prof. Seeley is president of the Ethical Society.

Segond (Louis August), French physician and Positivist, author of a plan of a positivist school to regenerate medicine, 1849, and of several medical works.

Seidel (Martin), Silesian Deist, of Olhau, lived at the end of the sixteenth century. He held that Jesus was not the predicted Messiah, and endeavored to propagate his opinion among the Polish Socinians. He wrote three Letters on the Messiah, *The Foundations of the Christian Religion*, in which he considered the quotation from the Old Testament in the new, and pointed out the errors of the latter.

Sellon (Edward), English archaeologist, author of *The Monolithic Temples of India; Annotations on the Sacred Writings of the Hindus*, 1865, and other scarce works, privately printed.

Semerie (Eugène), French Positivist, b. Aix, 6 Jan. 1832. Becoming physician at Charenton, he studied mental maladies, and in '67 published a work on *Intellectual Symptoms of Madness*, in which he maintained that the disordered mind went back from Positivism to metaphysics, theology, and then to fetishism. This work was denounced by the Bishop of Orleans. Dr. Semerie wrote *A Simple Reply to M. Dupanloup*, '68. During the sieges of Paris he acted as surgeon and director of the ambulance. A friend of Pierre Lafitte, he edited the *Politique Positive*, and wrote *Positivists and Catholics*, '73, and *The Law of the Three States*, '75. Died at Grasse, May, 1884.

Semler (Johann Salomo), German critic, b. Saalfeld, 18 Dec. 1725. He was professor of theology at Halle and founder of historical Biblical criticism there. He translated Simon's *Critical History of the New Testament*. and by asserting the right of free discussion drew down the wrath of the orthodox. Died at Halle, 4 March, 1791.

Serafini (Maria Alimonda), Italian authoress of a *Catechism for Female Freethinkers* (Geneva, 1869), and a work on *Marriage and Divorce* (Salerno, '73).

Serveto y Reves (Miguel), better known as Michael Servetus, Spanish martyr, b. Villanova (Aragon), 1509. Intended for the Church, he left it for law, which he studied at Toulouse. He afterward studied medicine at Paris, and corresponded with Calvin on the subject of the Trinity, against which he wrote *De Trinitatis Erroribus* and *Christianismi Restitutio*, which excited the hatred of both Catholics and Protestants. To Calvin Servetus sent a copy of his last work. Calvin, through one Trie, denounced him to the Catholic authorities at Lyons. He was imprisoned, but escaped, and to get to Naples passed through Geneva, where he was seized at the instance of Calvin, tried for blasphemy and heresy, and burnt alive at a slow fire, 26 Oct. 1553.

Seume (Johann Gottfried), German poet, b. near Weissenfels, 29 Jan. 1763. He was sent to Leipsic, and intended for a theologian, but the dogmas disgusted him, and he left for Paris. He lived an adventurous life, travelled extensively, and wrote *Promenade to Syracuse*, 1802, and other works. Died at Teplitz, 13 June, 1810.

Sextus Empiricus, Greek sceptical philosopher and physician, who probably lived early in the third century of the Christian era. He left two works, one a summary of the doctrines of the sceptics in three books; the other an attack on all positive philosophy.

Shadwell (Thomas), English dramatist, b. Straton Hall, Norfolk, 1640. Although damned by Dryden in his *Mac Flecknoe* Shadwell's plays are not without merit, and illustrate the days of Charles II. Died 6 Dec. 1692.

Shaftesbury (Anthony Ashley Cooper), third Earl, b. London, 26 Feb. 1671. Educated by Locke, in 1693 he was elected M.P. for Poole, and proposed granting counsel to prisoners in case of treason. His health suffering, he resigned and went to Holland, where he made the acquaintance of Bayle. The excitement induced by the French Prophets occasioned his *Letters upon Enthusiasm*, 1708. This was followed by his *Moralists* and *Sensus Communis*. In 1711 he removed to Naples, where he died 4 Feb. 1713. His collected works were published under the title of *Characteristics*, 1732. They went through several editions, and did much to raise the character of English Deism.

Shakespeare (William). The greatest of all dramatists, b. Stratford-on-Avon, 23 April, 1564. The materials for writing his life are slender. He married in his 19th year, went to London, where he became an actor and produced his marvellous plays, the eternal honor of English literature. Shakespeare gained wealth and reputation and retired to his native town, where he died April 23, 1616. His dramas warrant the inference that he was a Freethinker. Prof. J. R. Green says, "Often as his questionings turned to the riddle of life and death, and leaves it a riddle to the last without heeding the common theological solutions around him." His comprehensive mind disdained endorsement of religious dogmas and his wit delighted in what the Puritans call profanity. Mr. Birch in his *Inquiry into the Philosophy and Religion of Shakespeare*, sustains the position that he was an Atheist.

Shaw (James Dickson), American writer, b. Texas, 27 Dec. 1841. Brought up on a cattle farm, at the Civil War he joined the Southern Army, took part in some battles, and was wounded. He afterwards entered the Methodist Episcopal ministry, '70; studied biblical criticism to answer sceptics, and his own faith gave way. He left the Church in March, '83, and started the *Independent Pulpit* at Waco, Texas, in which he publishes bold Freethought articles. He rejects all supernaturalism, and has written *The Bible, What Is It? Studies in Theology, The Bible Against Itself*, etc.

Shelley (Percy Bysshe), English poet, b. Field Place (Sussex), 4 Aug. 1792. From Eton, where he refused to fag, he went to Oxford. Here he published a pamphlet on the necessity of Atheism, for which he was expelled the University. His father, Sir Timothy Shelley, also forbade him his house. He went to London, wrote *Queen Mab*, and met Miss Westbrook, whom, in 1811, he married. After two children had been born, they separated. In '16 Shelley learned that his wife had drowned herself. He now claimed the custody of his children, but, in March, '17, Lord Eldon decided against him, largely on account of his opinions. Shelley had previously written *A Letter to Lord Ellenborough*, indignantly attacking the sentence the judge passed on D. I. Eaton for publishing Paine's *Age of Reason*. On 30 Dec. '16, Shelley married Mary, daughter of William Godwin and Mary Woolstonecraft. In '18, fearing their son might also be taken from him, he left England never to return. He went to Italy, where he met Byron, composed *The Cenci*, the *Witch of Atlas, Prometheus Unbound, Adonais*,

Epipsychidion, Hellas, and many minor poems of exquisite beauty, the glory of our literature. He was drowned in the Bay of Spezzia, 8 July, 1822. Shelley never wavered in his Freethought. Trelawny, who knew him well, says he was an Atheist to the last.

Siciliani (Pietro), Professor in the University of Bologna b. Galatina, 19 Sep. 1835, author of works on *Positive Philosophy, Socialism, Darwinism,* and *Modern Sociology,* '79; and *Modern Psychogeny,* with a preface by J. Soury, '82. Died 28 Dec. '85.

Sidney (Algernon), English Republican, and second son of Robert, Earl of Leicester, b. 1617. He became a colonel in the Army of Parliament, and a member of the House of Commons. On the Restoration he remained abroad till 1677, but being implicated in the Rye House Plot, was condemned by Judge Jeffreys to be executed on Tower Hill, 7 Dec. 1678.

Sierebois (P.) See Boissière.

Siffle (Alexander François), Dutch writer, b. Middleburg, 11 May, 1801. Studied law at Leyden, and became notary at Middleburg. He wrote several poems and works of literary value, and contributed to *de Dageraad.* He was a man of wide reading. Died at Middleburg, 7 Oct. 1872.

Sigward (M.), b. St. Leger-sur-Dhume, France, 15 April, 1817. An active French democrat and Freethinker, and compiler of a Republican calendar. He took part in the International Congress at Paris '89, and is one of the editors of *Le Danton.*

Simcox (Edith), author of *Natural Law* in the English and Foreign Philosophical Library; also wrote on the Design Argument in the *Fortnightly Review,* 1872, under the signature " H. Lawrenny."

Simon de Tournai a Professor at Paris University early in the XIIIth century. He said that " Three seducers," Moses, Jesus, and Muhammad, " have mystified mankind with their doctrines." He was said to have been punished by God for his impiety.

Simon (Richard), learned French theological critic, b. Dieppe, 15 May, 1638. Brought up by the Congregation of the Oratory, he distinguished himself by bold erudition. His *Critical History of the Old Testament,* 1678, was suppressed by Parliament.

He followed it with a *Critical History of the New Testament*, which was also condemned. Died at Dieppe, 11 April, 1712.

Simonis.—A physician, b. at Lucques and persecuted in Poland for his opinions given in an Atheistic work, entitled *Simonis Religio*, published at Cracow, 1588.

Simpson (George), of the Glasgow Zetetic Society, who in 1838 put forward a *Refutation of the Argument a priori for the being and attributes of God*, in reply to Clarke and Gillespie. He used the signature " Antitheos." Died about 1844.

Sjoberg (Walter), b. 24 May, 1865, at Borgo (Finland), lives near Helsingfors, and took part in founding the Utilistiska Samfundet there. During the imprisonment of Mr. Lennstrand he gave bold lectures at Stockholm.

Skinner (William), of Kirkcaldy, Deist, author of *Thoughts on Superstition or an attempt to Discover Truth* (Cupar, 1822), was credited also with *Jehovah Unveiled or the God of the Jews*, published by Carlile in 1819

Slater (Thomas), English lecturer, b. 15 Sept. 1820. Has for many years been an advocate of Secularism and Co-operation. He was on the Town Council of Bury, and now resides at Leicester.

Slenker (Elmina), née DRAKE, American reformer, b. of Quaker parents, 23 Dec. 1827. At fourteen, she began notes for her work, *Studying the Bible*, afterwards published at Boston, '70 ; she conducts the Children's Corner in the *Boston Investigator*, and has contributed to most of the American Freethought papers. Has written *John's Way* ('78), Mary Jones, *The Infidel Teacher* ('85), *The Darwins* ('79), Freethought stories. Resides at Snowville, Virginia.

Smith (Gerritt), American reformer, b. Utica (N.Y.), 6 March, 1799, graduated at Hamilton's College. He was elected to Congress in 1850, but only served one Session. Though of a wealthy slaveholding family, he largely devoted his fortune to the Anti-Slavery cause. In religion, originally a Presbyterian, he came to give up all dogmas, and wrote *The Religion of Reason*, '61, and *Nature the base of a Free Theology*, '67. Died, New York, 28 Dec. 1874.

Snoilsky (Karl Johan Gustav), *Count*, Swedish poet, b. Stockholm, 8 Sept. 1841. Studied at Upsala, '60. Displays

his Freethought in his poems published under the name of
" Sventröst."

Socinus [Ital. Sozzini] (Fausto), anti-trinitarian, b Siena,
5 Dec 1539. He adopted the views of his uncle, Laelio,
(1525–1562), and taught them with more boldness. In 1574 he
went to Switzerland, and afterwards to Poland, where he made
many converts, and died 3 March, 1604.

Sohlman (Per August Ferdinand), Swedish publicist, b.
Nerika, 1824. He edited the *Aftonbladet*, of Stockholm, from
'57, and was a distinguished Liberal politician. Died at
Stockholm, 1874.

Somerby (Charles Pomeroy), American publisher, b. 1843.
Has issued many important Freethought works, and is business
manager of the *Truthseeker*.

Somerset (Edward Adolphus SAINT MAUR), 12th *Duke of*,
b. 20 Dec. 1804. Educated at Eton and Oxford. He married
a daughter of Thomas Sheridan. Sat as M.P. for Totnes,
'34–35, and was Lord of the Treasury, '35–39, and First Lord of
the Admiralty, '59–66. In '72 he startled the aristocratic world
by a trenchant attack on orthodoxy entitled *Christian Theology
and Modern Scepticism.* He also wrote on mathematics and on
Monarchy and Democracy. Died 28 Nov. 1885.

Soury (Auguste Jules), French philosopher, b. Paris, 1842.
In '65 he became librarian at the Bibliothèque Nationale. He
has contributed to the *Revue des Deux Mondes, Revue Nouvelle*,
and other journals, and has published important works on
The Bible and Archæology, '72 : *Historical Studies on Religions,* '77 ;
Essays of Religious Criticism, '78 ; *Jesus and the Gospels,* '78, a
work in which he maintains that Jesus suffered from cerebral
affection, and which has been translated into English, together
with an essay on *The Religion of Israel* from his *Historical
Studies. Studies of Psychology,* '79, indicated a new direction in
M. Soury's Freethought. He has since written *A Breviary of
the History of Materialism,* '80 ; *Naturalist Theories of the World
and of Life in Antiquity,* '81 ; *Natural Philosophy,* '82 ; *Contemporary Psychological Doctrines,* '83. He has translated Noeldeke's
Literary History of the Old Testament, '73 ; Haeckel's *Proofs of
Evolution,* '79 ; and Preyer's *Elements of General Physiology,* '84.

Southwell (Charles), English orator, b. London, 1814. He served with the British Legion in Spain, and became an actor and social missionary. In Nov. '41 he started *The Oracle of Reason* at Bristol, for an article in which on " The Jew Book' he was tried for blasphemy 14 Jan. '42, and after an able defence sentenced to twelve months' imprisonment, and a fine of one hundred pounds. After coming out he edited the *Lancashire Beacon.* He also lectured and debated both in England and Scotland ; wrote *Christianity Proved Idolatry*, '44 ; *Apology for Atheism*, '46 : *Difficulties of Christianity*, '48 : *Super-stition Unveiled; The Impossibility of Atheism,* which he held on the ground that Theism was unproved, and *Another Fourpenny Wilderness*, in answer to G. J. Holyoake's criticism of the same. He also wrote about '45, *Confessions of a Freethinker*, an account of his own life. In '56 he went to New Zealand, and died at Auckland 7 Aug. 1860.

Souverain (N.), French author of *Platonism Unveiled* 1700, a posthumous work. He had been a minister in Poitou and was deposed on account of his opinions.

Sozzini See Socinus,

Spaink (Pierre François), Dutch physician, b. Amsterdam, 13 Dec. 1862, and studied at the city, wrote for a time on *De Dageraad*, with the pen names " A. Th Eist." and "F.R.S." Has translated Romanes' *Scientific Evidences of Organic Evo-lution.*

Spaventa (Bertrando), Italian philosopher, b. 1817. Since '61 he has been professor of philosophy at Naples. Has written upon the Philosophy of Kant, Gioberti, Spinoza. Hegel, etc. Died 1888.

Specht (Karl August), Dr. German writer, b. Lhweina, 2 July, 1845. Has been for many years editor of *Menschenthum* at Gotha, and has written on *Brain and Soul, Theology and Science* and a *Popular History of the Worlds Development*, which has gone through several editions. Dr. Specht is a leading member of the German Freethinkers' Union.

Spencer (Herbert), English philosopher, b. Derby, 1820. He was articled to a civil engineer, but drifted into literature. He wrote in the *Westminster Review*, and at the house of Dr. Chap-man met Mill, Lewes and " George Eliot." His first important work was *Social Statistics*, '51. Four years later appeared his *Principles of Psychology*, which with First Principles, '62; Principles of Biology, '64: Principles of Sociology, '76-85, and Data of Ethics, '79, form part of his "Synthetic Philosophy" in which he applies the doctrines of evolution to the phenomena of mind and society no less than to animal life. He has also published *Essays*, 3 vols, '58-74; a work on *Education* '61; *Recent Discussions on Science, Philosophy and Morals*, '71; *The Study of Sociology*, '72; *Descriptive Sociology*, '72-86, an immense work compiled under his direction. Also papers directed against Socialism; *The Coming Slavery*, '84; and *Man and the State*, '85, and has contributed many articles to the best reviews.

Spinosa (Baruch), Pantheistic philosopher, b. of Jewish parents, Amsterdam, 24 Nov. 1632. He early engaged in the study of theology and philosophy, and, making no secret of his doubts, was excommunicated by the Synagogue, 27 July, 1656. About the same time he narrowly escaped death by a fanatic's dagger. To avoid persecution, he retired to Rhinsburg, and devoted himself to philosophy, earning his living by polishing lenses. About 1670 he settled at the Hague, where he remained until his death. In 1670 he issued his *Tractatus Theologico-politicus*, which made a great outcry; and for more than a century this great thinker, whose life was gentle and self-denying, was stigmatized as an atheist, a monster, and a blasphemer. A re-action followed, with Lessing and Goethe, upon whom he had great influence. Though formerly stigmatized as an atheist, Spinosa is now generally recognised as among the greatest philosophers. He died in poverty at the Hague, 21 Feb. 1677. His *Ethics* was published with his *Opera Posthuma*. The bi-centenary of his death was celebrated there by an eloquent address from M. Rénan.

Spooner (Lysander), American writer, b. Athol (Mass.), 19 Jan. 1808. His first pamphlet was *A Deist's Reply to the alleged Supernatural Evidences of Christianity*. He started letter-carrying from Boston to New York, but was overwhelmed with prosecutions. He published many works against slavery, and in favor or Individualism. Died at Boston, 14 May, 1887.

Stabili (Francesco), see Cecco' d'Ascoli.

Stamm (August Theodor), German Humanist, wrote *The*

Religion of Action, translated into English, 1860. After the events of '48, he came to England, went to America, Aug. '54.

Standring (George), English lecturer and writer, b. 18 Oct. 1855, was for some years chorister at a Ritualistic Church, but discarded theology after independent inquiry in '73. He became hon. sec. of the National Secular Society about '75, resigning on appointment of paid sec., was auditor and subsequently vice-president. Started *Republican Chronicle*, April, 1875, this was afterwards called *The Republican*, and in Sept. '88 *The Radical*. He is sec. of the London Secular Federation, and has contributed to the *National Reformer, Freethinker, Progress, Our Corner, Reynolds's* and *Pall Mall Gazette*. His brother, Sam., b. 27 July, 1853, is also an active Freethinker.

Stanley (F. Lloyd), American author of *An Outline of the Future Religion of the World* (New York and London, 1884), a Deistic work in which he criticises preceding religions.

Stanton (Elizabeth, née **Cady**), American reformer, b. Johnstone, New York, 12 Nov. 1815. A friend of Ernestine Rose and Lucretia Mott, she was associated with them in the Anti-Slavery and the Woman's Rights crusades, of which last the first convention was held at her home in Seneca Falls, July '48. She edited with her friends, Susan Anthony and Parker Pilsbury, *The Revolution*, and is joint author of *History of Woman's Suffrage* ('80-86). She has written in the *North American Review* notably on "Has Christianity Benefited Woman," May, 1885.

Stap (A.), author of *Historic Studies on the origins of Christianity*. Bruxelles, 1864, and *The Immaculate Conception*, 1869.

Starcke (Carl Nicolay), Dr. and teacher of philosophy in the University of Copenhagen, b. 29 March, 1858. A decided disciple of Feuerbach on whom he published a dissertation in '83. This able Monograph on the whole doctrine of the German philosopher was in '85, published in a German edition. Prof. Starcke has since published in the "International Scientific Series," a work on *The Primitive Family*, in which he critically surveys the views of Lubbock, Maine, McLennan, etc. He is now engaged on a work on *Ethics* based on the doctrines of Ludwig Feuerbach.

Stecchetti (Lorenzo). See Guerini (O.)

Stefanoni (Luigi). Italian writer and publicist, b. Milan, 1842. In '59, his first Romance, *The Spanish in Italy* was suppressed by the Austrians. He joined Garibaldi's volunteers and contributed to *Unita Italiana*. In '66, he founded at Milan the Society of Freethinkers and the organ *Il Libero Pensiero*, in which he wrote *A critical History of Superstition*, afterwards published separately 2 vols. '69. He also compiled a Philosophical Dictionary, '73-75; and wrote several romances as *L'Inferno, The Red and Black of Rome*, etc. He translated Büchner's *Force and Matter*. Morin's *Jesus réduit*, La Mettrie's *Man-machine*. Letourneau's *Physiology of the Passions*, and Feuerbach's *Essence of Religion*.

Steinbart (Gotthelf, Samuel), German rationalist, b. Züllichau, 21 Sept. 1738. Brought up in a pietist school, he became a Freethinker through reading Voltaire. In '74, he became Prof. of Philosophy at Frankfurt-on-the-Oder, and wrote a *System of Pure Philosophy*, '78. Died, 3 Feb. 1809.

Steinthal (Hajjim), German philologist, b. Gröbzig, 16 May, 1823, has written many works on language and mythology.

Steller (Johann), Advocate at Leipsic, published an heretical work, *Pilatus liberatoris Jesu subsidio defensus*, Dresden, 1674.

"**Stendhal** (M. de)," Pseud, see Beyle (M. H.)

Stephen (*Sir* James FitzJames), English judge and writer, b. London, 3 March, 1829. Studied at Cambridge, graduated B.A. '52, and was called to the bar in '54. He was counsel for the Rev. Rowland Williams when tried for heresy for writing in *Essays and Reviews*, and his speech was reprinted in '62. He wrote in the *Saturday Review*, and reprinted *Essays by a Barrister*. From Dec. '69, to April, '72, he was Legal Member of the Indian Council, and in '79 was appointed judge. He is author of *Liberty, Equality, and Fraternity*, '73, and some valuable legal works. He has written much in the *Nineteenth Century*, notably on the Blasphemy Law '83, and Modern Catholicism, Oct. '87.

Stephen (Leslie), English man of letters, brother of preceding, b. London, 28 Nov. 1832. Educated at Cambridge. where he graduated M.A., '57. He married a daughter of

Thackeray, and became editor of the *Cornhill Magazine* from
'71-82, when he resigned to edit the *Dictionary of National
Biography*. Mr. Stephen also contributed to *Macmillan*, the
Fortnightly, and other reviews. Some of his boldest writing
is found in *Essays on Freethinking and Plainspeaking*, '73. He
has also written an important *History of English Thought in the
Eighteenth Century*, '76, dealing with the Deistic movement, and
The Science of Ethics, '82, besides many literary works.

Stern (J.), *Rabbiner*, German writer, b. of Jewish parents,
Liederstetten (Wurtemburg), his father being Rabbi of the
town. In '58 he went to the Talmud High School, Presburg
and studied the Kabbalah, which he intended to translate into
German. To do this he studied Spinoza, whose philosophy
converted him. In '63 he graduated at Stuttgart. He founded
a society, to which he gave discourses collected in his first
book, *Gottesflamme*, '72. His *Old and New Faith Among the Jews*,
'78, was much attacked by the orthodox Jews. In *Women in
the Talmud*, 79, he pleaded for mixed marriages. He has also
written *Jesus as a Jewish Reformer*, *The Egyptian Religion and
Positivism*, and *Is the Pentateuch by Moses?* In '81 he went to live
at Stuttgart, where he has translated Spinoza's Ethics, and is
engaged on a history of Spinozism.

"**Sterne** (Carus)"; pseud. See Krause (E).

Stevens (E. A.), of Chicago, late secretary of American Secular
Union, b. 8 June, 1846. Author of *God in the State*, and contributor to the American Freethought journals.

Stewart (John), commonly called Walking Stewart, b.
London before 1750. Was sent out in 1763 as a writer to
Madras. He walked through India, Africa, and America. He
was a Materialist. Died in London, 20 Feb. 1822.

"**Stirner** (Max)." See Schmidt (Kaspar).

Stosch (Friedrich Wilhelm), called also Stoss (Johann
Friedrich), b. Berlin, 1646, and studied at Frankfort-on-the-
Oder. In 1692 he published a little book, *Concordia rationis et
fidei*, Amst. [or rather Berlin]. It was rigorously suppressed,
and the possession of the work was threatened with a penalty
of five hundred thalers. Lange classes him with German Spi-
nozists, and says "Stosch curtly denies not only the inma-
teriality, but also the immortality of the soul." Died 1704.

Stout (*Sir* Robert), New Zealand statesman, b. Lerwick (Shetland Isles), 1845. He became a pupil teacher, and in '63 left for New Zealand. In '67 he began the study of the law, was elected to the General Assembly in '75, and became Attorney-General in March, '78. He has since been Minister of Education of the Colony.

Strange (Thomas Lumsden), late Madras Civil Service, and for many years a judge of the High Court, Madras. A highly religious man, and long an Evangelical Christian, he joined the Plymouth Brethren, and ended in being a strong, and then weak Theist, and always an earnest advocate of practical piety in life and conduct, and a diligent student and writer. When judge, he sentenced a Brahmin to death, and sought to bring the prisoner " to Jesus." He professed himself influenced, but at the gallows " he proclaimed his trust to be in Rama and not in Christ." This set the judge thinking. He investigated Christianity's claims, and has embodied the result in his works. *The Bible, Is it the Word of God?* '71 ; *The Speaker's Commentary Reviewed,* '71 ; *The Development of Creation on the Earth,* '74 ; *The Legends of the Old Testament,* '74 ; and *The Sources and Development of Christianity,* '75. A friend of T. Scott and General Forlong, he died at Norwood, 4 Sept. 1884.

Strauss (David Friedrich), German critic, b. Ludwigsburg (Wurtemburg), 27 Jan. 1808. He studied Theology at Tübengen, was ordained in '30, and in '32 became assistant-teacher. His *Life of Jesus Critically Treated,* '35, in which he shows the mythical character of the Gospels, aroused much controversy, and he was deprived of his position. In '39 the Zürich Government appointed him professor of church history, but they were obliged to repeal their decision before the storm of Christian indignation. His next important work was on the *Christian Doctrines* (2 vols.), '40 In '47 he wrote on *Julian the Apostle,* and in '58 an account of the *Life and Time of Ulrich von Hutten.* He prepared a *New Life of Christ for the German People,* '64, followed by the *Christ of the Creeds* and the *Jesus of History.* In '70 he published his lectures on *Voltaire,* and two years later his last work *The Old Faith and the New,* in which he entirely breaks not only with Christianity but with the belief in a personal God and immortality. A devoted servant of truth, his mind was always advancing. He died at his native place, 8 Feb. 1874.

Strindberg (Johan August), Swedish writer, known as the Scandinavian Rousseau, b. Stockholm, 22 Jan. 1849. He has published many prominent rationalistic works, as *The Red Chamber* and *Marriage*. The latter was confiscated. He is one of the most popular poets and novelists in Sweden.

Stromer (Hjalmar), Swedish astronomer, b. 1849. He lectured on astronomy and published several works thereon, and also wrote *Confessions of a Freethinker*. Died 1887.

Strozzi (Piero), Italian general in the service of France, b. of noble Florentine family 1500. Intended for the Church he abandoned it for a military career, and was created marshal of France by Henry II. about 1555. He was killed at the siege of Thionville, 20 June 1558, and being exhorted by the Duc de Guise to think of Jesus, he calmly declared himself an Atheist.

Suard (Jean Baptiste Antione), French writer, b. Besançon, 15 Jan, 1734. He became a devoted friend of Baron d'Holbach and of Garat, and corresponded with Hume and Walpole. He wrote *Miscellanies of Literature*, etc. He had the post of censor of theatres. Died at Paris 20 July, 1817.

Sue (Marie Joseph, called Eugène), French novelist, b. Paris, 10 Dec. 1804. He wrote many romances, of which *The Mysteries of Paris* and *The Wandering Jew*, '42-45, were the most popular. In '50 he was elected deputy and sat at the extreme left, but was exiled by the *coup d'etat*. He died as a Freethinker at Annecy (Savoy), 3 July 1857.

Sullivan (J.), author of *Search for Deity*, an inquiry as to the origin of the conception of God (London, 1859).

Sully Prudhomme (René François Armand), French poet, b. Paris, 16 March 1839. He studied law but took to poetry and has published many volumes. In '78 he was made Chevalier of Honor, and in '82 member of the Academy. His poems are of pessimistic cast, and full of delicacy of philosophical suggestion.

Sunderland (La Roy), American author and orator, b. Exeter (Rhode Island), 18 May, 1803. He became a Methodist preacher and was prominent in the temperance and anti-slavery movements. He came out of the Church as the great bulwark of slavery and opposed Christianity during the forty years preceding his death. He wrote many works against slavery and Pathetism, '47; *Book of Human Nature*, '53, and *Ideology*, 3 vols., '86-9. Died in Quincy (Mass.) 15 May, 1885.

Suttner (Bertha von), *Baroness*, Austrian author of *Inventory of a Soul*, 1886, and of several novels.

Sutton (Henry S.), anonymous author of *Quinquenergia; or, Proposals for a New Practical Theology*, and *Letters from a Father to a Son on Revealed Religion.*

Swinburne (Algernon Charles), English poet and critic. b. London, 5 April, 1837, educated at Oxford, and went to Florence, where he spent some time with W. S. Landor. *Atalanta in Calydon*, a splendid reproduction of Greek tragedy, first showed his genius. *Poems and Ballads*, 1866, evinced his unconventional lyrical passion and power, and provoked some outcry. In his *Songs before Sunrise*, 1871, he glorifies Freethought and Republicanism, with unsurpassed wealth of diction and rhythm. Mr. Swinburne has put forward many other volumes of melodious and dramatic poems, and also essays, studies, and prose miscellanies.

Symes (Joseph), English lecturer and writer, b. Portland, 29 Jan. 1841, of pious Methodist parents. In '64 he offered himself as candidate for the ministry, and was sent to the Wesleyan College, Richmond, and in '67 went on circuit as preacher. Having come to doubt orthodoxy, he resigned in '72, preached his first open Freethought lecture at Newcastle, 17 Dec. '76. Had several debates, wrote *Philosophic Atheism, Man's Place in Nature, Hospitals not of Christian Origin, Christianity a Persecuting Religion, Blows at the Bible*, etc. He contributed to the *Freethinker*, and was ready to conduct it during Mr. Foote's imprisonment. He went to Melbourne, Dec. '83, and there established the *Liberator*, and has written *Life and Death of My Religion*, '84; *Christianity and Slavery, Phallic Worship*, etc.

Symonds (John Addington), English poet and author, b. Bristol, 5 Oct. 1840, educated at Harrow and Oxford, and was elected in '62 to a Fellowship at Magdalen College, which he vacated on his marriage. His chief work is on the *Renaissance in*

Italy, 7 vols., completed in '86. He has also written critical sketches, studies, and poems. Ill health compels his living abroad

Taine (Hippolyte Adolphe), D.C.L., brilliant French man of letters, b. Vouziers, 21 April. 1828. Educated at the College Bourbon (now the Condorcet Lyceum), in '53 he took the degree of Doctor of Letters. In '56 appears his *French Philosophers of the Nineteenth Century,* in which he sharply criticised the spiritualist and religious school. He came to England and studied English Literature; his Hand History of which was sent in for the Academy prize, '63, but rejected on the motion of Bishop Dupanloup on account of its materialist opinions. Also wrote on *English Positivism,* a study of J. S. Mill. In '71 Oxford made him D.C.L., and in Nov. '78, he was elected to the French Academy; his latest work is *The Origins of Contemporary France.*

Talandier (Alfred), French publicist, b. Limoges, 7 Sept. 1828. After entering the bar, he became a socialist and took part in the revolution of '48. Proscribed after 12 Dec. he came to England, started trades unions and co-operation, translated Smiles's Self-Help, and wrote in the *National Reformer,* Returned to Paris in '70 and became professor at the Lycée Henri IV. In '74 he was deprived of his chair, but elected on the Municipal council of Paris, and two years later chosen as deputy, and was re-elected in '81. In '83 he published a *Popular Rabelais* and has written in *Our Corner* on that grea Freethinker.

Taubert (A.), the maiden name of Dr. Hartmann's first wife She wrote *The Pessimists and their Opponents,* 1873.

Taule (Ferdinand), M.D., of Strassburg, author of *Notions on the Nature and Properties of Organised Matter.* Paris, 1866.

Taurellus (Nicolaus), German physician and philosopher, b. Montbéhard, 26 Nov. 1547, studied medicine at Tübingen and Basle. For daring to think for himself, and asking how the Aristotlelian doctrine of the eternity of the world could be reconciled with the dogma of creation, he was stigmatised as an atheist. Wrote many works in Latin, the principal of which is *Philosophiæ Triumphans,* 1573. He died of the plague 28 Sept. 1606.

Taylor (Robert), ex-minister, orator, and critic, b. Edmonton 18 Aug. 1784. In 1805 he walked Guy's and St. Thomas's Hospital, and became M.R.C.S., 1807. Persuaded to join the Church, he entered St. John's, Cambridge, Oct. 1809, in Jan. '13 graduated B.A., and soon after took holy orders. He was curate at Midhurst till '18, when he first became sceptical through discussions with a tradesman. He preached a sermon on Jonah which astonished his flock, and resigned. He then went to Dublin and published *The Clerical Review* and started "The Society of Universal Benevolence." In '24 he came to London and started "The Christian Evidence Society," and delivered discourses with discussion; also edited the *Phil_alethian*. In '27 he was indicted for blasphemy, tried Oct. 24, after an able defence he was found guilty, and on 7 Feb. '28 sentenced to one year's imprisonment in Oakham Gaol. Here he wrote his *Syntagma* on the Evidences of Christianity, and his chief work, *The Diegesis*, being a discovery of the origins, evidences, and early history of Christianity. He also contributed a weekly letter to *The Lion*, which R. Carlile started on his behalf. On his liberation they both went on "an infidel mission" about the country, and on May 30 the Rotunda, Blackfriars, was taken, where Taylor attired in canonicals delivered the discourses published in *The Devil's Pulpit*. He was again prosecuted, and on 4 July, '31, was sentenced to two year's imprisonment. He was badly treated in gaol, and soon after coming out married a wealthy lady and retired. Died at Jersey, 5 June, 1844.

Taylor (Thomas), known as "The Platonist," b. London, 1758. He devoted his life to the elucidation and propagation of the Platonic philosophy. He translated the works of Plato, Aristotle, Porphyry, five books of Plotinus, six books of Proclus, Gamblichus on the Mysteries, Arguments of Celsus taken from Origen, Arguments of Julian against the Christians, Orations of Julian, etc. He is said to have been so thorough a Pagan that he sacrificed a bull to Zeus. Died in Walworth, 1 Nov. 1835.

Taylor (William), of Norwich, b. 7 Nov. 1765. He formed an acquaintance with Southey, with whom he corresponded. His translations from the German, notably Lessing's *Nathan* *the Wise*, brought him some repute. He also wrote a *Survey of German Poetry* and *English Synonyms*, 1830. He edited the Norwich *Iris*, 1802, which he made the organ of his political and religious views. In '10 he published anonymously *A Letter Concerning the Two First Chapters of Luke*, also entitled *Who was the Father of Jesus Christ?* 1810, in which he argues that Zacharias was the father of Jesus Christ. Also wrote largely in the *Monthly Review*, replying therein to the Abbé Barruel; and the *Critical Review* when edited by Fellowes, in which he gave an account of the rationalism of Paulus. Died at Norwich, 5 March, 1836.

Tchernychewsky (N. G.) See Chernuishevsky.

"**Tela** (Josephus)," the Latinised name of Joseph Webbe who in 1818 edited the *Philosophical Library*, containing the Life and Morals of Confucius, Epicurus, Isoscrates, Mahomet, etc., and other pieces. Webbe is also thought to have been concerned in the production of *Ecce Homo*, '13. Cushing, in his *Initials and Pseudonyms*, refers Tela to " Joseph Webb," 1735-87 ; an American writer ; Grand Master of Freemasons in America ; died in Boston." I am not satisfied that this is the same person.

Telesio (Bernardino), Italian philosopher, b. of noble family at Cosenza, 1509. He studied at Padua, and became famous for his learning, optical discoveries, and new opinions in philosophy. He wrote in Latin *On the Nature of Things according to Proper Principles*, 1565. He opposed the Aristotleian doctrine in physics, and employed mathematical principles in explaining nature, for which he was prosecuted by the clergy. He died Oct. 1588. His works were placed in the *Index*, but this did not prevent their publication at Venice, 1590.

Telle (Reinier), or Regnerus Vitellius, Dutch Humanist, b. Zierikzee, 1578. He translated Servetus *On the Errors of the Trinity*, published 1620. Died at Amsterdam, 1618.

Testa (Giacinto), of Messina, Italian author of a curious *Storia di Gesù di Nazareth*, 1870, in which he maintains that Jesus was the son of Guiseppe Pandera, a Calabrian of Brindisi.

Thaer (Albrecht Daniel). German agriculturist, b. Celle, 14 May, 1752. Studied at Gottingen, and is said to have inspired Lessing's work on *The Education of the Human Race* Died 28 Oct. 1828.

Theodorus of Cyrene, a Greek philosopher, whose opinions resembled those of Epicurus. He was banished fer Atheism from his native city. He resided at Athens about 312 B.C. When threatened with crucifixion, he said it mattered little whether he rotted in the ground or in the air.

Theophile de Viau, French satiric poet, b. Clerac, 1590. For the alleged publication of *Le Parnasse Satyriques*, he was accused of Atheism, condemned to death, and burnt in effigy. He fled, and was received by the Duc de Montmorency at Chantilly, where he died, 25 Sept. 1626.

Thompson (Daniel Greenleaf), American author of works on *The Problem of Evil*, '87 ; *The Religious Sentiments*, etc. He is President of the Nineteenth Century Club.

Thomson (Charles Otto), Captain, b. Stockholm, 3 Jan. 1833. Went to sea in '49 and became a merchant captain in '57, and was subsequently manager of the Eskilstuna gas works. At Eskilstuna he started a Utilitarian Society in '88, of which he is president. He has done much to support Mr. Lennstrand in his Freethought work in Sweden; has translated articles by Ingersoll, Foote and others, and has lectured on behalf of the movement. He shares in the conduct of *Fritänkaren*.

Thomson (James), Pessimistic poet, b. Port Glasgow, 23 Nov. 1834. Educated at the Caledonian Asylum, London, he became a schoolmaster in the army, where he met Mr. Bradlaugh, whom he afterwards assisted on the *National Reformer*. To this paper he contributed many valuable essays, translations, and poems, including his famous " City of Dreadful Night," the most powerful pessimistic poem in the English language, (April, '74, afterwards published with other poems in '80). " Vane's Story " with other poems was issued in '81, and " A Voice from the Nile," and "Shelley" (privately printed in '84). Thomson also contributed to the *Secularist* and *Liberal*, edited by his friend Foote, who has published many of his articles in a volume entitled *Satires and Profanities*, which includes " The Story of a Famous Old Jewish Firm," also published separately. Thomson employed much of his genius in the service of Free-thought. Died 3 June, 1882.

Thomson (William), of Cork. A disciple of Bentham, and author of *The Distribution of Wealth*, 1824; *Appeal for Women*, '25; *Labor Reward*, '27, and in the *Co-operative Magazine*.

Thorild (Thomas), or THORÉN, Swedish writer. b. Bohuslau, 18 April, 1759. In 1775 he studied at Lund, and in 1779 went to Stockholm, and published many poems and miscellaneous pieces in Swedish, Latin, German, and English, in which he wrote *Cromwell*, an epic poem. In 1786 he wrote *Common Sense on Liberty*, with a view of extending the liberty of the press. He was a partisan of the French Revolution, and for a political work was imprisoned and exiled. He also wrote a *Sermon of Sermons*, attacking the clergy, and a work maintaining the rights of women. Died at Greifswald; 1 Oct. 1808. He was a man far in advance of his time, and is now becoming appreciated.

Thulie (Jean Baptiste Henri), French physician and anthropologist, b. Bordeaux, 1832. In '56 he founded a journal, "Realism." In '66 he published a work on *Madness and the Law*. He contributed to *La Pensée Nouvelle*, defending the views of Büchner. He has written an able study, *La Femme*, Woman, published in '85. M. Thulie has been President of the Paris Municipal Council.

Tiele (Cornelis Petrus), Dutch scholar, b. Leyden, 16 Dec. 1830. Although brought up in the Church, his works all tell in the service of Freethought, and he has shown his liberality of views in editing the poems of Genestet together with his life, '68. He has written many articles on comparative religion, and two of his works have been translated into English, viz., *Outlines of the History of Religion*, a valuable sketch of the old faiths, fourth ed. '88; and *Comparative History of the Egyptian and Mesopotamian Religions*, '82.

Tillier (Claude), French writer, b. of poor parents, Clamecy, 11 April, 1801. He served as a conscript, and wrote some telling pamphlets directed against tyranny and superstition, and some novels, of which we note *My Uncle Benjamin*. Died at Nevers, 12 Oct. 1844. His works were edited by F. Pyat.

Tindal (Matthew), LL.D., English Deist, b. Beer-ferris, Devon, 1657. Educated at Oxford, and at first a High Churchman, he was induced to turn Romanist in the reign of

James II., but returned to Protestantism and wrote *The Rights of the Christian Church.* This work was much attacked by the clergy, who even indicted the vendors. A defence which he published was ordered to be burnt by the House of Commons. In 1730 he published *Christianity as Old as the Creation*, to which no less than 150 answers were published. He died 16 Aug. 1733, and a second volume, which he left in MS., was destroyed by order of Gibson, Bishop of London.

Toland (John), Irish writer, b. Redcastle, near Londonderry, 30 Nov. 1669. Educated as a Catholic, he renounced that faith in early youth, went to Edinburgh University, where he became M.A. in 1690, and proceeded to Leyden, studying under Spanheim, and becoming a sceptic. He also studied at Oxford, reading deeply in the Bodleian Library, and became the correspondent of Le Clerc and Bayle. In 1696 he startled the orthodox with his *Christianity not Mysterious*, which was " presented " by the Grand Jury of Middlesex and condemned by the Lower House of Convocation. The work was also burnt at Dublin, Sept. 1697. He wrote a *Life of Milton* (1698), in which, mentioning *Eikon Basilike*, he referred to the "suppositious pieces under the name of Christ, his apostles and other great persons." For this he was denounced by Dr. Blackhall before Parliament. He replied with *Amytor*, in which he gives a catalogue of such pieces. He went abroad and was well received by the Queen of Prussia, to whom he wrote *Letters to Serena* (1704), which, says Lange, " handles the kernel of the whole question of Materialism." In 1709 he published *Adeisidæmon* and *Origines Judaicæ*. In 1718 *Nazarenus*, or Jewish, Gentile and Mahommedan Christianity, in which he gave an account of the Gospel of Barnabus. He also wrote four pieces entitled *Tetradymus* and *Pantheisticon*, which described a society of Pantheists with a liturgy burlesquing that of the Catholics. Toland died with the calmness of a philosopher, at Putney, 11 March, 1722. Lange praises him highly.

Tollemache (*Hon.* Lionel Arthur), b. 1838, son of Baron Tollemache, a friend of C. Austin, of whom he has written. Wrote many articles in *Fortnightly Review*, reprinted (privately) as *Stones of Stumbling*, '84. Has also written *Safe Studies*, '84; *Recollections of Pallison*, '85; and *Mr. Romanes's Catechism*, '87.

Tone (Theobald Wolfe), Irish patriot, b. Dublin, 20 June, 1763. Educated at Trinity College in 1784, he obtained a scholarship in 1786, B.A. He founded the Society of United Irishmen, 1791. Kept relations with the French revolutionists, and in 1796 induced the French Directory to send an expedition against England. He was taken prisoner and committed suicide in prison, dying 19 Nov. 1798.

Topinard (Paul), M.D., French anthropologist, b. Isle-Adam 1830. Editor of the *Revue d'Anthropologie*, and author of a standard work on that subject published in the Library of Contemporary Science.

Toulmin (George Hoggart), M.D., of Wolverhampton. Author of *The Antiquity and Duration of the World*, 1785 ; *The Eternity of the Universe*, 1789 ; the last being republished in 1825.

Tournai (Simon de). See Simon.

Traina (Tommaso), Italian jurist. Author of a work on *The Ethics of Herbert Spencer*, Turin, 1881.

Travis (Henry), Dr., b. Scarborough, 1807. He interested himself in the socialistic aspect of co-operation, and became a friend and literary executor to Robert Owen. In '51—53 he edited *Robert Owen's Journal*. He also wrote on *Effectual Reform, Free Will and Law, Moral Freedom and Causation*, and *A Manual of Social Science*, and contributed to the *National Reformer*. Died 4 Feb. 1884.

Trelawny (Edward John), b. Cornwall, Nov. 1792. Became intimate in Italy with Shelley, whose body he recovered and cremated in August, 1822. He accompanied Byron on his Greek expedition, and married a daughter of a Greek chief. He wrote *Adventures of a Younger Son*, '31 ; and *Records of Shelley, Byron, and the Author*, '78. He died 13 Aug. 1881, and was cremated at Gotha, his ashes being afterwards placed beside those of Shelley. Trelawny was a vehement Pagan despising the creeds and conventions of society. Swinburne calls him " World-wide liberty's lifelong lover."

Trenchard (John), English Deist and political writer, b. Somersetshire, 1669. He studied law, but abandoned it, and was appointed Commissioner of Forfeited Estates in Ireland. In conjunction with Gordon he wrote *Cato's Letters* on civil and

religious liberty, and conducted *The Independent Whig*.   He sat
in the House of Commons as M.P. for Taunton ; he also wrote
the *Natural History of Superstition*, 1709 ; but *La Contagion
Sacree*, attributed to him, is really by d'Holbach.   Died 17 Dec.
1723.

Trevelyan (Arthur), of Tyneholm, Tranent, N.B , a writer
in the *Reasoner* and *National Reformer*.   Published *The Insanity
of Mankind* (Edinburgh, 1850), and some tracts.   He was a
Vice-President of the National Secular Society.   Died at
Tyneholm, 6 Feb. 1878.

Trezza (Gaetano), Italian writer, b. Verona, Dec. 1828.
Was brought up and ordained a priest, and was an eloquent
preacher.   Study led him to resign the clerical profession.   He
has published Confessions of a Sceptic, '78 ; Critical Studies,
'78 ; New Critical Studies, '81.   He is Professor of Literature
at the Institute of High Studies, Florence.   To the first number of the *Revue Internationale* '83, he contributed *Les Dieux s'en
vont*.   He also wrote Religion and Religions, '84 ; and a Monk
on St. Paul.   A study on Lucretius has reached its third
edition, '87.

Tridon (Edme Marie, Gustave), French publicist, b. Chatillon
sur Seine, Burgundy, 5 June, 1841.   Educated by his parents
who were rich. he became a doctor of law but never practised.
In '64 he published in *Le Journal des Ecoles*, his remarkable study
of revolutionary history *Les Hébertistes*.   In May, '65 he founded
with Blanqui, etc., *Le Candide*, the precursor of *La Libre Pensée*,
'66, in both of which the doctrines of materialism were
expounded.   Delegated in '65 to the International Students
Congress at Liége his speech was furiously denounced by
Bishop Dupanloup ; he got more than two years' imprisonment
for articles in *Le Candide* and *La Libre Pensée*, and in Ste Pelagie
contracted the malady which killed him.   While in prison he
wrote the greater part of his work *Du Molochisme Juif*,
critical and philosophical studies of the Jewish religion,
only published in '84.   After 4 Sept. '70, he founded *La Patrie
en Danger*.   In Feb. '71 he was elected deputy to the Bordeaux
Assembly, but resigned after voting against declaration of peace
He then became a member of the Paris Commune, retiring after

the collapse to Brussels where he died 29 Aug. 1871. He received the most splendid Freethinker's funeral witnessed in Belgium.

Truebner (Nicolas), publisher, b. Heidelberg, 17 June, 1817. After serving with Longman and Co., he set up in business, and distinguished himself by publishing works on Freethought, religions, philosophy and Oriental literature. Died London, 30 March, 1884.

Truelove (Edward), English publisher, b. 29 Oct. 1809. Early in life he embraced the views of Robert Owen, and for nine years was secretary of the John Street Institution. In '44 and '45 he threw in his lot with the New Harmony Community, Hampshire. In '52 he took a shop in the Strand, where he sold advanced literature. He published Voltaire's *Philosophical Dictionary* and *Romances*, Paine's complete works, D'Holbach's *System of Nature*, and Taylor's *Syntagma* and *Diegesis*. In '58 he was prosecuted for publishing a pamphlet on *Tyrannicide*, by W. E. Adams, but the prosecution was abandoned. In '78 he was, after two trials, sentenced to four months' imprisonment for publishing R. D. Owen's *Moral Physiology*. Upon his release he was presented with a testimonial and purse of 200 sovereigns.

Trumbull (Matthew M.), American general, a native of London, b. 1826. About the age of twenty he went to America, served in the army in Mexico, and afterwards in the Civil War. General Grant made him Collector of Revenue for Iowa. He held that office eight years, and then visited England. In 1882 he went to Chicago, where he exerted himself on behalf of a fair trial for the Anarchists.

Tschirnhausen (Walthier Ehrenfried), German *Count*, b. 1651. He was a friend of Leibniz and Wolff, and in philosophy a follower of Spinoza, though he does not mention him. Died 1708.

Tucker (Benjamin R.), American writer, b. Dartmouth, Mass., 17 April, 1854. Edits *Liberty*, of Boston.

Turbiglio (Sebastiano), Italian philosopher, b. Chiusa, 7 July, 1642, author of a work on *Spinoza and the Transformation of his Thoughts*, 1875.

Turgeuev (Ivan Sergyeevich), Russian novelist, b. Orel, 28 Oct. 1818. In his novels, *Fathers and Sons* and *Virgin Soil* he has depicted characters of the Nihilist movement. Died at Bougival, near Paris, 3 Sept. 1883.

Turner (William), a surgeon of Liverpool, who, under the name of William Hammon, published an *Answer to Dr. Priestley's Letters to a Philosophical Unbeliever*, 1782, in which he avows himself an Atheist.

Tuuk (Tilia, Van der), Dutch lady, b. Zandt, 27 Nov. 1854. Was converted to Freethought by reading Dekker, and is now one of the editors of *De Dageraad*.

Twesten (Karl), German publicist and writer, b. Krcl, 22 April, 1820. Studied law, '38-41, in Berlin and Heidelberg, and became magistrate in Berlin and one of the founders of the National Liberal Party. Wrote on the religious, political, and social ideas of Asiatics and Egyptians (2 vols.), '72. Died Berlin, 14 Oct. 1870.

Tylor (Edward Burnet), D.C.L., F.R.S., English anthropologist, b. Camberwell, 2 Oct. 1832. He has devoted himself to the study of the races of mankind, and is the first living authority upon the subject. He has wrote *Anahuac*, or Mexico and the Mexicans, '61; *Researches into the Early History of Mankind*, '65; *Primitive Culture*; being researches into the development of mythology, philosophy, religion, art, and custom (2 vols.), '71. In this splendid work he traces religion to animism, the belief in spirits. He has also written an excellent handbook of *Anthropology*, an introduction to the Study of Man and Civilisation, '81; and contributed to the *Encyclopædia Britannica*, as well as to periodical literature. He is President of the Anthropological Society.

Tyndall (John), LL.D., F.R.S., Irish scientist, b. near Carlow, 1820. In '47 he became a teacher in Queenswood College (Hants), and afterwards went to Germany to study. In '56 he went to Switzerland with Professor Huxley, and they wrote a joint work on glaciers. He contributed to the *Fortnightly Review*, notably an article on Miracles and Special Providence, '66. In '72 he went on a lecturing tour in the United States, and two years later was president of the British Association. His address at Belfast made a great stir, and has been published. In addition to other scientific works he has published popular *Fragments of Science*, which has gone through several editions.

Tyrell (Henry). See Church.

Tyssot de Patot (Simon), b. of French family in Delft, 1655. He became professor of mathematics at Deventer. Under the pen name of "Jacques Massé" he published *Voyages and Adventures*, Bordeaux, 1710, a work termed atheistic and scandalous by Reimmann. It was translated into English by S. Whatley, 1733, and has been attributed to Bayle.

Ueberweg (Friedrich), German philosopher, b. Leichlingen 22 Jan. 1826; studied at Göttingen and Berlin, and became Professor of Philosophy at Königsberg, where he died 9 June, 1871. His chief work is a *History of Philosophy*. Lange cites Czolbe as saying "He was in every way distinctly an Atheist and Materialist."

Uhlich (Johann Jacob Marcus Lebericht), German religious reformer, b. Köthen 27 Feb. 1799. He studied at Halle and became a preacher. For his rationalistic views he was suspended in 1847, and founded the Free Congregation at Magdeburg. He wrote numerous brochures defending his opinions. His *Religion of Common Sense* has been translated and published in America. Died at Madgeburg, 23 March, 1872.

Ule (Otto), German scientific writer, b. Lossow 22 Jan. 1820. Studied at Halle and Berlin. In '52 he started the journal *Die Natur*, and wrote many works popularising science. Died at Halle 6 Aug. 1876.

Underwood (Benjamin F.). American lecturer and writer, b. New York 6 July, 1839. Has been a student and a soldier in the Civil War. He fought at Ball's Bluff, Virginia, 21 Oct. '61. was wounded and held prisoner in Richmond for nine months. In '81 he edited the *Index* in conjunction with Mr. Potter, and in '87 started *The Open Court* at Chicago. He has had numerous debates; those with the Rev. J. Marples and O. A. Burgess being published. He has also published *Essays and Lectures, The Religion of Materialism, Influence of Christianity on Civilisation*, etc. His sister, Sara A., has written *Heroines of Freethought*, New York, 1876.

Vacherot (Etienne), French writer, b. Langres, 29 July, 1809. In '39 he replaced Victor Cousin in the Chair of Philosophy at the Sorbonne. For his free opinions expressed in his *Critical History of the School of Alexandria*, a work in three vols. crowned by the Institute, '46-51, he was much attacked by the clergy and at the Empire lost his position. He afterwards wrote *Essays of Critical Philosophy*, '64, and *La Religion*. '69.

Vacquerie (Auguste), French writer, b. Villequier, 1819. A friend of Victor Hugo. He has written many dramas and novels of merit, and was director of *Le Rappel*.

Vaillant (Edouard Marie), French publicist, b. Vierzon, 26 Jan. 1840. Educated at Paris and Germany. A friend of Tridon he took part in the Commune, and in '84 was elected Muncipal Councillor of Paris.

Vairasse (Denis) d'Alais, French writer of the seventeenth century. He became both soldier and lawyer. Author of *Histoire des Sevarambes*, 1677: imaginary travels in which he introduced free opinions and satirised Christianity.

Vale (Gilbert) author, b. London, 1788. He was intended for the church, but abandoned the profession and went to New York, where he edited the *Citizen of the World* and the *Beacon*. He published *Fanaticism; its Source and Influence*, N.Y. 1835, and a *Life of Paine*, '41. Died Brooklyn, N.Y. 17 Aug. 1866.

Valk (T. A. F. van der), Dutch Freethinker, who, after being a Christian missionary in Java, changed his opinions, and wrote in *De Dageraad* between 1860-70, using the pen name of " Thomas."

Valla (Lorenzo), Italian critic, b. Piacenza, 1415. Having hazarded some free opinions respecting Catholic doctrines, he was condemned to be burnt, but was saved by Alphonsus, King of Naples. Valla was then confined in a monastery, but Pope Nicholas V. called him to Rome and gave him a pension. He died there, 1 Aug. 1457.

Vallee (Geoffrey), French martyr, b. Orleans, 1556. He wrote *La Béatitude des Chréstiens ou le Fléo de la Foy*, for which he was accused of blasphemy, and hanged on the Place de Gréve, Paris, 9 Feb. 1574.

Valliss (Rudolph), German author of works on *The Natural History of Gods* (Leip., 1875); *The Eternity of the World*, '75; *Catechism of Human Duty*, '76, etc.

Van Cauberg (Adolphe), Belgian advocate. One of the founders and president of the International Federation of Freethinkers. Died 1886.

Van Effen. See Effen.

Vanini (Lucilio, afterwards JULIUS CÆSAR), Italian philosopher and martyr, b. Taurisano (Otranto), 1585. At Rome and Padua he studied Averroism, entered the Carmelite order, and travelled in Switzerland, Germany, Holland and France making himself admired and respected by his rationalistic opinions. He returned to Italy in 1611, but the Inquisition was on his track and he took refuge at Venice. In 1612 he visited England, and in 1614 got lodged in the Tower. When released he went to Paris and published a Pantheistic work in Latin *On the Admirable Secrets of Nature, the Queen and Goddess of Mortals*. It was condemned by the Sorbonne and burnt, and he fled to Toulouse in 1617; but there was no repose for Freethought. He was accused of instilling Atheism into his scholars, tried and condemned to have his tongue cut out, his body burned and his ashes scattered to the four winds. This was done 19 Feb. 1619. President Gramond, author of *History of France under Louis XIII.*, writes "I saw him in the tumbril a they led him to execution, mocking the Cordelier who had been sent to exhort him to repentance, and insulting our Savior by these impious words. '*He* sweated with fear and weakness, and I die undaunted.'"

Vapereau (Louis Gustave), French man of letters, b. Orleans 4 April, 1819. In '41 he became the secretary of Victor Cousin. He collaborated on the *Dictionnaire des Sciences Philosophiques* and the *Liberté de Penser*, but is best known by his useful *Dictionnaire Universel des Contemporains*. In '70 he was nominated prefect of Cantal, but on account of the violent attacks of the clericals was suspended in '73 and resumed his literary labors, compiling a *Universal Dictionary of Writers*, '76, and *Elements of the History of French Literature*, 1883-85.

Varnhagen von Ense (Karl August Ludwig Philipp), German author, b. Dusseldorf, 21 Feb. 1785. He studied medicine and philosophy, entered the Austrian and Russian armies, and served in the Prussian diplomatic service. He was an intimate friend of Alex. von Humboldt, and shared his

Freethinking opinions. Died in Berlin, 10 Oct. 1858. He vividly depicts the men and events of his time in his *Diary.*

Vauvenargues (Luc de CLAPIERS), Marquis ; French moralist, b. Aix, 6 Aug. 1715. At eighteen he entered the army, and left the service with ruined health in 1743. He published in 1746 an *Introduction to the Knowledge of the Human Mind, followed by Reflections and Maxims,* which was deservedly praised by his friend Voltaire. Died at Paris 28 May, 1747. His work, which though but mildly deistic, was rigorously suppressed, and was reprinted about 1770.

Velthuysen (Lambert), Dutch physician, b. Utrecht, 1622. He wrote many works on theology and philosophy in Latin His works, *De Officio Pastorum* and *De Idolatria et Superstitione* were proceeded against in 1668, but he was let off with a fine. Died 1685.

Venetianer (Moritz), German Pantheist, author of *Der Allgeist,* 1874, and a work on *Schopenhauer as a Scholastic.*

Vereschagin (Vasily), Russian painter, b. Novgorod, 1842 He studied at Paris under Gerome, took part in the Russo-Turkish war, and has travelled widely. The realistic and anti-religious conceptions of his *Holy Family* and *Resurrection* were the cause of their being withdrawn from the Vienna Exhibition in Oct. '85, by order of the archbishop. In his Autobiographical Sketches, translated into English, '87, he shows his free opinions.

Vergniaud (Pierre Victurnien), French Girondist orator, b. Limoges, 31 May, 1759. He studied law, and became an advocate. Elected to the Legislative Assembly in 1791, he also became President of the Convention. At the trial of the King he voted for the appeal to the people, but that being rejected, voted death. With Gensonné and Guadet, he opposed the sanguinary measures of Robespierre, and, being beaten in the struggle, was executed with the Girondins, 31 Oct. 1793. Vergniaud was a brilliant speaker. He said : " Reason thinks, Religion dreams." He had prepared poison for himself, but as there was not enough for his comrades, he resolved to suffer with them.

Verlet (Henri), French founder and editor of a journal,

La Libre Pensée, 1871, and author of a pamphlet on *Atheism and the Supreme Being.*

Verliere (Alfred), French author of a *Guide du Libre-Penseur* (Paris, 1869); collaborated *La Libre Pensée, Rationaliste,* etc. To Bishop Dupanloup's *Atheisme et Peril Social* he replied with *Deisme et Peril Social,* for which he was condemned to several months' imprisonment.

Vermersch (Eugène), French journalist, b. Lille about 1840. Took part in the Commune, and has written on many Radical papers.

Vernes (Maurice), French critic, b. Mauroy, 1845. Has published *Melanges de Critique Religieuse,* and translated from Kuenen and Tiele.

Veron (Eugène), French writer and publicist, b. Paris, 29 May, 1825. He wrote on many journals, founded *La France Republicaine* at Lyons, and *l'Art* at Paris. Besides historical works he has written *L'Esthetique* in the " Library of Contemporary Science," '78; *The Natural History of Religions,* 2 vols., in the Bibliothèque Materialiste, '84; and *La Morale,* '84.

Viardot (Louis), French writer. b. Dijon, 31 July, 1800 came to Paris and became an advocate, but after a voyage in Spain, left the bar for literature, writing on the *Globe National* and *Siècle.* In '41 he founded the *Revue Independante* with " George Sand," and Pierre Leroux. He made translations from the Russian, and in addition to many works on art he wrote *The Jesuits,* '57; *Apology of an Unbeliever,* translated into English, '69, and republished as *Libre Examen,* '71. Died 1883.

Vico (Giovanni Battista), Italian philosopher, b. Naples 1668. He became Professor of Rhetoric in the University of that city, and published a *New Science of the Common Nature of Nations.* 1725, in which he argues that the events of history are determined by immutable laws. It presents many original thoughts. Died Naples, 21 Jan. 1743.

Virchow (Rudolf), German anthropologist, b. Schivelbein Ponnerania, 13 Oct. 1821. Studied medicine at Berlin and became lecturer, member of the National Assembly of '48, and Professor of Pathological Anatomy at Berlin. His *Cellular Pathology,* '58, established his reputation. He was chosen deputy and rose to the leadership of the Liberal opposition. His scientific views are advanced although he opposed the Haeckel in regard to absolute teaching of evolution.

Vischer (Friedrich Theodor), German art critic, b. Ludwigsburg, 30 June, 1807. Was educated for the Church, became a minister, but renounced theology and became professor of and is *Jahrbücher der Gegenwart,* '44, was accused of blasphemy and for his Freethinking opinions he was suspended two years. At the revolution of '48 he was elected to the National Assembly. In '55 he became Professor at Zürich. His work on *Æsthetic,* or the Science of the Beautiful, '46-54, is considered classic. He has also written, *Old and New*, '81, and several anonymous works. Died Gmunden, 14 Sept. 1887.

Vitry (Guarin de) French author of a *Rapid Examination of Christian Dogma*, addressed to the Council of 1869.

Vloten (Johannes van), Dutch writer, b. Kampen, 18 Jan. 1818; studied theology at Leiden and graduated D.D. in '43. He has, however, devoted himself to literature, and produced many works, translating plays of Shakespeare, editing Spinoza, and writing his life—translated into English by A. Menzies. He edited also *De Levensbode*, 1865, etc.

Voelkel (Titus), Dr., German lecturer and writer, b. Wirsitz (Prussian Poland) 14 Dec. 1841. Studied (59-65) theology, natural philosophy, and mathematics, and spent some years in France. He returned '70, and was for ten years employed as teacher at higher schools. Since '80 has been " sprecher " of Freethought associations and since '85 editor of the *Neues Freireligioses Sonntags-Blatt*, at Magdenburg. In '88 he was several times prosecuted for blasphemy and each time acquitted. He represented several German societies at the Paris Congress of Freethinkers, '89.

Voglet (Prosper), Belgian singer, b. Brussels, 1825. He was blinded through his baptism by a Catholic priest, and has in consequence to earn his living as a street singer. His songs, of his own composition, are anti-religious. Many have appeared in *La Tribune du Peuple*, which he edited.

Vogt (Karl), German scientist, b. Giessen, 5 July, 1817, the on of a distinguished naturalist. He studied medicine and became acquainted with Agassiz. In '48 he was elected deputy to the National Assembly. Deprived of his chair and exiled, he became professor of Natural History at Geneva. His lectures on *Man, His Position in Creation and in the History of the Earth*, '63, made a sensation by their endorsement of Darwinism. They were translated into English and published by the Anthropological Society. He has also written a *Manual of Geology, Physiological Letters, Zoological Letters, Blind Faith and Science*, etc., and has contributed to the leading Freethought journals of Germany and Switzerland.

Volkmar (Gustav), Swiss critic, b. Hersfeld, 11 Jan. 1809. Studied at Marburg '29—32; became *privat docent* at Zurich, '53, and professor '63. He has written rationalist works on the Gospel of Marcion, '52; Justin Martyr, '53; the *Origin of the Gospels*, '66; *Jesus and the first Christian Ages*, '82, etc.

Volney (Constantin François CHASSEBOUF de), Count, French philosopher, b. Craon (Anjou) 3 Feb. 1757. Having studied at Ancenis and Angers, he went to Paris in 1774. Here he met D'Holbach and others. In 1783 he started for Egypt and Syria, and in 1787 published an account of his travels. Made Director of Commerce in Corsica, he resigned on being elected to the Assembly. Though a wealthy land-lord, he wrote and spoke for division of landed property. In 1791 his eloquent *Ruins* appeared. During the Terror he was imprisoned for ten months. In '95 he visited America. Returning to France, Napoleon asked him to become colleague in the consulship but Volney declined. He remonstrated with Napoleon when he re-established Christianity by the Concordat, April 1802. Among his other works was a *History of Samuel* and the *Law of Nature*. Died 25 April, 1820.

Voltaire (François Marie. AROUET de), French poet, historian and philosopher, b. Paris 21 Nov. 1694. Educated by the Jesuits, he early distinguished himself by his wit. For a satirical pamphlet on the death of Louis XIV he was sent to the Bastille for a year and was afterwards committed again for a quarrel with the Chevalier de Rohan. On his liberation he came to England at the invitation of Lord Bolingbroke, and became acquainted with the English Freethinkers. His *Lettres Philosophiques* translated as "Letters on the English," 1732, gave great offence to the clergy and was condemned to be burnt. About 1735 he retired to the estate of the Marquise de Châtelet at Cirey, where he produced many plays. We may mention *Mahomet*, dedicated to the Pope, who was unable to see that its shafts were aimed at the pretences of the church. In 1750 he accepted the invitation of Frederick II. to reside at his court. But he could not help laughing at the great king's poetry. The last twenty years of his life was passed at Ferney near the Genevan territory. which through his exertions became a thriving village. He did more than any other man of his century to abolish torture and other relics of barbarism, and to give just notions of history. To the last he continued to wage war against intolerance and superstition. His works comprise over a thousand pieces in seventy volumes. Over fifty works were condemned by the Index, and Voltaire used no less than one hundred and thirty different pen-names. His name has risen above the clouds of detraction made by his clerical enemies. Died 30 May, 1778.

Voo (G. W. van der), Dutch writer, b. 6 April, 1806. For more than half a century he was schoolmaster and teacher of the French language at Rotterdam, where he still lives. He contributed many articles to *De Dageraad*.

Vosmaer (Carel), Dutch writer, b. the Hague 20 March, 1826. Studied law at Leyden. He edited the *Tydstroom* (1858—9) and *Spectator* (1860—73), and wrote several works on Dutch art and other subjects. Died at Montreaux (Switzerland), 12 June, 1888.

Voysey (Charles), English Theist, b. London 18 March, 1828. Graduated B.A. at Oxford, '51, was vicar of Healaugh, Yorkshire, '64—71, and deprived 11 Feb. '71 for heresy in sermons published in *The Sling and the Stone*. He has since established a Theistic Church in Swallow Street, Piccadilly, and his sermons are regularly published. He has also issued *Fragments from Reimarus*, '79, edited *The Langham Magazine* and published *Lectures on the Bible and the Theistic Faith*, etc.

Vulpian (Edme Felix Alfred), French physician, b. 5 Jan. 1826. Wrote several medical works and upon being appointed lecturer at the School of Medicine, '69, was violently opposed on account of his Atheism. He was afterwards elected to the Academy of Sciences. Died 17 May, 1887.

Wagner (Wilhelm Richard), German musical composer and poet, b. Leipsic, 22 May, 1813. From '42-49 he was conductor of the Royal Opera, Dresden, but his revolutionary sentiments caused his exile to Switzerland, where he produced his "Lohengrin." In '64 he was patronised by Ludwig II. of Bavaria, and produced many fine operas, in which he sought that poetry, scenery, and music should aid each other in making opera dramatic. In philosophy he expressed himself a follower of Schopenhauer. Died at Venice, 13 Feb. 1883.

Waite (Charles Burlingame), American judge, b. Wayne county, N.Y. 29 Jan. 1824. Educated at Knox College, Illinois, he was admitted to the Bar in '47. After successful practice in Chicago, he was appointed by President Lincoln Justice o the Supreme Court of Utah. In '81 he issued his *History of the Christian Religion to the year* A.D. 200, a rationalistic work, which explodes the evangelical narratives.

Wakeman (Thaddeus B.), American lawyer and Positivist, b. 29 Dec. 1834, was one of the editors of *Man* and a president of the New York Liberal Club. A contributor to the *Freethinkers' Magazine.*

Walferdin (François-Hippolyte), b. Langres, 8 June, 1795. A friend of Arago he contributed with him to the enlargement of science, and was decorated with the Legion of Honor in 1844. He published a fine edition of the works of Diderot in '57, and left the bust of that philosopher to the Louvre. Died 25 Jan. 1880.

Walker (E.), of Worcester. Owenite author of *Is the Bible True?* and *What is Blasphemy?* 1843.

Walker (Edwin C.), editor of *Lucifer* and *Fair Play*, Valley Falls, Kansas.

Walker (Thomas), orator, b. Preston, Lancashire, 5 Feb. 1858. Went to America and at the age of sixteen took to the platform. In '77 he went to Australia, and for a while lectured at the Opera, Melbourne. In '82 he started the Australian Secular Association, of which he was president for two years when he went to Sydney. In '85 he was convicted for lecturing on Malthusianism, but the conviction was quashed by the Supreme Court. In '87 he was elected M.P. for Northumberland district. Is President of Australian Freethought Union.

Walser (George H.), American reformer, b. Dearborn Co. Indiana, 26 May, 1834. Became a lawyer, and a member of the legislature of his State. He founded the town of Liberal Barton Co. Missouri, to try the experiment of a town without any priest, church, chapel or drinking saloon. Mr. Walser has also sought to establish there a Freethought University.

Ward (Lester Frank). American botanist, b. Joliet, Illinois, 18 June, 1841. He served in the National Army during the civil war and was wounded. In '65 he settled at Washington and became librarian of the U.S. bureau of statistics. He is now curator of botany and fossil plants in the U.S. national museum. Has written many works on paleo-botany, and two volumes of sociological studies entitled *Dynamic Sociology*. He has contributed the *Popular Science Monthly*.

Ward (Mary A.), translator of *Amiel's Journal*, and authoress of a popular novel *Robert Elsmere*, 1888.

Warren (Josiah). American reformer, b. 26 June, 1798. He took an active part in Robert Owen's communistic experiment at New Harmony, Indiana, in '25-6. His own ideas he illustrated by establishing a "time store" at Cincinnati. His views are given in a work entitled *True Civilisation*. Died Boston, Mass. 14 April, 1874.

Washburn (L. K.), American lecturer and writer, b. Wareham, Plymouth, Mass., 25 March, 1846. In '57 he went to Barre. Was sent to a Unitarian school for ministers, and was ordained in Ipswich, Feb. '70. He read from the pulpit extracts from Parker, Emerson, and others instead of the Bible. He went to Minneapolis, where he organised the first Freethought Society in the State. He afterwards resided at Revere, and delivered many Freethought lectures, of which several have been published. He now edits the *Boston Investigator*.

Waters (Nathaniel Ramsey), American author of *Rome v. Reason*, a memoir of Christian and extra Christian experience.

Watson (James), English upholder of a free press, b. Malton (Yorks), 21 Sept. 1799. During the prosecution of Carlile and his shopmen in 1822 he volunteered to come from London to

Leeds. In Feb. '23 he was arrested for selling Palmer's *Principles of Nature*, tried 23 April, and sentenced to twelve months' imprisonment, during which he read Gibbon, Hume, and Mosheim. When liberated he became a compositor on the *Republican*. In '31 Julian Hibbert gave him his type and presses, and he issued Volney's *Lectures on History*. In Feb. '33 he was sentenced to six months' imprisonment for selling *The Poor Man's Guardian*. Hibbert left him £450, which he used in printing d'Holbach's *System of Nature*, Volney's *Ruins*, F. Wright's *Lectures*, R. D. Owen's pamphlets, Paine's works, and other volumes. Died at Norwood, 29 Nov. 1874.

Watson (Thomas), author of *The Mystagogue*, Leeds, 1847.

Watts (Charles), Secularist orator, b. Bristol, 28 Feb. 1835 Converted to Freethought by hearing Charles Southwell, he became a lecturer and assistant editor on the *National Reformer*. Mr. Watts has had numerous debates, both in England and America, with Dr. Sexton, Rev. Mr. Harrison, Brewin Grant, and others. He started the *Secular Review* with G. W. Foote, and afterwards *Secular Thought* of Toronto. He wrote a portion of *The Freethinker's Text Book*, and has published *Christianity: its Origin, Nature and Influence; The Teachings of Secularism compared with Orthodox Christianity*, and other brochures.

Watts (Charles A.), a son of above, b. 27 May, 1858. Conducts *Watts's Literary Gazette* and edits the *Agnostic Annual*.

Watts (John), brother of Charles, b. Bedminster, Bristol. 2 Oct. 1834. His father was a Wesleyan preacher, and he was converted to Freethought by his brother Charles. He became sub-editor of the *Reasoner*, and afterwards for a time edited the *National Reformer*. He edited *Half Hours With Freethinkers* with "Iconoclast," and published several pamphlets, *Logic and Philosophy of Atheism, Origin of Man, Is Man Immortal? The Devil, Who were the Writers of the New Testament*, etc. Died 31 Oct. 1866.

Watts (of Lewes, Sussex), author of the *Yahoo*, a satire in verse (first published in 1833), also *The Great Dragon Cast Out*.

Webber (Zacharias), Dutch painter, who in the seventeenth century wrote heretical works *On the Temptation of Christ* and *The Seduction of Adam and Eve*, etc. He defended Bekker, whom he surpassed in boldness. Under the pen name J. Adolphs he wrote *The True Origin, Continuance and Destruction of Satan.* Died in 1679.

Weber (Karl Julius), German author, b. Langenburg, 16 April, 1767. Studied law at Erlangen and Göttingen. He lived for a while in Switzerland and studied French philosophy, which suited his satirical turn of mind. He wrote a history of *Monkery*, 1818-20; *Letters of Germans Travelling in Germany,* '26-28; and *Demokritos, or the Posthumous Papers of a Laughing Philosopher,* '32-36. Died Kupferzell, 19 July, 1832.

Weitling (Wilhelm), German social democrat, b. Magdeburg, 1808. He was a leader of " Der Bund der Gerechten," the League of the Just, and published at Zürich *The Gospel of Poor Sinners.* He also wrote *Humanity, As It Is and As It Should Be.* He emigrated to America, where he died 25 Jan. 1871.

Wellhausen (Julius), German critic, b. Hameln 17 May, 1844, studied theology at Göttingen, and became professor in Griefswald, Halle, and Marburg. Is renowned for his *History of Israel* in progress, '78, etc., and his *Prolegomena* to the same, and his contributions to the *Encyclopædia Britannica.*

Westbrook (Richard Brodhead), Dr., American author, b. Pike co., Pennsylvania, 8 Feb. 1820. He became a Methodist preacher in '40, and afterwards joined the Presbyterians, but withdrew about '60, and has since written *The Bible: Whence and What?* and *Man: Whence and Whither?* In '88 Dr. Westbrook was elected President of the American Secular Union, and has since offered a prize for the best essay on teaching morality apart from religion.

Westerman (W. B.) During many years, from 1856—68, an active co-operator on *De Dageraad.*

Westra (P.), Dutch Freethinker, b. 16 March, 1851. Has for some years been active secretary of the Dutch Freethought society, " De Dageraad."

Wettstein (Otto), German American materialist, b. Barmen, 7 April, 1838. About '48 his parents emigrated. In '58 he set up in business as a jeweller at Rochelle. He contributed to the *Freethinkers' Magazine, The Ironclad Age,* and other journals, and is treasurer of the National Secular Union.

White (Andrew Dickson), American educator, b. Homer, N.Y., 7 Nov. 1832. He studied at Yale, where he graduated in '53 ; travelled in Europe, and in '57 was elected professor of history and English literature in the University of Michigan. He was elected to the State Senate, and in '67 became first president of Cornell, a university which he has largely endowed. Among his works we must mention *The Warfare of Science* (N.Y., '76) and *Studies in General History and in the History of Civilisation*, '85.

Whitman (Walt), American poet, b. West Hills, Long Island, N.Y., 31 May, 1819. Educated in public schools, he became a printer, and travelled much through the States. In the civil war he served as a volunteer army nurse. His chief work, *Leaves of Grass*, with its noble preface, appeared in '55, and was acclaimed by Emerson as "the most extraordinary piece of wit and wisdom that America has yet contributed." It was followed by *Drum Taps, November Boughs* and *Sands at Seventy*. This "good gray poet" has also written prose essays called *Democratic Vietas* and *Specimen Days and Collect*.

Wicksell (Knut), Swedish author and lecturer, b. Stockholm, 30 Dec. 1851, studied at Upsala, and became licentiate of philosophy in '85. Has written brochures on Population, Emigration, Prostitution, etc., and anonymously a satirical work on Bible Stories, as by Tante Malin. Represented Sweden at the Paris Conference of '89.

Wieland (Christopher Martin), German poet and novelist, b. near Biberach, 5 Sept. 1733. A voluminous writer, he was called the Voltaire of Germany. Among his works we notice *Dialogues of the Gods, Agathon*, a novel, and *Euthanasia*, in which he argues against immortality. He translated Horace, Lucian and Shakespeare. Died Weimer, 20 Jan. 1813. His last words were "To be or not to be."

Wiener (Christian), Dr., German author of a materialistic work on the *Elements of Natural Laws*, 1863.

Wiessner (Alexander), German writer, author of an examination of spiritualism (Leipsic, 1875).

Wigand (Otto Friedrich), German publisher, b. Göttingen, 10 Aug. 1795. In 1832 he established himself in Leipsic, where he issued the works of Ruge, Bauer, Feuerbach, Scherr, and other Freethinkers. Died 31 Aug. 1870.

Wightman (Edward), English anti-Trinitarian martyr of Burton-on-Trent. Was burnt at Lichfield 11 April, 1612, being the last person burnt for heresy in England.

Wihl (Ludwig), German poet, b. 24 Oct. 1807. Died Brussels, 16 Jan. 1882.

Wilbrandt (Adolf), German author, b. Rosbock, 24 Aug. 1837. Has written on Heinrich von Kleist, Hölderlin, the poet of Pantheism, and published many plays, of which we may mention *Giordano Bruno*, 1874, and also some novels.

Wilhelmi (Hedwig Henrich), German lectnress and author of *Vortrage*, published at Milwaukee, 1889. She attended the Paris Congress of '89.

Wilkinson (Christopher), of Bradford. b. 1803. Wrote with Squire Farrah an able *Examination of Dr. Godwin's Arguments for the Existence of God*, published at Bradford, 1853.

Williams (David), Welsh deist, b. Cardiganshire, 1738. He became a dissenting minister but after publishing two volumes of *Sermons on Religious Hypocrisy*, 1774, dissolved the connections. In conjunction with Franklin and others he founded a club and drew up a *Liturgy on the Universal Principles of Religion and Morality*, which he used at a Deistic chapel opened in Margaret Street, Cavendish Square, 7 April, 1776. He wrote various political and educational works, and established the literary fund in 1789. Died Soho, London, 29 June, 1816.

Willis (Robert), physician and writer, b. Edinburgh, 1799. He studied at the University and became M.D. in 1819. He soon after came to London, and in '23 became M.R.C.S. He became librarian to the College of Surgeons. Besides many medical works he wrote a Life of Spinoza, '70, and *Servetus and Calvin*, '77. He also wrote on *The Pentateuch and Book of Joshua in the face of the Science and Moral Senses of our Age*, and *A Dialogue by Way of Catechism*, both published by T. Scott. Died at Barnes, 21 Sept. 1878.

Wilson (John), M.A., of Trin. Coll., Dublin, author of *Thoughts on Science, Theology and Ethics*, 1885.|

Wirmarsius (Henrik), Dutch author of *Den Ingebeelde Chaos*, 1710.

Wislicenus (Gustav Adolf), German rationalist, b. Saxony,

20 Nov. 1803. He studied theology at Halle, and became a minister, but in consequence of his work *Letter or Spirit* (1845) was suspended and founded the Free Congregation. For his work on *The Bible in the Light of Modern Culture* he was, in Sept. '53, sentenced to prison for two years. He went to America, and lectured in Boston and New York. He returned to Europe in '56, and stayed in Zürich, where he died 14 Oct. 1785. His chief work, *The Bible for Thinking Readers*, was published at Leipsic in '63.

Wittichius (Jacobus), Dutch Spinozist, b. Aken, 11 Jan. 1671. Wrote on the Nature of God, 1711. Died 18 Oct. 1739.

Wixon (Susan H.), American writer and editor of the "Children's Corner" in the *Truthseeker*, has for many years been an advocate of Freethought, temperance, and women's rights. She was a school teacher and member of the Board of Education of the City of Fall River, Mass., where she resides. She contributes to the *Boston Investigator.*

Wollny (Dr. F.), German author of *Principles of Psychology* (Leipsic, 1887), in the preface to which he professes himself an Atheist.

Wollstonecraft (Mary), English authoress, b. Hoxton, 27 April, 1759. She became a governess. In 1796 she settled in London, and began her literary labors with *Thoughts on the Education of Daughters.* She also wrote a *Vindication of the Rights of Man*, in answer to Burke, and *Vindication of the Rights of Woman.* In 1797 she married William Godwin, and died in childbirth.

Wooley (Milton), Dr., American author of *Science of the Bible* 1877; *Career of Jesus Christ*, '77; and a pamphlet on the name God. Died Aug. 1885.

Woolston (Thomas), Rev. English deist, b. Northampton, 1669. He studied at Cambridge, and became a Fellow at Sydney College and a minister. He published in 1705 *The Old Apology*, which was followed by other works in favor of an allegorical interpretation of Scripture. In 1726 he began his *Six Discourses upon the Miracles*, which were assailad in forcible, homely language. Thirty thousand copies are said to have been sold, and sixty pamphlets were written in opposition. Woolston was tried for blasphemy and sentenced (March, 1729) to one year's imprisonment and a fine of £100. This he could not pay, and died in prison 29 Jan. 1733.

Wright (Elizur), American reformer, b. South Canaan, Litchfield Co., Connecticut, 12 Feb. 1804. He graduated at Yale College, '26. Having warmly embraced the principles of the Abolitionists, he became secretary of the American Anti-Slavery Society, and edited the *Abolitionist* and *Commonwealth*. He was a firm and uncompromising Atheist, and a contributor to the *Boston Investigator*, the *Freethinker's Magazine*, etc. Died at Boston, 21 Dec. '85. His funeral oration was delivered by Col. Ingersoll.

Wright (Frances), afterwards D'ARUSMONT, writer and lecturess, b. Dundee, 6 Sept. 1795. At the age of eighteen she wrote *A Few Days in Athens*, in which she expounds and defends the Epicurean philosophy. She visited the United States, and wrote *Views on Society and Manners in America*, 1820. She bought 2,000 acres in Tennessee, and peopled it with slave families she purchased and redeemed. She afterwards joined Owen's experiment; in part edited the *New Harmony Gazette*, and afterwards the *Free Inquirer*. A *Course of Popular Lectures* was published at New York in '29, in which she boldly gives her views on religion. She also wrote a number of fables and tracts, and assisted in founding the *Boston Investigator*. Died at Cincinnati, 14 Dec. 1852.

Wright (Henry Clarke), American reformer, b. Sharon, Litchfield co. Connecticut, 29 Aug. 1797. A conspicuous anti-slavery orator, he was a friend of Ernestine Rose, Lucretia Mott, etc. He wrote *The Living, Present and the Dead Past*. Died Pawtucket, Rhode Island, 16 Aug. 1870.

Wright (Susannah), one of Carlile's shopwomen. Tried 14 Nov. 1822, for selling pamphlets by Carlile. She made a good defence, in the course of which she was continually interrupted.

Wundt (Wilhelm Max), German scientist, b. Neckaran (Baden), 16 Aug. 1832. His father was a clergyman. He studied medicine at Tübingen, Heidelberg, and Berlin, and became professor of physiology at Heidelberg in '64, and has since held chairs at Zurich and Leipsic. His principal works are *Principles of Physiological Psychology*, '74; *Manual of Human Physiology; Logic*, '83; *Essays*, '85; *Ethik*, '86.

Wuensch (Christian Ernest), German physician, b. Hohenstein, 1744. Was Professor of Mathematics and Physics in Frankfort on the Oder, 1828.

Wyrouboff (Gr.), Count; Russian Positivist, who established the *Revue de Philosophie Positive* with Littré, and edited it with him from 1867—83.

Xenophanes, Greek philosopher, b. Colophon, about 600 B.C. He founded the Eleatic school, and wrote a poem on Nature and Eleaticism, in which he ridiculed man making gods in his own image.

Ximines (Augustin Louis), *Marquis de*, French writer, b. Paris, 26 Feb. 1726. Was an intimate friend of Voltaire, and wrote several plays. Died Paris, 31 May, 1817.

York (J. L.), American lecturer, b. New York, 1830. He became a blacksmith, then a Methodist minister, then Unitarian, and finally Freethought advocate. He was for some years member of the California Legislature, and has made lecturing tours in Australia and through the States.

Yorke (J. F.), author of able *Notes on Evolution and Christianity*, London, 1882.

Youmans (Edward Livingstone), American scientist, b. Coeymans, N. Y., 3 June, 1821. Though partially blind he was a great student. He became M.D. about 1851, and began to lecture on science, popularly expounding the doctrines of the conservation of energy and evolution. He popularised Herbert Spencer, planned the "International Scientific Series," and in '72 established the *Popular Science Monthly*, in which he wrote largely. Died at New York, 18 Jan. 1887.

Zaborowski Moindrin (Sigismond). French scientific writer, b. La Crèche, 1851. Has written on *The Antiquity of Man*, '74; *Pre-historic Man*, '78; *Origin of Languages*, '79; *The Great Apes*, '81; *Scientific Curiosities*, '83.

Zambrini (Francesco). Italian writer, b. Faenza, 25 Jan. 1810. Educated at Ravenna and Bologna. He devoted himself to literature and produced a great number of works. Died 9 July, 1887.

Zarco (Francisco). Mexican journalist, b. Durango, 4 Dec. 1829. Edited *El SigloXIX* and *La Ilustracion*, in which he used the pen-name of "Fortun." He was elected to Congress in '55, and imprisoned by the reactionaries in '60. Juarez made him Secretary of State and President of Council. He was a friend of Gagern. Died Mexico, 29 Dec. 1869.

Zeller (Eduard), German critic, b. Kleinbottwar (Würtemberg), 22 Jan. 1814. Studied theology at Tübingen and Berlin, became professor at Berne, '47. He married a daughter of Baur; gave up theology for philosophy, of which he has been professor at Berlin since '72. Has written a memoir of Strauss, '74; *Outlines of the History of Greek Philosophy*, '83; *Frederick the Great as a Philosopher*, '86; and other important works.

Zijde (Karel van der). Dutch writer, b. Overschie, 13 July, 1838. Has been teacher at Rotterdam. Under the pen-name of M. F. ten Bergen he wrote *The Devil's Burial*, 1874. Besides this he has written many literary articles, and is now teacher of Dutch and German at Zaandam.

Zimmern (Helen), b. Hamburg, 25 March, 1846. Has lived in England since '50, and is naturalised. She has written lives of Schopenhauer and Lessing, and a paraphrase of Firdusi's *Shah Nahmeh*.

Zola (Emile), French novelist, b. of Italian father, Paris, 2 April, 1840. By his powerful collection of romances known as *Les Rougon Macquart*, he made himself the leader of the "naturalist" school, which claims to treat fiction scientifically, representing life as it is without the ideal.

Zorrilla (Manuel Ruiz), Spanish statesman, b. Burgo-de-Osma, 1834, became a lawyer, and in '56 was returned to the Cortes by the Progressive party. For a brochure against the Neo-Catholics he was prosecuted. In '70 he became President of the Cortes, and has since been exiled for his Republicanism.

Zouteveen (H. H. H. van). See Hartogh.

Zuppetta (Luigi), Italian jurist and patriot, b. Castelnuovo, 21 June, 1810. He studied at Naples, took part in the democratic movement of '48, was exiled and returned in 1860, and has been Professor of Penal Law in the University of Pavia.

SUPPLEMENT.

Those which have already appeared are marked ∗

Abd al Hakk ibn Ibrahim ibn Muhammad ibn Sabin.
See Sabin.

Abu Abd'allah Muhammad ibn Massara al Jabali.
Arabian pantheist b. 881. He lived at Cordova in Spain and
studied the works of Empedocles and other Greek philosophers·
Accused of impiety, he left Spain and travelled through the
East. Returned to Spain and collected disciples whom he led
to scepticism. He was the most eminent predecessor of Ibn
Rushd or Averroes. Died Oct. 931. His works were publicly
burned at Seville.

∗**Acosta** (Uriel), the name of his work was *Examen Tradi-
torum Philosophicarum ad legem Scriptam.*

Acuna (Rosario de), Spanish writer and lecturess, b. Madrid
about 1854. Contributes to *Las Dominicales* of Madrid. Has
written *The Doll's House*, and other educational works.

∗**Adams** (Robert C.), American Freethought writer and
lecturer, the son of the Rev. Needham Adams, b. Boston 1839.
He became a sea-captain, and was afterwards shipper at
Montreal. Has written in *Secular Thought* the *Truthseeker* and
the *Freethinkers' Magazine*, and published rational lectures
under the title *Pioneer Pith,* '89. In '89 he was elected President of the Canadian Secular Union.

Admiraal (Aart), Dutch writer, b. Goedereede 13 Oct. 1833.
At first a schoolmaster, he became in '60 director of the
telegraph bureau at Schoonhoven. He wrote from '56 for
many years in *De Dageraad* over the anagram "Aramaldi."
In '67 he published *The Religion of the People* under the
pseudonym "Bato van der Maas," a name he used in writing to
many periodicals. A good mind and heart with but feeble
constitution. He died 12 Nov. 1878.

339

Airoldi (J.) Italian lawyer, b. Lugano (Switzerland), 1829 ; a poet and writer of talent.

Albaida (Don Jose M. Orense), Spanish nobleman (marquis), one of the founders of the Republican party. Was expelled for his principles ; returned to Spain, and was president of the Cortes in 1869.

* **Alchindus.** Died about 864.

* **Aleardi** had better be deleted. I am now told he was a Christian.

Alfarabi. See Alpharabius.

Algeri (Pomponio), a youth of Nola. Studied at Padua, and was accused of heresy and Atheism, and burnt alive in a cauldron of boiling oil, pitch, and turpentine at Rome in 1566.

Alkemade (A de Mey van), Dutch nobleman, who contributed to *De Dageraad*, and also published a work containing many Bible contradictions, 1862 ; and in '59 a work on the Bible under the pen name " Alexander de M."

Allais (Denis de). See Vairasse.

Allais (Giovanni), Italian doctor, b. Casteldelfino, 1847.

Almquist (Herman), Swedish, b. 1839, orientalist ; professor of philology at the University of Upsala. An active defender of new ideas and Freethought.

Altmeyer (Jean Jacques), Belgian author, b. Luxembourg, 20 Jan. 1804. Was professor at the University of Brussels. He wrote an *Introduction to the Philosophical Study of the History of Humanity*, '36, and other historical works. Died 15 Sept. 1877.

Amari (Michele), Sicilian historian and orientalist, b. Palmero, 7 July, 1806. In '32 he produced a version of Scott's *Marmion*. He wrote a standard History of the Musulmen in Sicily. After the landing of Garibaldi, he was made head of public instruction in the island. He took part in the anticlerical council of '69. Died at Florence, July 1889.

* **Amaury de Chartres.** According to L'Abbè Ladvocat his disciples maintained that the sacraments were useless, and that there was no other heaven than the satisfaction of doing right, nor any other hell than ignorance and sin.

Anderson (Marie), Dutch lady Freethinker, b. the Hague, 2 Aug. 1842. She has written many good articles in *de Dageraad*, and was for some time editress of a periodical *De Twintigste Eeuw* (the twentieth century). She has also written some novels. She resides now at Würmburg, Germany, and contributes still to *de Dageraad*. As pen-name she formerly used that of " Meirouw Quarlès " and now " Dr. Al. Dondorf."

*** Anthero de Quental**. This name would be better under Quental.

Apono. See Petrus de Abano. This would probably be best under Abano.

*** Aquila**. Justinian forbade the Jews to read Aquila's version of the Scriptures.

Aranda (Pedro Pablo Abarca de Bolea), *Count*, Spanish statesman, b. of illustrious family, Saragossa, 18 Dec. 1718. Was soldier and ambassador to Poland. He imbibed the ideas of the Encyclopædists, and contributed to the expulsion of the Jesuits from Spain in 1767. He also disarmed the Inquisition. In 1792 he was elected Spanish minister to France. He was recalled and exiled to Aragon, where he died in 1799.

Argilleres (Antoine), at first a Jacobin monk and afterwards a Protestant preacher, was tortured several times, then decapitated and his head nailed to a gibbet at Geneva, 1561—2, for having eight years previously taken the part of Servetus against Calvin at Pont-de-Veyle in Bresse.

*** Arnould** (Victor). Has continued his Tableau in the Positivist *Revue* and *La Societé Nouvelle*. From 1868 to '73 he edited *La Liberté*, in which many a battle for Freethought has been fought.

Ascarate (Gumezindo de), Spanish professor of law at the University of Madrid and Republican deputy, b. Leon about 1844. One of the ablest Radical parliamentary orators; in philosophy, he is a follower of Krause. He has written *Social Studies, Self-Government and Monarchy*, and other political works.

Aszo y Del Rio (Ignacio JORDAN de), Spanish jurist and naturalist, b. Saragossa, 1742. Was professor at Madrid, and left many important works on various branches of science.

In his political works he advocated the abolition of ecclesiastical power.   Died 1814.

*** Aubert de Verse** (Noel) had probably better be omitted, although accused of blasphemy himself, I find he wrote an answer to Spinoza, which I have not been able to see.

Auerbach (Berthold), German novelist of Jewish extraction, b. Nordstetten, 28 Feb. 1812.   Devoted to Spinoza, in '41 he published a life of the philosopher and a translation of his works, having previously published an historical romance on the same subject.   Died Cannes, 8 Feb. 1882.

*** Aymon** (Jean). *La vie et L'Esprit de M. Benoit Spinoza* (La Haye, 1719) was afterwards issued under the famous title *Treatise of Three Impostors.*

*** Bahrdt** (Karl Friedrich).   The writings of this *enfant terrible* of the German Aufklarung fill 120 volumes.

*** Bailey** (William Shreeve) was born 10 Feb. 1806.   He suffered much on account of his opinions.   Died Nashville, 20 Feb 1886. Photius Fisk erected a monument to his memory.

*** Bancel** (Francis Désiré).   In his work *Les Harangues de l'Exil*, 3 vols., 1863, his Freethought views are displayed.   He also wrote in *La Revue Critique.*

Barnaud (Nicolas), of Crest in Dauphiné.   Lived during the latter half of the sixteenth century.   He travelled in France, Spain, and Germany, and to him is attributed the authorship of a curious work entitled *Le Cabinet du Roy de France*, which is largely directed against the clergy.

Barreaux.   See des Barreaux.

Barth (Ferdinand), b. Mureck, Steyermark Austria, 1828. In '48 he attained reputation as orator to working men and took part in the revolution.   When Vienna was retaken he went to Leipzig and Zurich, where he died in 1850, leaving a profession of his freethought.

Bartrina, Spanish Atheistic poet, b. Barcelona, 1852, where he died in 1880.

Bedingfield (Richard, W. T.), Pantheistic writer, b. May, 1823, wrote in *National Reformer* as B.T.W.R., established *Freelight*, '70.   Died 14 Feb. 1876.

342

* **Berigardus** (Claudius), b. 15 Aug. 1578.

* **Bertillon** (Louis Adolphe). In a letter to Bp. Dupanloup, Apil, '68, he said, You hope to die a Catholic, I hope to die a Freethinker. Died 1883.

* **Berwick** (George J.) M.D., Dr. Berwick, I am informed, was the author of the tracts issued by Thomas Scott of Ramsgate. with the signature of " Presbyter Anglicanus."

Blein (F.A.A.), *Baron*, French author of *Essais Philosophiques*, Paris, 1843.

Blum (Robert), German patriot and orator, b. Cologne, 10 Nov. 1807. He took an active part in progressive political and religious movements, and published the *Christmas Tree* and other publications. In '48 he became deputy to the Frankfort Parliament and head of the Republican party. He was one of the promoters at the insurrection of Vienna, and showed great bravery in the fights of the students with the troops. Shot at Vienna, 9 Nov. 1848.

* **Blumenfield** (J. C.), this name I suspect to be a pseudonym.

Bolin (A. W.), a philosophic writer of Finland, b. 2 Aug. 1835. Studied at Helsingford, '52, and became Doctor of Philosophy in '66, and Professor in '73. He has written on the Freedom ofthe Will, The Political Doctrines of Philosophy, etc. A subject of Russian Finland; he has been repeatedly troubled by the authorities for his radical views on religious questions.

Bolivar (Ignacio), Spanish professor of natural history at the University of Madrid, and one of the introducers of Darwinian ideas.

Boppe (Herman C.), editor of *Freidenker* of Milwaukee, U.S.A.

Borsari (Ferdinand), Italian geographer, b. Naples, author of a work of the literature of American aborigines, and a zealous propagator of Freethought.

Bostrom (Christopher Jacob), Swedish Professor at Upsala, b. 4 Jan. 1797. Besides many philosophical works, published trenchant criticism of the Christian hell creed. Died 22 March, 1866.

Boucher (E. Martin), b. Beaulieu 1809. Conducted the *Rationaliste* at Geneva, where he died 1882. His work *Search for the Truth* was published at Avignon, 1884.

Bourneville (Magloire Désir), French deputy and physician, b. Garancières, 21 Oct. 1840. Studied medicine at Paris, and in '79 was appointed physician to the asylum of Bicêtre. He was Municipal Councillor of Paris from '76 to '83. On the death of Louis Blanc he was elected deputy in his place. Wrote *Science and Miracle*, '75; *Hysteria in History*, '76; and a discourse on Etienne Dolet at the erection of the statue to that martyr, 18 May 1889.

Boutteville (Marc Lucien), French writer, professor at the Lycee Bonaparte. Wrote to Dupanloup on his pamphlet against Atheism, 1867; wrote in *La Pensée Nouvelle*, '68: is author of a large and able work on the *Morality of the Church and Natural Morality*, '66; and has edited the posthumous works of Proudhon, 1870.

* **Bovio** (Giovanni), b. Trani, 1838, Dr. of law and advocate. Author of a dramatic piece, *Cristo alla festa di Purim*, and of a *History of Law in Italy*. Signor Bovio delivered the address at unveiling the monument to Bruno at Rome, 9 June, 1889.

Boyer. See Argens.

* **Bradlaugh** (Charles), M.P. In April, 1889, he introduced a Bill to repeal the Blasphemy Laws.

Braga (Teofilo), Portuguese Positivist, b. 24 Feb. 1843. Educated at Coimbra. Has written many poems, and a *History of Portugese Literature*. Is one of the Republican leaders.

Branting (Hjalmar), Swedish Socialist, b. 1860. Sentenced in '88 to three months' imprisonment for blasphemy in his paper *Social Democraten*.

Braun (Eugen), Dr. See F. W. Ghillany.

Braun (Wilhelm von), Swedish humoristic poet, b. 1813. He satirised many of the Bible stories. Died 1860.

Brewer (Ebenezer Cobham), English author. Has written numerous school books, and compiled a *Dictionary of Miracles*, 1884.

Brismee (Desiré), Belgian printer, b. Ghent, 27 July, 1822. As editor of *Le Drapeau* he underwent eighteen months' imprisonment. The principle founder of *Les Solidaires*, he was the life-long secretary of that society, and his annual reports are a valuable contribution towards the history of Freethought in Belgium. An eloquent speaker, many of his Freethought orations were printed in *La Tribune du Peuple*. Died at Brussels 18 Feb. 1888.

* **Brothier** (Léon), Died about 1874.

* **Brown** (G. W) Dr. Brown's new work is published at Rockford, Illinois, and entitled *Researches in Jewish History*, including the rise and development of Zoroastrianism and the derivation of Christianity.

* **Bruno** (Giordano), b. Nola, 21 March, 1548. The *Avisso di Roma* of 19 Feb. 1600, records the fact of his being burnt, and that he died impenitent. Signor Mariotti, State Secretary to the Minister of Public Instruction, has found a document proving that Bruno was stripped naked, bound to a pole, and burnt alive, and that he bore his martyrdom with great fortitude.

Buen (Odon de), Spanish writer on *Las Dominicales*, of Madrid, b. Aragon, 1884. Professor of Natural History at the University of Barcelona. Has written an account of a scientific expedition *From Christiania to Treggurt*, has translated *Memoirs of Garibaldi*. He married civilly the daughter of F. Lozano, and was delegate to the Paris Freethought Conference, 1889.

Calderon (Alfredo), Spanish journalist and lawyer, b. 1852. He edits *La Justicia*. Has written several books on law.

Calderon (Laurcsmo), Professor of Chemistry in the University of Madrid, b. 1848. Is a propagator of Darwinian ideas.

Calderon (Salvador), Spanish geologist and naturalist, b. 1846; professor at the University of Seville. Has made scientific travels in Central America, and written largely on geological subjects.

Calvo (Rafael), Spanish actor and dramatic author, b. 1852. A pronounced Republican and Freethinker.

* **Canestrini** (Giovanni), b. Revo (Trente), 26 Dec. 1835.

Cassels (Walter Richard), a nephew of Dr. Pusey, is the author of *Supernatural Religion*, a critical examination of the worth of the Gospels (two vols. 1874 and three '79). Has written under his own name *Eidolon* and other poems, 1850, and *Poems*, '56. In '89 he published *A Reply to Dr. Lightfoot's Essays*.

345

Castro (Fernando), Spanish philosopher and historian. He was a priest, and on his death-bed confessed himself a Freethinker, and had a secular burial. Died about 1874, aged 60 years.

Cavia (Mariano), Spanish journalist and critic, b. 1859, editor of the *Liberal* of Madrid.

***Coke** (Henry), author of *Creeds of the Day*, is the third son of the first Earl of Leicester, and was born 3 Jan. 1827. He served in the navy during the first China War, 1840-42. Published accounts of the siege of Vienna, '48, at which he was present, also " Ride over Rocky Mountains," which he accomplished with great hardships in '50. Was private secretary to Mr. Horsman when Chief Secretary for Ireland in '54-'58. Married Lady K. Egerton, 1861.

Cornette (Henri Arthur Marie), Belgian professor of Flemish literature at Antwerp, b. Bruges, 27 March, 1852. A writer in *L'Avenir* of Brussels and the *Revue Socialite*, he has published separate works on *Freemasonry*, 1878 ; *Pessimism and Socialism*, '80 ; *Freethought Darwinism*, etc.

Curros (Enriquez), living Spanish poet, who was prosecuted by the Bishop of Santiago, of Galicia, for his collection of poems entitled *Airs of my Country*, but he was acquitted by the jury.

Czerski (Johannes), German reformer, b. Warlubien, West Prussia, 12 May, 1813. He became a Catholic priest in '44, broke with the Church, associated himself with Ronge, married, and was excommunicated. Has written several works against Roman Catholicism, and is still living at Schneidemükl-Posen.

D'Ercole (Pasquale), Italian professor of philosophy in the University of Turin, author of a work on Christian Theism, in which he holds that the principles of philosophic Theism are undemonstrated and at variance both with reality and with themselves.

Deschanel (Emile Auguste), French senator, b. Paris, 19 Nov. 1819. He wrote in the *Revue Independante, Revue des Deux Mondes* and *Liberté de Penser ;* for writing against clericalism in the last he was deprived of his chair. After 2 Dec. he went to Belgium.   He has been Professor of Modern Literature at the College of France, and written many important works.

Desnoiresterres (Gustave le Brisoys), Frenchman of letters, b. Bayeux, 20 June, 1817, author of *Epicurienes et Lettres XVII. and XVIII. Siecles,* 1881, and *Voltaire et la Société Française au XVIII. Siecle,* an important work in eight vols.

* **Desraimes** (Maria), b. 15 Aug. 1835.

Diogenes (Apolloinates), a Cretan, natural philosopher, who lived in the fifth century B.C.   He is supposed to have got into trouble at Athens through his philosophical opinions being considered dangerous to the State.   He held that nothing was produced from nothing or reduced to nothing; that the earth was round and had received its shape from whirling. He made no distinction between mind and matter.

Donius (Augustinus), a Materialist, referred to by Bacon. His work, *De Natura Dominis,* in two books, 1581, refers the power of the spirit, to motion.   The title of his second book is "Omnes operationes spiritus esse motum et semum."

Dosamantes (Jesus Ceballos), Mexican philosopher; author of works on *Absolute Perfection,* Mexico, 1888, and *Modern Pharisees and Sadducees* (mystics and materialists), '89.

Druskowitz (Helene), Dr., b. Vienna, 2 May, 1858.   Miss Druskowitz is Doctor of philosophy at Dresden, and has written a life of Shelley, Berlin, '84 ;   a little book on *Freewill,* and *The New Doctrines,* '83.

Dufay (Henri), author of *La Legende du Christ,* 1880.

Duller (Eduard), German poet and historian, b. Vienna, 18 Nov. 1809.   He wrote a *History of the Jesuits* (Leipsic, '40) and *The Men of the People* (Frankfort, '47-'50).   Died at Wiesbaden, 24 July, 1853.

***Du Marsais** (César Chesneau).   He edited Mirabaud's anonymous work on *The World and its Antiquity* and *The Soul and its Immortality,* Londres, 1751.

***Fellowes** (R.)   Graduated B.A. at Oxford 1796, M.A. 1801. Died 6 Feb. 1847.

Figueras-y-Moracas (Estanilas), Spanish statesman and orator, b. Barcelona, 13 Nov. 1810.   Studied law and soon manifested Republican opinions.   In '51 he was elected to the

347

Cortes, was exiled in '66, but returned in '68. He fought the candidature of the Duc de Montpensiér in '69, and became President of the Spanish Republic 12 Feb. '73. Died poor in 1879, and was buried without religious ceremony, according to his wish.

Fitzgerald (Edward), English poet and translator, b. near Woodbridge, Suffolk, 31 March, 1809. Educated at Cambridge and took his degree in '30. He lived the life of a recluse, and produced a fine translation of Calderon. His fame rests securely on his fine rendering of the *Quatrains* of Omar Khayyam. Died 14 June, 1883.

Galletti (Baldassare), *cavalier* Pantheist of Palermo. Has translated Feuerbach on *Death and Immortality*, and also translated from Morin. Died Rome, 18 Feb. 1887.

Ganeval (Louis), French professor in Egypt, b. Veziat, 1815, author of a work on Egypt and *Jesus devant l'histoire n'a jamais vécu*. The first part, published in '71, was prohibited in France, and the second part was published at Geneva in '79.

Garrido (Fernando), Spanish writer, author of Memoirs of a Sceptic, Cadiz 1843, a work on *Contemporary Spain*, published at Brussels in '62, *The Jesuits*, and a large *History of Political and Religious Persecutions*, a work rendered into English in conjunction with C. B. Cayley. Died at Cordova in 1884.

Gerling (Fr. Wilhelm), German author of *Letter of a Materialist to an Idealist*, Berlin 1888, to which Frau Hedwig Henrich Wilhelmi contributes a preface.

Geroult de Pival, French librarian at Rouen; probably the author of *Doutes sur la Religion*, Londres, 1767. Died at Paris about 1772.

Goffin (Nicolas), founder of the Society La Libre of Liége and President of La Libre Pensée of Brussels, and one of the General Council of the International Federation of Freethinkers. Died 23 May, 1884.

Goldhawke (J. H.), author of the *Solar Allegories*, proving that the greater number of personages mentioned in the Old and New Testaments are allegorical beings, Calcutta 1853.

Gorani (Guiseppe), count, b. Milan, 1744. He was intimate with Beccaria, D'Holbach, and Diderot. He wrote a treatise on *Despotism*, published anonymously, 1770; defended the French

Revolution and was made a French citizen. Died poor at Geneva, 12 Dec. 1819.

Govett (Frank), author of the *Pains of Life*, 1889, a pessimistic reply to Sir J. Lubbock's *Pleasures of Life*. Mr. Govett rejects the consolations of religion.

Guimet (Etienne Emile), French traveller, musician, anthropologist and philanthropist, b. Lyons, 2 June, 1836. the son of the inventor of ultramarine, whose business he continued. He has visited most parts of the world and formed a collection of objects illustrating religions. These he formed into a museum in his native town, where he also founded a library and a school for Oriental languages. This fine museum which cost several million francs, he presented to his country, and it is now at Paris, where M. Guimet acts as curator. In 1880 he began publishing *Annales du Musée Guimet*, in which original articles appear on Oriental Religions. He has also written many works upon his travels. He attended the banquet in connection; with the International Congress of Freethinkers at Paris, 1889.

Guynemer (A. M. A. de), French author of a dictionary of astronomy, 1852, and an anonymous unbelievers' dictionary, '69, in which many points of theology are discussed in alphabetical order.

Hamerling (Robert), German poet, b. Kirchberg am Wald, 24 March, 1830. Author of many fine poems, of which we mention Ahasuerus in Rome '66. The King of Sion ; Danton and Robespierre a tragedy. He translated Leopardis' poems '86. Died at Gratz, 13 July, 1889.

Heyse (Paul Johann Ludwig), German poet and novelist, b. Berlin, 15 March, 1830. Educated at the University, after travelling to Switzerland and Italy he settled at Munich in '54. Has produced many popular plays and romances, of we specially mention *The Children of the World*, '73, a novel describing social and religious life of Germany at the present day, and *In Paradise*. 1875.

Hicks (L. E.) American geologist, author] of *A Critique of Design Arguments*. Boston, 1883.

Hitchman (William), English physician, b. Northleach,

Gloucestershire, 1819, became M.R.C.S. in '41, M.D. at Erlangen, Bavaria. He established *Freelight*, and wrote a pamphlet, *Fifty Years of Freethought*. Died 1888.

Hoeffding (Harald), Dr., Professor of Philosophy at the University of Copenhagen, b. Copenhagen, 1843. Has been professor since '83. Is absolutely free in his opinion and has published works on the newer philosophy in Germany, '72, and in England, '74. In the latter work special attention is devoted to the works of Mill and Spencer. German editions have been published of his works *Grundlage der humanen Ethik* (Basis of Human Ethics '80), *Psychologie im Umries* (Outlines of Psychology '87). and *Ethik* 1888.

Holst (Nils Olaf), Swedish geologist. b. 1846. Chairman of the Swedish Society for Religious Liberty.

Ignell (Nils), Swedish rationalist, b. 12 July, 1806. Brought up as a priest, his free views gave great offence. He translated Renan's *Life of Jesus*, and did much to arouse opposition to orthodox Christianity. Died at Stockholm, 3 June, 1864.

Jacobsen (Jens Peter), Danish novelist and botanist, b. Thistede, 7 April, 1847. He did much to spread Darwinian views in Scandinavia, translating the *Origin of Species* and *Descent of Man*. Among his novels we may name *Fru Marie Grubbe*, scenes from the XVII. century, and *Niels Lyhne*, in which he develops the philosophy of Atheism. This able young writer died at his birth place, 3 April 1885.

Kleist (Heinrich von), German poet, b. Frankfurt-on-Oder, 18 Oct. 1777. Left an orphan at eleven, he enlisted in the army in 1795, quitted it in four years and took to study. Kant's Philosophy made him a complete sceptic. In 1800 he went to Paris to teach Kantian philosophy, but the results were not encouraging. Committed suicide together with a lady, near Potsdam, 21 Nov. 1811. Kleist is chiefly known by his dramas and a collection of tales.

Letourneau (Charles Jean Marie), French scientist, b. Auray (Morbihan), 1831. Educated as physician. He wrote in *La Pensée Nouvelle*, and has published *Physiology of the Passions*, '68; *Biology*, '75, translated into English by W. Maccall; *Science and Materialism* '79; *Sociology based on Ethnography*, '80; and the

350

Evolution of Marriage and the Family, '85. He has also translated Büchner's *Man According to Science, Light and Life* and *Mental Life of Animals,* Haeckel's *History of Creation* and, *Letters of a Traveller in India,* and Herzen's *Physiology of the Will.*

Lippert (Julius), learned German author of works on *Soul Worship,* Berlin, 1881 ; *The Universal History of Priesthoods,* '83 ; and an important Culture History of Mankind, '86-7.

Lloyd (William Watkiss), author of *Christianity in the Cartoons,* London 1865, in which he criticises Rafael and the New Testament side by side. He has also written *The Age of Pericles,* and several works on Shakespeare.

Lucian, witty Greek writer, b. of poor parents, Samosata, on the Euphrates, and flourished in the reign of Marcus Aurelius and Commodus. He was made a sculptor, but applied himself to rhetoric. He travelled much, and at Athens was intimate with Demonax. His principal works are dialogues, full of wit, humor, and satire, often directed against the gods. According to Suidas he was named the Blasphemer, and torn to pieces by dogs for his impiety, but on this no reliance can be placed. On the ground of the dialogue *Philopatris,* he has been supposed an apostate Christian, but it is uncertain if that piece is genuine. It is certain that he was sceptical, truth-loving, and an enemy of the superstition of the time which he depicts in his account of Alexander, the false prophet.

Maglia (Adolfo de), Spanish journalist, b. Valencia, 3 June, 1859, began writing in *La Tronada* at Barcelona, and afterwards published *L'Union Republicana.* He founded the Freethinking group "El Independiente" and edits *El Clamor Setabense* and *El Pueblo Soberano.* Was secretary for Spain at the Anti-clerical Congress at Rome in '85, and in '89 at Paris. During this year he has been condemned to six years' imprisonment and a fine of 4,000 francs for attacking Leo XIII. and the Catholic dogmas.

disciples, whom he conducted from faith to scepticism. He was the most eminent predecessor of Ibn Roschd or Averroës. Died Oct.—Nov. 931. His works were publicly burned at Seville.

Mata (Pedro), Spanish physician, professor at the University of Madrid. Author of a poem, *Glory and Martyrdom*, 1851 ; a Treatise on Human Reason, '58—64 ; and on *Moral Liberty and Free Will*, '68.

Mendizabal (Juan Alvarez), Spanish Liberal statesman, b. Cadiz, 1790. Was minister during the reign of Cristina, and contributed to the subjugation of the clerical party. He abolished the religious orders and proclaimed their goods as national property. Died at Madrid, 3 Nov. 1853.

*** Meredith** (Evan Powell), b. 1811. Educated at Pontypool College, he became a Baptist minister, and was an eloquent preacher in the Welsh tongue. He translated the Bible into Welsh. Investigation into the claims of Christianity made him resign his ministry. In his *Prophet of Nazareth* he mentioned a purpose of writing a work on the gospels, but it never appeared. He died at Monmouth 23 July, 1889.

Miralta (Constancio), the pen name of a popular Spanish writer, b. about 1849. Has been a priest and doctor of theology, and is one of the writers on *Las Dominicales*. His most notable works are *Memoirs of a Poor Clerical*, *The Secrets of Confession*, and *The Sacrament Exposed*. His work on the *The Doctrine of Catholicism upon Matrimony* has greatly encouraged civil marriages.

Moraita (Miguel), Spanish historian, b. about 1845. Is Professor of History at Madrid, and one of the most ardent enemies of clericalism. Has written many works, including a voluminous *History of Spain*. In '84 he made a discourse at the University against the pretended antiquity of the Mosaic legends, which caused his excommunication by several bishops. He was supported by the students, against whom the military were employed. He is Grand Master of the Spanish Freemasons.

Moya (Francisco Xavier), Spanish statistician, b. about 1825. Was deputy to the Cortes of 1869, and has written several works on the infallibility of the Pope and on the temporal power.

Nakens (José), Spanish journalist, b. 1846. Founder and editor of *El Motin*, a Republican and Freethought paper of

Madrid, in connection with which there is a library, in which he has written *La Piqueta*—the Pick-axe.

Nees von Esenbeck (Christian Gottfried), German naturalist, b. Odenwald. 14 Feb. 1776. He became a doctor of medicine, and was Professor of Botany at Bohn, 1819. and Breslau, '31. He was leader of the free religious movement in Silesia, and in '48, took part in the political agitations, and was deprived of his chair. Wrote several works on natural philosophy. Died at Breslau, 16 March, 1858.

Nyblaus (Claes Gudmund), Swedish bookseller, b. 1817, has published some anti-Christian pamphlets.

Offen (Benjamin), American lecturer, b. England, 1772. He emigrated to America and became lecturer to the Society of Moral Philanthropists at Tammany Hall, New York, and was connected with the Free Discussion Society. He wrote *A Legacy to the Friends of Free Discussion*, a critical review of the Bible. Died at New York, 12 May, 1848.

Palmaer (Bernhard Henrik), Swedish satirist, b. 21 Aug. 1801. Author of *The Last Judgment in the Crow Corner*. Died at Linkoping, 7 July, 1854.

Panizza. (Mario). Italian physiologist and philosopher; author of a materialist work on *The Philosophy of the Nervous System*, Rome, 1887.

Perez Galdos (Benito), eminent living Spanish novelist. b· Canary Islands lived since his youth in Madrid. Of his novels we mention *Gloria*, which has been translated into English, and *La Familia de Leon Roch*, 1878, in which he stoutly attacks clericalism and religious intolerance. He has also written *Epizodes nacionales*, and many historical novels.

Regenbrecht (Michael Eduard), German rationalist, b. Brannsberg, 1792. He left the Church with Ronge, and became leader of the free religious movement at Breslau, where he died 9 June, 1849.

Robert (Roberto). Spanish anti-clerical satirist, b. 1817. Became famous by his mordant style, his most celebrated work being *The Rogues of Antonio, The Times of Mari Casania, The Glimmer of the Centuries.* Died in 1870.

Rupp (Julius), German reformer, b. Königsberg, 13 Aug. 1809. Studied philosophy and theology, and became in '42 a minister. He protested against the creeds, and became leader of the Free-religious movement in East Prussia.

Ryberg (Y. E.) Swedish merchant captain, b. 16 Oct. 1828. He has translated several of Mr. Bradlaugh's pamphlets and other secular literature.

Sachse (Heinrich Ernst), German atheist, b. 1812. At Magdeburg he did much to demolish the remains of theism in the Free-religious communities. Died 1883.

Sales y Ferre (Manuel), Spanish scientist, b about 1839. Professor at the University of Seville. Has published several works on geology and prehistoric times.

Schneider (Georg Heinrich), German naturalist, b. Mannheim, 1854. Author of *The Human Will from the standpoint of the New Development Theory* (Berlin, 1882), and other works.

Schreiner (Olive), the daughter of a German missionary in South Africa. Authoress of " The Story of an African Farm," 1883.

Serre (...de la), author of an *Examination of Religion*, attributed to Saint Evremond, 1745. It was condemned to be burnt by the Parliament of Paris.

Suner y Capderila. Spanish physician of Barcelona, b. 1828. Became deputy to the Cortes in 1829, and is famous for his discourses against Catholicism.

Tocco (Felice), Italian philosopher and anthropologist, b. Catanzaro, 12 Sept. 1845, and studied at the University of Naples and Bologna, and became Professor of Philosophy at Pisa. He wrote in the *Rivista Bolognese* on Leopardi, and on "Positivism " in the *Rivasta Contemporanea.* He has published works on *A. Bain's Theory of Sensation,* '72 ; *Thoughts on the History of Philosophy,* '77 ; *The Heresy of the Middle Ages,*' 84 ; and *Giordano Bruno,* '86.

Tommasi (Salvatore), Italian evolutionist, author of a work on *Evolution, Science, and Naturalism,* Naples 1877, and a little pamphlet in commemoration of Darwin, '82.

Tubino (Francisco Maria), Spanish positivist, b. Seville, 1838, took part in Garibaldi's campaign in Sicily, and has contributed to the *Rivista Europea*.

Tuthill (Charles A. H.), author of *The Origin and Development of Christian Dogma*, London, 1889.

Vernial (Paul), French doctor and member of the Antropological Society of Paris, author of a work on the *Origin of Man*, 1881.

Wheeler (Joseph Mazzini), atheist, b. London, 24 Jan, 1850. Converted from Christianity by reading Newman, Mill, Darwin, Spencer, etc. Has contributed to the *National Refor mer Secularist, Secular Chronicle, Liberal, Progress,* and *Freethinker* which he has sub-edited since 1882, using occasionally the signatures "Laon," "Lucianus" and other pseudonyms. Has published *Frauds and Follies of the Fathers* '88, *Footsteps of the Past,* a collection of essays in anthropology and comparative religion '86; and *Crimes of Christianity,* written in conjunction with G. W. Foote, with whom he has also edited *Sepher Toldoth Jeshu.* The compiler of the present work is a willing drudge in the cause he loves, and hopes to empty many an inkstand in the service of Freethought.

ERRATA.

Preface V. line 30, *for* Dal Volta *read* Dalla Volta.

Page 8, line 17, *for* translated *read* translated.

P. 16, line 1, *for* Anaxagorus (some copies) *read* Anaxagoras.

P. 24 *for* Rennaisance *read* Renaissance.

P. 30, line 18, *for* National Science *read* Natural Science.

P. 85, line 15, *for* Count *read Count*.

P. 101, line 29 *read* lived near Wiesbaden.   Died 19 Feb. '87

P. 102, line 3, *for* Ouida *read* Ramée.

P. 105, line 12, *for* 1836 *read* 15 Aug. 1835.

P. 107, line 18, *for* Dyons *read* Lyons.

P. 107, line 26, *delete* " before."

P. 112, line 17, *for* Williams *read* William.

P. 122, line 27, *after* Toronto *insert* 1839.

P. 131, line 18, *for* 8 May *read* 3 May.

P. 158, line 18, *for* Honton *read* Hontan.

P. 162, line 16, *for* surveyor *read* surgeon.

P. 171, line, 4, *for* HIDENIN *read* HEDIN.

P. 172, line 7, *for* de voilée *read* devoilée.

P. 182, line 21, *after* Massara *insert* in Supplement.

P 217, line 28, *for* Dupins *read* Dupuis.

P. 229, line 26. *for* Herzogenbusch *read* Herzogenbosch.

P. 230, line 18, *for* Pelusuin *read* Pelusium.

P. 249, line 6, *insert* 11 Aug. *before* 1805.

P. 255, line 21, *for* Dijp *read* Rijp.

P. 259. line 17, *for* National *read* Natural.

P. 282, line 2, *for* Laland *read* Lalande.

P. 284, line 33, *for* 1715 *read* 1745.

P. 289, line 25, *for* 1821 *read* 1851.

P. 313, line 36, *for* Guiseppe *read* Giuseppe.

P. 318, line 18, *for* Monk *read* work.

P. 319, line 35, *for* 1642 *read* 1842.

P. 320, line 7, *for* Tilia *read* Titia.

www.ingramcontent.com/pod-product-compliance
Lightning Source LLC
Chambersburg PA
CBHW021730110726
47902CB00005B/1411